THE ACCIDENTAL SPY

A Novel

TOM RATTRAY

PATRIOT PRESS

An Imprint of LILLIPUT PRESS

DAYTON, OH

THE ACCIDENTAL SPY
Copyright © 2020, 2022 by Tom Rattray
Published by Patriot Press, an Imprint of Lilliput Press
Dayton, OH

Publishers Cataloging-in-Publication Data
Name: Rattray, Tom, author
Title: the accidental spy / by Tom Rattray; edited by Linore Burkard
Description: Previous version published as Mayday: USA, 2016
Summary: A simple pleasure sail leads to one man's accidental discovery of a threat to the United States—which he alone must solve.

Identifiers: Library of Congress Control Number: 2020904296
ISBN : 978-1-7333111-3-7 (EPUB) / ISBN: 978-1-7333111-5-1 (PRINT) /
Subjects: 1. Fiction—Christian 2.Fiction—Mystery and Suspense
 3. International Intrigue 4.Spy and Espionage

What Readers Are Saying About
The Accidental Spy

A clean, action-packed read filled with
unexpected twists and turns.
Midwest Book Review

Realistic characters facing overwhelming conflict. I was
hooked pretty quick and had a hard time putting this one down!
Jody Burgin

Great thriller. Many unexpected twists and turns. Once I
started it, I couldn't wait to get back to it and see what
happened next. Keeps you hanging right to the end.
Robert J. Fritz, Jr.

Move over, Tom Clancy! Excitement, humor and heart.
This book will have you holding your breath! I look forward to
reading more from this author.
Deb Mitchell

A satisfying page-turner of ocean peril and adventure
woven with resourceful intelligence, courage, faith, and
determination. Great visual descriptions.
Amy Weinstein

It was hard to put down! And you didn't overwhelm me with
technical details (Tom Clancy did that sometimes).
Chuck Clevenger, Recruiting Consultant

"Riveting, suspenseful thriller captured my interest from the opening lines and didn't let me go until the exciting and unexpected resolution...Don't start it at bedtime as I did. You'll lose more sleep than you bargained for!"
Gary L. Breezeel, Reviewer

"Action-packed...full of energy, excitement, intensity...and emotion! My hands were sweating and my heart was racing more than once!! And who doesn't love a book with a little romantic intrigue in the midst of espionage?"
Anne M. Smith, Reviewer

"Suspense-ridden, fast-paced, international intrigue... I was hooked from the start."
Grant Stauffer

"I was as hooked on the unfolding adventure as Phil Shepherd was to the net. I would certainly recommend *The Accidental Spy* to anyone who enjoys an action-packed believable adventure and knows that faith and trusting God will come to a satisfying conclusion."
Cliff Kuhnell, Reviewer

"The book was exciting, a real page-turner from page one to the very end...and I didn't want it to end. However, the ending was perfect!"
Patricia Krueger, Reviewer

"Intense and engaging plot! Some lesser works seem to use bad language or salacious situations to bolster an otherwise mundane storyline. Not this one.. (And) well-hidden end of story! Bravo!"
Ted W. Smith, Reviewer

"We should not trust in ourselves, but in God."

1 Corinthians 1:9 NKJV

CHAPTER 1

"Dad, Dad! Wake up! I think we're sinking!"

Phil Shepherd snapped awake, tore out his earplugs, and pushed a knit cap off his eyes as he sprang from the cabin couch where he'd hoped to sleep until his midnight-to-four watch. He and his son Dave and four of Dave's friends were on a rented forty-foot Beneteau, a beauty of a boat, for a spring break cruise. They'd only been out a few hours.

"What happened!" He felt for his deck shoes and found them—underwater.

"I think we hit a shipping container! Starboard—forward berth and storage locker. It's really pouring in, Dad!" Dave, tow-haired, tall, and worried—swallowed. "What do we do?"

Dave was usually level-headed, but Phil could see he was shaken. That was the real danger—panic. He'd have to keep both of them calm.

"Easy there. Let me take a look. We'll have time to abandon ship if we have to. Where are we?"

"Maybe 25 miles out from Miami—maybe 18, 20 miles to Cat Cay."

"Who's driving?" Phil kept his voice even.

"Nancy, I think."

Nancy seemed to be a mature, level-headed young lady, which gave Phil confidence. "Have her put us into the wind, release the sails, and put the engine in neutral." He grabbed a mini-Maglite, hung the lanyard around his neck, and hurried into a jacket. He sloshed across the cabin in water already calf-deep and flipped on the light over the galley sink. He opened the lower doors to expose the inside of the fiberglass hull. One look sent his heart pounding. Water streamed through a long gash that ran from the galley sink to the forward berth. This was way more than they could hope to plug. Dave was back for more orders, so Phil asked, "Are both bilge pumps running?"

"Yeah, I think so."

Phil strained to hear their quiet hum but wasn't sure, and there was no time to check. They'd only buy a little time, anyway. They were meant for small leaks, not gaping rips in the hull.

"Attention! Everybody up!" he called. "This is not a drill! We've hit something and we're taking on water!" He turned to Dave. "Get everyone into life jackets. Tell 'em to get their passports, money, keys—" he was thinking fast—" and get on deck. Then get Josh and launch the dinghy." Josh was Dave's best friend.

As Dave turned to go, Phil added, "Don't mess with untying the dinghy. Cut it loose—just be careful. You could be in it for hours; even a small nick will deflate it. Put it over starboard and hang on to the bow line. I'll ease the boat to port so you can get off on starboard and not get caught in the rigging when she goes down." Phil hoped Dave was getting all the instructions. "I'll take the dive dink off the stern for myself later. Seven in the big dinghy is too much," he finished.

"No, Dad, no!" Dave gripped his arm, "We can all fit. That little raft is too old."

Phil shook his head, "It's too crowded. The last thing we need in the dark is a man overboard. The one-man will work fine for me." Dave's eyes pleaded, so he took him by the shoulders. At 25, Dave was the spitting image of a younger Phil, with sandy-blonde hair and blue eyes.

"Don't panic. You can do this. I'll call the Coast Guard." He scooped up a few items from the navigation station. "Here—shove these in your pockets. You'll need 'em. Now get your jacket and life vest and stuff and get everyone else ready." He hugged him hard. "I love you. It'll be okay. You can do this."

Phil's eyes were teary. He had sailed with his sons for years, from when they were little in Cub Scouts. Dave was now six-foot-one, one hundred and ninety pounds and a graduate student at Asbury Seminary. In minutes, he'd be in charge of the dinghy that had to keep him and his friends safe. *Lord, it's in your hands.*

Josh staggered out of his cabin, rubbing sleep from his eyes. "This for real, Cap'n?" Tall and rangy, he was affable but impetuous. He came from Minnesota—*hopefully from good Viking stock*, Phil thought, as he considered what was ahead of them.

"Get dressed and in your life jacket—pronto!" Phil grabbed a flare gun. "Take this. You and Dave need to launch the dinghy in the *next four minutes.*" He couldn't overstress the urgency of the situation.

"Aye aye, Captain," Josh said with a mock salute. "I'm on it! Bye-bye, Bahamas spring break." He dove back to the forward cabin to get his gear.

If they could launch and load the dinghy quickly, they'd be okay, and the boat could go down without trapping anyone beneath it. If not, those kids would be floundering in the water in the dark trying to find it.

Phil strapped his safety harness on and grabbed the "abandon ship" fanny pack he'd prepared years ago when they'd first started making these trips. He never thought he'd need it. He clipped it around his waist and glanced at the time. 11:10 PM.

The girls came out of the aft cabins, scared but dressed and ready to go with big red life jackets around their necks. Yesterday they'd all thought the life jacket practice was silly; people always do. Now they understood.

"Good work, ladies. Get yourselves on deck right now, and do not come back for *anything*."

Phil waded to the navigation station in water knee-deep. Pizza crusts, candy wrappers, and soda cans swilled around the cabin. He picked up the radio mic and prayed that the battery and connection would last a few more minutes.

"Mayday! Mayday! Mayday! This is the sailing yacht, *Amazing Grace*, out of Ft. Lauderdale, with six people on board! We've been hulled. We're sinking fast!" He looked quickly at the GPS. "Our position is 79 degrees, 40 seconds west, 25 degrees 39 seconds north." He repeated the message, adding that they were about 25 miles due east of Key Biscayne. "Over."

No reply.

Finally, he heard a scratchy female voice, *"Amazing Grace, Amazing Grace,* this is the Coast Guard. What is your emergency?"

"Coast Guard, we hit something, tore a chunk out of our hull, and have maybe five or ten more minutes afloat. Did you get my position? Over."

"*Amazing Grace*, we have your position and will get you help as soon as possible. Stand by, *Amazing Grace*."

The operator sounded shaky. *Just what they didn't need—an emergency operator who was unsure of herself. No way, lady,* Phil thought. *I'm getting out of here!*

He flipped on the deck and anchor lights so the young folks could see while they boarded the dinghy. Amazingly, the boat engine was still running, and all electrical equipment was working. *Thank you, Jesus!*

It was time to get on deck and let this puppy go. Phil's heart ached at the thought, for the Beneteau was a beautiful boat, only three years old and in great shape. It had an autopilot and all the bells and whistles. *Darn shame.*

The Coast Guard hadn't called back.

He made sure he was the last person below deck before he stepped up the companionway to the cockpit. Someone had lowered the Bimini sunshade during the night to see the stars, and even now, Phil had to gawk for a second. He never ceased to be awestruck at the heavens' starry display. With no other light in any direction, the stars were spectacular. *Nobody,* he thought, *puts on a show like God.*

The engine coughed and stopped—the carburetor was probably submerged. The kids' voices as they prepared to disembark were the only sounds he heard. *Praise God the deck lights were still on! This escape would have been a bear in the dark.*

"Okay, everyone," Phil called. "Get in the dinghy, and get clear of the boat. Dave, you're dink captain."

He went to locate his ride—the dive-dinghy, a one-man inflatable military surplus life raft. They usually used it as a snorkeling and scuba station. He yanked open the port cockpit locker. Yep—there she was, with the foot pump. He slipped it out, coupled up the pump, and tromped on the foot treadle. It inflated quickly with no apparent leaks.

As Phil stepped to the stern and hoisted a leg over the transom, *Amazing Grace* slowly turned to port and was already settling low in the water. She wouldn't be with us much longer.

Lord, he prayed, *YOU be with us!*

CHAPTER 2

Cadet Leticia Carter, USCG, only four nights at her job at the Miami Beach Coast Guard station, was already rethinking her career. What was an East St. Louis black girl doing alone at a computer and radar console in Miami? Several of her Academy classmates were out on patrol, but she was stuck at a desk. Suddenly the radio barked, *Mayday! Mayday! Mayday!* She scanned the console as she punched the record button—her pulse racing into triple digits. She couldn't miss a single detail of this call.

Listening to the message from the *Amazing Grace,* her stomach churned. The boat was sinking fast? Her hand shook as she wrote down the coordinates. *The man sounded calmer than she was.* Seven people would soon be in the water. She glanced at the clock. 11:15 PM. *Was there even a moon out tonight?*

Leticia's thoughts raced. Miami Station's crew was already all deployed! They had two boats out on search and rescue, one down for maintenance, and the rest on a massive drug interdiction exercise with ATF, DEA, and Customs— using all the South Florida Coast Guard stations from Miami to the Florida panhandle. *What should she do?* She swallowed down a sense of panic and kicked into gear, snatching up her microphone: "*Amazing Grace*, we have your position, and will get you help as soon as possible. Stand by, *Amazing Grace*."

She called her boss. *No answer!* She called the break area but the phone just rang. Finally, she resorted to her last option, and screamed. "Lieutenant, Lieutenant Rojas! I need help!"

In seconds, Lieutenant Luis Rojas came charging through the door looking irritated. "Cadet Carter, is there a problem?" He frowned at her while tucking in the back of his shirt.

"I've got a sailboat sinking out near the Bahamas, sir, and I don't know what to do. I think all our assets are already out. There's nobody here!"

The lieutenant stepped forward and peered over her shoulder at the radar screen. "Hmm, you're right about our assets, but that doesn't matter. We start this kind of search by air, Cadet. You got the Mayday on screen?"

Leticia raised a shaky finger and pointed to the very edge of the screen. "You can barely see it; it's right here. I'm pretty sure this is the one that called. They gave me the coordinates."

"Well, do the coordinates match that position?" he asked brusquely.

"I haven't had time to cross-check it, sir. Do you want me to do that now?"

"No, no. Did you at least record the call?"

"Yes, sir. Want me to play it?" She looked up at him hesitantly.

Rojas paused before answering, "No, not yet. They may still be trying to call us. See if you can raise them."

"*Amazing Grace, Amazing Grace.* This is the US Coast Guard. Over." She waited, but there was only silence. She repeated the call two more times. Glancing at the radar, she noticed their blip near the edge of the screen had vanished.

She pointed at the screen. "Sir, I think they're gone," she said sadly.

"Yeah, looks like they are. Okay, let me hear their call."

"Yes, sir," she said and reached for the replay button. She played it once. Rojas hit the replay to hear it again. He looked at Leticia. "This is your first one, isn't it?"

Leticia took a deep breath and sighed. "Yes, sir, it sure is."

"That's okay, Cadet. You're doing fine. Sorry I wasn't here sooner to help." He smiled briefly and patted her shoulder.

"Thank you, sir," she said with relief. "Sir, what are we going to do? They're out there in the dark. We don't even know if they have a lifeboat. Don't we have to help them somehow?" she asked, blinking back tears. Rojas nodded reassuringly. "Absolutely, Cadet, that's what we're here for. Bad night for this. Normally in a situation like this, Sector would put up a helo out of Miami Air Station. I'll get District 7 on the horn and see what they can do."

Leticia frowned. "Yes, sir. What should I do? To help, I mean?"

"Oh," he responded, almost as if he'd forgot her. "Copy off those coordinates for me, and the name of the craft. Probably a charter. I'll be in my office." He glanced at her badge. "Ah, right, *Carter*," he said. "And, uh, get out a clean chart. Plot their coordinates and probable path with the Gulfstream and the wind." His gaze pierced hers as if he was wondering if she could handle doing that.

Leticia said, "Yes, sir," and tried not to show that she was wondering herself. The lieutenant flicked out his phone and called the Coast Guard District Seven Command Center. Although headquartered just up the road and around the corner, they were responsible for monitoring all of Florida, Georgia, and South Carolina.

"District Seven, CPO Foster." Leticia heard the crisp voice from the other end.

"Chief Foster, Lieutenant Luis Rojas here. Miami Boat—you guys get that Mayday a few minutes ago?"

"Sure did, Lieutenant. Lousy timing. Miami Air's all out on the drug sweep. They've got a couple HH-65 helos on the ground, and I think an HC-144 Turboprop ready to go, but no crews. We gotta find your sailboat people pretty soon before the Gulfstream takes them to Canada."

The lieutenant nodded, thinking.

Chief Foster said, "Okay, choice one: pull back a helo from the DEA thing. They won't like it, but lives come first. It'll probably take an hour to come back, refuel, and switch out the drug bust gear for a search and rescue. Probably more than an hour. Choice two: get on the horn and wake up a new crew. Also an hour, maybe more. Choice three: get an HC-130 out of Clearwater to at least locate them."

The lieutenant suggested, "Chief, won't Clearwater be on the drug mission too? How about options one and two—start calling for a crew? If we can raise one, fine; if not, call back a helo and get ready for a fast launch?"

"Sounds like a plan, Lieutenant. Any way you slice it, we won't be on scene for at least an hour and a half. Can you eyeball where they'll be by then?"

Lieutenant Rojas inhaled through his teeth and responded, "Sure." *Sure, I know where they'll be,* he thought. *Somewhere in the middle of nowhere.*

CHAPTER 3

Earlier

After Dave and Josh sawed off the lashings and got the dinghy into the water, the next challenge was getting the four girls in, Nancy, Kim, Jane, and Sheila. Nancy surprised Dave by suddenly jumping in the water. She stroked her way to the side of the dinghy and hoisted herself up.

"Good job, Nancy," Dave said. Nancy was strong—an asset at a time like this. He turned around to see the other young women lined up along the starboard lifelines. "All right, ladies, you saw Nancy. That's how it's done. Who's next?"

They hesitated. Sheila, the youngest, shrank back. Dave turned to Kim; her no-nonsense attitude would be helpful. "Kim, if you step over the lifeline, you'll be able to get right into the dinghy. Can you give it a try?"

Kim took a breath and nodded. Stepping forward, she put a leg cautiously over the line. Then, hanging onto Dave's hand, she lifted her other leg over and plopped into the dinghy.

"Not very ladylike, but I'm in it," she quipped.

Dave thought, *not quite what I had in mind, but it worked!* "Josh," he said. "Get in next. Release the bow line and take a loop around the cleat to hold us next to the boat until everyone's in."

The *Amazing Grace* suddenly listed to port as she took on more water, making the girls gasp and reel until they regained their footing. Now the dinghy was further from the deck rail, so they could no longer step right down into it.

"Come on, girls, we've got to move quickly!" Dave said.

Below in the dinghy, Nancy stood to help her friends get in. Dave yelled, "Stay low, Nancy! You can't stand up in a rubber dinghy. You'll capsize it!"

Jane stepped forward over the lifeline and slid down the exposed bow into the dinghy. Nancy stuck out a hand to help her gain her balance; Jane sank to a seat against the side. Sheila, still on deck, was literally frozen. Her small hands gripped the lifeline, white knuckles showing.

"Sheila, let's go," Dave prodded, holding out a hand to her.

She shook her head. "I can't swim!" she gasped.

Dave recognized her panic, but didn't know how to calm her. "We can't stay here. This boat is going down. We have to go now!" He tried to keep his voice calm though he felt anything but. Easy, easy, he told himself. Firm, but calm—like Dad.

Sheila tried to bend over the lifelines but stopped. "I can't, I can't! I just can't do it!"

A sudden loud bang made her scream, while a rushing sound filled the air. Dave turned just in time to see Josh ready to launch a second flare as the first one started to fizzle out a hundred yards away in the dark.

"Josh, no!"

Too late. Josh pulled the trigger on the flare gun and Dave watched it with a sinking heart. "Save those until we know someone's out there, man!" Josh sheepishly stuffed the gun back into his pocket along with the remaining flares.

Dave turned back to Sheila. She wasn't gonna move. He gently but firmly pried her hands off the lifelines, and then scooped her into his arms. By now, the Grace was leaning markedly to port. He had to brace himself against the cabin top to keep from sliding across the deck and down the port side onto the half-submerged jib sail. If the boat went down while they were still tangled in the sail, it would easily take them with it.

Stepping over the lifeline as he held onto Sheila, she screamed again, and her fingers clawed his arm as he slid the two of them into the water. He rolled her onto her back and into a lifesaver carry, then put his head next to hers. "It's okay. I have you," he said softly. "You're safe, see? Your life jacket is keeping your head above water. I'm gonna swim us over to the dinghy and get you in." Sheila stopped sobbing and her body relaxed against him. He asked, "Can you help me help you into the dinghy?"

"I—I can try," she said shakily.

Dave side-stroked the two of them over. He called, "Josh, release the bow line off the boat and push us away from it! The Grace is gonna sink any moment." While Josh did so, he added, "Guys we're gonna need your help getting Sheila in."

Sheila grabbed his arm and hung on for dear life. The others cheered while they helped hoist her into the dingy, and Dave gave a silent breath of relief.

But suddenly the lights went dark on the boat, leaving them floating in nothing but starlight. Sheila screamed; the others gasped.

"Listen up!" Dave commanded. Years of his father's strong lead during lesser calamities must have trained him for such a situation, for he calmly said, "Everybody is fine. We're okay here. Give yourself a couple of moments. Your eyes will adjust. All we need do is sit tight in the dinghy. Everybody up for that?"

A chorus of sheepish "Amens" and one "Yes, sir," came from the dinghy, as well as a weak "I think so," from Sheila.

"I'll come in over the transom at the back," he called. He walked his hands around the edge of the dinghy, but as he prepared to lift himself over, he paused, listening. A gentle swirling and slapping told him the Amazing Grace had rolled over on her port side. Stopping to look back, Dave could now see the fatal gash along the hull that the container had made.

"We did the right thing. There was no plugging that," he said as if to convince himself. He hoisted his six-foot frame over the side. The others were watching the *Grace*. He found himself tearing up as he saw the beautiful craft slipping beneath the waves. One of the girls cried softly, but otherwise, it was suddenly strangely quiet.

The dinghy bobbed peacefully in a gentle breeze as if a beautiful new boat hadn't just sunk in the maw of the sea. Dave suddenly remembered—*Dad!* He'd disappeared in a one-man life raft off the stern of the boat.

"My father!" he cried. "I forgot about him! Dad? Dad! Are you okay?" he shouted. "Mr. Shepherd!" the others called, and then everyone fell silent to listen. Dave's ears strained as he heard what seemed like the distant sound of an engine somewhere southwest of them. Was it another boat? But there was no reply from his father.

"Dad! Dad! Are you there?" Panic rose in his throat.

A faint voice wafted out of the darkness. "I'm fine, son!"

Dave let out a gasp of relief. "Thank you, Jesus," he said softly.

His father continued, "I hear an engine. I'm gonna paddle over to it and get us some help. Not to worry!"

Thank God his father was okay, but his voice had sounded far off. "I think we should pray," he said.

Nancy said, "Good idea. But can we start by singing a hymn?"

CHAPTER 4

Earlier (11:16 PM)

When Phil eased the little life raft into the water, he realized he'd never actually sat in it before. They'd only used it to hold fish or scuba gear, or to carry the dive flag—never as a lifeboat. It was an Air Force surplus life raft, so he should be okay in it, he thought. But his mouth was dry, his breath, shallow. No sense denying it—he was scared. His heart tripped as he settled in the raft and pushed away from the Amazing Grace.

He'd heard the kids getting into the dinghy, and thanked God that the lights had lasted long enough. Then the darkness enveloped him. The sounds of the others grew fainter. He didn't like being separated from the kids but figured they'd be safe until help arrived. Looking up, Phil was struck by the cosmic mantle of stars. Spectacular. Since they ventured to sail the Gulf only once every year or two, he'd never got used to it.

He tried to relax so he could think. Maybe he should have tried tying the two dinghies together? That would have made sense. Why didn't I think of that? He'd do it now. He'd paddle over and tie onto the dink. But his eyes had grown accustomed to the dark, and now he saw the Grace had rolled much farther to port. If he went to the bow of the boat, he'd have to keep well clear of her keel. It could roll up and capsize him as she went over.

Instead, he decided he'd backstroke the raft like he did as a kid in an inner tube at the Michigan lake where his family used to spend their summers. He'd stroked away from the Grace to give himself clearance, and now he'd backtrack. But he heard something and paused, listening. An engine of some sort was approaching. His spirits soared. That's help! He started stroking toward it when he heard Dave calling, his voice desperate.

"I'm fine, son!" he called. "I hear an engine. I'm gonna paddle to it and get us some help. Not to worry!" He listened hard, turning his head to better locate the direction of the noise. It seemed to be coming closer, southwest of him. This was wonderful!

Phil kept stroking toward it so he could be in its path when it came by. He turned and strained to see lights, running lights, any light. Nothing. Hmm, must be a clandestine fishing boat. Approaching it could be tricky. He kept heading toward it. Now it sounded like a very big engine but had a peculiar note to it. They probably put mufflers on it to avoid detection. He wondered if he should turn on a flashlight, and realized he had to, or they'd never stop.

Glancing behind him, he could barely see as the Grace slipped over horizontally into the water. He swallowed a gulp as her masts and sails rattled in a final farewell, and then watched sorrowfully as she slid under the waves and was gone. Good thing for rental insurance! He listened for sounds of the kids but heard nothing. Had they been trapped in the boat as she went down? Oh no, Lord!

But then he heard, wafting along the night air, voices in song. They were praising God! Thank you, God! They're okay!

The mystery boat sounded closer. He had to get almost next to it without getting run down. He twisted on his light and saw something like a bow wave—but no bow or boat! He had no clue what was making the wave.

"Hello! Help!" When there was no answer, he shouted louder. "Hello? Help me! Help me! Mayday! Mayday!" Still no response. In the blackness, Phil felt it going by but saw nothing—except it seemed to be dragging something! Of course! A fishing line. He stroked hard to get behind it, working with all his strength. He swung in behind and felt a ripple under his raft. Something—that fishing line—was in the water. He reached in and grabbed it, a slimy line sliding underneath the raft. It yanked him and he settled back to keep his grip. It began towing him, raft and all. When he had a good grip, he shone the beam of light on it and saw there were floats tied on it. It was some kind of net. It looked huge.

This boat was definitely fishing, but how? He needed to be very careful because they obviously didn't want to be discovered.

He shoved the Maglite in his mouth to keep the beam ahead while pulling hard to get closer to the boat. He figured he wasn't more than 40 feet behind them now—close enough for them to see him. He spit out the light, cupped his hands around his mouth, and screamed. "Hello! Ahoy there! Mayday! Mayday!"

He wondered suddenly if they might speak Spanish. "¡Hola! ¡Señors! ¡Ayúdeme, por favor! ¡No puedo nadar!" He hoped he got that right. But there was no response. No lights, not even a cigarette—no movement at all. But whatever this craft was, it picked up speed, and the net tightened. The hair on Phil's neck rose. He bit his lip and felt suddenly breathless.

Part of him wanted to get closer and find out what was pulling him.

Part of him wanted to just let go—before it was too late.

CHAPTER 5

Dave and the others were praying quietly, when he cried, "Listen up! Listen! What do you hear?"

Nancy said, "An engine, I think! Must be a boat!"

Someone else started to speak but Dave said "Shhh. *Listen!*"

They heard Phil shouting, "Mayday," "Help me," and maybe something in Spanish.

Josh said, "It *is* a boat!"

Dave's heart lifted. He wasn't gonna let himself get too excited, though. Something seemed strange. There were no lights—no running lights or cabin lights, nothing—just the sound of an engine. And even that sounded funny.

They continued to listen for sounds. After a few minutes of silence, Dave said, "You would think if there were people there, my dad would keep yelling. Or he'd tell us we're gonna be saved." But there was only quiet, except for the engine which was getting louder. "Sounds like a diesel, not some little outboard," he added.

Jane asked, "Dave, what do you think it is?

Dave didn't answer immediately. "I'm———I'm not sure." He paused, thinking. "But I think it will be all right. My dad said he would get help. I believe him. He knows what he's doing."

"Then why are we floating around in the dark in a little

rubber boat?" Sheila asked bitterly. "He doesn't sound overly competent to me. You sure you've done this before?"

Dave stiffened. "Look, I know how it seems. But nothing like this has ever happened to us before. This is only my third trip on the Gulf. And I think it's my dad's seventh. We sailed the Great Lakes, the Chesapeake, Tampa, and other places. But nothing like this has ever happened before. Not even close. There's no way we could have foreseen that container floating in the ocean. It was a freak accident." He thought for a moment, "And here we are, all safe. Right?"

Sheila sounded teary. "I just want to go home! I don't like this anymore. Which way is Florida? Let's go that way."

Nancy put an arm around her. Speaking softly, she said, "I think we'll be okay. Mr. Shepherd radioed the Coast Guard. They know we're here. They'll be coming."

They sat in silence then, crowded together in the little rubber boat and rocking to the rhythm of the waves. A gentle breeze pushed them along. Someone started humming softly to the tune of "Amazing Grace." The others picked up on it and started singing. It felt surreal to Dave—floating under the stars, singing that classic hymn with the namesake of the boat; a boat that had just sunk beneath them.

Dave looked at his fellow passengers. *Gotta get their minds on something else here,* he thought. He looked up at the stars and asked, "Can anyone see the Big Dipper?"

Nancy and Josh spotted it immediately. "There it is!" they said in unison.

Dave asked, "And what does it point to? Where is the North Star?" He felt like a teacher in a classroom. God's classroom!

After a pause, Nancy said uncertainly, "Isn't that what the two ends of the Dipper point to?" She pointed up. "That must be the North Star, right there."

"That's right," Dave said. "Think about it. This is how sailors navigated for thousands of years—by the stars. They didn't even have a compass."

Sheila said, "Okay, if that's the North Star, then where's Miami?"

Dave pointed behind them. "You see that glow? That hint of a glow right on the very edge of the horizon?"

Sheila said, "Yeah, I see it. So if that's Miami, let's go that way!"

Dave took a long breath, letting it out slowly. "I'm sorry, but we don't have the ability to choose where we go. We're on the Gulfstream, propelled by this breeze. We're pretty much floating north, paralleling the Bimini islands."

"What?" Sheila said. "You mean we just have to sit here? Can't we do something?" Her voice rose with each word. "I want to go home! Dave—do something!"

Josh had been quiet but spoke up. "Dave, you have any idea how fast we're going? Where will we be when it's daylight?"

"Good question," Dave said. He thought over their position and likely destination. "The Gulfstream here is probably about 2 knots. And the raft makes headway in a breeze, even a light one like this, so I would add another knot, maybe knot and a half, to that. So let's say 3 knots max."

Several people asked at the same time, "What's a knot?"

"Sorry," Dave said. "I've been around boats all my life. A knot is one nautical mile an hour. That's 1.15 land miles per hour. So, 3 knots would be about 3.5 miles an hour. That's the same speed as a moderately brisk walk."

Josh asked, "What about the Coast Guard? Your dad called in our position, but that was back there. We've already moved, and we're still moving. We're gonna move all night. How do they find us in the dark?"

"The Coast Guard knows all about that. It's what they do. But hey, I just remembered something!" Dave reached into his pocket and pulled out a gadget that looked like a cross between a portable radio and a parking meter. He held it up, trying to read the fine print. "I need some light to see how to work this thing," he said.

Jane asked, "What is it?"

"It's an EPIRB—an Emergency Position Indicating Radio Beacon. It sends out an electronic emergency signal! Airplanes pick up the signal, maybe other people too, like the Coast Guard or the navy, maybe even satellites. They home in on the signal and find us! Since the *Grace* was new, this is probably a new EPIRB. That means it'll send out our GPS position. But I've gotta see how to work it."

Sheila said, "I've got a little light on my keychain."

"Great! Hold onto your keys while you shine the light so you won't risk dropping them."

Sheila fumbled in her pocket and pulled out her keys. It wasn't much of a light, but when Dave held up the EPIRB, it was enough to read the directions. "Sheila, you're a lifesaver. Good work!" Dave exclaimed.

"Thanks," she said. She sighed and added, "I guess I've been kind of a baby tonight. I've never experienced anything like this before. I'm from Nebraska. And I didn't think it was gonna be like this at all."

Dave took her hand to steady the light—and to reassure her. "None of us expected this." He unwound the cord wrapped around the EPIRB, snapped it to an eyebolt on the transom, and dropped the device in the water. The girls gasped. Nancy demanded, "Why did you do that?"

Dave said, "Sorry, I should've explained. This thing is activated by water. It won't work unless it's in the drink. See, it floats just fine. See that little nubbin thing sticking up the top? That's the antenna. That's what they home in on when they come to find us."

Josh gave Dave a high five. "All right, my man!"

"Thanks." He turned to the rest of them. "Remember folks, no standing or quick movements. We're comfortable; we're riding well. But this is quite a load for this dinghy, and we need to stay low in case the wind picks up or we get a stray wave. We'll never get an ocean view of the night sky like this back in Wilmore. So, let's sit tight and enjoy the ride." He hoped he sounded more confident than he was.

"And pray," Kim said. "Maybe we should pray for your dad."

"If I know my dad," Dave replied, "I think he's probably praying for us."

CHAPTER 6

Amanda Hardwicke reached groggily for the ringing phone on her nightstand. "Hello."

"Lieutenant Hardwicke? Pete Larkin, operations duty officer. Need you to come in. We've got a Mayday on the Gulfstream."

Amanda reluctantly threw off her covers, swung around to sit up, and said, "Yes sir, Lieutenant. I'll be there." She staggered into the bathroom, ran a brush through her unruly blond locks, and turned on the shower. *Gotta wake up.* Minutes later, she slipped into her dark green flight suit— hanging as always on the back of the bathroom door—and hurried along to rush out. But she stopped in the kitchen and sniffed. *Jake, you're a sweetheart!* "Sleep well, sweetie," she said aloud as she snatched up the thermos of fresh coffee he'd left, then her keys, and stepped into the garage.

Forty-five minutes later, she pulled into the Coast Guard Air Station parking lot at the Opa-Locka Airport. Charlie Erickson's bright red Miata slid into the slot next to hers. They exited their cars simultaneously. Both a shade shy of 6 feet, trim and athletic, they looked like brother and sister.

"Evening, Mandy," Charlie said. "How you doing?"

"I'm here. Just came off day shift—two search and rescues. Any idea what we've got here?" she asked, as they walked into the operations center.

"Not a clue. Let's find out."

As they pushed the door open, they saw that rescue swimmer Wilford Heimatt was there, but no flight mechanic yet. A standard Coast Guard helicopter crew needed a pilot (her, tonight), copilot, flight mechanic, and rescue swimmer. As Amanda and Charlie sat down, she hoped the others would arrive shortly if this was an emergency.

The operations officer, Chief Larkin, slid into the table opposite them. "Okay, Crew. Sailboat halfway to the Bahamas, hit something and sank quickly. We have an initial GPS position, and that's about it. Been in the water," he looked at his watch, "an hour plus. There were seven on board. Your flight mechanic," he paused, looked up to see a squat little man approaching and added, "is coming in as I speak. Wally! How's the leg? All healed up?"

The little man arrived. "Absolutely, Chief. Got a full check-out and green light from the base medico this afternoon. I'm ready to go!" He turned to Amanda. "Hi, Mandy." He shook hands with Charlie. "Lieutenant, I don't think we've officially met before, although I've seen you around. I'm Wally O'Reilly, your flight mechanic."

"O'Reilly. How are you?" Charlie said, nodding. "What's the story with the leg?" Amanda and Chief Larkin suppressed smiles. When Wally was silent, Larkin leaned over and quietly said, "He sprained it in his toilet. He was standing on the seat to swat a hornet, and he slipped." Wally raised his eyes to the ceiling, but the Chief rubbed his hands together.

"Showtime, people. I've got an HC-144 crew coming too. They'll be a few minutes behind you."

The HC-144, Amanda knew, was the Coast Guard's medium-range propeller aircraft for wide-area searches. It could stay aloft up to ten hours and had a wide array of highly sensitive search electronics, including a full-time "Forward Looking Infrared Radar" (FLIR) operator.

The HC-65 helicopter crew finished preparations and ran through the checklists. As they strapped into their five-point combination safety/harness life vests for takeoff, Chief Larkin walked quickly out to Amanda. As pilot, she was in command. "Got an update from Sector. We have an EPIRB in the water, same approximate position as the Mayday call. We'll patch you in." He looked in the back at the mechanic. "Wally, did you load a SLDMB?"

"Yes, sir, right here," he said as he slapped a long cylinder that was strapped to the helicopter bulkhead. The SLDMB, a satellite locating marker buoy, sent position, wind, and water current data to the Sector computers. It enabled them to predict the movement of victims in the water over time.

Minutes later, Amanda tightened her helmet and started her twin turbine engines. They were 853 horsepower Turbomeca Arriel 2C2-CG, which gave her confidence. When she was satisfied they were running properly, she lifted off, keyed her mike, and announced, "Be advised, be advised; Coast Guard chopper is airborne pursuing EPIRB signal."

Turning east, she quickly passed over the brightly lit North Miami and Florida coast and headed out over the moonlit ocean. A few minutes later, Amanda's voice came over the intercom, "All eyes outside. We're coming up on the latest GPS position." The crew flipped on their night vision goggles and took up their pre-assigned watch positions, ensuring a 360-degree observation of the ocean below.

Amanda slid into a 300-foot hover over the datum—the point where the GPS showed the victims. She turned on the spotlight, "Midnight Sun," and looked down. Seeing nothing, she turned the helicopter slowly around while easing the spotlight out in a gradually increasing circle.

"Mark, Mark! EPIRB beacon, seven o'clock, one hundred fifty yards!" Wally yelled.

Amanda crabbed the helo sideways, spotted the EPIRB's little strobe light flashing in the night, and restarted a slow turn over it. They all studied the circle, a radius of about one hundred yards. After a few moments, Amanda asked, "Anybody see anything?"

Three "nos" crackled through the intercom. Her eyes hurt, she stared so hard. *There were people on board that boat!* But finally, she had to accept the evidence. "There's nothing here."

CHAPTER 7

Phil stared into the darkness. He let up on the tow rope, his hands in the water, but didn't let go. He needed to make a decision. Evidently, if there were human beings ahead of him, they were not going to respond. This was a type of a craft like nothing he'd ever seen before. His hands felt shaky, his mouth dry. His breaths were in gulps but felt shallow. *All right! I'm either going to let go right now or find out what this is.*

He slowly reeled in more of the net, drawing gradually closer and closer to whatever was towing him. He was soon 35 feet, 30 feet, 25 feet from the thing, whatever it was. The water was warmer and more turbulent. Was it an exhaust, an underwater exhaust? He cried, "Lord, give me strength. Give me wisdom. Keep me safe!"

He was going for it.

He paused, thinking about Dave and the rest of the kids in the dinghy. The thing ahead of him had been streaming along at about 3 knots. He was probably a couple of miles north of their dinghy by now and getting farther with every minute. But he'd made his decision: there was no going back. If he let go now, he'd be in a one-man raft in the middle of the Gulfstream going nowhere. He'd be extremely difficult to find, even after they knew to start looking for him—which probably wouldn't happen until well after daylight—assuming that Dave and the raft were found soon and that whoever found them could look for him as well. Too many long shots. He was committed to this thing ahead of him.

He pulled in another 10 or 15 feet of net and grabbed the light. For a Mini-Mag, it threw out a good little beam. He twisted it on and splayed it against the net ahead, but now saw that it angled gradually up toward the top of whatever was towing it—and him. This was very strange. He shut off the light, convinced the net was long, perhaps hundreds of feet, maybe even more. Phil had heard of these things—drift nets, they were called. It had a heavy top line with floats every few feet on the surface, which probably held many yards of coarse mesh netting below it. And now he could see the bottom line where it was bunched up by the snorkels. It had weights on its lower line, he supposed, to keep the net hanging down below the float line.

Okay, Phil, you can figure this out. Whatever was pulling him seemed to be on autopilot—like a nautical drone. *I bet that whatever or whoever is controlling this has no idea I'm here—at least until I get closer.*

He tried to relax. He had to pull himself up to this thing and see what it was. Then he'd decide what to do next.

He pulled himself closer, hand over hand. The exhaust was bubbling up around the raft now like a warm breeze. It felt good. The engine was roaring steadily. But it still sounded like it was at the end of a tunnel, or in a cave—not on the surface.

He held the net with one hand and twisted the light on again to examine the thing more closely. He saw a tapered cylinder about the size and shape of an inverted trash can on the end of a large tube, plowing through the ocean. There was something ahead of it that broke the waves and created the bow wave. The top stood about 5 feet above the surface with the net draped around it, cascading off both sides of the trash can part.

Phil froze. He realized what this was—it could only be one thing. He was looking at a snorkel—a breathing tube from a submarine! It was obviously being propelled from beneath the surface. It couldn't be anything else!

He was positive the U.S. no longer had any snorkel subs. This had to be what they called a diesel-electric sub—one that ran on a diesel engine snorkeling on the surface at night while charging its batteries—and on electric motors while submerged during daylight. The Germans first launched them late in World War II.

He was sure the U.S. fleet was now all nuclear. He believed other major seagoing nations like Britain, Russia, and France were also all nuclear. So whose submarine was it? And why was it snorkeling up the Gulfstream past Florida and the Bahamas?

Maybe it was a friendly nation on a seagoing exercise. Or a commercial research vessel. Worst case scenario? It was an unfriendly nation up to no good. Phil tried to calm his racing heart while thinking it over.

The research vessel idea was benign but sounded pretty unlikely. And what friendly nation with diesel-electric submarines would conduct an exercise in the Florida Strait? Maybe Brazil? But did they have diesel-electric subs? Phil thought he'd read somewhere that India did, but no way would they come all this way just for an exercise. What about Venezuela? They had a navy. Maybe they had diesel-electric subs. Probably not friendly, though, if they did.

Hello! Another possibility hit him—drug runners. He

remembered seeing a TV special showing that Colombian drug cartels actually were building submarines to smuggle drugs into the U.S. The ones on the show didn't totally submerge. They just rode *almost* submerged with a little bubble on top—just enough to steer the sub. This could be one of their ventures! Or maybe they bought a surplus sub from somebody...

Phil couldn't be sure, but he figured it had to be an entity up to no good, smuggling drugs, or landing spies, or—he had no idea. But it was right in front of him.

Okay, Phil, let's take a good look at this thing. Take your time, be careful.

He pulled his little raft up next to the snorkel. Most of the exhaust was now bubbling out behind him. The net draped behind the snorkel on both sides. They'd obviously snorkeled through the net and got hung up on it without realizing it. He took out his light and splayed it on the surface. It was black, but not metallic. He reached out and touched it. It had a rubber kind of feel to it, a familiar feel. It reminded him of what he'd felt on the wingtip of the SR-71 spy plane in the Dayton Air Force Museum where the surface was used to reflect radar! This was definitely not a research vessel! No research vessel would want to go undetected by radar. It also seemed pretty sophisticated for a drug cartel. On the TV special, their submarines were very rudimentary—spartan— and much simpler in design.

He examined the shape of it. The top was like a shroud—a covering to keep water from cascading down the intake duct into the engine room of the sub. He reached a hand underneath the edge. It concealed an open space. He moved slowly around the sides of the snorkel with his hands to feel out the opening. He bumped into a support, slid his hand around it, and continued moving in.

He wanted to get a look at the top but standing up in the little one-man raft would be extremely hazardous. Even hanging onto the net was risky: he could easily fall over the side and lose the raft.

He settled back down into the raft—took the bow line and tied it to the top line of the net, wondering if it would support his weight. He reached up on either side of the snorkel, got a good firm grip on the net there, and gave it a yank. It seemed to be steady. He supposed the net had to be strong to withstand the rigors of ocean fishing. *Sure hope so.* He boosted himself up slowly, hand over hand on each side of the net until his head was above the top of the snorkel. If only he could get a firm enough grip to free one hand to use the light! He reached across the top and grabbed the net on the far side. That held him in position as long as he stayed centered. *Thank goodness this was a submarine. The rocking of a fishing boat would have thrown him off for sure.* Instead, it rode very, very steadily.

He carefully moved his free hand across the top of the snorkel. There was something on in it! He couldn't tell what it was. He found the lanyard for the light—around his neck, thankfully—and gradually pulled it up. Twisting it on, he splayed the light across the top. There were some rivets or bolts holding it together, and something written on it. He couldn't make out what it said. He had to get higher.

Phil let his feet slide out of the raft completely and felt for a toehold in the net. There were lots of them. He pulled himself up very gradually until he could raise his elbows on top of the thing. Now he could see the writing. But it wasn't in a script or language he knew, and in fact, seemed to be in two different languages. One of them was stamped into the metal with backward letters. It looked like Russian writing—Cyrillic, he believed it was called. The other looked like Arabic or a similar language. He had no idea what they said.

Weariness ran through him. Phil realized tension was sapping his energy. He slowly eased back down the snorkel, took one foot out of the net, and felt for the raft. He couldn't find it!

Searching behind him, he barely saw it--still attached to the net. *Thank You, God!* But it had slid back a couple of feet and was bobbing off to the left in the snorkel's foamy wake. How was he going to get back to it? He guessed the trick would be to climb across the net and get next to the raft. He slowly eased back from the snorkel, keeping a grip on the top lines. His feet found toe holds in the net, and he crept closer to the raft. Soon his feet were underwater.

He could see now that he should have positioned the raft between the two sides of the net that were wrapped around the snorkel. He worked his way down until he was waist-deep in moving water. The current tugged against him, trying to drag him away. He reached the raft, let go of the net, and rolled over into it, but it started tipping to one side and he almost spilled out again. Phil pulled himself and the raft back upright with the net. He let out a huge sigh. *That was close.*

The little Air Force surplus raft felt like home, like safety. He smiled at the thought of the many times he'd told his kids and his boat crews the mantra: *Safety is not doing dangerous things carefully; it is not doing them at all.* If they could only see him now!

He gathered his thoughts and reviewed his situation to decide what to do next. First, this was almost certainly an unfriendly submarine. It was snorkeling up the coast of the U.S., destination unknown. It was recharging its batteries and would pull the snorkel down—and in a few hours convert to battery and run on its electric motor all day.

He hated to think it but couldn't escape a growing hunch: these were terrorists! He could think of no other explanation. He set his jaw firmly and pursed his lips, but tears escaped and rolled down his cheeks. Phil was suddenly back in time, back to a devastating phone call from the New York City Fire Department. His wife, Mary, his brother, Peter, and his son, Caleb were in the Windows of the World restaurant in the South Tower having a late breakfast on 9/11. They were in New York because Caleb was interested in Columbia, Mary's alma mater. She was going to show him around.

They were never found.

"That was once, you heartless butchers! Never again!" Phil ground out the bitter words, directed at the nefarious craft ahead of him. "If I'm going to count for anything in this life, it's going to be *now*. One way or another, I'm going to stop you!"

CHAPTER 8

"Dave!" Kim cried. "I heard something! Look, see the flashing lights? Over there, there!" She sat up pointing, but the dinghy began tipping and Sheila shrieked. Kim quickly sat back down. "Oops. Sorry."

"Easy, everyone," Dave said, as he twisted around to look. In a moment he cried, "Sounds like a chopper! Must be the Coast Guard. They'll be homing on our EPIRB." He felt for the eyebolt on the transom that he clipped the EPIRB to. "Uh oh. There's no eyebolt," he said solemnly.

"What does that mean?" Sheila asked, gripping his arm with one hand. "Does that mean they can't find us?"

"I'm not sure," he said. "I know I clipped the EPIRB to the eyebolt! Sometime in the last couple of hours, it must have come off." He sighed. "The Coast Guard will go to the EPIRB. We have no way of knowing when it came loose. Josh, how many flares do we have left?"

Josh felt in his pocket. "Um. Two. Should I send one off now?"

"Not yet. Let's watch what they do. They're way too far out yet."

The six fell silent, all eyes on the approaching helicopter. Jane said softly, "Yea, though I walk through the valley of the shadow of death, I will fear no evil; For You are with me; Your rod and Your staff, they comfort me. All things are possible with You, Lord. So let the Coast Guard find us and get us home safely."

Sheila started weeping. Nancy put an arm around her, "They'll find us, sweetie. Don't you worry."

Josh piped up, "Look, they've got a light on! They're looking in the water! Hey, over here, over here!" he yelled, waving his arms.

"Send up a flare now, Josh!" Dave ordered. "Make it count."

"Alright!" He readied his flare gun, raised it in the direction of the helicopter, and sent it flying. "Come on, Coast Guard! Come and get us!" The rocket flew skyward, leaving a bright red trail behind it. A few seconds later it went out and dropped into the sea. They all studied the helicopter expectantly.

"Oh no," Nancy said. "They didn't see it. Josh, send another one."

"No, no," Dave said. "We have to wait until we're sure they'll see it. I think with that light on, they'll all be looking down in the water, not out here. We should have saved that flare. We must be a couple miles away, maybe more. Let's be patient, people; have faith."

Aboard the helo, Amanda snapped off the spotlight and spoke over the intercom: "Wally, drop the buoy. We'll commence a standard pie search."

"Copy, Lieutenant. Buoy going into the water—" he paused as he maneuvered the buoy to the door and pushed it out— "now!" The buoy dropped, shed its outer casing, and its spring arms popped out, four vertical vanes that caught the current with minimal interference of wind or waves. It ran through its start-up routine and began broadcasting position data.

"Thanks, Wally," Amanda said. "Okay, folks, all eyes on the water. Let's find our vic, er, vic*tims*. We're looking for seven." She pitched the helo forward and slowly followed her compass heading out 2 miles, all the while scanning the ocean for survivors with night vision goggles. Then she turned abruptly 120 degrees, and followed that for a mile, before turning again and headed back for the marker buoy. She went beyond the buoy 2 more miles, before turning another 120 degrees. She slowly traced triangles over the ocean, like pieces of pie, with the center at the marker buoy. Over time, they would thoroughly examine a circle of ocean roughly 4 miles in diameter.

Watching the helicopter from a distance, Sheila cried, "What are they doing? They're going the wrong way! Can't they see us? Can't Josh send up another flare?" Her voice cracked as she held back tears.

"Yeah, why not?" cried Nancy and Kim.

"No, he can't. Not yet," Dave said. "We only have the one flare left. They're flying a pattern. We just have to wait." After a moment he added, "Our best bet is to wait until they're flying toward us. Then they'll be looking ahead." He turned to the others. "See, they fly to the left, then turn, fly away from us, then back to the right. I bet when they turn this time it will be toward us. So Josh has to wait because they're still pretty far away. Faith, people, faith. We're gonna be okay."

They rocked silently in the waves as the breeze moved them along. The helicopter's *flucketa-flucketa* increased and dimmed, almost as if on schedule. Then it seemed louder than before.

"Josh, get your flare ready!" Dave called. "They're coming almost directly at us. We need to fire just before they turn. That's the closest they'll be. *Lord, let this work! Let them see our flare.* Thank you, Jesus!"

"Amen," Josh replied, as he fired off the flare. For a second, they all watched and then Josh moaned, "Oh no! They're turning already! I waited too long. *Please, Lord, please!*"

Sheila burst into sobs.

Charlie said from the co-pilot seat, "Mandy, got a flare, ten o'clock, maybe a mile or a little more,"

"Got it, Charlie, thanks. I saw it too." Amanda said as she pulled back on the stick and rotated the helo to the left. She eased the stick forward and moved gradually in the direction that Charlie indicated.

"Look! Sheila, look!" Dave said excitedly. "They're turning! I think they saw us. Hey, get that key chain light you had. Maybe they can see it."

Sheila said, "It's awfully small. But here—you try it." She handed him the key chain.

Sitting on the transom, Dave was closest to the helicopter. He switched on the light, held it over his head, and waved back and forth. He thought to himself, *If they see this, it'll be a miracle.* "Man, I wish we had another flare," he lamented.

"Mark!" Amanda cried. "Got a light, 10 degrees to the right. About half a mile. Going to spotlight in a minute. Willie, you ready for a swim?" she added, to Wilfred, the rescue swimmer, as she altered course toward the little light waving in the darkness. She leaned forward to see better as they came aloft of it.

"Looks like a rubber raft full of people." She switched on the "midnight sun" and illuminated *Amazing Grace's* dinghy and its six occupants.

She gave a sigh and smiled. *Thank God,* she thought.

CHAPTER 9

Phil settled into the raft and tried to get comfortable. It wasn't riding well. Somehow, he had to center it between the two sides of the net coming off the snorkel. He turned onto his knees and untied the bow line from the net. Slowly he maneuvered the raft between the sides of the net and let it slide back 10 or 15 feet out of the exhaust from the sub. He laced the bow line between the sides of the net, and suddenly the raft rode well. Although they were moving through waves 1 to 2 feet high, he could barely feel them. He slid down into the little life raft, rolled over, and looked at the stars.

Lord, what am I doing here? How am I going to stop this sub? Phil's eyes searched the heavens as if the answers were there. Falling back to a favorite coping strategy, he gave himself a lecture. *Okay, buddy, you can figure this out. Think. What do you know?*

He closed his eyes, resting, and slowly felt tension flow from his body. He hadn't realized how stressed he'd been for the last—what—hour? Since Dave woke him up. He glanced at his watch—it was well over an hour. He prayed the kids had been rescued by now. But for him, it wasn't immediately an urgent situation. The submarine would be operating on snorkel for hours, probably until close to sunrise—or at least dawn—4 AM at the earliest.

He took a deep breath, stared at the stars, and found himself smiling. *This was an awesome ride!* If he thought only about this very moment, what was happening right now, it was near miraculous. If someone had told him that morning that he'd spend the evening dragging through the Gulfstream behind a submarine in a little rubber raft staring at the stars, he would've said he was nuts. He could hardly believe he was there, now. *Thank you, Lord, for protecting me. Thank you, Lord, for putting Dave and the others on the big dinghy. But now, Lord, time to get serious. How am I going to stop this thing? I haven't the foggiest idea.*

He had no idea what their intentions were, either. Did they hope to land enemy agents? Highly doubtful. There were far easier ways to get people into the country—like buy a plane ticket. *Uh-oh*, he thought. This could be another 9/11, literally, another suicide mission! They might be planning to go into some harbor and blow themselves up. On the East Coast, it would either be Norfolk—to destroy all the navy vessels there—or New York harbor. In any case, his job was to somehow make sure that the sub was detected, stopped, and destroyed before anything like that could happen.

Suddenly, Phil's eyes snapped open with an idea. He obviously couldn't stop the sub, but what if he could stop it from submerging? He thought about how the vessel probably worked. They were currently operating on a diesel engine and recharging their batteries; the snorkel was for air intake; which meant it must have some sort of valve or gate to shut off the air when the ship submerged. In fact, this valve had to be very substantial to withstand the depths to which the submarine could dive. Otherwise, it would be like having a fifteen-inch hole in the top of the boat. The question was, where was this valve, how did it work, *and could he jam it open?*

That's it! He had to jam that snorkel wide open—the way it was now. In a few hours, they'd try to submerge and would get the surprise of their lives! The ocean would come rushing in.

But would it really be that simple, he wondered? He remembered something about submarines having "light boards." They called them the Christmas tree, at least the U.S. subs did. And before they could dive, all the lights had to be green. Any open valve or hatch or whatever would show up as a red light. So there must be a system, a switch or something, to show when the valve was shut.

He lay there thinking it over. *Okay, if I can do it, the objective would be achieved; they wouldn't be able to dive.* Another thing he could do was cut off the rubber cloaking stuff on the snorkel so it gave a prominent radar reflection.

He rolled onto his knees to look at the snorkel. The moon was up, almost full. *Thank you, Lord.* Step one: find out how the snorkel valve worked. Step two: figure out a way to override or wedge it open.

Phil, baby, time to get to work. You got a plan; now execute it. He untied the raft from the drift net and pulled himself up to the snorkel. Tension crept back, making his breathing shallow, and sending his pulse racing. *Gotta relax. Think of this like service—mowing the lawn or changing the car's oil—just something you have to do. They don't know you're here. And if all else fails, you cut loose and float.*

He pulled through the warm turbulence of the exhaust right next to the snorkel. He wasn't sure whether he should work from the raft or try to climb onto the thing. He'd start from the raft. He turned on the Maglite and inspected beneath the outer cowling that covered the intake tube. Slowly he worked his way around to one side. The bracket looked like a hinge. He wondered if the other side was the same and slid around to it. It was. The cowling was meant to be *pivoted* open to get access to the intake tube.

He wondered what held it down and shone the light across it again. *Ah! How had he missed it?* A bracket lay on the centerline of the snorkel with a bolted connection to the cover. The other brackets were welded, so this was how they released the cover to get at the intake tube.

Now he had to figure out how to get the bolt loose. He grabbed the nut with his hands and tried to turn it but almost laughed at the futile effort. Was there something in the little raft that would help? He had a Swiss Army knife in his pocket, but didn't remember everything he'd put in the abandon ship bag. He'd packed it years ago, for their first cruise. But he knew there were no wrenches in it.

He lowered himself and sat back into the raft--and bumped into something hard. *The raft anchor!* He'd forgotten about it. The raft came with a small, collapsible folding anchor and 80 feet of line that they used when diving. He pulled it out of its storage pocket on the side of the craft and examined it. It had a center shaft and folding flukes or blades, and probably weighed about five pounds. If he hit the nut with a glancing blow using the anchor like a hammer, could he get it loose?

Holding the anchor, he climbed back up, got on his knees, and examined the nut. Marine growth and rust blanketed it, evidence of years in the water. He should try to break it free from that gunk before anything else. He took the army knife out and opened the small penknife blade. As he traced the edges of the nut, the rust broke off; he continued scraping and soon the algae or whatever the growth was, came off too. *So far, so good.*

Sitting up tall on his knees, Phil hung onto the snorkel shroud with one hand while taking a whack at the nut with the anchor.

Oh man, that was loud! Could they have heard it down below? He paused, listening, but decided they couldn't have. Not by a longshot. The diesel from the intake tube was roaring so loud, he could probably run a jackhammer up there and they wouldn't know. He tried a few more oblique hits on the nut, but it didn't seem to be loosening. Phil returned to the raft to think.

He examined the folding anchor again, hoping for inspiration. If he used one of the blades like a giant plier against the shaft, he could get enough grip on the nut to make it move. He hoped so, anyway. It was worth a try.

He climbed back up, "stood" on his knees, and tried positioning the anchor blade and shaft around the nut using both hands. But the raft began bouncing unsteadily. If this was going to work, he'd have to steady the craft somehow. Fortunately, though the raft was rocking, the snorkel was steady. So was the net. He'd have to step off the raft—off his life vessel— and *stand on the net*. Would it hold his weight? Could he get in position to do what he needed to do?

He eased the raft back a couple of feet, and put the anchor on top of the snorkel, letting the line hang down. He put his left foot on the left net, his right foot on the right net. He pulled himself up to the snorkel. And took a deep breath.

It felt nice and steady, but he'd need both hands to hang on to the snorkel. He knew what to do—his safety harness had two six-foot safety lines attached to it. Normally, he kept them coiled and held in position with elastic bands, neat and out of the way. But he could see himself hanging on the snorkel like a lineman working off a telephone pole.

He hung on to the snorkel with one hand and freed the safety line with the other. Reaching up, he flipped it over the far side of the snorkel. He wasn't sure whether one safety line would be long enough, but it just made it. He clipped it onto the harness and leaned back cautiously—but when he let go of the snorkel, the harness took his weight—and held. *Thank you, Jesus!*

Now he was attached to the submarine and had both hands free to try and loosen the cantankerous nut. He felt the top of the snorkel and pulled the anchor down in front of him. Positioning the shaft on one side of the nut and a blade on the other, he slid them to the end of the shaft, wanting to get the most leverage possible. Squeezing the blade around the nut, he applied pressure, praying beneath his breath. The shaft slipped off.

That was the bad news. The good news was that if he could get this right, it was going to work! He turned the anchor blade on edge and after three more attempts, felt the nut move. It was tedious, but gradually it budged to the point that he could turn it by hand. Phil sighed.

This was just the beginning. Now he had to lift the shroud somehow. He unclipped one end of the safety line and hung it onto the snorkel tube. He tried raising the shroud with his free hand. It wanted to move but was heavy. And the hinges were probably corroded and stiff like the bolt was. If he could strap himself to the intake tube instead of the shroud, and if the net continued to hold, he might be able to lift it up. He'd push with his back and both arms.

It's worth a try. He took the safety line, squatted down in front of the intake tube—his chin was almost in water—and hugged the tube. He reached around the sides but couldn't quite get the carabiner to clip to the line. He flipped it back and forth and finally caught it. Then he pulled it in and clipped it back onto his harness. He leaned back again to check the steadiness—*yes!* This was going to work!

He squatted underneath the edge of the shroud and tried to stand. It felt like it was bending, but not moving. Suddenly, it broke loose and flipped open. He grabbed the edge of the intake tube to steady himself.

Wow! I actually did it!

Curiously, Phil took a look at the inside of the tube, hooking his elbow over it and splaying the Maglite. *Thar she is, me hearties!* Sure enough, there was a large, heavy-duty, flapper-like disc on edge in the tube. It had a mechanism that moved it, kind of like the closer on a commercial door. Attached to this mechanism was a cylinder with a piston pointing up. The piston was fully extended, obviously in the full open position. *Oh yes!* There was a switch, a button encased in rubber that depressed when the flapper shut. That was how they knew the valve was shut.

He needed to jam that thing open. The piston rod extending from the cylinder looked about the same length as the shaft on his little anchor. *Old peanut brain here has an idea.*

He eased down off the snorkel and settled back into the raft. Fatigue was catching up with him. And he absolutely could not afford to fall off and miss the net. It was going to be a darn nuisance, but he needed to clip himself either to the net or the raft. Right now, it had to be the net. He clipped the safety line to the top of it and felt around in the raft for the anchor. As he hoped, the blades came off as he slid them down the shaft. They only came off part way at first, but he jiggled them around until they were completely loose.

He checked his watch, pressing on the light. Almost 3:00 AM. He had at least an hour more before the sub should try to submerge.

He climbed back to the snorkel with the anchor shaft, and wondered: *What would happen if he just dropped the shaft down the intake duct? Would it foul up their engines?* But he squashed that idea. It was a nice fantasy but wouldn't work. He hooked his elbows over the edge of the intake duct, held the Maglite in his mouth, and positioned the anchor shaft next to the piston rod. *Praise God!* The anchor shaft was just a little bit shorter than the extended piston rod.

He lashed the anchor shaft and piston tightly together. Afterward, he tried to dislodge the shaft but was gratified to find it nice and secure. When they finished snorkeling and tried to retract the piston on their flapper valve, his little anchor shaft would jam it open!

Phil slid off the intake tube and pulled the shroud back down into position. He replaced the nut, finger tight, since he no longer had the shaft for a makeshift wrench. He found the raft with his feet. And collapsed into it.

CHAPTER 10

Hovering above the water and the little dinghy, Wally reported progress to Amanda. "Rescue swimmer halfway down…ten feet…in the water! Hoist coming back up."

"Copy that," Amanda said as she pulled the helo back to reduce the prop wash on the dinghy. She maintained "Midnight Sun's" spotlight on the little raft and watched while Wilfred swam to about 10 feet of the dinghy.

Dave, Josh, and the girls in the boat hooted with excitement, though they had to shield their eyes from the strong spotlight.

"I can't believe it!" Sheila murmured, blinking away tears. "We're actually getting rescued!"

"Of course," Dave said. They watched as a man was lowered into the water and approached them, swimming.

"You the guys that ordered pizza?" he asked. Wilfred always started with a joke to reduce tension.

"Only if it's got anchovies," Dave said, smiling.

"You want anchovies, Dave? Take a swim!" Nancy quipped.

Wilfred came up next to the dinghy. "I'm Wilfred; Call me Willie. I'm your full-service rescue swimmer," he said with a grin. But his face grew serious when he added, "Anyone here sick or injured, or need immediate medical attention?"

A chorus of "nos" ensued.

"Good. Here's what's gonna happen. We can only take three people at a time. We'll hoist you one by one into the helicopter. I'll stay here. The helo will take you to the nearest airport where you'll get checked by medical professionals. It will refuel, come back, and get the rest of us. Is that clear?"

A chorus of enthusiastic "yeses" ensued.

"Who's in charge here?" he asked.

"I guess that would be me," Dave said. "What do you need?"

"I need you to tell me who goes in the first round."

Dave looked at his fellow passengers. "I'd ask for volunteers, but he said only three."

"Me, me, me, me, me!" cried Sheila. "Please!"

Dave nodded. "Absolutely."

Sheila gave him an impromptu hug. "Thank you! I'm sorry I was so much trouble. You were great."

"Thanks. You were fine too," Dave said. "Okay, who else?"

"Ladies first," Josh said.

"There's three more of us," Jane said. "Only two more can go."

"I'll wait for the next round," Nancy said.

As the others thanked her, Dave turned to Sheila. "You know what's next, right? You have to get in the water with Willie. He'll help you to the basket. Okay?"

She nodded, but with eyes clouded with worry. "Okay."

Willie said, "Once we lower the rescue basket, I'll take you out to it, load you into it, and they'll hoist you up." He unclipped a radio from his life vest and said, "65, 65, ready for the basket."

"Willie," Dave said. "Sheila's going with you first, but she can't swim, and she's not comfortable in the water." He gave her a sideways glance. "She's learning fast."

Willie said, "Not to worry, Sheila. I do this for a living. Now, just ease into the water, and I'll be right here with you."

A few minutes later as the basket rose, swinging back and forth to the helicopter, Sheila called out, "Who-wee! Momma's never gonna believe this!"

"Good to see she's not afraid of heights!" Nancy said.

Twenty minutes later, Jane and Kim had joined Sheila aboard the helicopter, after which it disappeared into the night.

Willie climbed into the dinghy. "You guys have had quite a night. What happened, anyway?"

Dave said, "We hit something in the water—some kind of floating container. We started taking on water fast, so I woke up my dad and he told us to abandon ship."

"Your dad?" Willie asked, concerned. "Aren't you the captain? Where's your dad?"

"My dad's the captain. He took a one-man life raft off the stern. I wanted him in this raft, but he said it was too small. He was right. We heard an engine back there, so he said he'd paddle to it and try to get some help. We haven't seen him since." Dave swallowed, hit with a sudden concern for his father.

"Oh man!" Wilfred exclaimed as he snatched up his radio. "65? 65? Do you copy?" He listened. Nothing. He tried it again. Still nothing. "My radio range is too short. We'll have to wait until they come back for us. We thought you were the whole crew. We had no idea there was another person." He looked up at Dave's stricken face in the moonlight. "Don't worry, sir. We'll find him. That's what we do."

CHAPTER 11

Now that he'd wedged the snorkel valve open, Phil lay back to enjoy the victory and think over his next move. He was exhausted but exhilarated, as if he'd just scored a touchdown. He thought of his father and how proud he'd be at this feat. Phil had never liked farming, but he was glad now that he'd learned how to fix all kinds of beat-up equipment on the farm.

He tried to concentrate on what to do next. When the sub skipper tried to dive, he'd discover the problem. He'd surface to fix the valve, and Phil didn't want to be anywhere close when that happened.

He figured the sub was probably 30 or 40 feet below the water—and its propeller—but if he surfaced, the net would hang off the top of the ship and hit the blades. He had to get away before that happened. Just imagining the submarine surfacing in front of him sent his pulse racing. He moved the dinghy further and further down the net; he didn't know how much.

When he had gained some distance, he turned for a last look at the snorkel in the moonlight. "Okay, mister sub skipper; your move."

Sometime later Phil woke with a start. It took him a moment to get oriented, and then he realized something had changed. It was quiet, very quiet. *The diesel engine was off.* His pulse quickened and he was suddenly a ball of tension. This was the proverbial moment of truth.

The nap had refreshed him, though. Before drifting off, he'd positioned the raft in the exhaust wake of the submarine. Its warmth and gentle bubbling had acted like a continuous massage as he'd caught up on some rest. He scrambled to his knees and prepared to release the net quickly if necessary.

What would they do first? Close the flapper valve and lower the snorkel, he supposed. He heard a sudden *thunk*— and then silence. Phil waited, half-enjoying the play that must have been unfolding below him. He was sure they'd tried to close the valve; and would do so again, perhaps two or three times. And it wouldn't work. An officer would get involved to see what was wrong. There'd be a discussion. The captain would be informed and demand a clear answer on what was malfunctioning.

His nerves tingled with excitement and a breath of fear. *I'm in Your hands, Lord!*

Thirty-five feet below the surface, an engineering mate tried to decide what to do. He heard the *thunk* but got no confirming green light that the flapper valve was closed.

In the sub's engine compartment, the captain stood uncomfortably close to the machinist mate. His jaw hardened and his dark eyes flashed. "What do you mean, 'It won't close?"

Back in the raft, Phil thought, *Okay, Skipper, let's see what you're made of. Are you gonna surface, or are you gonna take a chance that the switch is malfunctioning and the snorkel valve is okay?* He watched for a sign of activity from the sub but saw only the surface of the water, unbroken except for occasional swells and the net.

I pick door two. Do a test dive. And that means I need to give you some space. I don't know how fast you're gonna go down, or how far. But you're not taking me with you! Phil let the dinghy drift further down the net, and away from the sub.

He was now about 100 feet behind the submarine, ready to release the net completely if need be. He glanced to the east. No sign of dawn yet.

He supposed the snorkel would go up and down like a periscope. *Uh oh—the periscope! That's what the skipper will use first, try to look at the snorkel.* He and his little raft might be seen, too.

Sure enough, no sooner than he'd thought of it, the periscope came up and rotated around. It pointed straight at him as well as the snorkel. He threw himself to the floor of the raft as flat as he could get. The periscope seemed to be directed to the right of the snorkel, so perhaps they hadn't seen him. If they did see him, he was toast. In fact, if they saw just the net, he was still probably toast.

It was dark, at least. *Unless they had night vision on the scope!* His pulse quickened again, but he thought, *No, no reason for that. The scope looked for ships and airplanes. Night vision was no good for that.* As he slowly grew calmer, he kept his eyes on the device, still pointed in his direction. *Okay, Skipper, pull your scope down. And then try pulling your snorkel down. Keep your hand on the switch, or whatever it is, because you're in for a very wet surprise!*

Phil swallowed a sense of unreality. It felt like he was orchestrating a terrorist submarine's actions--right in front of him! But this part was predictable. The next was not.

As if on cue, the periscope dropped out of sight and the snorkel powered down. Its speed surprised him. He guessed it worked quickly to avoid detection by enemies. *But that meant they were gonna get a real deluge down their intake too!*

He figured there must be fair terror down in that submarine about now. A 15-inch hole through the top brought a lot of seawater. He wondered where the water went and caught himself smiling. It wasn't his problem. By now the skipper would be screaming to raise the snorkel. Lo and behold, the snorkel popped back up. *Yes!* Phil stifled a sense of glee.

He wondered about the captain, who the guy was, where he'd come from. *By the grace of God, I'll never find out.* He was surprised at his detachment as he watched the drama play out ahead of him. Somehow, he didn't feel threatened. He had an almost supernatural calm. *Lord, thank you for watching over me, keeping me safe. Give me wisdom. Let the submarine be detected and destroyed or sent away.*

Thirty-five feet below, a great debate raged. The captain was fuming, but underneath his façade, he was downright frightened. His executive officer beseeched him to surface immediately.

"No!" The captain turned on him. "We have come all this way without detection. Our mission is almost complete! Subject closed."

The executive officer, an experienced and very strong-willed man, though physically unimposing, shook with rage. "Captain, if there is a problem, we have only until sunrise to fix it, before someone might see us!" He moved back as if he'd overstepped his bounds.

The third man in the compartment, the engineering officer, stood by anxiously. The captain whirled toward him. "Can you start your engines again? Has the water damaged them?" he demanded. "Well?"

"I--I think so. I mean, I think I can start the engines. And no, the water will not have reached them. We will pump it out."

The captain straightened, looked fixedly into the executive officer's eyes, and said very firmly, "Here's what we are going to do, Executive Officer Purali. We are going to restart the engines and make sure they are okay. Then you are going to bring the boat to neutral with minimal forward motion, snorkel depth. Next, I want you to get Lieutenant Asgari. He's a dedicated believer and cruised through commando training. Send him up through the escape hatch in the forward torpedo room with a flashlight and a wrench or something. Tell him to find and fix whatever is wrong with that snorkel head valve. If he cannot fix it, then we surface. Not before."

The executive officer started to say something, but the captain interrupted, "Is that clear?"

"Yes, sir." The exec responded, snapping a crisp salute. He turned to make preparations.

Phil sat patiently in the little raft, waiting to see what happened next. If they surfaced, he'd need to release the net and get out of sight. This caper would be over.

"Showtime, Skipper," he said aloud.

The diesel started back up with a cough and stutter, and then ran steadily. But their forward motion was negligible. His muscles tightened as he strained to watch what was happening. The moon still provided some light through a thin, patchy cloud cover.

Suddenly Phil saw a splash ahead of the snorkel. It was a man! *Oh boy, they sent somebody up to repair it. This will not do.* He started to reel in the raft, counting on the darkness and the man's focus on the snorkel to distract him as Phil approached.

The man discovered the net. Would he start cutting it loose, or would he look at the snorkel first? He chose the snorkel. Someone had surely briefed him on how it was built, for he worked his way around to the aft side with his back to Phil. *Perfect.* He would have to attack him. But he hadn't been in a fight since grade school. He hoped that having a lot of water polo under his belt would come in handy!

The man was fumbling to find the locknut on the snorkel's cover tilt mechanism. Phil came up quietly behind him. This wasn't going to be easy. His whole body tensed as he anticipated what he had to do. Whatever his move, it had to be fast and dominating. The guy had breathing apparatus on his chest. Phil reached up, sank a hand into the waistband of the guy's shorts and his other hand in his hair. He yanked with all his might, using his weight as leverage. They both crashed into the water.

Phil knew he should drown him but couldn't bring himself to do it. They were both sinking, the man fumbling for Phil's arm around his neck. Phil ripped the little scuba rig off him and let it sink. He realized with amazement that the guy was a lousy swimmer—or at least a lousy water polo player. If he could get him away from the sub and away from the net, maybe he could just release him. That would take care of him without Phil having to take his life.

The man thrashed and struggled to get loose. Phil came to the surface and let him catch a breath. He sputtered and gagged as he sucked in air. Phil slipped into a lifesaver carry with his arm around his neck and side-stroked away from the sub. The man tried to rip Phil's arm away so he could turn over to face him, but Phil grabbed a breath and took him underwater again.

Amazing, what lack of air did to a person. The guy panicked. They came back up, but Phil maintained an iron grip around his neck. The man continued to struggle but seemed disoriented.

A few minutes later Phil figured they were at least fifty yards from the net and the sub—and that his prisoner was exhausted. He took a deep breath, released him, and swam away underwater, back toward the net. When he reached it, he reeled himself to the raft which was still right behind the snorkel and climbed in. He was shaking—a mixture of adrenaline, anger, and fear. He searched for a sign of the guy out on the water and saw nothing. But he heard him. He was coughing and gasping and yelling something, probably for help. If he was smart, he'd get himself under control, tread water, and hope that someone found him before the sharks did. If he wasn't smart…Phil didn't want to think about that.

He returned his attention to the submarine. When this guy didn't come back, if they surfaced, he had to be long gone. He released the raft and let it drift. The sub's diesel stopped. Phil froze, listening. He heard banging sounds and then a muffled yell. They'd probably opened an access plate to the intake duct and were calling the surface to see if their guy was still there—or if he'd found anything.

The captain and the exec sat over coffee in the war room. "What do you think is happening?" the captain asked.

The exec returned his gaze with a tentative one. "I know how much you like Lieutenant Asgari and have confidence in him, but from what I know, he isn't a very good swimmer. He has many necessary skills, but not that one. I'm sorry to say, sir, but he has probably drowned."

The captain shrank into his chair as if daunted. "I didn't know," he said quietly. "I wish you had told me." Then, looking back at the exec, he continued, "But I guess I was not in a very receptive mood just then." He smiled slightly and added, glancing at his watch, "Okay, we have time to do this once more. Who is our best swimmer?"

"You're not going to like this, sir, but it's Asad. Without a doubt."

"Asad? That *kafir!* I'm to trust this boat to that pagan infidel?" The captain stopped himself. "Okay, we have to move. Get him in here. Give him whatever he asks for, and get him out there. If that doesn't work, we surface."

CHAPTER 12

Connie Morello cruised up Miami's 8th Avenue behind the wheel of her Volkswagen Beetle convertible, heading for home. She straightened the pillow on the seat to help her see over the steering wheel. At 2:30 AM, she was tired, frustrated, and apprehensive. Plus, her feet were sore. She fumbled in her purse for a cigarette. If she didn't sell a story to the Miami Herald or somebody else—soon—she would have to move back in with her mother.

Tonight had been a fiasco. She'd gotten a tip about a political refugee flying in on LAN from Caracas. Although the plane had landed two hours ago, she'd only just discovered—thanks to time-consuming security restrictions— that he wasn't on board.

She took a deep inhale and let the smoke out slowly as she rolled to a stop at a red light. She started to take another drag but stopped to listen. "A helicopter, at this hour?" she said. "Has to be the Coast Guard." She looked ahead at the Opa-Locka airport, home of the Miami Coast Guard Air Station. Flights were unusual at two AM. She searched the eastern sky and made out a chopper's red and green flashing strobe lights as it approached the airport. *This might be a new story.*

She checked traffic either way and gunned her VW through the light. *Definitely a story!*

She snaked her way through the approach roads and parked right up by the fence. She snatched her purse and rushed from the car. Standing on tiptoe to elevate her 4 foot,

10 inches, she spotted the Coast Guard hangar and the likely landing place for the copter and headed through an open gate in that direction. Soon she began jogging, watching as the Opa-Locka Fire Department's Advanced Life Support Squad rolled past her and around a corner.

She rounded the hangar just as the Coast Guard helicopter hovered above the ground, preparing to land. Heading quickly for the copter, she couldn't believe her good fortune. As the rotor spooled down, a red-clad crewman jumped out of the side door. He turned and helped a young lady step down on the tarmac.

Gotta find out what happened, Connie thought, as two more young women, all looking tired but relieved, appeared after the first. She approached the group, reaching in her purse as a crew member came toward her.

"Miami Herald." She held up an identification card. In the dim light, she hoped he couldn't see that it was her health club ID.

The man said, "We need to check these ladies out first. Then you can talk to them."

Connie flashed her brightest smile at him, knowing it was one of her best features. "Thanks very much. I'll be right here." She listened as the paramedics talked to each woman, took their blood pressure, checked their heart and lungs with a stethoscope—and got their stories. She heard enough to know they'd been on a sailboat that had sunk and left them floating in the ocean in a rubber raft. She thought she heard one of the girls say there were more people yet to be rescued. She tagged along as they walked toward the hangar. The helicopter began spooling up its rotor.

She approached the group of women. "Hi, I'm Constanza Morello, but you can call me Connie. I'm a reporter with the Miami Herald. I'd love to spend a few minutes with you and your friends, getting your story to put in the morning paper."

The girls looked at each other, and one of them said, "Okay, that sounds great."

Connie's heart soared. *She'd have a story to sell for sure!*

Later, though she'd interviewed the girls in a deserted break area, she realized she'd only gotten half the story. There were three more people to come in, and they had to find a seventh person, the captain. But it was better than nothing. She clicked speed dial for the night editor of the paper, holding her breath.

"Hi, Connie Morello. Yeah, I'm a stringer. I'm at the Opa-Locka airport, and I just got a story about a sailboat that sank out near the Bahamas. We have six people being rescued by the Coast Guard, and one more is missing." She nodded. "Uh-hum, they're all students except the missing guy. Number seven is apparently the father of one of the students. They say he's on a little raft by himself trying to get help from a boat they heard in the dark. Coast Guard's already out again, so his son should be in soon."

She listened again and her eyes lit up. "Thank you so much! Four-column inches is great. You think it will make the front page?" she asked hopefully. And then, biting back a smile, "It *will*? *¡Gracias Dios!* Whoops, I mean thank you, thank you so much! Any chance of a byline?" she asked, grinning broadly now. She could already see the headline: "Six Students Rescued from Ocean, One Missing."

CHAPTER 13

Back in the raft, Phil tried to rest but couldn't relax. The sub was evidently still trying to decide how to proceed, but the odds of surfacing had to be high. If they did surface, he'd have to get scarce in a hurry, slide into the water to lower his profile, perhaps, while he stroked away with the raft somehow.

He maintained a constant watch on the snorkel which was moving slowly ahead and saw another swimmer pop his head up. *Gutsy move, skipper.* He liked that. He studied him—this guy knew how to swim. As he reeled in the raft and prepared for action, he heard the strangest thing.

"Don't kill me, don't kill me!" the man yelled at Phil in English.

An American? How could that be? But he yelled back, "Okay, Okay, I didn't kill the last guy." He reached the snorkel. Phil pulled his life raft to within 20 feet of it, and said, "Who are you? Where are you from?"

"My name is Asad. It means lion. But in the states, they call me Ace. I'm from Iran. This is the *Yunes*, in the Iranian Navy."

Phil was dumbfounded. An Iranian speaking perfect English atop a submarine snorkel moving down the Gulfstream—*Lord, how could this be?* He yelled, "Where did you learn English? It sounds perfect."

"I grew up in the states, in Michigan."

Wow. "Where in Michigan?"

"Dearborn, outside Detroit."

"Where did you go to high school?"

"Fordson."

Phil was astounded. "Fordson? I've raced in their swimming pool; marched on the football field. I've played drums in the auditorium. I'm from Wyandotte."

Asad smiled. "No way, man. I was on the Fordson swim team. I swam in their pool too!" He looked Iranian with dark hair and tan skin, but his words were American all the way.

Phil began to feel safe with the guy and reeled in his raft so they could talk face-to-face. "So, what's the story here? What are you guys doing?"

His face sobered. "We've come from Iran. This used to be a Russian Kilo sub. There's something wrong with the snorkel. I have to try to fix it."

"I know, I blocked it so it wouldn't close. I figured your sub was up to no good." He paused. "Is that true?"

Ace hesitated, sizing up Phil. "Yeah, actually it is true." Quietly, he continued. "There are missiles on the aft deck in watertight compartments. I think we're going to shoot them off before very long." In a more strident voice, he added, "But look, man, I've got to fix the snorkel. If I don't, they'll kill me, and kill my family back in Iran. I really *have* to fix it. I don't have much time. And I have to get rid of this net, too."

Phil hesitated. He liked this guy. He believed what he said about being killed, and his family too. He made a decision. "Okay, Ace. By the way, my name is Phil. I understand. We'll take off the block I put on the valve, but the net stays. I'm using it to follow your sub until our navy can intervene. I don't want to kill you or your family, or really anyone on your sub. But I must protect my country. We can slide the net down below the head of the snorkel but no more."

Asad nodded. "Fair enough," he said.

Phil climbed to the snorkel, and they stood on the net together and hinged open the cover.

"If you grew up in Michigan, how did you wind up in Iran?" he asked, as he twisted on his light. He reached in to start unstrapping the anchor shaft from the snorkel valve piston rod.

"My dad immigrated to the States to get away from the Shah before I was born," Ace said. "But after the revolution, he decided to go back to Iran. It's his homeland. So that's where I live now. I'm kind of—kind of an outcast. The captain doesn't like me. But maybe after this, he'll take me off his dump list."

Suddenly the diesel engine stopped. They heard the access plate being opened from the lower end of the intake duct.

"Asad, Asad!" someone yelled. Asad replied, starting a short conversation in what I guessed was Farsi. The access plate was slammed back into position.

"That was the captain. I told him I was almost done and had it fixed. I said it was a fishing net. Come on, let's finish this up, I need to get back down there."

"Okay, but what's the story with these missiles?" The more he'd thought about it, the more concerned he'd grown. "What do you know about them?"

"Not much; except they don't want anybody to get near them, even on deck. We have a couple of missile experts camped out in the torpedo room with us. They don't say much. But they check these little meters from time to time. I think they're Geiger counters."

"Are they nuclear?" Phil asked.

"Hmm," Ace said, thinking. "I really don't know. I guess they must be." His gaze leveled sadly on Phil. "You're right. We're up to no good."

"When are you going to launch them? Where?"

"Not a clue. Sorry. Look, we're done here. I gotta go, okay?" He turned to swim back down to the sub. Phil grabbed his elbow. When Asad looked back, Phil took his sheath knife, cut out a few squares of the net, and said, "Here; take this down as evidence." Then he offered his hand, and they shook. "Good luck, Ace. This was not a coincidence. God bless you."

"Yeah, I guess you're right. Good luck to you too." He took a deep breath, popped in his breather, and disappeared.

CHAPTER 14

Naval headquarters at Bandar Abbas,
Gulf of Hormuz, Iran

"Admiral, Mr. Zamani from the Ministry of Information is here to see you. He does not have an appointment. Should I show him in?" the secretary asked.

Mustafa Karim Radan, Admiral and Commander of the Islamic Republic of Iran's navy, sat up ramrod straight. A large, florid man, he was a former Greco-Roman wrestler, but now visibly overweight. "Zamani? He's not *from* the Ministry of Information, he *is* the Ministry of Information. Show him in. Bring tea, and some sort of cakes or sweets," he added.

Zamani was the supreme leader's go-to person, a spymaster and hatchet man. Radan had no idea why he'd come from Teheran to the Gulf just to see him, but it could not be good.

The door opened and the minister walked in—a thin, middle-aged, unassuming man in a gray, Western-style business suit. He looked keenly at the admiral with piercing eyes. "Admiral, thank you for seeing me."

Radan almost leapt to his feet and came around his ornate desk to bow and shake hands with Zamani. He motioned to two chairs in front of the desk. "Please, it is my pleasure, definitely my pleasure. We'll have tea in just a moment if that is acceptable."

He returned to his chair and sank back in it, aware that he'd exhibited none of his usual confidence as Commander of the navy. He leaned forward to face the spymaster. "So, Minister, what brings this most pleasant surprise to my humble office?"

Zamani smiled—one could never tell whether it was an expression of menace or pleasure, the Admiral thought.

"I am here about your submarine venture. If I remember correctly, the *Yunes* should be very near its objective." He looked at the admiral, waiting.

"Yes, sir, that's correct," the admiral replied.

"The Ayatollah Karameini, our supreme leader, would like an update on its position and when we may expect its final action. As you may suspect, our newly elected President Akbari knows nothing of this venture, in keeping with the need for absolute security. However, the supreme leader must be in an informed position to explain the situation to the president."

The Admiral relaxed. When Zamani first mentioned the Ayatollah, his heart sped as if it would stop, as the supreme leader was the head of all military forces in Iran. He said "To be honest, Minister, I'm relieved to hear you say that. First of all, I can assure you that this mission has been kept secret. As you know, we went to great lengths to disguise it, both inside and outside the country. With the change in presidents, however, one never knows whether we are still secure."

"And can we get an update from the captain?"

The Admiral inhaled sharply. "That, Minister, is not possible at this time. I don't believe you and I have ever spoken about it before, but the reality of a submarine operating underwater is that it's impossible to communicate with them. They'll be snorkeling in a few hours, and we will of course send your request to them. However, I must tell you that although the *Yunes* is very close to its final objective, it is still under absolute radio silence. Our best information is that they should be advancing along the East Coast of the United States as we speak. Obviously, this is the most hazardous portion of this long, long trip. I would not be surprised if the captain decided not to raise his communications mast above the surface—to minimize his radar exposure."

He continued, "Our last communication with them was three and a half weeks ago, at the supply ship rendezvous off the coast of Brazil. Other than the usual small mechanical problems and minor crew complaints, everything was on track. I was pleasantly surprised to hear how well they were doing. A trip of this length puts a Kilo sub and its crew to a test. It has already traveled almost twice its normal cruising range. And that's without the trip home." The admiral looked at his guest questioningly.

Zamani squinted and his mustache twitched. He said quietly but through tight lips, "So, am I to tell the Ayatollah that we cannot provide what he asked for?"

Admiral Radan raised his hands and forced a smile. "Please, Minister, understand my limitations. If it is humanly possible, I will provide you with everything you ask for. Please tell the supreme leader that we have every reason to believe the mission will be entirely successful."

The minister fell silent. He would let the admiral dig through his deepest fears to be sure there was no recourse. The door opened, and the secretary started to back in with the tea service on a tray.

"Not now!" the Admiral barked. The secretary scooted back out, his eyes bulging.

Radan looked back at Zamani with fake confidence. "Please, Minister, please understand. Captain Golzar was specifically selected for his skill, experience, and devotion to Islam. He has brought this submarine almost 12,000 miles without detection. That in itself is a major feat for our navy—for anyone's navy. He is so close to the final attack that nothing will deter him. He will not jeopardize the mission's success to give updates. The American satellites pick up everything.

"In addition, we have been monitoring the weather and it looks excellent for the next few days, very mild. As you know, he cannot launch in rough weather." The admiral watched his guest closely but saw only an unreadable countenance.

"You and the supreme leader can be completely confident that in," he paused and looked at his watch, "about three days from now we should receive reports of our successful attack from the Western news services—and the *Yunes*. After our years of planning and preparation, this hazardous voyage will bring our fondest hopes of bringing the Great Satan of the West to its knees."

Zamani nodded curtly, rose, and quietly walked out without a word.

CHAPTER 15

Phil felt sad watching Ace slip between the waves and return to his submarine. He was a young man trapped between two cultures. *Strange.* In fact, this whole night was getting stranger and stranger. *God, what are you doing here? I'm a high school history teacher, not a Navy SEAL!*

His thoughts jolted back to his predicament as he realized the sub would submerge soon. *Gotta move—now!* He wondered how long it would take Ace to get back in, and hoped he'd make it. It was probably a tricky procedure and rarely practiced, much less even contemplated.

He quickly untied the raft and let it float back in the sub's wake. He had no idea how far back he should go. And how long was the net? He grabbed it to keep it from running out, and slowly let it slide through his hands as the sub moved on.

When he was roughly a hundred yards behind it, he stopped letting the net loose and just hung on. He heard the diesel engine stop and then the clank as the snorkel valve slammed shut. The snorkel disappeared beneath the waves. With a pounding heart, he watched the net disappearing underwater, ready to release it and let more out if needed. He did not want to be dragged down with the sub.

After ten tense minutes when the net didn't go any deeper, he figured they'd reached their cruising depth. He took a deep breath and relaxed. There was about 50 feet of net floating on the surface ahead now, before it angled down into the water which slipped past the raft in gentle laps. The sub evidently moved a lot slower on battery than when snorkeling on diesel.

Phil swung his arms and shook his shoulders to ease out the remaining tension. *Forty-three is a little old for this stuff. Okay, I know what I need to do now—sleep.* The raft had a cover, a shroud, tucked in around the edges, and he pulled it out and wrapped himself in it. He settled down with his head on the forward end of the tube, and his feet tucked at the other end. Even with the warm Gulfstream, the night was chilly. He had no idea when he'd be rescued, and figured he'd best get comfortable. He'd need to think about food and water, too— but not now. *Sleep Phil, sleep.*

Staring up at the heavens, he noticed the stars were getting hazy. *Thank you, God, for the moonlight when I needed it. Lord, I have no idea what you're doing here, but I trust in you and believe in you.*

He contemplated what should be happening by now on shore. The Coast Guard would have found David and the others. Dave had the EPIRB, so should have been easy to find. He'd tell the Guard about Phil, and they'd start looking for him. He was way north of the normal drifting position that the Coast Guard would expect, but it would be daylight soon, making him easier to find—except for that growing haze.

Whatever happened, he couldn't abandon the sub until the Coast Guard started tracking it. But a terrible thought hit him. *Nuts!* He'd forgotten to carve off the anti-radar coating on the snorkel. *Anti-radar or anti-sonar?* He guessed anti-radar. But it didn't matter. If he was still dragging along when darkness fell, he'd peel it off then.

He wondered where they were and searched the west. He could barely see the glow of city lights through the mist. Was that Fort Lauderdale? The stars looked fainter, especially in that direction. *Fog.* He hoped it didn't get thick, but there was nothing he could do about it. *It's in Your hands, Lord.*

Snuggled down in the raft, he realized he was actually enjoying the adventure. It was truly a trip of a lifetime. He drifted off to sleep, lulled by the waves and the sound of the water slipping past.

Phil awoke to the sensation of something bumping his butt through the bottom of the raft. Was something caught in the net? He pushed back the shroud and peered into the darkness. The moon and stars were fully masked by clouds now. How long had he been asleep? He fumbled for the light and twisted it on, then leaned over the side of the raft to try to see underneath.

Oh God! His pulse raced as he recoiled back. Terror gripped him. *Be calm, Phil, be calm.*

He'd seen a fin, a large dorsal fin—at arm's length. As he peeked again, he saw it lazily kept with him in the water. He could have reached out and touched it. *Bad idea.* Could he see the tail? He slid the light back. Six feet behind the fin, he saw it weaving languidly back and forth. This shark could have him for breakfast with a couple of bites.

God—help me!

CHAPTER 16

Dave, Josh, Nancy, and Wilfred the rescue swimmer, sat floating in the dinghy in the dark. The first three girls had been flown back to the mainland over an hour ago, but Wilfred's presence was reassuring, despite a dense fog closing in. Soon, however, it covered the stars, sealing them in a very, very, dark night.

"How are they gonna find us in this fog?" Josh asked.

"They'll home in on my beacon," Wilfred explained. "When they get close, I'll talk them in with my trusty handheld radio," he added, while holding it up.

Dave said, "I should've asked Sheila to leave her little penlight with us. I never thought the clouds would come in and turn the lights off."

"Not to worry, Captain Dave, the Coast Guard is here," Wilfred said. He snapped on his flashlight and shone it around.

"You guys are all Boy Scouts at heart, aren't ya?" Dave said. "You follow their motto, 'Be Prepared.'"

"Yeah, I guess," Wilfred said.

"I hear the helicopter!" Nancy cried.

The others heard it and hooted with excitement. Wilfred searched the sky. "Okay, let's get this rescue underway."

Amanda tracked Wilfred's beacon. When she reached the

area, she dropped to 300 feet. "All eyes outside," she said. "Let's find them."

With night vision goggles in place, the crew searched for the little raft.

"Rescue swimmer, rescue swimmer, copy?" She waited, and then repeated, "Rescue swimmer, rescue swimmer. This is 65 Alpha. Do you copy?"

"Copy loud and clear!" Wilfred's strong voice came crackling over the line. "We can't see you yet, but you sound due east of us. It's foggy, so I'll talk you in. Over."

Amanda turned west, switched on her spotlight, and dropped down to 200 feet. Her rotor wash cleared the mist away from the surface of the ocean.

"Mark! Light at two o'clock." Wally, the flight mechanic said. "A hundred fifty yards."

"Got the mark!" Amanda confirmed, as she slowed down even more and shifted slightly to the right. The raft came into view below them. She eased the chopper down to a 50-foot hover over it. "Wally, you ready?" she asked.

"Just a sec. Okay, basket going down," he replied as he lowered the rescue basket near the raft.

Wilfred turned to his companions. "Okay, you know how it's done!" he called, over the noise of the chopper. "Shall we say ladies first?" He looked at Nancy.

"Works for me!" Nancy exclaimed. "Nice warm towel, hot chocolate, dry clothes," she continued, "and a bed! *I am ready*!" She slid off the raft and swam to the basket. Wilfred slid in behind her and swam hard to catch up. By the time he got to the basket, she was already settled in it.

"Ready to hoist," Wilfred called.

In seconds, Nancy began rising steadily and was soon helped into the copter. After Dave and Josh were likewise hoisted up, Wilfred followed.

"Lieutenant, you know we're missing one, right?" he asked.

Amanda was startled, "No—no I didn't. Who's missing?"

"My dad!" Dave exclaimed.

"The captain of the boat that went down," Wilfred added. "His name is Phil—Phil Shepherd. He took a one-man life raft so the kids could fit in the dinghy. Dave says they heard an engine nearby, and Phil was gonna paddle to it and get help. That's the last they know."

Amanda replied, "I had no idea. We've already sent the CASA home. I guess the search will have to begin from the original sinking point. Okay, I'll call it in to District. Is everyone aboard?"

"Aye, Lieutenant, ready to go," Wilfred said.

"Tell me again exactly what we're looking for," Amanda asked as she wheeled the helicopter back toward Miami.

Wilfred looked at Dave. He'd be able to describe his father's raft better than he could, but it was deafening in the cabin; he handed Dave the intercom headset.

Dave nodded at him. "Hello, hello," he said, into the mic. He heard nothing. He gave Wilfred a quizzical look. Wilfred grinned and pointed to the "talk" button. Pressing the button, Dave tried again. "Hello, Dave Shepherd here, can you hear me?"

"I can," Amanda responded. "Okay, hang on a minute, Dave. I'm gonna patch you into District Seven in Miami, and ask you to describe exactly what happened with your father, okay?"

Dave never answered. He looked down at the black ocean whizzing beneath them, and felt his throat tighten. His dad was floating around somewhere down there in that ocean, in the dark, in that…that little, tiny life raft. How were they ever, ever going to find him? *Oh, Dad!* he thought. *I don't want to lose you!*

CHAPTER 17

"ASAD OMIDI TO THE WARDROOM." The command reverberated from the submarine intercom. A few moments later, Asad shuffled into the room and leaned against the bulkhead to steady himself. He was exhausted. The return swim to the sub and entry through the escape chamber had been harrowing. His breathing regulator had malfunctioned, and he almost hadn't made it. He'd since managed to don a clean shirt but was still in wet shorts and barefooted. *What did they want from him now?*

But at his entry Captain Golzar and Executive Officer Masood Pourali looked up at him with a smile. "Sit—sit, sailor," the captain said. "Would you like coffee?"

"That would…that would be fine," Asad stuttered.

"Seaman Omidi, you did a good job out there. I am impressed. Tell me what you found," the captain said in a friendly tone.

Asad swallowed. "It was a net, sir. A big fishing net—one of those long ones that hangs down from the surface. I guess we must've snorkeled through it sometime during the night. It jammed everything up," he added, hoping they'd believe him. He remembered something and reached into his pocket. "Here." He held out the piece of net that Phil gave him. "I brought this to show you. I guess I forgot when I came in. I'm sorry, Captain."

Both officers reached for the net, but the XO quickly withdrew his in deference to the captain. The captain exclaimed, "Well, look at that!" He fingered and stretched the net. "Strong. I wonder where we picked it up? XO, where were we when we first began snorkeling tonight?"

"I can check the chart, but from memory I would say off the Florida Keys, north of Cuba," the XO responded.

"So, you found this and cleared it away, is that right?" the captain asked Asad.

"Yes, sir. It was a mess. The net was huge and had floats and weights on it. I had to get underneath the cover of the snorkel to get everything cleared out," he explained shakily. His anxiety was uncontrollable. If they ever found out he'd spoken to an American… he'd be a goner.

"Ah, yes! I spoke to you through the snorkel access plate." The captain thought for a moment, then continued, "Okay, you've done a fine job. Go and rest. We'll find someone to take your next watch. Dismissed."

"Yes, sir," Asad replied, in great relief.

After he'd gone, the Captain and Executive Officer sat quietly for a few moments, sipping coffee. The XO said calmly, "Captain, I owe you an apology. I didn't think the swimmer idea had a chance of working, especially after we'd lost Hesam. I was wrong. This was a far better way to rectify the situation than surfacing."

"Thank you, Masood," the captain said. "I was wrong too—about this Asad kid. He's alright." He continued, "You know, we've been through a great deal here. Eventually, this mission will go down in the annals of marine history for hundreds of years to come—like the Twin Towers. It's too bad we won't be able to tell anyone about it though. When you think about all the trouble, all the planning, the preparation—and here we are—just a few miles off the American coast." He smiled and leaned back in his seat.

"When I first heard the proposal of launching missiles from the surface of a Kilo sub, I thought it was crazy. And then—sneak out of Iran? Load the missiles in their housings at sea, in the dark? Not possible!" He smiled again. "But we did it. And somehow, I believe we even kept this whole thing under wraps. As you know, our zealot competitor, the Iranian Revolutionary Guard Navy, is always sniffing around our docks and facilities, trying to find out what we're doing and how to cut us down. This mission will elevate the Islamic Republic's Navy! Commodore Radan's vision and guidance in this project have paid off."

"I know exactly what you're talking about, Captain," the XO replied, nodding. "I felt very honored to be selected for a special, secret mission. But when I heard what the mission was, I struggled. I knew they would never let me walk away from it—not after I knew what it was. But you're right, it's all working out. I often wonder how they managed to train and equip the supply ship that met us, so far three times, to keep us going."

"Allah's blessing is surely upon us. We will bring honor to him," the Captain said, with eyes far off. Shifting gears, he continued, "Okay, what about our charts? We're getting close to our objective. We must be prepared for anything." He held up the piece of net, adding, "Who would have expected this?"

"Nobody, sir." The XO shook his head. "Captain, now that you ask about the charts, I would be happier if we could get American charts. They will have all the latest notices to mariners and navigation aids. Once we finally surface to attack, we will want to be as well-informed as possible."

"And how, sir, do you suggest we get American charts?" The captain asked, sneering. "We can't exactly put in at the Navy Yard in Charleston and buy a set." His anger grew. "Do you have any idea what you're talking about?"

The XO smiled to himself. "Actually, sir, I have an idea—the Internet. I believe we can probably find American charts on the Internet. The Americans say they can find anything that exists on the Internet. If you agree, I believe it's worth checking."

The captain cocked a brow at his subordinate. "How would you propose to do this—later tonight when we snorkel again? How do we keep the Americans from finding us if we try it?"

The XO inwardly exulted. Here was a great chance to prove his worth to the captain. "I took the liberty of subscribing to a French satellite Internet service before we left our base on Bandar Abbas. I believe we can go online when we snorkel and not be identified."

"And whom do we have on board that knows about this American Internet?" the captain challenged.

"Captain, I think we were just talking to him—Asad."

The captain nodded—and smiled.

CHAPTER 18

Phil fell backward, stumbling over the right side of the raft and almost falling out as he recoiled from the shark.

Get control of yourself. But his hands shook, and his heart raced. *Lord, help me! What do I do?*

He settled back into the raft, keeping his light on the shark as it patrolled alongside. He thought about the net—was it okay? He shone the light at the bow and saw what happened. *That's what I'm to do!* Both sides of the net had shifted to the right side. *That's it, Lord! Thank you!* He needed to put the net between the shark and himself—the raft, rather—like a fence.

When he tied to the net before the sub stopped snorkeling, he really hadn't thought much about how it should be done. Now it was critical. He turned over slowly, getting on his hands and knees so he could grasp the net. He shifted the light back to the left to check on the shark. *Oh no! He was gone!*

Phil waited and decided it was underneath the raft. He kept still but nothing happened. Slowly he untied the raft from the net. But then— *Ouch!* His knee got the brunt of a shark bang right through the bottom of the raft. Was he testing to see if Phil was edible? If so, that was a problem, because he was! He tried to speed up the task, but his fingers shook as he struggled with the wet lines and net.

Though still on hands and knees, Phil figured he was riding way too high in the raft. He'd be easy to tip over, and that would be disastrous.

He had no choice but to get on his belly. This left his feet dangling out the back above the water, but it couldn't be helped. *Lord, don't let him see my feet and attack them!*

He finally got the net loose and separated the two sides. He flashed the light on the water to the left and was relieved to see the shark swimming there—*better there than underneath him.* It was almost twice as long as the raft. Apparently, it was still uncertain about what Phil was.

But he needed to put this net in position, pronto, before it figured it out. He tied one side of the net to a small ring on the side of the raft. He'd never know who designed the raft, but he felt they did a great job. They'd tried to cover all possibilities. But he'd bet they never thought of this one— trailing an enemy sub!

He grabbed a float and tried to push it and its line under the raft. He had to get it to the left side. He tucked the light in his mouth and turned to check if the shark was still there— *gone again!*

Phil's hand slipped off the float, and the raft skewed sideways just as a gigantic mouth snapped out of the water, engulfing the float he'd just been holding. "Jesus, help me!"

Phil vomited into the ocean. *Where did that come from? Could this get any worse? Thank you, Lord, that my hand slipped just as the shark attacked! He must've seen my hand or sensed it moving in the water and gone for it.*

Phil played the light around, searching for the monster. He saw it several feet away on the left, thrashing. It looked like there was blood there, too. He found himself smiling in spite of it all.

"Mr. Shark, you've literally bit off more than you can chew," he said, staring at the thing. Its teeth had gone through the glass float.

"Aw, did you cut your mouth? Serves you right, trying to mess with me!" He was practically shouting. He wondered if it might be precipitating another attack, a more serious one, or if the injury would drive it off. He turned his attention back to the net. He had to repair the gap in the left float line. He pulled himself closer to the submarine, groped down in the water, and found the piece of net. Lying on his belly was killing his back, though, so he carefully rolled over and sat up. He hung onto the float line and slid an arm through a couple squares of the netting—just so he wouldn't lose it again. Now he could use both hands. He pulled in the torn section until he found the other end of the line.

The shark had taken out more than a foot. Phil tried not to think about how big its mouth must be. He pulled the ends of the severed line into his lap and tied them as firmly as possible. Some of his earlier sailing trips floated across his mind, images of docking line knots coming apart. So he tied a double granny knot. A granny knot was usually a big no-no because it was so hard to untie. But right now, he wanted a knot that would last until the end of time.

So, where was Mr. Shark? He shone the light around but didn't find him. He visualized the net as an underwater fence, protecting him on both sides from predatory intruders. He got back to his hands and knees, facing forward, and tied up the other side of the net to hold the raft firmly between them.

Finally, he let go and sat back to watch how the net affected the raft. How would it ride now? To his relief, it seemed fine. The sub was moving north at about the same speed as the waves, so the raft's motion was gentle. *Praise God for a south wind.*

Phil recalled a Gulf Stream crossing they'd attempted with the wind out of the north. It was like sailing inside a washing machine. The wind fought the Gulfstream, and the waves were crazy. He'd never make it through that in this little raft. They'd been in a 40-foot sailboat, then. Still apprehensive about another sudden bump in his butt, he waited, trying not to anticipate it.

He felt lousy. Besides exhaustion, he was surely getting dehydrated. The vomiting hadn't helped. His hands were still shaky. Now that he thought about it, his whole body felt weak, and he was lightheaded—almost woozy. He slid down with his knees up. He dragged the waterproof shroud over him, leaving only his face showing. He felt around for his knit cap and realized he still had it on! It even felt reasonably dry.

A light glow to the east through the fog and mist appeared. Dawn. Finally—a new day was nearing. What did it hold in store? *A little less action would be nice. A lot less action would be wonderful—and a rescue!*

Phil knew he had to sleep; it was mandatory. As he relaxed, he felt tension flow from his body like air from an air mattress. But as he softly recited Scripture to himself, a surprising release of tears crossed his cheeks.

"The Lord is my shepherd; I shall not want."

Lord, he prayed, *that's true. You are my shepherd; I shall not want for help or rescue. I feel safe under Your protection. Thank you, Jesus.*

CHAPTER 19

Captain Shine stood on the bridge of his Hatteras 38 charter fishing vessel, *Jessica Bell,* as it rocked gently in its slip in the Port Lucayo Marina near Freeport, Grand Bahama Island. The dawn light illuminated the controls on his piloting station. Shine, whose real name was Shinjuku, a third-generation Japanese Bahamian, took great pride in his vessel and had an excellent reputation as a deep-sea fishing charter captain. Over the years, he'd customized the boat, but had kept the original piloting station on the main deck with wheel, engine controls, compass, and VHF radio.

His passengers would be arriving soon: eager, probably loaded with equipment and who knows what. He flipped through lighting switches, verifying each one as they flicked on and off. The cooler was filled with ice chips to keep the day's catch cool until they returned to port. Everything seemed ready.

He looked up as he heard flip-flops coming down the dock runway. Here they were, *Frick and Frack,* he called them—two men, both on the short side, lots of middle in their middle age, long on enthusiasm, and short on stamina—not brothers, but they could be. They were good-hearted, good customers.

Dr. Winston Olson, DDS, and Dr. Marvin Robinson, DDS,

of Des Moines, Iowa, strode down the runway swinging a refrigerated cooler between them, filled with beer and sandwiches. They each toted a couple of fishing rods and were looking forward to competing in the Bahamas Bill Fishing Championship.

"Too bad Harvey couldn't make it today," Olson said. "But better for us to catch a whopper."

"Or maybe a whopper apiece," Robinson responded with a sly grin, "and I don't mean the Burger King kind." They chuckled as they came to a stop at the dock beside the *Jessica Bell*.

"Permission to come aboard, sir?" Olson asked, looking up at Shine on the flying bridge. Like most charter fishing boats, the forward-facing windows were covered in fiberglass to prevent leaks and reduce maintenance. This meant the boat had to be operated from the bridge above the main piloting station since there was no forward visibility from the main deck.

"Of course, gentlemen. Come aboard and make yourselves comfortable. I thought there were three of you today?"

Robinson said, "Harvey's not feeling so good today. Frankly, I think he's worried about getting seasick. He never did have a steady stomach. It's just the two of us."

Shine slid down the ladder with his hands on the rails, shook hands with them, and said with a grin, "All right! Why don't you stow your gear in the cabin, set up your rods on the fantail, and we'll get this beautiful luxury fishing vessel underway?"

A few minutes later, the twin 283 horse Detroit Diesel engines growled into action and the *Jessica Bell* backed out of the slip, turned toward the west, and slowly moved out to sea.

Olson brought up a thermos of hot coffee and a couple of cups. "Hey Skipper, want a cup of Iowa's finest special brew?"

Shine looked over his shoulder from the bridge. "No thanks, Winn. I'm a tea drinker—a cultural thing, you know. Where did you guys say you want to go?"

Robinson looked at Olson. "We were thinking of going south for 30 or 40 miles. Then fish our way back and finish up here by four o'clock."

Championship rules prescribed no lines in the water before eight AM. Shine said, "You know, guys, no fishing before eight o'clock, right?"

Olson said, "No problem, Skipper. During my lonely winter hours in Des Moines, I put together a few new lures I want to try. I'm gonna do some test tows on the surface to see how their action is. We won't go deep for the big ones or really start fishing before eight o'clock."

"Works for me," the captain said.

An hour later, they were well out from the islands into the Gulfstream. Shine, on the flying bridge, was high enough to see the islands, but on the deck below, Robinson and Olson could only see fog. Marv got out a large tackle box, filled with bits of colored plastic ribbons, steel leaders, and serious-looking hooks. They were fishing for white or blue marlin or spearfish—all of which required heavy-duty equipment to hook and land, despite the competition rules, which limited the line strength to 100 pounds.

After trying out two of his homemade lures with disappointing results, Winn selected a third, hoping for better action in the water. Marv joked, "So what's this one? Howdy Doody goes fishing? I see everything but the freckles."

"Wait and see, ye of little faith," Winn replied. "This one has trophy fish written all over it. Let's see how it acts." He reeled out a few feet of line, stepped to the side of the boat, lowered his rod tip almost to the surface, and released the lure. He watched keenly for its action as it coursed through the water. "Skipper, can you take us down to just 1 or 2 knots?" Winn called. "I think I found the best of the lot here."

Satisfied with the action of the lure, Winn released about 300 feet of line and let it run for a while. He settled down in one of the dual fighting chairs, imagining a big catch.

Shine called down, "We're well into the Gulfstream. You want me to speed it up to get farther south? Or just let it run at fishing speed?"

"Fishing speed will be fine," Winn said. "Let's let this run for twenty or thirty minutes to see how it holds up."

"Aye, aye, boss," Shine replied, as he scanned the horizon for other vessels. Nothing in sight at the moment. He noticed a fog bank off to the west.

Marv glanced at his watch: 6:30 AM. He reached in his backpack for sunblock and started applying it. "Now the *coup de grace*," he said as he put on his fishing hat.

"In your dreams, Paisano," Winn retorted, glancing at the tip of his rod in the holder at the back of the boat. He stood and tried to see his lure 300 feet behind the boat. Suddenly the rod bent over, and the reel screamed out line. "I've got something!" he shouted.

Shine shifted into neutral.

Winn yanked his rod out of the holder and started cranking on the heavy-duty reel.

Marv grabbed his arm, frowning. "Hold up! Hold up! There's something wrong—listen!"

Both men listened. "Oh, man! Someone's yelling! You hooked somebody in the water!" Marv cried. Winn squinted toward the sound. He could just make out a human head and an arm waving. They were yelling but the words were unintelligible. Winn cried, "Skipper! I've hooked somebody swimming! What do we do?"

Shine turned from the wheel, binoculars in hand. Focusing them, he said, "You're right, there's somebody there. Okay, maintain just enough tension on your line so it doesn't foul my props. I'm gonna back and turn toward him so that we don't put any more pressure on the line than we need to. Then we'll motor up to him, nice and slow. No point in ripping this guy up with that hook of yours."

Shine put both props in reverse, giving the starboard side more revolution to turn as they backed up. Winn walked carefully to the corner of the fantail, keeping the line clear of the props and open to the person on the end.

As they approached the swimmer, Marv called, "Shine? How are we gonna get this guy in the boat? You got a boarding ladder? What if he's not strong enough to climb it?"

"I've got a folding ladder in the port locker," he said. "Hang it over the stern rail." He peered through the binoculars again. "Good Lord! He doesn't have a life jacket! Marv! Open the starboard locker; find a life jacket and a long docking line. Tie the line to the jacket and get ready to throw it."

The man was floundering in the water, struggling to swim toward the boat. Winn thought he looked young and healthy. That was good. Marv called out, "We'll come to you. I'll throw you a life jacket! You put it on, and I'll pull you to the boat."

But it seemed the man didn't understand. Winn said, "I wonder if he speaks English." He looked up at the captain.

"Skipper, how's your Spanish? I don't think this guy speaks English."

Shine looked down at him and responded, "*Muy malo, señor*. Sorry about that."

Marv threw the life jacket, missed him, and tried again. This time it reached him, and he got it on. *At least he knew how to put on a life jacket.* The guy yelled something, but none of them understood it. "*Habla usted Español?*" Winn called, as under his breath he added, "If he does, I have no idea what to say next." But the man didn't respond.

Shine put the engines in neutral and called down, "Get that ladder in position and pull him around with the docking line. Let's see if he's strong enough to climb up."

As the man reached to take hold of the sides, it was obvious he was exhausted. Winn and Marv reached down, grabbed him under the armpits, and lifted. He got up to the railing, bent over it, and could go no further. Winn and Marv half lifted, half dragged him the rest of the way into the boat. Winn saw his hook deeply embedded in the back of the man's shoulder, which was bleeding slightly. The man leaned over the edge and vomited into the ocean.

"Okay," Winn said, taking charge. "We need to get that hook out, bandage him, hydrate him, and treat him for exposure. Shine, you have any blankets? A first aid kit?"

Shine slid down the ladder to the deck, took one look at the man, and disappeared into the cabin. Moments later he returned with a pillow, a blanket, and a first aid kit. "Let's start treating him here, and then move him down below."

"Good plan," Marv said as he examined the man. He looked to be in his early twenties with a dark complexion, jet black hair and mustache, tan shirt, and shorts—kind of like a uniform—and bare feet. Not the kind of shorts you usually saw in the Bahamas. He had a large tattoo on his left arm of an ancient warrior or maybe a king. "This guy must've fallen off some foreign freighter," Marv said. "I wonder where he's from?"

Shine returned to the back deck with a couple of bottles of spring water. He unscrewed the cap on one and offered it. The man's eyes opened wide, and he muttered something unintelligible, reaching for it. He drank thirstily. Shine cautioned, "Not too much, man. You'll make yourself sick." Then chuckling, he added, "I wonder why I'm talking to him? He obviously doesn't understand anything I'm saying."

Winn stood up, patted himself on the chest, and said loudly, "Winn, Winn." Then he patted Marv on the shoulder, and said, "Marv, Marv." Then he pointed to the man.

The man replied quietly, "Hesam."

Winn beamed. "Hesam?" The man nodded in assent.

Winn then looked around, pointed to the cabin, and motioned to go there as a group. "Okay gents, let's get him down below." Using grunts and sign language, they shuffled him to the forward cabin and eased him to an open berth.

Winn said, "I think he's gonna be okay. I want to stay with him for a while to be sure." He noticed that Hesam had a large knife in a sheath strapped to his belt. As he reached down to remove it to make him more comfortable, Hesam grabbed his wrist, and said something sharply. Winn was surprised at how strong he was. "Okay, okay, it's all yours," Winn said as he backed off and forced a smile. Hesam relaxed and lay down.

Shine said, "Gentlemen, I'm obliged to take this man back to port. And with what time remains, I will bring you out to do your fishing, but this takes priority. I have to call the Coast Guard and inform them we found a sailor. If there's been a man overboard, they've probably already gotten notice of it." Marv and Winn murmured their assent. They went to the back deck and started packing up their fishing gear.

Shine moved over to the main navigation station, checked it was on channel 16, and keyed it on. "Pan, pan, pan, this is the *Jessica Bell*. We just picked up a man out of the water." He paused as he noticed some motion at his side. He turned just in time to see Hesam's knife aiming for his throat. Shine tried to call out but could only gurgle as the razor-sharp blade slipped through his larynx and carotid artery.

Winn charged up the cabin steps behind Hesam and ran straight into that same wicked blade as it entered his abdomen and pulled up toward his heart. Hesam hung on to the boat with one hand as he turned and looked for Marv.

Marv was frozen in terror as he watched the bloody scene unfold. "What the—?" was all he managed to say. He held up his hands, trying to protect himself. Sinking to his knees, he knew his fate. "No, no, no!" he cried softly, as he looked pleadingly into Hesam's dark eyes. Hesam stepped toward him, lost his balance, and crashed into Marv, sinking the knife between his ribs into his heart.

The radio sputtered, "*Jessica Bell, Jessica Bell*. This is the United States Coast Guard. Please repeat your transmission."

Nobody answered.

CHAPTER 20

On Shore

"District 7, Duty Officer Lieutenant Kusmarak. May I help you?"

"Lieutenant, this is Petty Officer Vincent Forelli, Fort Lauderdale Boat Station. Did you guys hear the pan call about a man picked up in the Gulfstream?" Vincent sat back and rested his eyes on the view of the Port Everglades harbor with Ft. Lauderdale beyond. It was one of his favorite scenes— especially with the rising sun just starting to illuminate the masts and topsides of the bigger boats at dock.

"Petty Officer Forelli—no, no we didn't," the lieutenant responded.

Forelli straightened up and reached for a pen in his windowless office in the Brickell Plaza Federal Building of downtown Miami.

"What did they say? Has the man been identified?"

"No, sir. It was very short, sir. All they said was that it was the *Jessica Bell* calling, and they'd picked up a man out of the ocean—no position, no further information, and we lost them. When we tried to get them back, there was no response. Their radio must have gone out. We have no idea where *Jessica Bell's* home port is. We really have no more additional information. Have there been any reports of a man overboard?" Forelli asked.

"No, no there haven't…wait a minute! Yes, there was—sort of. We had a sailboat sink last night, halfway between Miami and Cat Cay. We thought we'd picked up the whole crew, but we learned that the captain is in a one-man life raft that we have yet to locate. I've got an HC 144 up, mowing the lawn for him."

"Mowing the lawn, sir?"

"It's a search pattern term, Officer. Going back and forth over a fairly large area with slightly overlapping passes. It's foggy down there, so their FLIR, the forward-looking infrared radar, is all we have to go by. Finding one guy in a one-man raft out there is like looking for a basketball in Montana. I'm thinking your call must be the same guy. What was the name of that boat again?"

"*Jessica Bell,*" Forelli answered.

The phone went silent for a few moments. Finally, Kusmarak said, "Okay, we'll do a boat name search and hope it's registered. I'll also call our friends in the Bahamas and ask them to do the same in case it came from one of their ports. I'd like to tell our search plane what kind of boat to look for, but we have no idea yet".

"I understand, Lieutenant," Vincent responded. "It's a long shot, but we've got local radar coverage here. We can try to identify everything that shows up. If we get some blanks, I'll give you a call, and maybe you can send your plane to check it out."

"Excellent," Lieutenant Kusmarak responded. "Okay, Petty Officer Forelli, I've got to get busy. Call me if you find anything."

A few minutes later

At the Royal Bahamas Defense Force Navy in Nassau, Lionel Higgenbotham, age nineteen, had been playing solitaire on his computer as he watched the clock, waiting for his shift to end. Tonight, like most nights, was boringly slow. But suddenly a call got his attention.

"This is Lieutenant Walter Kusmarak, U.S. Coast Guard. Our Fort Lauderdale station got a distress call of picking up a man from the Gulfstream. All we know is the name of the boat, *Jessica Bell*. I'm calling to see if you folks can identify that as a possible Bahamian vessel."

"Hmm. We didn't catch the call here in Nassau. Must've been too far away. Okay, let me see," Higginbottom said. He woke up his keyboard with a tap. "*Jessica Bell,* that's what they said, right?" he asked.

"That's correct."

"I'm going into our vessel registration files. Give me a moment." He entered a search, waited, and said, "Well, wow, we do have a *Jessica Bell*."

"Excellent! Do you have a boat description?"

"Coming up, sir. Here it is. Sport fisherman. Hatteras 38. It's registered to Captain Shinjuku Takeo of Freeport Fishing Tours. Must be a charter boat. Its home port is Port Lukayo Marina. That's out of Freeport, Grand Bahama Island."

"Color? We'll be searching by air."

"Sorry, no color listed, but they're almost always white or light cream," Higgenbothom said. "Would you like me to call the harbormaster to confirm that the *Jessica Bell* is not in port? I suppose it's possible that there is more than one vessel with that name."

"Yes, please, that would be very helpful," Kusmarak responded.

A few minutes later, Higgenbotham confirmed that *Jessica Bell's* slip was vacant.

Time to confer with the boss, Kusmarak thought. He keyed in a new number.

A sleepy voice answered, "Martin."

"Captain, Lieutenant Kusmarak here. Sorry to disturb you, sir, but we have a situation. Last night we got a mayday from a sailboat that sank halfway between Miami and Cat Cay. The skipper of the boat is in a one-man life raft. We've had a CASA up for a few hours, but it's very foggy and no sightings. Thirty minutes ago, the Fort Lauderdale boat station got a distress call from a Bahamian sport fisherman saying they picked up somebody from the ocean. Their radio apparently went bad, and we couldn't get more information. We do have the name of the boat, a charter out of Freeport. I'm thinking this must be the guy we're looking for. I think we should tell the CASA to stop looking for a life raft and to start looking for the sport fisherman."

"Sounds right to me, Lieutenant. Anything else?"

"That's it, sir. I'll take care of it. Thank you very much, sir, and I'm sorry I bothered you."

"No problem, Lieutenant, you did the right thing. Can I go back to sleep now?"

"Of course. Thank you, sir. Good night, sir," Walter said. And now he had a few more calls to make. He was guessing Miami Air stashed the crew of the boat that sank in the nearest

Howard Johnson. In ten minutes, he was calling David Shepherd's room.

"Hullo," A very sleepy voice answered.

"Is this David Shepherd? This is the Coast Guard calling."

David struggled to wake up. "Yeah, I'm Dave Shepherd."

"Mr. Shepherd, I'm Lieutenant Kusmarak, Duty Officer. I want to let you know we received a radio report that a fishing boat picked up a man out of the Gulfstream. We believe this to be your father. We haven't located the boat yet, but I'm sure we will soon." He listened—and heard quiet sobbing.

"Thank you, thank you so much!" Dave choked out.

"You're very welcome. We'll keep you posted. Are there other family members we should notify?"

"No, it's just me, my dad, and my brother—and he's backpacking in Alaska right now."

"I see," Kusmarak said. "Okay, good night, Mr. Shepherd. You try to get some rest."

He thought, *I love this part of the job*.

CHAPTER 21

Hesam surveyed the carnage on the boat. He could hardly think straight. He was exhausted, splattered with blood, and frightened. His instincts said to get away from there as soon as possible. He knew that he should get rid of the bodies but didn't have the strength.

And where could he go? Not the United States! That must be over to the west. And to the east were the Bahamas. He knew little of them, but thought they would be friendly to the U.S. How about Cuba? Maybe that was safer. He went to the navigation station. Shine's body was slumped across the deck in front of the captain's chair. Grabbing Shine's hair, Hesam dragged his body to the back deck. Then he shoved the first infidel's body down the short steps that led to the forward cabin to give himself room, staggered back to the navigation station, and hoisted himself into the captain's chair.

How did this boat operate? How could he get it south toward Cuba? The station was loaded with confusing electronics. The red light on the VHF radio was on. He twisted the volume until it clicked off. He didn't know if the Americans could locate the radio even when it wasn't transmitting.

The engines were idling at low speed. Two large levers protruded from the deck of the station. He eased them away from himself, heard the engines speed up, and felt the boat surge forward in response. Hesam smiled. Progress.

Studying the compass, he concluded the boat was going

west, toward the mainland. That would never do. He eased the wheel in front of him slowly left and watched the compass as it rotated gradually until the "S" stood at the top. Then he straightened out the wheel to maintain a southerly course and looked for some way to lock it in position.

He stepped over to Shine's body and pulled off his deck shoes. He put them on the navigation station surface and removed the leather laces, then tied them together and lashed the wheel to a drawer knob.

At last, he began to relax. He leaned out to scan the water ahead but saw only fog. He glanced up at the bridge and thought about climbing up to get a better view. But he didn't have the energy.

After a few minutes of motoring south, Hesam concluded the boat would operate without his attention. He was getting dizzy. He needed fluid, and stumbled down to the cabin, almost tripping over the body that he'd pushed down the steps. He found a small galley, and a cooler filled with sandwiches wrapped in plastic—along with cans of beer and Dr. Pepper. He popped open one of the Dr. Peppers and tasted it. He grimaced at its flavor but continued to drink. He needed more fluid and definitely did not want beer. He brought more Dr. Pepper cans and a couple of sandwiches to the navigation station and climbed back in the chair. Leaning with his elbows on the station, head on his arms, he fell asleep…

Sometime later, there was a sudden loud crunching sound, which jerked him awake. The bow was high in the air, and the boat came to a precipitate stop. Hesam tried to evaluate what happened. The engines were racing, but the boat wasn't moving. It was in a peculiar position—angled up and tilted to the side. He was aground! Looking around, he was shocked to see a shoreline 50 meters to his left. He could make out palm trees and low houses thru the mist—probably a Bahamas island. He pulled the engines to neutral to reduce the noise, but someone must've heard him by now—or heard his boat crash into the rocks.

He had to get out of there. He wolfed down one of the sandwiches and followed it with another can of Dr. Pepper. Then, tightening his life jacket, he walked to the stern. Stepping around the other infidel's body, he hoisted himself over the transom onto the ladder, and down into the water. The saltwater stung the wound in his back, but he swam as best he could toward shore.

A few minutes later, he tested for bottom and was relieved when his feet found sand. Wading the rest of the way, he looked up and down the beach for a place to hide. He had to rest before he could figure out what to do next. He saw low, colorful buildings, fences, and a few gardens—a small town. Glancing down the beach to his right, he panicked. There was a pack of feral dogs sniffing around the water's edge, occasionally wandering to one of the backyards, moving gradually in his direction. Hesam had been scarred by dogs as a child—something he never, ever got over. Fortunately, in his commando training, they never discovered it or they would have rejected him.

He struggled out of the water and started walking. Looking over his shoulder, he saw the dogs had spotted him and were beginning to trot in his direction! He took off running as fast as his exhausted body would take him. Ahead was a large tree with low branches. He reached it just as the dogs got to him. One of them snapped at his heel but missed. He forced himself to climb high and tried to hide in the foliage. The dogs circled and barked beneath him, watching him. If he stayed still, perhaps they would lose interest and go away. He didn't know where he was, but he guessed it wasn't Cuba.

He knew one thing for sure: he was in big, big trouble.

CHAPTER 22

Freddie Smith looked out his bedroom window overlooking the Gulfstream. "Yes!" he said, as he spied a fishing boat on the rocks offshore. He hurried into shorts and a tee-shirt and raced through the house to the backyard.

He reached his 18-foot aluminum boat and started dragging it to the beach but stopped. "Forgot the tools!" he said, as he turned and raced back to the shed to get them. If this boat was abandoned, it would be stripped of all salable devices, instruments, and equipment in a very short time. Freddie was only sixteen but had a reputation for being light-fingered, quick to seize easy-money opportunities. Pushing the boat into the light waves, he jumped in, gave the starter a quick jerk, and motored the short distance to the wreck. He circled around it once to see if there were any signs of life aboard. Seeing none, he killed his engine, coasted up to the back of the boat, and grabbed on. Standing up so he could peek on deck, he froze. There were two bodies lying on the deck around the fighting chairs—bloody bodies. Besides his grandfather's funeral, he'd never actually seen a dead body.

No way I'm going on this. He tried to see as much as he could without going aboard. He saw the navigation station on the main deck, and another one up on the flying bridge. "Oh man!" he said. "What a haul. I could've made a bundle."

He looked around to see if anyone else was approaching. It was still misty, so the wreck was not highly visible. It was a beautiful boat. Someone had taken great care of it.

Who should he tell? There really was only one choice: the police. Freddie didn't have a cordial relationship with Bimini's Constables. In fact, he was sure his name was in their files, probably several times. But he had to do this.

As he prepared to head back to shore, he thought, *how did this get here? These two stiffs sure didn't drive it. It was too high up on the rocks to have just drifted there.*

He looked at the cabin door. *Oh my God! Was the killer still in there?* He pushed off the *Jessica Bell* as hard as he could, slipped his lean body to the motor, and raced back to the beach. Leaping out, he pulled his boat above the high tide line and took off running.

North Bimini Island, Commonwealth of the Bahamas, boasted 2,012 permanent residents. Most of them lived in its only municipality—Alice Town. There, the Government Administration Centre housed the Royal Bahamas Police Force, Post Office, Immigration, District Council and Bimini Administrator.

Freddie slowed as he reached the door of the Centre. His instinct was to keep as much distance between himself and the law as possible. He peeked inside. *Oh no, Clevvie!*

Officer Warren Clevenger, the only office on duty, looked up in surprise. "Freddie?" he asked in amazement. "What are you doing here?" He knew that something must have happened for Freddie to come in voluntarily.

"You gotta' come, Clevvie!" Freddie gasped. He pointed toward the west side of the island, "Out there, on the rocks. There're dead bodies on the boat!"

"What boat?" Clevenger asked.

"It's a wreck! A fish charter ran aground on the rocks, offshore of my house," Freddie said. "I went out to...check it out...you know? In case somebody needed help."

Officer Clevenger smiled. "Sure, Freddie. So what is this about bodies?"

Freddy shuddered as he remembered the site. "Clevvie, I mean Constable, I pulled up to the transom. There were two dead guys lying there. There's blood all over the place. I didn't go on board; I figured somebody drove the boat because it's pretty high up on the rocks. I wasn't sure if the...you know...the killer, was still on board!"

Clevenger snapped into action. He picked up the phone and called the officer in charge, getting the answering machine. "Freddie Smith is here with a story about two bodies in a fishing boat hung up on the rocks offshore of his house. I'm going to investigate right now." Then, turning to Freddie, he said, "One minute, Freddie. Then we'll go." He unlocked a cabinet behind him and strapped on a Glock 40 automatic.

Freddie's eyes opened wide. In his sixteen years, he had never seen a constable wearing a sidearm. "We can take my boat," Freddie said and started running back to the beach.

"Sweet Jesus," Constable Clevenger said as he surveyed the two bodies on the deck of the *Jessica Bell*. Turning to

Freddie, he said quietly, "Stay here while I go aboard. If I get in trouble, get help as soon as possible."

Freddie couldn't remember when he'd been so scared. "Yes, sir," he said.

Clevenger pulled out his sidearm and carefully stepped over the transom into the stern. Flipping the safety off and jacking a shell into the chamber, he approached the open cabin door. He peered into it and saw a body. "Royal Bahamas Police!" he called. "Come out with your hands up."

Nothing happened. After repeating the call, he entered the cabin and soon determined that the only people aboard were the murdered. Careful to touch as little as possible, he returned to Freddie.

"This is a multiple homicide. It's far more than I can investigate myself. Stay here while I go back to the office for help. Your job is to keep anyone else from coming aboard. And don't touch *anything*."

"No way! No way I'm gonna get on that boat with those dead guys!" Freddie wailed.

Clevenger stifled a smile. "Okay Freddie, tell you what. You run me into shore and then come back and hang out like you're doing now. Somebody has to stand guard over this boat. This is a crime scene. Other officers will be out here soon to investigate." He thought a moment, worried that Freddie would leave the boat open to scavengers. "I'm gonna make you a temporary deputy, Freddie, to guard this crime scene. Can you handle that?"

"*Me?* A deputy?" Freddie asked, astounded.

"Yes, I know we've had our little problems, but I need you to help me now. Will you do that?"

"Yeah, yeah I guess so." He straightened up, squared his shoulders, and asked, "Do you—do you have to like, swear me in or anything?"

Clevenger again stifled a smile. What he was about to do wasn't going to make it into his report, but he said, "Raise your right hand, Freddie. Do you, Frederick, Frederick Smith, swear to uphold the laws of the Commonwealth of the Bahamas and to assist all designated law enforcement officers in pursuit of that?"

"I do," Freddie answered solemnly.

"I hereby deputize you, Frederick Smith, Royal Bahamas Police, temporary deputy." Clevenger stepped back into Freddie's boat. "Okay, back to shore. I gotta get help."

"Yes, sir!" Freddie cried. He raced the two of them back to the beach. The constable got out and gave Freddie's boat a little push off the sandy bottom.

Freddie wondered if he should have saluted.

CHAPTER 23

Phil awoke with a start. *What was that?* He pushed his knit cap off his eyes and was startled to see a seabird hovering just overhead. It soared off when he moved. *Probably looking for breakfast.* He sat up, stretched, and yawned. *Wow!* He felt 1,000 percent better. The sun was burning off the hazy fog. He glanced at his watch—almost 10 AM.

They were cruising along comfortably. In the daylight, he could clearly see the net stretching out behind him, its floats bobbing along on the water. It went for a long, long way—at least 100 yards, probably much more. That was a relief. He'd been concerned about running off the end and being stranded.

The water was a deep blue, the waves keeping pace with the little raft as they gurgled along. A few yards ahead of him, the net angled down to the submarine. Turning south, Phil scanned the sky for aircraft. It was concerning to see none. He'd have thought they'd be searching for him by now. But he felt good. A couple scrambled eggs, some hash browns or maybe corned beef hash, a glass of fresh-squeezed orange juice, and a steaming cup of black coffee was all he needed, and he'd be good to go! *Who was he kidding?*

He scanned the water and the horizon, looking for signs of life. *Hey! A flying fish.* He guessed that meant something down below was chasing it—probably his old friend the shark. He remembered a previous crossing when a flying fish smacked into the cabin top. They'd had it for breakfast. It was delicious. He didn't want one smacking into him just now, though.

Hello? He saw fins approaching, bobbing up and down. Dolphins—on both sides of the net! He'd bet they didn't like it any better than the shark did. They came right along beside him. *Dolphins are fascinating,* Phil thought. He wondered if they were thinking about food—just like he was. One of them dove under and came up moments later with part of a fish in his mouth. Another one on the other side of the boat looked like—yes—he was doing the same thing. He dipped underneath, and in moments came up with part of a fish in his mouth. Phil wondered how they'd caught fish so quickly. And come up with only part of them, not the whole fish.

It was the net! There were fish caught in the net! *Of course, Phil, duh!* He wondered how long this net had been in the water—where was it first put out? Who put it out? How long had these fish been stuck in it? Were they still getting caught as we trailed along behind the sub? Probably. And if there were fish for dolphins, wouldn't there be fish for him?

With the mist burned off and the sun getting higher, it was easier to see into the water. He looked over the side and could see where the net hung down into the gloomy deep. *Yes!* There were things stuck in it. And one of them seemed to be moving. *Thank you, Jesus!*

He scanned the water for sharks, then scooped up a couple of feet of net. Reeling it slowly in, he let the slack fall back in the water. He was greeted by the half remains of a fish. The other half was undoubtedly in one of the dolphin stomachs. He pulled the fish's head loose and flipped it in the water. A dolphin snatched it up.

Phil kept reeling in more net until a nice-sized red snapper practically fell in his lap, still alive. He grabbed it fast, but what was he gonna do with this thing? He let the net go and tried to hold it under the gills with one hand. It almost got loose, but he pinned it against his legs with both hands. As it thrashed around, Phil thought, *You don't need to rush this.* He scanned the water and saw another shark approaching! A smaller one, thankfully. He wondered if his activity had attracted it—or maybe the fish head. He stayed still and watched, but the shark soon lost interest and veered off for better pickings.

Phil looked down at his snapper. How was he gonna kill it without stabbing himself or punching a hole in the raft? *Answer: very carefully!* He managed to get it by the gills with one hand, and carefully unclasped his knife. He slid the tip under the gill toward the spine. Meeting resistance, he pushed harder and twisted the blade. The fish went limp.

He laid it on his lap and pulled his hand loose to make sure it was dead. Yep—*as a doornail. That worked well.*

A few minutes later, half-covered with scales and fish guts, he was enjoying a sushi breakfast. It was incredibly tasty. Talk about fresh fish! Red Lobster would never be the same.

He washed off his knife in the water and carefully snapped it securely into its sheath on his hip. Thank goodness he'd remembered to hone a razor-sharp edge on it before leaving Indiana. Funny, he hadn't thought of it the night before when he'd fought that guy from the sub—not that he wanted to or could've killed him anyway.

He ate his fill of snapper and threw the remains into the ocean—feeding another dolphin in the process. He tried his best to rinse off the fishy residue from the shroud.

The sky was beginning to appear blue. Still no sound of aircraft.

He decided to inventory everything on the raft, discovering he'd totally forgotten about the fanny pack he'd taken from the *Amazing Grace*. He wasn't sure what he'd put it in, as he'd packed it years ago—for their first Gulfstream crossing. He unzipped it. To his surprise, there was his cell phone in a plastic bag! He wasn't as rested as he thought, for he'd totally forgotten that he'd put it in there when they'd left Port Miami yesterday afternoon. It seemed ages ago, now.

He made sure his hands were good and dry and unzipped the plastic bag. He took out the phone and turned it on. It worked! Of course, it worked; it was supposed to. But was there any reception out there? He waited until it booted up but saw "no service" in the upper left-hand corner. No surprise.

But I bet the GPS works, he said to himself, thumbing to get it. In seconds it showed his exact latitude and longitude. He stretched the map until he could see land on both edges. He was about even with Delray Beach, north of Fort Lauderdale. Next, he went to messages. He'd put in a text and leave the phone on in the Ziploc bag. If he got close enough to Grand Bahama Island or the mainland, it might get picked up.

He texted Dave:

Hi son,

I'm safe and healthy. It's a long and incredible story, but I'm being towed by a fishing net that got stuck in the top of an Iranian submarine. The sub is going north and is gonna launch missiles on the U.S., I think New York City, and maybe Washington DC or Norfolk. Please tell the authorities. I haven't seen or heard the Coast Guard yet, but I'm sure they're looking for me. My present position at

10:20 AM is 79 degrees, 32 minutes west, 26 degrees, 27 minutes north, and we're moving north at about 3 knots. I'm safe and under God's protection. I love you, and I'm sure I will see you soon!
Love, Dad.

Lord, let that message go out, let him get it! Phil made sure his ringer was still on—in case, by some miracle, Dave called or texted back. He turned the phone over and carefully positioned it in his lap so the solar charger faced the sun. The phone was new; he'd gotten it shortly before they left home to try it out. *There'd never be a better chance to try it, that was for sure!*

He searched the rest of the pack, pulling out the contents. He blew the whistle a few times—just in case somebody could hear it. He held the signal mirror, remembering how he'd learned to use it in Scouts. If he saw a ship on the horizon, he'd try it. He examined himself in it. He looked a little worse for wear, but not too bad. He raked a hand through his hair and rubbed his stubby chin. Then he examined the paracord. *Good thinking, Phil, to pack it.* It looked like 50 or 100 feet. This was strong stuff—four-hundred-pound test, he thought. Might come in handy. Finally, in another plastic bag, he found a photocopy of his passport photo and cover page.

Now that he'd completed the "morning inspection" and breakfast, he faced his weakness—being a human being instead of a human doing. He never was very good at sitting still. As Mary used to remind him. *God, he missed her.* It didn't hurt as much when he was busy—he'd gotten really good at keeping busy.

He took a deep breath, relaxed, and let it out. It was a beautiful, beautiful, morning. The salt air, occasional birds doing aerial ballet, and dolphins escorting him along—this was a unique situation. *Thank you, Lord, thank you.*

How incredible the last twelve hours had been—the net, the submarine, fighting with that sailor and encountering Ace from Dearborn—of all places. That couldn't have been a coincidence. *Lord, you do work in mysterious ways.* He chuckled, realizing he was still trying to take matters into his own hands, when, in fact, he was entirely in His hands. Phil's plan was to be rescued by the Coast Guard, tell them about the submarine, and have them capture it or drive it away. *That may not be Your plan, Lord. If it isn't, I yield to you.*

An old song, "Lord, make me an instrument, make me an instrument of mercy and love," came to mind. How he could possibly be that—trailing along behind a terrorist sub, was beyond him. *But that's why You're in charge, isn't it God?*

So, Lord, I will enjoy this beautiful morning that you have given me, cruising along, courtesy of the Iranian Navy. I will sing praises to you here—where no one can hear what a lousy singer I am.

He was comfortable, well-fed, and with plenty of fresh fish literally beneath his feet.

He had only one worry. If he was to be here for an extended period, he'd need water. Even with the snapper, he was thirsty. How long could somebody go without water? He thought it was two or three days. But in the hot sun with little protection and a continual breeze, he'd dehydrate even more quickly.

So, Lord, have You chosen me to track this submarine that's going to attack the country? I know You choose the least likely of people. I know I'm not up to this. But I can do all things through Christ who strengthens me. I put myself in Your hands, Lord, and ask that You provide me with water and whatever else I need to be here for as long as You require. Thank you, Jesus.

Little did Phil know how much that prayer would be tested.

CHAPTER 24

"Nassau Port Authority, Waugh speaking."

"Ms. Waugh, this is Constable Warren Clevenger, Bimini Police. We have a boat run aground just offshore with a triple homicide, the *Jessica Bell*. Looks like a charter fishing boat. Can you find the home port and particulars of this craft?"

Ashley Waugh practically dropped the telephone in surprise. She had never gotten a request like this. "Yes, yes of course, just a moment," she said, as she turned to her computer console. "The name was what? The *Jessica Bell*?"

"Yes. It says it's out of Freeport on the transom."

"That's right! Here it is. Shinjuku Takeo, owner. Licensed as a charter. Been in business—let's see—fourteen years." She noticed an unusual symbol next to the listing. "Just a moment, Constable," she said. "There's a recent notice about this vessel. Let me look it up."

"Yes, please."

"Here it is," she said. "This was just posted today. The U.S. Coast Guard is looking for information about a person aboard the *Jessica Bell*; somebody picked up out of the ocean. Do you have the identities of the people on board?"

"Actually, I don't, but I'm sure the CDU people have them by now."

"CDU?" she asked.

"Sorry, ma'am, Criminal Detective Unit. There was a triple homicide you know—all stabbed—gutted really,"

Constable Clevenger added, with distaste. "I'll get back to you in a few minutes with those names."

As promised, he rang her back up.

"Thanks, Constable," she greeted him. "You have the names?"

"The captain is Shinjuku Takeo, per your registration. The other two must be charter customers—two dentists from Iowa—Dr. Winston Olson, and Dr. Marvin Robinson, both DDS's."

"Thank you. I don't think the person the Coast Guard is looking for is one of these, but I'll forward this information to them immediately," she said.

Moments later, a phone rang in the Brickell Plaza Federal Building on First Avenue, Miami. "District 7, Duty Officer Reedy. May I help you?"

"Officer Reedy, this is Ashley Waugh, Nassau Port Authority. It says here that you're looking for the *Jessica Bell*?"

"Yes! You found her?" Warren Kusmarak had briefed Officer Reedy at their shift change. Reedy was anxious to reunite Mr. Shepherd with his son.

"Apparently, she ran aground on some rocks off the west shore of North Bimini Island sometime earlier this morning."

"Excellent! Tell me that Philip Shepherd was aboard, and he's safe," Matt said.

"I'm sorry, sir. I can't do that. There was nobody by that name found on the boat. There were two American dentists from Iowa and the charter boat captain from Freeport." She paused. "But all were murdered—stabbed to death."

"My God! How gruesome. Okay, thank you, Ms. Waugh."

"I'm sorry we don't have your man. I'll ring off now and let you get hunting. Good luck. I know you'll find him; you guys always do," Ms. Waugh said.

"Thank you, ma'am," said Officer Reedy. *More bad news,* he thought. *We've still got a man missing somewhere out in the Gulfstream.*

In seconds he was back on the phone calling the district commander.

"Captain, Matt Reedy. I just heard from Nassau Port Authority. The *Jessica Bell*—the boat we thought had picked up Phil Shepherd, the missing sailor, has been found. He wasn't on it. They have three dead bodies, none of them his. We need to resume the search."

"Three dead bodies? Wow. Okay, how many hours ago did Shepherd's boat go down?" the captain asked.

"That would be…almost twelve, sir. We'll have to develop a new search pattern," Matt suggested.

"We should get our CASA 144 up, and one from Clearwater Air. Walter was gonna try to get in touch with the missing man's son, who was also on board. Do you know if he did?" Martin asked.

"Yes, sir. He said he woke him up at the Howard Johnson. I'll call over there and see if they're still there."

He dreaded this next call.

In the Howard Johnson coffee shop, Dave and his five companions were finishing up a leisurely breakfast courtesy of Connie Morello. Copies of the morning *Miami Herald* with Connie's article were strewn around the table. Connie thought the AP wire had picked it up as well—and hoped it might appear in some afternoon papers around the country.

The waitress came over. "Is one of you David Shepherd?"

Dave smiled. "That would be me."

"You have a call, sir, at the front desk. It's the Coast Guard."

Dave jumped up. "I bet they found him! Lord, let this be good news!" He stepped quickly to the front desk. Connie followed him, trailed by the rest of the crew.

"Hello, this is Dave Shepherd."

He listened quietly, then hung up and turned to the group. Connie knew by the look on his face that it hadn't been good news.

"We gotta keep praying, people," Dave said, blinking hard and swallowing a huge lump in his throat. "My dad's still missing."

CHAPTER 25

"Nigel! Come on deck, please? And bring the binoculars!" Olivia Braxton called as she scanned ahead of their Westerly 36 sailboat. She was trying to make out something in the water. Tan, slim, with medium-length sun-bleached hair in a ponytail, and in white duck short-shorts, tee-shirt, and sandals, Olivia looked like the long-distance sailor that she was.

In moments her husband came up the companionway, his hair still tousled from sleep. His piercing blue eyes and streaky brown hair accented a narrow face and trim body.

He handed her the binoculars. She rested her elbows on the cabin top as she focused them. "It's a man! In a little raft! He seems to be moving under some sort of power, to the north." She paused, then exclaimed, "Look! He's waving at us."

Nigel shook his head to dislodge the last cobwebs from his morning nap and moments later was focusing on Phil moving across their bow, three hundred yards or so ahead of them. "That's amazing! Let's go alongside and—I guess—rescue him. He must be off a ship or something." Olivia had eased the jib and mainsail to slow the boat, and they approached the little raft.

The Braxtons were on their first leg of what they hoped would be a round-the-world trip. They'd been saving for years and put enough together to get a seaworthy boat and take time off their jobs. They were out from Liverpool for well over a month, with a brief stay in Bermuda. Their plan was to bypass the Bahamas and go straight into Fort Lauderdale as their first, and perhaps only, U.S. port.

Nigel went to the bow and cupped his hands to his mouth. "I say there! Do you need assistance?"

The man called back, but they were too far to make out what he was saying. Nigel turned to Olivia. "Let's get alongside him, dear."

"Righto," she responded. She disconnected the mechanical steering vane from the rudder and took the wheel. The man was so low on the water that it was hard for her to see his exact location. She peered over the boat's deck. There he was, already passing to their right. "What on earth is moving him?" she muttered.

As they came alongside, she released more sail to slow down to his speed. "Good morning, sir. How are you?" she asked in amazement.

Phil smiled broadly. "I'm doing okay. I could use some water, but it's a beautiful morning. I'm enjoying the ride."

Nigel returned and put his arm around Olivia. "Would you like to come aboard and go to the States?" he asked.

"I'd love to! But I can't! Thank you—if you could radio the Coast Guard with my name, Phil Shepherd, and my position, I'd appreciate it. I'd like them to take over so I can get off."

Nigel and Olivia looked at each other. A man in a raft who didn't want to be rescued! "Oh dear," Olivia said. "I'm afraid a storm has taken out our antennae. All we have is a handheld VHS with just a few miles' range. Out here, nobody would hear us." She paused and then asked, "But I must ask, sir, what is pulling you?" She saw the net stretching ahead of Phil's raft and trailing out behind it.

Phil responded joyfully, "I wish I could say it was Moby Dick! Unfortunately—and you're not going to believe this—it's an Iranian submarine. I actually spoke to one of the sailors last night. It's a long story—do you have time to hear it?" he asked.

"Yes, absolutely!" They responded in unison. "We've got all the time in the world." Nigel paused. "Excuse my bad manners; Nigel Braxton, and this is my wife, Olivia. As you can tell, we're British. We're on the first leg of a trip that we *hope* will take us around the world. We expected an adventure, but never anything like this."

From where he sat, Phil went through the detailed story of the *Amazing Grace* sinking, his discovery of the net, being pulled by a snorkel, talking to Ace—and getting the sub's story—and his intention to ensure the sub didn't succeed in launching an attack on the U.S. "So that's my story, and I'm sticking to it," he finished.

Nigel said, "Unbelievable. If I were to call this into the Coast Guard, they wouldn't believe it, either. Except—you *are* being towed through the ocean by something underwater." Olivia had ducked down into the cabin to fetch her camera but now reappeared.

"Do you mind if I take a few photos?"

"No, not at all," Phil said. "In fact, now that you remind me, I'd like to get a couple of pictures of you on my cell phone. Is that okay?" He reached for his iPhone.

"Certainly," Nigel responded. "Olivia, can you get some video with your camera as well?"

"Excellent idea!" Olivia said as she zoomed in on Phil and his raft. She panned out to include the net pulling him along.

With the photo op done, Nigel asked, "Would you like to come aboard for a while? Is there anything we can give you?"

Phil said, "That drink! I sure could use it! Water, that is. If you could spare a bottle or two, that would be great. I've got plenty of fresh fish here, but they don't satisfy my thirst."

"We'd be delighted to," Olivia responded. "Since we'll be in port soon, we don't need to be sparing of water. Let me see what I can find." She disappeared down the companionway. A few moments later she returned with a three-liter plastic jug of water.

"You two are an answer to prayer," Phil said. "I asked the Lord to provide fresh water somehow—having no idea how He'd do it."

She hooked the jug handle with her boat hook. "Then, thank you, Lord, for using us," she said cheerfully. She reached over to transfer it. "I included a little gift. I think you'll need it."

Phil smiled broadly as he received it. "Thank you. I'll use it right now." It was a ball cap, with "Manchester United" embroidered across the front. "Hey, thanks a million." He almost got choked up. "You folks are a real blessing. God bless you both."

"Happy to help," Olivia said.

Nigel said, "Indeed we are." But his face sobered. "I'm sorry, Phil, but we'd best be heading south now. This Gulfstream is getting us too far north to make Fort Lauderdale easily."

"I understand. For what it's worth, when I motor-sail across the Gulf, I use a 30-degree offset to my compass course. If you're going to Fort Lauderdale, you might wait 'til you get through the worst of the current before you head south. It's not nearly as strong near the coast. Also, watch out for the net." He pointed to the net trailing along behind him. "Don't try to sail across it. It goes down for 30 or 40 feet, maybe more. I assume you have a spade rudder. You'll get hung up on it."

Nigel said, "We do. All right, good advice. I guess we need to fire up the engine, and jibe around to get behind your net," he said as he pressed the button to start their diesel engine. Waving to Phil, he said, "Cheerio!"

Phil waved back, tears appearing on his cheeks. *Lord, you are incredible. I asked for one thing—water. And You brought it all the way from England!* He watched Nigel and Olivia until their boat, *The Wanderlust*, vanished over the horizon. He felt unbelievably protected and content.

But Lord, three liters of water? How long am I going to be here?

CHAPTER 26

Aboard the Yunes

Emad Jabrani, *Yunes's* sonar technician, was midway through his watch. He felt honored to be allowed to use the new sonar system—a MGK-519EM Rubikon, which had been added to the sub after they'd acquired it from the Russians. The 1996 sub's advantage was stealth, but its disadvantage was vision. When submerged, it was a blind man. And like all blind men, it relied on hearing.

Unfortunately, like all subs with sensors on the bow, it couldn't hear anything directly behind it. This deaf area--called the baffle--required a sub to occasionally turn left or right to hear what might be there in a procedure called 'clearing the baffles'.

For weeks and weeks, Jabrani and his two sonar colleagues had routinely been clearing the baffles and yet heard almost nothing—a distant freighter at best. However, since turning the corner of South America and entering the Caribbean, traffic had picked up. They'd gotten quite used to the low power diesel engines of local fishing boats, or the occasional high-speed whine of a pleasure boat. In the Florida Strait, these were now accompanied by a steady stream of nearby freighters and cruise ships.

The morning had been relatively quiet until moments ago. Suddenly, from overhead a diesel engine started up and moved slowly aft and off to the west. It was very loud. Everyone in the boat must have heard it. It sounded like a three bladed propeller, and a 40 or 50 horsepower engine. This was not a typical fishing boat. Emad was perplexed—trying to explain to himself how this craft suddenly appeared—basically on top of the *Yunes*. Had it been drifting unpowered?

He was about to page the executive officer on the intercom when he walked in.

"Jabrani, what was that?" the XO asked. "It sounded very close."

"I was just going to call you, sir. It was right on top of us. It surprised me. I have no idea what it was doing right above us. But I have it as a low-power diesel, three-bladed prop, not moving fast. It moved south of us for a few hundred meters and then turned through our baffles to the west, toward the U.S... It doesn't fit the normal profile of a fishing boat or the behavior of a pleasure craft."

"Do we need to clear our baffles?" the XO asked.

"No, sir. He's gone right through them."

The XO mused, "Probably brilliant sunshine up there. I'd love to take a look, but it's gone by now, right?"

"Possibly not, sir. I'd estimate it's two or three kilometers from here. If you raise the scope, you could see it," Emad responded.

"And how many people would see us? You got anything else in the area?"

Emad pressed his earphones and was silent, listening. "Nothing close, sir. We've got a medium-sized cargo ship coming down from the north—at least 5 miles from here now. That's the closest thing."

"Very good, Jabrani," the XO responded. "But if we're going to do this, we've got to do it immediately. I'll see the skipper."

Asad, or "Ace," as Phil knew him, sitting next to the sonar station, had heard the conversation. Although he wasn't assigned as a sonar tech, they liked to have him nearby in case they picked up any English conversation.

Asad had no idea what kind of boat Emad had heard. But he knew what they would see if they put up the periscope now: plain as day—Phil trailing along behind them in his little rubber raft. If that happened, Asad was a dead man—and so was his family back in Iran. There was no way he could explain how a man in a raft suddenly showed up after he allegedly cleared the snorkel of the fishing net.

He thought frantically how he could avoid this, what he might say—and came up empty. He started to sweat and noticed his hands were shaky.

He went to his bunk. As he lay on his back, Asad surprised himself by uttering an unplanned prayer. *God, the God of Phil, if you are real—prevent the periscope inspection. Keep Phil safe! Keep me safe!*

To his further surprise, his panic subsided.

CHAPTER 27

Hesam clung to the top of the tree until the feral dogs lost interest and moved on. Then, very cautiously, he climbed down, checking for the dogs and anyone who might see him. He had to get someplace safer, someplace he could rest.

He went back to the beach and headed north, away from the boat. The other direction would go toward the little town. His exhaustion was catching up with him, but he walked about a quarter of a mile and found a space with overgrown bushes and a few trees. He followed a narrow path into the woods and, seeing a glade of heavy bushes, veered off the path and crawled into the underbrush. He was at the base of a large tree, so even if the dogs returned, he could climb it and escape. He heard sounds of civilization—motorbikes, voices, an occasional horn. But he *had* to rest. Then he'd figure out how to get out of there, hopefully to Cuba.

A light plane flew low overhead, coming in as if for a landing. He gave it no more thought. In seconds, he'd drifted off to sleep.

A few miles away, Lincoln Washington, Florida State Trooper, climbed out of the Royal Bahamas Police Grand Cessna Caravan 208B and stretched the kinks out of his 6-foot 3-inch frame. Lean and trim in the tan uniform, he carefully positioned a Stetson on his head, and turned to the cabin door. The rear seat had been removed to make room for his dog's cage. The pilot came around and helped ease the cage through the narrow opening. Washington unlatched the cage door. "Come on, buddy. Let's go find our bad guy."

Rufus, a large bloodhound, bounded from the cage, shook himself, and licked Washington's hand as the trooper snapped a leash on him. Washington turned to find Inspector Forsyth of the Royal Bahamas Police standing there, hand extended.

"Mr. Washington, Inspector Abraham Forsyth, Bimini Criminal Investigation Division. Glad to have you with us. How was your flight?" he asked politely. Medium build with a chocolate brown complexion, the inspector also dressed in a tan uniform, but with a Glock sidearm and a hat with a red band and "Royal Bahamas Police" crest. He seemed genuinely glad to see Washington and his dog.

"Flight was fine. Rufus is a pretty good traveler. This is our first time in the Bahamas." He looked around at the sandy terrain and brilliant blue water. "I must say, this sure beats trudging through snake infested swamps in the Everglades." He leaned down by the dog. "Rufus, this is Inspector Forsyth." He noticed the inspector wore body armor and momentarily wondered if he should be following suit.

"I'm happy you could get here so quickly," Forsyth said as he motioned toward a police Jeep. "If you'll follow me, we'll get you to the last known location of our assailant. It'll be aboard a boat that ran aground this morning," he added, as they climbed into the Jeep.

Moments later, they pulled up to a dock and stepped aboard the Bimini Police patrol boat. It powered them out into deep water.

"Bimini is two islands, you know—South, where you landed, and North. Most of the residents live on the North, in Alice Town. We're going into the Gulfstream now, and there, as you can see ahead of us, is the boat on the rocks. As we mentioned, it ran aground sometime early this morning. We believe the killer was on board and killed the captain and two charter passengers. We found all three bodies, savagely stabbed. They've been removed." He paused and added, "I suppose you'll need to get your dog aboard to get a sniff of the killer."

"Either that, or if you have some of his clothing, or if you know a track on the ground that is definitely his—Rufus has to know what he's looking for."

The inspector said, "We believe the killer used one of the berths in the forward part of the boat. There's a little blood on it, making us think he's got an injury. It will take a few days to get DNA done, though."

The police boat idled to the stern of the *Jessica Bell*, which had two officers already on board. Rufus eagerly leapt aboard, almost knocking Washington down. "Okay, Inspector, you lead the way."

The inspector pointed to an outline on the deck. "This was victim number one, gutted. The killer has a large knife—and knows what he's doing. Each of the three bodies was killed with a single cut—one through the abdomen to the heart, one through the ribs, and the captain through the carotid, jugular, and larynx.

He pointed to the other side of the afterdeck at a second outline. "That's number two, the captain." Stepping through the cabin door, he said, "And here's number three. We believe he was stabbed at the control station and then pushed down." They moved on. "Here's the bunk we believe held the killer. You can see there's a little blood there on the sheet. We also found bandage wrappings."

Washington led Rufus to the berth and let him get a good, strong whiff. "Okay, let's get on land and find this guy. The fresher the track, the better." Proudly he added, "Although Rufus can follow trails that are days old." He noticed a crowd of onlookers standing on the beach and frowned. "You got a lot of people in this area. I hope they haven't obscured this guy's tracks."

A few minutes later they were dropped off at the beach where Constable Clevenger waited. Freddie Smith stood behind him watching. Washington asked, "Does anyone have any idea which way the man went?"

Clevenger said, "Sorry, sir. I boarded first except for Freddie here," he motioned at the boy. "The killer was already gone."

Freddie stepped forward. "Excuse me, sir, but when I came back to shore after finding those bodies, I saw a set of tracks leading up through the sand into the grass." He pointed north. "There."

"Excellent!" Washington said. "Thank you, young man. The tracks may be wiped, but if you're right, Rufus will find them." He looked at the crowd. "Inspector," he said, "If you don't mind, I think we need some crowd control here. Your killer is a violent person. He could be hiding close— especially since he's injured. We don't want people following us when we start tracking. A couple more of your officers wouldn't be a bad idea—armed, of course."

The men ordered the crowd back to their homes, cautioning them to be careful. Formal notices were meanwhile being issued and posted about town, and local radio broadcasts confirmed that a violent killer was on the loose. Washington hoped that people's curiosity wouldn't keep them from staying home.

He put Rufus on a longer leash, and they moved up the beach. The hound instinctively went into the grass, sniffing busily back and forth as they slowly moved north. Suddenly he yelped and almost yanked the leash from Washington's hand.

"He's on it!" Lincoln cried. He opened his jacket. "I don't know if this is legal here, but I brought a little protection." The inspector saw a 9 mm Sig-Sauer was in his belt.

Forsyth smiled. "We welcome law enforcement personnel of the two-legged variety as well as four. No problem."

Rufus led them at a trot along the grass in and out of the beach area to the north. Washington noticed lots of dog tracks. Soon they found a life jacket with *Jessica Bell* stenciled on it, and a bloodstain inside the right shoulder. They covered about fifty yards when the trail turned inland. Rufus's excitement was growing, and he dragged them hurriedly on, coming to a stop and barking at a large tree. Dog tracks circled the base.

"Y'all have a lot of dogs here?" Washington asked.

"They're rarely a problem, semi-feral," Forsyth said, defensively.

They saw nothing among the branches and Rufus tugged to lead them back toward the beach. Minutes later they approached a wooded area.

Hesam awoke from the baying of the bloodhound. His phobia of dogs sent him scrambling up the tree, all the way to the topmost branches. This tree, unfortunately, wasn't full and lush like the first one he'd climbed.

But he was stuck.

Rufus took them through a narrow animal trail in scrubby woods and then barked excitedly. Washington reeled him in, held out his arm to signal a stop to the others behind him, and pointed to a tree ahead "I think that's our man."

The inspector shaded his eyes and squinted. Yup. There he was, crouching near the top. He looked questioningly at Washington. "You're the expert. What now?"

"Rufus and I'll confirm that this is the man we want. Then you tell him to come down. It's time he faces the music."

The inspector grinned. "An American way of putting it," he said. He and his men circled the tree like a human net. He pulled out a two-way and said, "Bimini base, Inspector Forsyth here."

"Bimini base. Go ahead, Inspector."

"Commander, we've the suspect in the top of a tree in the woods in Bailey Town. Could you bring the van down the road toward the patch of woods, and we'll bring him out in a few minutes?"

"Copy, Inspector. Good work. See you soon."

"Okay Rufus, let's finish this, buddy," Washington said, as he shifted the leash to one hand and pulled his sidearm. He released the safety, jacked a shell in the chamber, and moved slowly toward the tree. Rufus bayed enthusiastically.

"He's your man!" Washington called. "Rufus and I 'll leave the rest to you." The man clinging to the branches looked terrified. "Good job, Rufus," Washington said, as he re-holstered his sidearm. He pulled some doggie treats from a pocket and gave them to the animal.

Around the base of the tree, the officers drew their weapons. The inspector studied the man. "He's scared—good. But he's got a large knife. No other weapons in sight."

As Washington and Rufus left the scene, the inspector called, "You up there! We have you surrounded! You have no chance of escape. Come down. You will not be harmed. You are under arrest for suspicion of murder."

Hesam yelled in Farsi from the tree, saying he'd never be taken.

Inspector Forsyth looked at his fellow officers, "Anybody understand that?"

They shook their heads.

"Hmm. It appears we have a standoff. I wonder how we're gonna get him out of there."

Freddie Smith, who'd been following along behind the constable piped up, "You could always cut down the tree."

CHAPTER 28

Aboard the Yunes

Captain Golzar almost bumped into Executive Officer Purali in the narrow companionway. He'd heard the engine that had passed overhead. "Do we know what it was?" he asked.

"Not sure. Sonar said three-bladed props—40 or 50 horsepower. Doesn't fit the pattern of commercial fishing boats or pleasure boats. It went south of us slowly for a couple hundred meters and then turned west. Want to take a look at it?"

"Of course not. But I think we must. Don't you?"

The executive officer winced. "I'm afraid we do."

Few things are kept secret in a 240-foot submarine for long. The word spread through the crew that they'd be putting up the periscope in daylight to see the craft they'd all heard overhead.

Asad hunkered in his bunk, dreading what was probably going on in the control room. He muttered his little prayer again, in English.

The captain and executive officer returned to the control room. "Up scope, 58 feet periscope depth," the captain commanded.

On the surface, one hundred yards behind them, Phil was lying in his little raft, experimenting with his signal mirror. It was a beautiful, clear afternoon. The sun blazed in the sky, so he should have been able to get a good reflection to anybody west of him. The mirror was a heavy plated glass rectangle, 4 by 5 inches, with a clear cross in the middle. On the other side was a second mirrored circle.

Phil remembered that he had to line up the sun coming through the cross with the ship he was trying to signal. This was tricky; getting it precisely at the horizon required a steady hand. As he held up the mirror, he saw reflected the sub's periscope going up behind him. "Oh no!" He slouched down as low as possible and froze. Very, very carefully, he lifted the mirror to peek.

The captain saw something in the water, but it was small, not what he was looking for. He turned the periscope west. Suddenly, the radio operator called. "Airplane, sir! From the south, sounds low!"

"Down scope!" the captain ordered. "I think what we heard was a sailboat. I got a very brief glimpse of it… I think we're okay," the captain said. "Return to cruising depth."

Phil heard the plane and scanned the sky for it. Looking over his shoulder in the mirror, he saw the periscope dip below the surface. "Must have scared him off," he said, returning his attention to the plane. He could see now it wasn't Coast Guard; probably private.

"I wonder," he said as he raised the mirror to his cheek and tried to find the plane through the little cross in the middle. "This will be a long shot."

As expected, his attempts to signal didn't work. They flew right on past him.

Asad felt a calm so strong it had to be supernatural. He rolled out of the bunk and headed to the control room. One of his crewmates, coming the other way, whispered conspiratorially, "They didn't find anything. A plane came by, and they had to put the scope down."

Asad couldn't erase a broad smile as he moved on. A wave of relief went through him. *Maybe Phil's God is real.*

CHAPTER 29

Phil calmed down after the periscope scare, still searching the southern sky for any sign of the Coast Guard. They probably hadn't learned about the sub yet, but Nigel and Olivia should tell them soon.

He got his cell phone and tapped the position app. *Uh oh,* He was pretty far north. The Brits would have their hands full fighting the Gulfstream to get into harbor before dark. He hoped they'd radio ahead with their little handheld VHS when they got in range, though.

He thought about what might be happening on land. Dave and the rest of the kids were no doubt safe in Florida. He felt suddenly hollow inside remembering how their trip had been aborted. The last few years—when he'd organized and taken similar trips with one or both of his boys and their friends—had been the highlight of his life, especially since he'd lost Mary, his second half for 27 years. 9/11 at the Twin Towers—would he ever forget? The boys were all he had, now. Church friends had been encouraging him to start looking for a new wife. As he sat there alone and lonely on the raft, Phil had to admit the idea was appealing

The face of Louise Heureux was suddenly before him. Louise was a good friend, a member of Phil's church. Since the death of her husband to cancer five years ago, he and Louise understood each other's loneliness in a way most people didn't get. But like Phil, Louise was still mourning her loss. Maybe one day they'd find a way to move on...*if I ever get off this raft alive!*

Thoughts of Louise and her quick laughter only made him feel lonelier, so Phil forced his mind back to the situation.

As he contemplated it, he signaled with the mirror. However unlikely the chance of someone seeing it, he had to keep trying. He thought about how the Coast Guard would have notified the charter company, Marakesh, and the owner of the *Amazing Grace*. Phil felt awful thinking about the poor guy. Had the boat been just a tax shelter? Or had he been saving and scrimping for it for years? He'd probably never talk to that owner, but Phil wished he could apologize—even though there was nothing they could have done. Maybe, when it was all over, he could ask Marakesh who he was. His insurance company would want to investigate—maybe then he'd make contact.

But what was there to investigate? There would be no trace of the boat anymore, only a few cockpit cushions floating around, perhaps. And the dinghy—what would the Guard have done with it after the rescue? Probably nothing—let it go. It was worth three or four thousand dollars but be miles from where they'd gone down. Such a shame it was. *Unless it was all meant so that Phil would help avert a nuclear attack!*

The sun sank lower and lower. Phil marveled that the pristine ocean wasn't so pristine. Junk floated by—boards, bottles, weeds and tar—or maybe it was crude oil, but so much! Occasionally, he saw freighters and tried to target their bridge with the mirror. But they were miles away; and probably running on autopilot, trusting radar to alert them to problems. No way would he and his little raft show up. The snorkel wouldn't even show.

As darkness fell, he thought, *You know what, God? I don't want to spend another night here. One night was kind of a cool experience, but it was enough. I'm ready for home. Any time soon would be just fine.*

Hunger gnawed at him. He'd already eaten the fish trapped in the net within reach, so he untied the dinghy and slid back a few yards to get a fresh section of it. The sun was too low to see into the water. And the dolphins had gone. It looked like even the birds were turning in for the evening.

Phil reeled in the net, looking for fish. *Praise God!* A nice pompano came up, trapped and still wiggling, with shimmering, silvery skin. He was getting better at killing and cleaning fish without smearing scales and guts over himself.

The pompano was excellent, really tasty. He'd have to try to catch more of those. *Ha! Who was he kidding? Whatever was down there was already caught, thank you, Lord!*

He washed down the fish with a few careful swigs from the water jug. He didn't know what signs of dehydration to watch for. If he ever got a signal from a cell tower, he'd look it up. He checked his phone just in case, but there was no signal.

He wondered suddenly if Ace knew they'd put up the periscope. "Ace," he said, "I hope you're okay down there. You could have gotten in a lot of trouble if they saw me." *What if they* had *seen him? They could be planning to surface after dark to kill him!*

Phil chose to believe the best. "Thank you, Jesus, for protecting Ace—and for protecting me."

CHAPTER 30

Bimini Island

Inspector Forsyth called for a chainsaw. When it came, and they started it up, the man in the tree yelled and waved. They turned it off and motioned him down, watching his every move during the descent. When he reached the ground, the inspector motioned for him to put his knife down, and step away from it. The man looked hostile, glaring at them. He wasn't tall, but lean and wiry. He had a thick, black mustache, a full goatee, and the dark complexion of a Middle Easterner.

Forsyth motioned for him to lie on his stomach. Four policemen stood nearby, revolvers pointing from two-handed grips.

When he was down, the inspector turned to Clevenger. "Constable, straddle him. You other two—take an arm and put it behind his back, so the constable can handcuff him. I'll keep my gun on his head. Don't block my line of fire."

The man resisted but was overpowered and eventually handcuffed. They rolled him over, sat him up, and got him on his feet. With one constable on each arm and Clevenger behind him, Inspector Forsyth led the way to the road. After radioing an update, it was only a few minutes before a stretch Jeep Wrangler arrived for the suspect. They sandwiched him between two officers in the back and returned to the Government Administration Center.

Since the police department shared the building with the island's other administrative offices, there was great interest when the suspect came in. Assistant Superintendent Smedley, the highest-ranking police officer on Bimini, came out to greet them. Smedley studied the man. "You speak any English?" he asked. The man just glared.

Turning to Inspector Forsyth, Smedley said, "Looks like a nasty customer. Okay, let's book him as a John Doe. We'll need to transfer him to Nassau as soon as possible. Triple murder on the high seas by a foreigner is beyond our bailiwick."

"Right," Inspector Forsyth said, as he ushered the man inside.

The single jail cell was occupied. Willie Nelson—not the singer—was its frequent resident, usually after enjoying excessive libations and chasing female tourists. The superintendent looked at his new prisoner, then at Willie, and said, "We're gonna give Willie a little furlough here. I don't want to put this new guy in with him."

"Thank you, Your Honor, good man!" Willie said from the cell. "I heard your radio this morning about this guy. No way do I want to share a cell with him! And your luxury accommodations only afford one bed."

A lady jail keeper opened the cell. "Okay Willie, that's enough. You get out of here and behave yourself."

They moved the new prisoner into the cell, locked it, then, reaching through the bars, removed his handcuffs. Now it was only a matter of time: they'd find out who this guy was and what he'd been up to.

CHAPTER 31

Nigel Braxton rolled in the self-furling jib as Olivia piloted the boat through the navigation lights toward the entrance channel to Fort Lauderdale's harbor, Port Everglades. It had taken them arduous hours, longer than anticipated, to sail upstream, tacking back and forth into the south wind of the Gulf.

As Olivia swung the boat to starboard to enter the main shipping channel, their mainsail filled with a light evening breeze. Turning left would have put them among the cruise liners, freighters and US Navy warships—and prompted an invitation from the Coast Guard to turn around—so Olivia kept course. They'd downloaded the cruising guide for Port Everglades from the Internet, and knew they'd have to wait for the 17th Street Bridge to open before proceeding into the small boat harbor.

Running on their Volvo engine, they idled with several other sailboats waiting. A few minutes later, the bell rang; they watched the gates drop on the highway, and then the bridge as it opened. Olivia powered through.

Minutes later, as they entered the fairly spacious inlet, Nigel dropped the mainsail, lashed the boom amidships, and started stowing it for the night. They were tired and hungry, but he gave Olivia a big grin.

"We made it, dear."

Olivia put an arm around him while hanging onto the wheel. She eased the boat toward the pilings in front of the Lauderdale gas dock. Nigel said, "Uh-oh, I forgot to throw the three-way valve on the sewage discharge!" He scooted below deck and reached beneath the marine toilet. There was a significant fine if they didn't discharge into their holding tank. While at sea, it could have gone into the ocean—but not here.

He came back to the cockpit as Olivia put the engine in neutral. He hurried to position a fender and threw a line to the attendant on the dock.

A few minutes later, with the boat docked securely, they topped up the diesel and freshwater tanks. Nigel stepped ashore to call U.S. Customs, as required by law, then got directions for berthing overnight from the attendant.

Back on the boat, it took twenty minutes to navigate the Inland Waterway, watching for the inlet to Lake Sylvia where they could anchor legally. The many lights along and around it made it difficult to pinpoint the navigation lights.

"There!" Olivia said, pointing ahead.

Nigel reminded her to stay near the eastern shore and watch for the sandbar in the middle of the little lake.

"Looks like we've got some good anchoring spots—not too crowded," Olivia murmured. "I'll go forward and drop the hook."

Olivia motored slowly, watching her depth gauge. Passing the sandbar, she checked depths, put the boat into a light breeze, and gave it just a touch of reverse to stop the forward motion. Nigel knew from years of experience that this was the precise moment to lower the anchor and let out enough line so it wouldn't drag.

Afterward, he extracted their small, inflatable dinghy. "I would say, love, that our first night in the U.S.—probably our only night on the East Coast—calls for a dinner at one of Fort Lauderdale's finer restaurants."

"And I would say, my wonderful husband, that you have a smashing idea."

"First things first," he said, as he eased the dinghy off their stern and clamped their little outboard on it.

It was before dawn when Olivia, nestled comfortably beside Nigel in the master berth of the boat, awoke with a start. "Good God! We forgot to call the Coast Guard about that guy!"

CHAPTER 32

Dave Shepherd and Connie Morello ate dinner at a little Cuban restaurant and then returned to a Lagoon 44-foot catamaran in the Marakesh Marina in Fort Lauderdale. The Yacht Charter company had graciously offered Dave the use of the beautiful boat while the search for his father continued. Josh and the rest of the crew had headed for home, but Dave would stay until the Coast Guard found his dad.

It was a balmy and pleasant South Florida evening, but he was tired and disheveled and in no mood to appreciate it. He needed a shave and a change of clothes, but everything from the *Amazing Grace* was on the ocean's bottom.

Connie not only had permission from the *Herald* to follow his story, but the paper would even cover some of her expenses. She was on cloud nine—she'd landed a good story, a byline, and with a good-looking guy! It would have been perfect but for the seriousness of Dave's missing father.

"I'm not gonna be good company this evening," Dave said. "We can chat a few minutes, but then I have to try to get some sleep."

"I'm a reporter but I'm also a friend," Connie said. "I don't want to keep you from your sleep. We can pick up tomorrow. Maybe they'll have some news of your dad by then." She paused to study him. His blue eyes were bloodshot, his mouth drawn. "You'll feel better with a good night's rest." She reached across the table to put her hand on his but caught herself and drew it back. There was just something about

Dave Shepherd. He was smart, but vulnerable like a boy. She felt drawn to him but hadn't seen anything to indicate that he felt likewise.

"I thought they'd have found my dad by now," he said. "It was a clear day—they should've easily seen him."

"There was heavy fog," Connie said, gently.

"But it dissipated. I think they got thrown off by that other guy being picked up by a fishing boat. So there was a gap in the air search. But even so—" he stopped. He pursed his lips and looked out at the marina and water. "You know, when I talked to the Coast Guard, they treated me like a surrogate captain, which was right because Dad listed me as the first mate on the charter application. But it was like they didn't believe me about using two dinghies. They didn't believe my dad had gone off by himself to look for help. "

Connie frowned, wishing she had words of comfort. She felt a small thrill when Dave suddenly settled his gaze upon her and then reached for her hand.

"But that's what happened," she said. "The others confirmed it."

He nodded. "I know! But the officer didn't want to believe it or something. He even asked me if I actually saw my dad in the dive dink. What's up with that?"

Connie shook her head. "It's just unusual." She smirked and said, "That's what makes it a great story."

Dave nodded. "Right. I'm not blaming the Coast Guard. Those people are super—really good at what they do. They were all very professional during the rescue. And when I asked how long they'd keep looking for Dad, they said at least a week." Suddenly his eyes got watery.

Without thinking, Connie slid around the bench and put an arm around his shoulder. She leaned in close and whispered, "They'll find him. You've got to believe."

He turned somber eyes upon her and nodded. "I appreciate that." Connie suddenly felt self-conscious and removed her arm. She slid back from him, but he surprised her by taking her hand again.

"You sound like a Christian," he said. "I'm a Christian. Are you?"

She nodded. "Yes!"

Dave squeezed her hand and smiled gently. "That's great."

"As a reporter, I wish I could write about this, having faith in God—how He watches over and protects us—but it almost never makes it into print. But I believe He is watching over your dad, and you two will be back together soon."

"Thanks very much. I agree. But we gotta keep praying. By now, people back at school will be praying for him as well."

Dave scooted closer to Connie and put his arm around her shoulder. He drew her toward him until their cheeks touched. Connie practically held her breath, wondering if he was about to kiss her. He only gave her a long, gentle hug, but she returned it. She had surprisingly strong feelings for him!

Pulling back so they could see each other's eyes, Dave said, "I think we best call it an evening. I'll see you tomorrow." He smiled. Connie smiled back, aware that Dave Shepherd had never given her a full smile before. And that she really, really liked it when he did.

Before turning to leave she said, "Okay—reporter hat back on. You have my cell number. If anything comes in during the night, call me. We can probably make the morning edition if it's not super late. And…" she hesitated and met his eyes. His clear blue gaze looked approving, so she said, "I'll take you to breakfast—my treat."

CHAPTER 33

The Yunes

"Asad Omidi to the control room," the intercom blared. Moments later Asad hurried in, tucking in his shirt. He was greeted by a smiling XO—*strange*.

"Yes, sir?" he asked hesitantly, wondering why they'd paged him.

"Asad, you have experience with the U.S. Internet—yes?"

Asad was taken aback, but he mastered his expression. "Yeah. I mean, yes, sir. I used it all the time before we emigrated."

"Excellent! I thought so. Let me explain what we want."

Asad swallowed. In spite of his effort to blend in with Iranian society, including the all-Iranian crew on the sub, they still thought of him as an American. It wasn't an image he relished.

"In a few minutes we'll be at snorkel depth to recharge batteries," the XO said. "At that time, we'll put up a communications mast to check for messages from Bandar Abbas. We'll expect you to get on the American Internet and get the latest updates to mariners for the East Coast. We want to make sure our information is current—no surprises."

Asad nodded with relief. "I'll give it my best, sir. It's been a few years, but I'm sure it's not much different than what we have in Teheran and Bandar Abbas."

Minutes later at snorkel depth, the two 3,650 horsepower diesel engines fired up, starting the recharge and propelling them forward at three times their underwater battery speed.

Shaya Nikahd, the grim-faced radio operator at the communications console, put his hands on his earphones for better sound. He jotted some notes. Then, more relaxed, he turned and motioned to the XO to come over.

"Sir, we just received a message from Bandar Abbas. Commander Radan has been asked by the Ayatollah for an update. Glancing at his notes, he said, "They want our location, condition, and expected launch date."

The XO frowned. The *Yunes* had been on strict radio silence since rounding the horn of Africa. The commander's request would require a transmission from dangerous waters. Their answer would be encoded, but he had no doubt that American spies--satellites and listening stations-- would pick it up.

Asad noticed the men talking, wondering what it was about; but he had no clue other than the stone faces of the officers. They looked grim.

The captain entered the control room and joined the two men. He and the XO had an urgent, whispered conversation which turned into a disagreement. How Asad wished he could hear it!

The captain scribbled a message on a pad and showed it to the XO, who reluctantly nodded agreement. He gave it to the radio operator.

"Nikahd, code this and send it immediately."

Minutes later, with the captain's message transmitted, Asad slid into the operator's seat at the console. This was his first opportunity to use it, and he hesitated. Looking up at the

XO, he said, "Sir, I need Shaya to get me started, since I don't know the passwords or protocol for this system."

"Of course," XO Purali murmured. He motioned to the radio operator.

Soon Asad was on Google. He entered "U.S. Atlantic Coast, notice to mariners." After several false leads, he located the relevant Coast Guard information and turned to the XO. "What areas of the East Coast do you want me to cover, sir? As you can see, they have a long list of charts available."

"Start from here—the West Coast of Florida and go to-"— he paused, "New York Harbor."

"All right." He turned to Shaya. "Can we print this out?"

Shaya threw a couple of switches, pushed a button, and said, "Printer ready to go."

Twenty-five minutes later, Asad had a sizeable stack of notices arranged in order from Miami to Long Island.

The XO patted Asad on the shoulder. "Excellent work. I'll have the navigation officer look them over."

When the officer, Lieutenant Commander Majid Behzadi, arrived, he said, "Omidi, thank you very much."

Asad cleared his throat. "Lieutenant, I noticed two things while finding the notices. First, there's a rare species of whale migrating through the area, and ships are warned to stay at least 500 yards away. Second, there is construction on an offshore wind project, 27 miles off the coast of Virginia Beach. Could those things be important?"

"They could be. I'll take note of them. Your work is done here. I need to confer with the XO and the captain."

Asad left quickly, relieved to be done.

Minutes later, the captain, XO, and navigation officer conferred, their corresponding charts before them in the wardroom.

Behzadi said, "Captain, I marked our course from here to the launch site. Notice the depths in the launch area. One fathom is the equivalent of 1.8 meters. Sir, this is very shallow for our operation. We'll be detected; if not when we first surface, then certainly when we fire a missile. It concerns me that the water remains shallow far from shore, until we reach the continental shelf." He paused, letting his information sink in. "I know the mission was painstakingly planned, but would it be possible to move the launch to deeper water?"

The captain studied the chart. He motioned from the two target cities to the planned launch locations. "What are these distances?"

"One hundred sixty kilometers each. As you recall, we wanted to launch equidistant from the two targets."

The captain frowned at Behzadi. Quietly, he said, "And that's why, Mr. Behzadi, the launch sites were chosen. As I recall, they are almost at the extreme range of our missiles. Do I have that right, Mr. Behzadi?"

The XO interrupted, "But Captain! Shouldn't we—..."

"Enough!" the captain barked. He glared at them. "Nobody said this mission would be easy. It's gone extremely well—frankly, better than I anticipated. We are two days from launch. The forecast is excellent. We will not jeopardize this mission."

He suddenly relaxed and even smiled at the officers.

"All it means, gentlemen, is that we'll have to be extra light on our feet to avoid detection."

CHAPTER 34

Phil checked the time: 9:40 PM. Wrapping himself in the shroud to ward off the evening chill, he fixed his knit cap lower and settled down for another night on the raft. He looked forward to the sub's snorkeling, when he'd be able to wallow in the warm exhaust of the big engines. His new idea was to rig a sort of slipknot up close to the sub. That way, if he fell asleep—which he hoped he would—and they stopped snorkeling, the sudden quiet would wake him. The problem was that when they stopped, if he didn't get loose from the net fast enough, he'd go down with them. Not a comforting thought.

But overall, it had been a good day. The Braxtons were an amazing gift from God. Phil had really felt His presence.

He came to attention, as the water motion changed. There was a long, slow roll, topping the waves from the south. He booted up the location app on his cell phone—it was slow but worked—his little solar charger was coming in handy! *Excellent*.

He saw they were now north of the protection of the Grand Bahama Island—in open ocean. He'd thought as much. He'd felt the bouncing of the long Atlantic rollers, coming all the way from Europe—France, he guessed. A ripple of consternation went through him, but he tried to stifle the fear.

Suddenly the snorkel popped up. He heard the *thunk* of the vent valve as it opened, followed by the roar of the diesels. He was excited as he reeled in the net up close to the snorkel. He laced the anchor line through the sides of the net and tied it with a slipknot to the tow ring of the raft. He needed to test its hold and gave the line a jerk. It came open and slid out from both sides of the net. Perfect! He loved it when a plan worked.

He suddenly thought to record the sub and opened his cell camera. Soon he'd snapped a few unsteady pictures of the snorkel, and a couple of the net with the water rushing around it. He wished there was enough light to make a movie, but he had only a flash. It probably took a lot of battery at that.

Phil wondered—could he get the writing on top of the snorkel? He pulled the raft up even closer to it, laced an arm around a support bracket, and carefully snapped a shot. He took a few more, this time holding the phone above his head for a better view.

A wave shook the raft, and he almost dropped the phone, sending his pulse racing. He couldn't lose that phone—his only connection with the world! He slid back to the raft and checked the photos. The snorkel came out great, but his attempts to catch the writing on top of it were blurry. No surprise, but too bad.

When the jitters from the near loss passed, Phil tried again. This time, when he raised the camera up, he rested an elbow right on the snorkel to steady it. *This ought to do it,* he thought.

Back in the raft, he was glad he'd tried again. He had nice, clear shots of the foreign signs. He wished he could read them.

Suddenly he thought of Dave, and how worried he must be. He figured it couldn't hurt to try and text him.

Hi, son. I don't know if you'll get my messages—he stopped and changed it to, *I don't know <u>when</u> you'll get my* *messages, but I'm* confident *you will*. He paused, added his position, and decided he should add a picture of the snorkel and himself in case Dave needed it to help the Guard find him. He scooted back up to the snorkel, steadied himself on the brace, and held out the camera. *Ooops,* he hadn't counted on being blinded by the flash. After his eyes adjusted, he checked the picture. It was great!

Here's your smiling father, he wrote, *standing next to an Iranian submarine snorkel, cruising through the ocean night on its way to attack the United States. Wish I wasn't here. Love Dad.*

Hah! He copied in some friends from the school where he taught, and some from church. Unfortunately, he had no signal, and the message stayed in the outbox. *It'll go eventually. I just don't know when.*

He felt good. Although the message hadn't been received yet, somehow writing it helped Phil feel connected to the world and less isolated. He put the phone in its plastic bag and zipped it, pressing out air as he did. He couldn't stay completely dry himself but keeping that bag tight was essential. He needed to keep that phone working.

As he eased down into the raft and prepared to sleep, he thought, *Oh no! He'd meant to carve the rubber radar shield off the snorkel!* He wondered if it would be difficult—but how hard could it be?

Okay, back to work, Phil. He returned to the snorkel, grabbing the usual brace, and pulled out his knife. He tried to slide it underneath the rubber coating and was pleased when it went in easily. He supposed the long trip from Iran had loosened it. Minutes later, he'd exposed most of the left side of the snorkel to bare metal. It was more strenuous than he anticipated, and he decided to call it a night. He'd peeled off the left side which faced the U.S., hoping our radar came from that direction.

All things considered, he felt good. He'd done everything he could that night. The weather still held. He was mostly dry, warm, well fed—and had plenty of water. This wasn't exactly a Lazy Boy recliner in front of the widescreen with a steaming cocoa, but really not too shabby.

Thank you, Lord. Sorry about complaining earlier. One more night—I can do this.

CHAPTER 35

"Pan, Pan, Pan. This is the *Wanderlust* with information about Phil Shepherd," the radio squawked in the Port Everglades Coast Guard station as the sun rose slowly in the horizon. CPO Vincent Forrelli snapped to attention. "*Wanderlust*, this is the Coast Guard. Switch to channel 22, please."

"Copy, Coast Guard. Calling 22," Nigel replied. Moments later, he continued, "Coast Guard, are you there? This is the *Wanderlust*."

"Go ahead, *Wanderlust*." Forelli sat with pencil poised over his pad, anxious to hear what they had to say about Phil Shepherd.

"Coast Guard, yesterday afternoon we crossed the Gulfstream, coming through the New Providence Channel from the Bahamas, when we came across Phil Shepherd in a one-man life raft being towed by something. He said his boat had sunk the previous night; the rest of his crew were in a larger dinghy; and that his raft was tied to a drift line fishing net—*being pulled by a submarine!*" Nigel carefully enunciated each word of the amazing story. "He said he'd talked with one of the sub's crewmen and found out it was an Iranian sub preparing to attack the U.S. in a few days with missiles!"

There was a long pause.

"I understand how this sounds rather preposterous. But I assure you, sir, this is exactly what Mr. Shepherd told us. He

168

didn't want to be rescued because he felt it necessary to stay with the sub so you can find it and stop it."

Forelli didn't know what to make of it. "Who is speaking, please?"

"Nigel Braxton of Manchester, England—captain of the *Wanderlust*. My wife Olivia and I are on a round-the-world sailing trip, and this is our second port of call. Bermuda was the first."

"Well, Mr. Braxton, we are searching for a Phil Shepherd, who was reported to be in a one-man raft. Can you give me the time and location that you encountered him?"

"Certainly. It was about three thirty in the afternoon. Our position was—just a minute—I wrote it down... 79 degrees, 24 minutes, 13 seconds west, 26 degrees, 45 minutes, 47 seconds north. He was going north, so that last figure kept changing. As I said, we came out of the New Providence channel and crossing to Fort Lauderdale.

"Please hold, sir," Forelli said.

Dave Shepherd aboard the catamaran was beside himself with excitement. He'd overheard the conversation between the *Wanderlust* and the Coast Guard and couldn't wait to radio the Braxtons. He called Connie to give her the good news.

CPO Forelli called his officer-of-the-day, Lieutenant Alisha Saxby, and quickly filled her in. She keyed the mike and said, "Mr. Braxton, this is Lieutenant Saxby, officer-of-the-day, Port Everglades Coast Guard. Would you mind telling me exactly what you told CPO Forelli about Phil Shepherd and the submarine? "

Nigel knew his story was bizarre but true. He repeated it from the beginning.

Lieutenant Saxby was dismayed and not a little skeptical. But the guy's story added up—he had the correct information about Phil Shepherd in a raft. It had been in the newspapers, but if the *Wanderlust* really just came into port last night, they wouldn't know that.

Glancing at a wall chart, she saw that the reported encounter with Phil Shepherd was much farther north than it should've been, had he been simply drifting from the sinking the previous night. But the sub story was hard to swallow.

"Mr. Braxton—you say you encountered Mr. Shepherd with your wife. Can she confirm what you're telling me? And where are you now?"

"I can confirm it!" Olivia cried in the background.

"We're anchored in a little pond off the inland waterway, almost adjacent to the entrance to Port Everglades," Nigel continued. "I think it's Lake Sylvia. And by the way, I failed to mention that we have photographs of Mr. Shepherd and his raft. I believe my wife even took a short movie of him being towed. "

"Photographs?" Lieutenant Saxby's brows rose, and she met Forelli's eyes and nodded. This could be a game-changer, weird as it was. "We need to see those photos, sir. Can you get them to us?"

"Well, I don't even know where you are, and I'm not sure how to do that since they're on my wife's camera. Can you come and look?"

"Sure, Mr. Braxton, thank you very much. We'll get the information on Phil Shepherd to District 7 right away." She paused and added, "I'm sure you realize this story about a submarine has implications far beyond rescuing Mr. Shepherd?"

She turned to Forelli and said, covering the mic with one hand, "It's imperative we get those photos!"

"I understand, Lieutenant," Nigel said, over the wire. "And—er—if you want hardcopies, you'll need to bring a printer.

He was growing weary of the process. "Unless there's anything else, Lieutenant, I'll return to monitoring channel 16 until you get here." He clicked off.

Forelli looked at Saxby, surprised that anyone would hang up on the Coast Guard.

"CPO, I'll call District 7. Give me the coordinates from the Braxtons." She looked at her watch and frowned. "It's been hours since they saw him. If he really is being towed by something, we have no idea how fast, so who knows where he is now."

Forelli said, "This Iranian submarine story—I don't know."

Saxby nodded, but then she smiled. "If it's true, it's way above our pay grade! Let's see what the boys with the big bucks do about it. Meanwhile, let's get a boat over to this Lake Sylvia and this British couple with their cockamamie story—and see what they've got." She glanced at the wall chart. "Do you know this place? Lake Sylvia?" She was a recent transfer from Mobile, Alabama, and unfamiliar with the intricacies of Port Everglades.

Forelli nodded. "I know it all right. I'll go myself."

Dave Shepherd ran down the dock and crashed through the door of the Marakesh Yacht Charter office. "Larry, you gotta' help me! I just overheard a conversation with a British boat that saw my dad yesterday afternoon! They're anchored in Lake Sylvia. They've got pictures! And they said my dad's being towed by an Iranian submarine!"

Larry Williams, co-owner of the charter company, leaned back and stifled a smile.

Dave said, "I know. Sounds wild. But that's what they said. Can I rent a dinghy and motor over there and find out what's going on?"

Larry's brows were still raised, but he smiled. "Sure, Dave." He paused. "Say, is that cute little reporter of yours still around? "

"She's on her way. Why?"

"I'll make you a deal: you get her, I'll get the dinghy. Then all three of us will go if we can get Marakesh's name in the story."

Dave grinned. "You got it!"

As he left, he reflected that Connie would be thrilled, almost as much as he, Dave, was. His father was still okay! And she'd get a great breaking story. *Thank You, Lord!*

CHAPTER 36

"Ahoy, *Wanderlust!* Ahoy!" Dave shouted from the Marakesh dinghy.

Nigel appeared on the companionway. "May I help you?"

"Mr. Braxton? My name is Dave Shepherd. Phil Shepherd is my father. Did I hear on the radio that you actually saw him yesterday?"

"We did, sir. And who are they?" Nigel asked, eying Larry and Connie.

"This is Connie Morello, from the *Miami Herald.* And this is Larry Wilcox, co-owner of Marakesh Yacht Charters—the company that chartered my dad's boat. May we ask you a few questions?"

"Of course; come aboard," Nigel said. He scanned the water toward the Intracoastal Waterway and noticed two other dinghies approaching. "Are they with you also?"

Dave and his companions scrutinized the dinghies. Larry said, "Nope; I know many boaters around here, but I've never seen them. Your radio call could have been picked up by anybody monitoring channel 16. If they switched to 22, they heard about your afternoon adventure yesterday. Probably just curiosity seekers."

"Right. I hope they won't cause trouble," Nigel said.

"If you like," Larry said, "I can stand guard. I'll tell them you're not available for comment. Sound good?"

Nigel nodded, relieved.

Minutes later, the foursome—Dave, Connie, Nigel and Olivia—were seated comfortably in the cockpit of the *Wanderlust,* talking.

"How did my dad look?" Dave asked. Eagerly, the questions poured out. "Was he in good shape? How long did you speak with him? Did he come on board?"

Nigel smiled. "Your father looked better than I would've expected from a man who'd spent fifteen hours on the open sea in a life raft. He wasn't hungry, which surprised us. That fishing net he was tied to had fish in it—all he had to do was pull it up, and he'd have sushi. The only thing he wanted from us was water—and to tell the Coast Guard about him." He eyed Dave soberly. "He told us more than I could say on the radio."

He went on to tell them about Phil's sabotaging the snorkel, fighting with a sailor who had been sent up to fix it, and talking to another man named Ace about the sub's mission. "So your dad is waiting for the Coast Guard to find him and turn the sub away or...I guess, sink it."

Dave and Connie were all ears. Soberly, Dave said, nodding, "I'm not surprised. My mom died in 9/11." He let out a relieved sigh. "Mr. Braxton, I can't tell you..." He stopped to compose himself. "I was really worried. I thought they should've found Dad long before you did. I couldn't understand what was taking so long. But I get it now. You have no idea how relieved I am."

Connie slid next to Dave and put a hand on his arm. She said in his ear, "I know he's okay."

Nigel seemed uncomfortable. "Oh my, well, we're so glad to be able to reassure you."

"We are," Olivia echoed, nodding.

Connie said, "As Dave mentioned, I'm with the *Miami Herald*." She reached in her jacket and pulled out a camera. "Do you mind if I get your photo? Perhaps you and Dave together, and your beautiful boat here?"

Nigel chuckled. "When Olivia and I planned this trip—around the world you know—we expected some adventures, but we'd no idea they'd start so soon, or get us in the newspaper!" He smiled at Olivia who said, "Smashing!"

Dave said, "Mrs. Braxton, Could we see the photos you took? The movie, too?"

Minutes later, Dave, and then Connie, saw the smiling face of Phil in the life raft. "Oh, Dad!" Dave said, softly. "Be safe. Come home soon!" Larry had joined them, and he took a look into the viewfinder too.

He said, "I'll be darned! He really is tied to a net." He looked up at Nigel. "It sounded far-fetched when I first heard it."

"Frankly, Larry," Nigel said, "It still sounds far-fetched—and I saw it!" They all laughed. Olivia brought up two more photos she'd taken of Phil. Then she said, "I'll find the movie."

When she handed the camera to Dave, he watched the footage and said, "You guys were moving at a good clip. And look at that net! There *is* something pulling it—from underwater." They ran the movie for Connie, Larry, and even Nigel, who hadn't seen it yet.

Connie asked, "Can we download this to a computer?"

Olivia said, "I should've thought of that. It'll be much easier to see on the PC. Let me get the cable, and we'll do it now."

Minutes later they looked at it all again, this time seeing it clearly. Connie said, "May I download these on a flash drive? I have one with me."

"Excellent idea," Olivia said. She took Connie's drive and plugged it in.

Larry was looking around from the cockpit. He shooed away a round of sightseers but saw a white boat with a diagonal orange slash—he wouldn't shoo *that* one away. He turned to the others.

"Better get your download, Connie. The Coast Guard's here. And something tells me they're gonna want that footage."

CHAPTER 37

"Commander Radan, a message from the *Yunes*," Radan's secretary said, handing him a piece of paper.

The commander had been enjoying a cup of tea while reading the morning paper. His head came up and he took it impatiently. "Thank you. There will be no reply."

The message contained the time and coordinates of the sub, along with the reassuring words, "mission on schedule." The commander reached for his phone. "Get me Minister Zamani."

But when the call went through, a woman's voice said, "I'm sorry, Commander, but Minister Zamani has asked not to be disturbed. May I take a message?"

"Tell him the mission he asked about two days ago is on schedule."

"That's all?"

"That's all. He'll know what I'm talking about."

A few minutes later the commander's phone rang. "Minister Zamani for you, Commander."

"Minister, how are you?" the commander asked.

"I got your message. Excellent news—I think," Zamani responded.

"This is the confirmation you were asking for, isn't it?" asked the commander.

"It is—of course. But I'm still learning about our new president. The ayatollah wants him brought into this. How soon can you come to Tehran?"

The Commander glanced at his desk clock. "I could be there this afternoon, sir. Should I come to your office?"

"No," Zamani said. "Meet me at the presidential palace. How soon will you be leaving?"

"In just a few minutes. I'll take my navy plane. Could you have a car at the airport?" On the south side of Tehran, the airport was miles from the presidential palace on the north. An official car would speed the trip—not to mention being more pleasant than a cab.

Zamani was irritated by the request, but said curtly, "Yes."

The commander hurriedly put on his best uniform and left for the airport. He'd never met the new president, but he reviewed what he knew. Akbari had come from a rural area and begun his career as a businessman. He had several degrees, including one from a foreign university. He was undersecretary of commerce and worked his way up. His campaign focused on improving Iran's status with the outside world--especially the West—and ending their economic sanctions.

When the government car dropped the commander in front of the palace, he noted how impressive it was. Inside, Persian carpeted steps, high ceilings, and ornate décor surrounded him. After showing his credentials, he was ushered to a side room. Zamani was making him wait—a typical power move. The commander had second thoughts about coming alone. Perhaps he should've brought one of his aides. It was too late, now. He wondered if the minister would come alone. As if in answer to his question, the Minister walked in—alone.

"Commander. Thank you for coming on such short notice." He motioned him to a chair. "I don't know how much the president knows about this mission. I will explain the origin and background, and you can fill in the details, the technical aspects."

"Of course," the commander said. He was relieved that Zamani would help explain. That would permit him to study the president's reaction.

An attractive young woman came in and announced, "President Akbari will see you now. This way, please." They rose and followed her to the president's office. Commander Radan had never been there before and wondered if Minister Zamani had. In fact, he'd never been beyond the formal reception hall for state functions.

President Akbari sat behind a desk covered with papers. His jacket hung from the back of the chair, and his sleeves were rolled up. His tousled gray hair offset an angular face with a dark mustache, but no beard. As they walked in, he stood and smiled, "Minister Zamani, Commander Radan—welcome, gentlemen."

He came around to shake hands, then indicated their chairs in front of his desk. By the time he took his seat again, the presidential smile was replaced with a look of concern. "Gentlemen, the little I know about this mission makes me uneasy." He looked back and forth at them. "Why don't you tell me how it got started?"

Zamani said, "Of course, sir. I believe Commander Radan gets credit for originating the first proposal—almost two years ago." He looked at the commander for confirmation. "The objective was to strike a decisive blow at the Great Satan—the United States." Zamani paused to study the president's reaction.

The president waited for more.

"The beauty of Commander Radan's proposal," Zamani continued, "is that it can't be traced to us. Nobody will believe the Iranian Navy is capable of sub-launched missiles, especially so far from our shores. One U.S. intelligence official is on record as saying it would be so easy for U.S. aircraft to find and destroy our subs that eliminating them would be little more than a 'live-fire exercise.'"

The commander smiled, realizing that Zamani had done his homework. "To be honest, Mr. President," Zamani said, "Our primary concern was internal security. This was a unique and dangerous mission, involving over a hundred people. I'm sure Commander Radan can detail how he managed it all. Suffice it to say, we have no indication of any leaks. The whole thing has been quite remarkable. Our submarine, the *Yunes,* left Bandar-Abbas,"—he looked at Radan— "Nine weeks ago, Commander?"

"Correct," Radan confirmed.

Zamani continued, "The *Yunes* went around the southern tip of Africa to avoid being seen in the Suez Canal—a trip several times its normal cruising range. Commander Radan arranged for it to be secretly met in the high seas periodically with a supply ship."

Proudly, he added, "Our latest information is that the *Yunes* is off the East Coast of the United States and expects to launch its missiles in two days. They took considerable risk sending this message and will be in radio blackout from here on. Washington, D.C., and New York City will be uninhabitable afterward."

The President nodded, frowning. "As I said, gentlemen, I'm very concerned about this mission. You pointed out,

Minister, that the key to our success is secrecy—including internal security. So—not only does your submarine have to launch these two missiles and escape undetected, but nobody in Iran can reveal anything they know about this mission—ever. Is that correct?" he asked, looking up at the two men opposite him.

The commander and minister nodded. Zamani said, "That's correct, sir."

The president looked at Radan. "Commander, I'm impressed with what you have done. I'm sure it is a major technical achievement. But do you feel certain the *Yunes* can complete this mission and come back without being discovered?"

"I do, Mr. President. I admit I've lost a few nights' sleep over it, but I firmly believe we have everything under control. The passage to the United States has been flawless," he said, hoping to sound confident. He didn't mention the contingency plan of sinking the *Yunes* with all hands after it fired its missiles.

The president pushed away from his desk and stood up. He walked behind his chair, as though to put a barrier between himself and the two men. He took a deep breath. "Can it be stopped?"

CHAPTER 38

As the Coast Guard pulled alongside the *Wanderlust,* Larry was surprised to see them in full muscle with a 41-foot patrol boat instead of the smaller, rigid hull inflatable they usually used for harbor work.

Nigel stepped into the cockpit to observe the boarding. A Coast Guard crewman in a dark blue uniform, cap, and life jacket said, "Request permission to come aboard, sir?"

"Welcome to the *Wanderlust,*" said Nigel, as a no-nonsense-looking female officer stepped from the other boat's cabin. She strode purposefully across the deck and stepped adroitly over both boats' lifelines.

"Are you Captain Braxton?" she asked.

"I am."

"Captain, I'm Lieutenant Alicia Saxby, Officer-of-the-Day, Port Everglades Coast Guard. Thank you for receiving us. I know we covered the basics of your incident yesterday over the radio, but I'd like to hear it again, in detail."

"Certainly, Lieutenant. Come into the cabin? Can I offer you a drink?"

As she stepped down, Lieutenant Saxby eyed the gathering with surprise. Dave and Connie introduced themselves, and soon, squeezed together, everyone had a seat.

The lieutenant produced a pocket recorder and asked Nigel, "Do you mind if I record this?"

"I guess not. I assume you'd like to start by me telling you what Mr. Shepherd said?"

Nigel went through everything he could remember about Phil's story, with occasional supplements from Olivia. When he got to the part about Phil sabotaging the snorkel and fighting with the sailor, the lieutenant looked skeptical. And when they told her about Phil's conversation with Ace, in English, she frowned and then covered a smirk with her hand.

Nigel ignored this, adding, "Mr. Shepherd said he wasn't willing to stop trailing the *Yunes*—that's the submarine—until the Coast Guard took over."

Lieutenant Saxby said, "I'm sorry, Captain, but this sounds beyond belief. I've never heard of such a thing."

Olivia looked at Nigel and winked. Then she positioned her laptop so that Lieutenant Saxby would get a good view of it. "Would you like to see the pictures, love?"

The lieutenant smiled. "I sure would. They'd better be good."

After silently viewing the photographs and short movie two times, the lieutenant said, "That's enough evidence to overrule my call. I think your story's verified. Thanks so much. How fast would you say the raft was moving?"

"I'd guess about 3 1/2 knots," Olivia said. Nigel nodded his agreement.

"That's important for the search," The lieutenant said. She motioned to a Coast Guard crewman on the companionway steps. "I brought Eddie to transfer your photos and movie to our computer if that would be all right."

While Olivia and Eddie managed the transfer, borrowing Connie's flash drive, the lieutenant looked at the group and said somberly, "This is big, very big. I need to pass this on to my higher-ups as soon as possible. If this missile threat is real—well, it'll require an immediate response, I should think. I must ask you not to repeat this part of your story, please." She squiggled out of her seat and asked Eddie, "All set?"

When he nodded, she said, "Thanks again. You've been very helpful." She paused and added, "Off the record?" She looked around conspiratorially and whispered, "This is too big for the Coast Guard. We don't do submarines." To Dave she said, "I hope you get your father back safely really soon."

The cabin was still as they listened to the Coast Guard roar away. Larry broke the silence. "Maybe I shouldn't say this Mr. Braxton, but I spent time in law enforcement before I got into the yachting business. I've got to say I don't think this is over for you. That officer has the tape and pictures, but when this hits the fan, they're gonna want you as well. An Iranian submarine getting ready to launch missiles—that's worldwide headlines if it gets out."

Connie grinned. "Don't I know it! I'm writing the piece in my head as I sit here, and I've got the pictures to prove it." She held up her little flash drive. But she frowned. "At least I think I do. That guy borrowed my drive. Olivia, could you plug this in and verify they're still on it?"

A few moments later, Olivia said, "It's blank, love. That nice young man erased it. Let me make you another copy."

"*Madre mia*, what a jerk!" Connie said. She looked at Larry and Dave. "You guys about ready? I need to talk to my editor. That lady said it. This is huge—TV for sure."

As they prepared to leave, Larry said, "Why don't you forget the Marakesh mention, Connie? I like free publicity, but not government attention." Then he looked at the Braxtons. "May I ask what your plans are?"

Nigel said, "We planned on spending a few days here, but—" he looked at Olivia— "I think we'll pull up anchor this afternoon. We don't want to stay for the feeding frenzy."

"And then?" Olivia asked.

"We'll go where they won't bother us."

She raised her brows at him, but in another second her eyes cleared. They nodded together and said in unison, "Cuba."

CHAPTER 39

As Dave peered from the catamaran in the morning, he saw Connie stepping out of her VW in Marakesh's parking lot. They waved to each other as she approached.

He'd found a chart of the Florida Straits in the navigation station and had it spread out on the table. Rather than spend the day just waiting around, he'd been doing some calculation on his father's most likely position.

Connie looked glum as she came up the dock carrying two cups of coffee. She looked glum as she greeted him and handed him one.

"I brought you a latte. Hope you like it—not sure what kind you go for."

"Thanks! I'm not fussy about much of anything in the food department." He studied her as she plopped down across the table from him. "Are you okay?" When she only frowned, he added, "Where's my perky ace reporter? You're looking kinda low."

She smiled wanly. "I am. I filed my story right after we got back from the Braxtons. My editor called me within the hour." She paused, visibly upset. "Bottom line—I have to rewrite it. The problem is the submarine—and the Iranian thing. As the Coast Guard Lieutenant said, this is getting really big—and with implications far beyond rescuing your dad. The editor and publisher want more confirmation than the pictures provided!" She met his eyes, hers filled with indignation. "Do you believe it? What better evidence can there be?" She crossed her arms and frowned. "In my opinion? He didn't actually say this—he wants to stay out of trouble with the authorities."

Dave nodded, looking at her with sympathetic eyes, his own sense of indignation growing. "That's incredible. How much more confirmation do they want? A signed affidavit from the sub captain?" He shook his head.

Connie chuckled. "Wouldn't that be great! Notarized and witnessed would be even better."

Dave moved closer to Connie. He said, "I don't get the problem. We all heard what Dad told the Braxtons. What else do they need?"

"That's just it. We only have the Braxtons' word for it. I try to think about it from my editor's standpoint. You have a few photographs of a guy in a little raft tied to a fishing net— and a very short clip of the net dragged through the water." She paused and sighed. "And then you have this incredible story about an Iranian submarine with missiles and this net attached to its snorkel. And your father having a conversation in English with an Iranian sailor raised in Dearborn, Michigan—give me a break."

Dave pursed his lips and took a breath. "We know it's hard to believe. The thing is, I know my dad, and he wouldn't make up anything like this. But your editor doesn't know my dad. So I guess they have to be careful."

He leaned back and sipped his latte. "I have to admit I can see his point. A lot of people would freak out over this. It could cause widespread hysteria. And if it was unfounded—I mean if the story turned out to be bogus or a hoax—I guess your editor could lose his job."

"That is not far from what he actually said," Connie replied, sardonically. "And the marina guy—what's his name? Larry? What he said about this not being over—I believe it. They'll want to talk to the Braxtons—and probably you. And if the Braxtons are gone—definitely you." Connie smiled at him sideways.

"I don't know how much I can help, but I'll do what I can." He took another sip of his latte. "You know, as I think about it, the best evidence is those pictures, so I'll bet they're gonna want to control them. Did you give them to the newspaper?"

"Had to," Connie said. "They went in ahead of the story. They're what make this real." She gave a sly smile. "But I'm no birdbrain—I still have copies."

Dave looked admiringly at his pretty friend, even prettier when she was being smart. "Good girl," he said, approvingly, and placed a hand over hers. Connie smiled again, this time with a slight blush on her cheeks.

"What about you?" she asked. "Did you do anything with your copies?"

Dave grinned. "I emailed them to everybody on the crew and some of my buddies back at school—along with the story from the Braxtons. I also copied my brother in Alaska—although I'm not sure when he'll get back to civilization to see them."

"Good boy," Connie said playfully. They shared a smile, then sat in silence sipping their lattes in the shade of the open cabin, enjoying the salt air. Connie touched Dave's arm and motioned to the chart on the table. "What's all this?"

"I wanted to see if I could approximate my dad's position. I researched how fast a sub would go—snorkeling, and on battery. Then I made a few assumptions—" He pointed to a place on the chart. "And I came up about here—roughly 86 miles from where the Braxtons found him."

Connie looked impressed. "Wow, good work!"

"Dad taught me basic navigation. And I couldn't understand why the Coast Guard hadn't found him. So when I found this chart here on the boat I decided to figure it out. The Coast Guard was off because they didn't know the sub was pulling him. By the time the Braxtons found him, he was way farther north than they expected."

"Interesting," Connie murmured while studying the chart. "I may weave that into my story as a teaser without saying anything overt about the submarine. I'm gonna give it a try."

They shared another smile.

Connie said, "You'll be my technical expert on this story, okay? I need to get this right."

"I don't know about the expert part, but I'll be glad to help."

Dave was still smiling at Connie, enjoying her proximity. She looked away, but said, "I got a job because of this. I'm on the *Herald* staff! I'm supposed to follow this lead wherever it goes." She paused and looked up at him. "That wouldn't have happened without you and your dad's story."

He squeezed her hand. "I'm glad! Couldn't have happened to a nicer—or prettier—reporter." With a sudden burst of courage, he leaned over and kissed her softly on the mouth. Afterward, Connie smiled at him with such a cute expression that he kissed her again.

But then his eyes grew sober. "When you say 'follow this story,' do you mean that literally? Because my dad is moving north, and I'm thinking about doing the same thing. The Coast Guard's search has been switched from Miami to Clearwater. They'll be the ones to find him. I want to be up there when they do."

Connie searched his eyes a moment as if wondering if he really wanted her along. Something in Dave's expression reassured her for she said, "I'd be happy to be your shadow, if that's what you want. I can even chauffeur you there in a yellow Volkswagen!"

"Great!" Dave exclaimed. He gave her another quick kiss. "I was afraid to ask…but since you're my chauffeur," he added with a grin, "Could you run me to Walmart? I need to expand this *snappy* wardrobe I've been wearing since Friday—and get some toiletries and stuff.

"All part of the service, sir," Connie said with a wink.

Dave was suddenly the happiest he'd felt since the rescue. He'd be able to spend a lot more time with Connie, and they were getting closer to when Dad would be rescued. As he helped Connie from the seat and they prepared to leave the boat, he glanced toward the parking lot. "Uh oh."

A Coast Guard SUV was pulling up near Connie's car. Two men got out—one looked like an officer—and looked around.

Dave went to the stern and called, "Can I help you?" As they approached, he added, "Are you looking for Dave Shepherd?"

"We are!" the officer responded.

"That would be me," Dave grinned. "Come aboard. How can I help you?" He introduced Connie as a friend with no mention of her occupation. "I suppose you're here to talk about my dad and the report we got from the British couple?"

"Yes, sir, we are." The officer noticed the chart and the sheet of calculations. "What's this?"

"I was trying to find my dad. Using the information from the Braxtons and what I found on the net about Iranian subs, I calculated where I think he should be about now." He pointed to the chart. "As you can see, he's about even with Savannah."

The two looked at each other. "How'd you figure that?"

"It wasn't very complicated. The sub is a diesel-electric, so it has a snorkel speed which I put at 10 knots, and a submerged speed which I put at 3 knots. I figured six hours of snorkeling at night, plus the Gulf Stream. The rest is simple arithmetic." Dave looked at them. "I have nothing to add about my dad, except that you can trust what he says. Your lieutenant recorded the Braxtons, and I don't know anything more than they did. What else can I tell you?"

"The raft. What are we looking for?"

"Haven't you seen the pictures? Your technician took copies from the Braxtons' computer. It's an Air Force surplus one-man life raft. I think it's kinda old. We used it as a SCUBA and snorkeling tender, and for the dive flag."

"Got it," The officer replied. "Okay, we're done here. Can we take a copy of your calculations?"

Dave grinned. "Go for it! Go find my dad!" he said with more passion than he intended.

When the visitors were out of earshot, Connie slid up to him and put her arms around him. "I think you're smarter than the Coast Guard, David Shepherd."

When they kissed, it was because this time Connie had the sudden burst of courage.

CHAPTER 40

Phil's plan to disconnect from the snorkel before they pulled it down worked like a charm. He awoke immediately when the engine stopped running, the line still wrapped around his hand. He gave it a single hard jerk and began floating back behind the sub while the snorkel disappeared beneath the waves.

It was 4:30 AM. He verified that the raft was riding well in its new position, then snuggled back under the shroud, pulled his cap down, and drifted back to sleep.

Several hours later Phil was greeted by the sun and the usual seabirds cawing overhead and dipping down to see if he was edible. He glanced to one side and felt a small thrill when he saw the dolphins were back. He didn't know why, but he always felt better when they were with him. He wondered if they were the same ones that had escorted him yesterday morning. When he got back home, he'd read up on dolphin ranges and find out if they might be.

Suddenly the net seemed to be jerking beneath the raft. *Fresh fish!* He reeled the net in carefully and found a beautiful sea bass struggling to get loose. "Sorry, Mr. Bass. Today you're breakfast." Minutes later, after sea bass sushi and a swig of water, Phil pulled up his cell phone to check the position app.

Wow—they were almost off the coast of Georgia. But something didn't feel right. Something had changed. He couldn't put his finger on it at first until he realized he was—cold! The sun felt warm; he put a hand in the water—it was colder.

Glancing at his watch, it seemed like the sun was in the wrong place. It should have been off his left knee, not his hip. The sub must have changed course. He opened a compass app and saw they were going 35 degrees northeast—not the usual straight north. *What were they up to?*

Watching the dolphins jump and dive, Phil thought it over. "I know what you're doing," he said. "You're cutting the corner."

North of Florida, the U.S. coast curved to the east. Rather than follow the curvy coast and stay parallel, the sub was shortening the trip by heading to the hump of Cape Hatteras.

But they'd pulled away from the Gulfstream. Phil had gotten so used to the Gulfstream that he never considered it wasn't ubiquitous, at least for this ride. He hoped they'd meet up with it again when they got to Hatteras because it was gonna be very nippy in the meantime. And if the good weather didn't hold, he could be in serious trouble. *Lord, keep me warm!*

Ninety feet below, the *Yunes's* navigator said, "Captain, may I show you something in the wardroom?"

"What do you have?" the captain asked, after following the man to the large sea chart on the wall.

"Sir, recall that we decided to head straight for Cape Hatteras once we got clear of the Bahamas;" he said, drawing a line across the chart.

"Is there a problem?" Captain Golzar asked.

"Not a problem, Captain, but an *opportunity*. Notice the path of the Gulfstream. Its expected speed is 3 1/2 knots along here."

The captain nodded slowly. "I think I see where you're headed."

The navigator smiled, "By going straight for Cape Hatteras, we gave up the benefit of the Gulfstream. I did some calculating, and I concluded that if we return to the Gulfstream, we will reduce our total transit time by several hours."

The captain hesitated, studying the chart. "It says the 'approximate course of the Gulfstream.' If I remember correctly from my marine hydrodynamics classes, ocean currents tend to wander—sometimes quite a bit. Which means you will need a scheme to ensure that we stay in the fastest part of the Gulfstream."

"I have one, sir—temperature."

"Temperature?"

"The Gulfstream is fastest where it's the least diluted, and therefore the warmest." The navigator smiled.

The captain laughed. "So, what you're proposing, Mr. Physicist, is that we navigate—not by the compass—but by the thermometer?"

"Precisely."

CHAPTER 41

Lieutenant Saxby was nervously excited. She was sitting on a situation with the potential to explode—she had to get it to her superiors as fast as possible. Her performance now would be under heavy scrutiny.

As they pulled up to the dock in the Port Everglades station, she was on her cell phone trying to reach Commander Bill French. *No answer.* It was Sunday afternoon; Bill was probably on a golf course someplace.

She hopped off the boat and hurried to her office, trying to get a grip on the situation. The photographs, the movie, and a transcript of the interview would all be requested. They'd want to speak to the Braxtons too. She grabbed her technician as he was coming in from the boat. "Eddie, can you run some prints of those photos and put them on my computer as well? And the little video?"

"Sure, no problem." He smiled mischievously and added, "And I took care of that lady's flash drive."

"Excellent! We need to control this stuff," she replied. She found Petty Officer Forelli eating lunch in the day room.

"Vincent, get a boat and go sit on the Braxtons' sailboat in Lake Sylvia. It's called the *Wanderlust*."

"What am I supposed to do with them?" Vincent asked.

"Keep them there. We'll need to talk to them again, and possibly move them to Miami. Legally we can't hold them, but I need them on standby for more talks. So if you see them getting ready to pull anchor—" She paused, thinking. "Ask them politely if they could stay until we can talk to them again."

Vincent shrugged. "Okay, Lieutenant, aye, aye." He wolfed down the last of his lunch and headed to the dock.

The lieutenant called District 7 Headquarters in Miami and reached "CPO Foster."

She introduced herself and said, "Mr. Foster, I need to speak to Captain Martin immediately—wherever he is. Do you have a home phone number or cell phone?"

"Actually, Lieutenant, I think I have both," the CPO responded as he flipped through his office directory. He proceeded to call his boss.

Seconds later, Captain Robert Martin's cell phone rang on his hip as he prepared to board his boat, the *Martin*.

The lieutenant explained her situation and the report she had just taken from the Braxtons. She spoke clearly and slowly about the Iranian sub and the snorkel. The captain stopped what he was doing, picked up his gear and hustled back to the parking lot. "And you took this interview yourself, personally?" he asked.

"Yes, sir, less than an hour ago."

"Did anybody else hear it?"

Alisha swallowed, "Mr. Shepherd's son, David, was there, with his girlfriend, a Connie somebody or other. Also, a guy named Larry Wilcox, the owner of the charter company that Phil Shepherd chartered his boat with. And my technician, Eddie."

"I'm heading to the office now. I'm gonna need a copy of your notes and the photographs as soon as possible."

"I didn't take notes, sir, but I'm preparing to send a recording. We're transcribing it as we speak. It wasn't a long interview, so by the time you get to your office I should be able to email the transcription."

"Good thinking, Lieutenant. Are we sure this is the right guy—the guy from the sinking? Could there be any doubt about that?" Martin asked.

"No doubt at all. As I mentioned, Mr. Shepherd's son David was there, and he instantly recognized him from the photos the Braxtons took. By the way, I've sent a boat to hold them there, since I assume you may want to speak to them."

"Good!" Captain Martin said. His thoughts were racing, as was his heart. "Anything else, Lieutenant? I want to get to my office and get the ball rolling. This is going to go to Atlantic Area for sure. Probably higher."

After the call, Lieutenant Saxby ran a mental checklist of what needed to happen next. She relaxed, feeling sure she had her bases covered. A cadet stuck her head in the door, "Lieutenant, PO Forelli on the radio."

She snapped her laptop shut and hurried into the communications room. "Vincent? What's up?"

"Lieutenant, I'm at Lake Sylvia. No sailboat *Wanderlust*. In fact, no sailboats here at all. The party seems to have left. You want me to look around for them?"

Oh no! thought the lieutenant. "I'll bet they went to a nearby marina," she said. "Check out the ones nearby including the budget ones. They might be on a tight string."

"Gotcha, Lieutenant. Ten-four."

The lieutenant muddled over whether there was any other way they could find the Braxtons. Of course—*the radio*! She grabbed the mic again and switched to channel 16. "Sailing yacht *Wanderlust*, sailing yacht *Wanderlust*. This is the U.S.

Coast Guard, over." No response. After trying it three more times, she gave up. If they were docked in a marina, they could have the radio off. She also didn't want the eavesdropping marine public to hear her calling too many times for the *Wanderlust*.

Back in her office, she noticed her technician had transferred the Braxtons' photographs and movie clip to her computer, so she emailed them to Captain Martin. She told him the transcript would follow as soon as it was ready.

Her phone rang. "Saxby? Martin. These photographs and video are bombshells. The only question is, what's pulling the guy? His story, that it's a sub, seems reasonable, as crazy as it is."

"I agree," the lieutenant said.

Martin fell silent, thinking. "Okay, I'm giving Atlantic Area in Portsmouth a heads up. They'll want to see the pictures and read your transcript—is it ready?"

"In ten or fifteen minutes."

"And what about this British couple? You said you had somebody sitting on them?"

"I sent somebody to sit on them," the lieutenant said regretfully, "but I was just informed they're gone."

"Gone?"

"Well, they're not where we left them in Lake Sylvia. I've got my patrol boat looking for them."

"I hope he finds them," said Martin. "In the meantime, I'll call this into Lantarea and send them your information. They'll want to talk to you, and that British couple too. Can you meet me at Opa-Locka Air Station in say, forty minutes? And be prepared to stay overnight? We'll take the Lear."

Alicia gulped silently and said, "Yes, sir." She added, "You know, we can't force the Braxtons to do anything. They haven't broken any laws, and they're not U.S. citizens. All we can do is ask for cooperation. But it's unlikely that I can find them *and* get them to the Air Station in forty minutes."

"I see. We can ease up on that departure time," Martin said decisively.

The lieutenant sighed with relief—and got a new idea. "Sir, we could impound their boat. Force a safety and customs search including a drug dog. That could take enough time for us to question them. To be honest, they were very cooperative, but if we need them and they don't want to cooperate further, this might encourage them." Alicia felt almost guilty about her suggestion, but the captain jumped on it.

"Get hold of customs and tell them what we need."

In minutes, Lieutenant Saxby was on the phone with an Officer Porter at U.S. Customs. She quickly explained that they needed help to keep "a recently arrived British boat in harbor for the next day or two—pending an investigation" that she couldn't reveal details of.

"Oh-kay," the voice said slowly. "What's the name of the vessel?"

"*Wanderlust.*"

"One moment please." Alicia could hear a keyboard typing. "It's here. They came in late last night, phoned us this morning...." Seconds later he added, "And they phoned again an hour ago to check out."

"Check *out*?"

"That's right. They're leaving our fair city—if they haven't gone already."

"Oh no!" Alicia said. She thanked the officer, called Captain Martin, and gave him the bad news.

"Do we have a physical description of this boat?"

"Unfortunately, it's a generic rigged sloop. About 35 feet long—white sails with blue trim. Nothing else to distinguish it from thousands of other sailboats, except the British ensign."

"Okay, thank you, Lieutenant. We'll do an air search. They can't be too far. I'll fly them up to Portsmouth when we find them. See you in an hour."

"Yes, sir," she said and slumped into her chair. *Girl, this is what you signed up for. Now go to it.*

CHAPTER 42

Phil stifled a sense of dismay at the thought that he was apparently going to spend a third night in the rubber raft. Inexplicably, the Coast Guard had yet to find him. He'd watched planes cross the sky many times that day, searching back and forth, but to the south. *What was their problem?* The Braxtons must've given them his position and approximate speed—why couldn't they find him?

As he finished another rice-less sushi dinner, he noticed the weather was changing. The sky was cloudy and the water grey, not the friendly blue-green it had been. He'd see no sunset tonight. Also, the breeze had shifted to the west and had a different feel to it. While he pondered this, waves splashed over the sides of the raft and washed over him. A wet night—just what he didn't need. He hoped the poncho shroud was tight enough. Fortunately, they seemed to be back in the Gulfstream, as the water was noticeably warmer than that morning.

Okay—position check. He extracted the phone, keeping it under the shroud, and found their location. *Just as he thought.* They were moving close to true north. Peeking from his cover, he saw over his shoulder the glow of Myrtle Beach and guessed they were near 30 miles out.

You can do this, Phil. One more night. "*I can do all things through Christ who strengthens me.*" He remembered years ago when he and his sons hiked a small stretch of the Appalachian Trail. He was so stiff and sore at one point he could hardly walk. But he kept walking—it was the only way out.

He was older now, quite a bit older—but in good shape. He could make it through the night. He continued to repeat the comforting verse of Scripture as the hours ticked past, reassuring himself that the Coast Guard would surely find him come morning. *Lord, please let the Coast Guard find me!*

He began bailing water from the raft a bit ineffectually with his hands, then pulled the shroud higher around his neck to keep the waves off.

9:15 PM—there was still over an hour before the snorkel would come up and he could move into its comforting warm exhaust. The usual diesel fumes which he'd had to ignore in the past should even be whipped away with the current breeze.

He dozed. He awoke when the snorkel valve *thunked* as the diesel roared up. *Excellent!* He got on his knees and reeled in the net, quickly managing the tie of the quick-release line, and positioned himself comfortably behind the snorkel. All he need do now was sleep. No more exercises with the snorkel. He'd done all he could.

He settled in the raft and searched the sky fruitlessly for stars or the moon. But sleep took over again until he awoke suddenly from sweet, memory-filled dreams. The engine had stopped. The ensuing silence was like an alarm. He hurriedly yanked the anchor line to free the raft from the net.

It jammed. *Nuts!* He spun to his belly to lower his profile, but continued to work at the knot, leaning over the front of the raft. He tore frantically at the tie-line as the net sank beneath him. Just as it would have pulled him and the raft with it, the tie came loose.

Phil took deep breaths. *That was close, very close.* Another few seconds and the sub would have pulled him and the raft under. He was soaking wet and would take hours to dry, but he was alive.

Settling beneath the shroud, he tried to go back to sleep. He'd dreamt earlier of times years ago when he and Mary had gone sailing, just the two of them. Those were wonderful days. He missed Mary. He loved her still, just as much as he ever had.

But his thoughts moved to Louise Heureux. Whenever he thought of how he missed Mary, he'd find himself thinking of Louise. He was lonely and knew it. He didn't want to live the rest of his life like a hermit—piggybacking on his sons' lives. It wasn't healthy for him or them.

It was remarkable, really—how often he and Louise had seen each other over the years, first at school and then church. She'd lost her spouse to cancer eight or nine years ago. And like his kids, hers were out of the house as well. He stood next to Louise when they sang in the church choir. Sometimes their arms brushed—Phil liked that. He liked *her*. *I like her a lot. I wonder what she's doing right now.*

Phil was jerked from his thoughts of Louise when suddenly the raft felt shaky. *Oh no, it had gotten soft! There was a leak!* His heart raced and his mouth went dry. If the raft deflated, he was a dead man. *Lord, help me find this leak and plug it!*

He remembered there was a manual inflation tube along the side somewhere. *He should have brought a foot pump.* And he should have practiced with the manual inflation thing. *Life is full of 'should haves.'*

Feeling along the edge of the shroud, he found a cap on the end of a tube—the inflation tube! He needed to pull it up remove the cap, and blow air in. If he dropped the cap, the raft would probably deflate in seconds.

Phil yanked it up and twisted the cap. It didn't move. It was old, the raft was old. Using the anchor shaft, he tapped the cap all around and tried it again. It broke loose! Now he saw there was a cord on it, so he couldn't drop it overboard. Nevertheless, this would be tricky in the dark.

He stuck the tube in his mouth and blew hard—as hard as he could. The raft was firming up. He didn't want to overinflate it and aggravate the leak, wherever it was, so he slapped the cap back on and screwed it tight. He checked the tube itself for a leak but found nothing. If it was daylight, he could put it in water and watch for bubbles. Perhaps in the morning....

He tried to rest, but his nerves were on edge. He'd been taking the little raft for granted. *Big mistake.* He wondered if he might have put a nick in it when cleaning fish. He'd always been careful to keep his knife away from the rubberized fabric—perhaps not careful enough.

The raft, he realized, was actually terribly old. If memory served, it was a product of World War II—used for downed aviators! The navy had provided them through Vietnam, and possibly beyond. When he'd bought it to use for snorkeling and SCUBA, he only needed something small and inexpensive. He sure didn't think he'd be betting his life on it. But now it was all he had—he had to deal with it.

He squeezed the tube gingerly to see if it had lost air. He couldn't detect a change. Whatever this leak was, so far it was slow. It would be hard to find it, especially if it was underwater. Even tire repair shops had trouble finding slow leaks. Phil prayed it wasn't deterioration of the rubber and fabric. He had no idea how he'd handle that. Truth is, he probably couldn't.

I should be okay until the Coast Guard finds me. Please, Lord, let them come soon!

CHAPTER 43

By the time Captain Martin and Lieutenant Saxby arrived at Lantarea in Portsmouth, Virginia, the Coast Guard's regional headquarters were just shifting to night duty. Commander Roger Behrens, a tall, slim man in uniform, waited to greet them.

"Bob, how are you?" Behrens asked the captain. His eyes flicked to the lieutenant. "And you must be Lieutenant Saxby. You've had quite a day, haven't you?"

The lieutenant blushed lightly. "Yes, sir, we certainly have."

"If you'll follow me to the conference room," the commander said briskly, "there's coffee, and we can send out for sandwiches if we run late."

They entered a room where several officers sat around a long table. They looked up expectantly.

Behrens said, "As you can see, your story has garnered attention." He introduced them to the officers and motioned them to sit.

"We've read the transcript of your interview, Lieutenant, and watched your little video clip and looked at the photos." He paused, looking around the room and then at the two of them, and continued. "We all realize, of course, that this is hard to believe."

"That's what we've said to each other all day," Captain Martin said. "But the evidence, you must admit, is compelling."

The commander looked at Saxby. "Lieutenant, is there any way this could have been fabricated? Like, a hoax?"

Saxby shook her head. "No, sir. We rescued six members from the *Amazing Grace* Friday night when we began the search for Mr. Shepherd. He was captain of the vessel. He was not in the crew that we rescued and all six of them said he left in a single-person raft looking for help. In fact, they also said they could hear an engine off the stern of their boat. Their stories are consistent, and I—I believe them."

She took a breath. "I also believe the Braxtons, the British couple. I interviewed them Sunday morning. Phil Shepherd's son David was on their sailboat. He'd overheard their radio transmission earlier and immediately went to meet them and get the full story. He identified his father in the photographs and the video. I don't believe this could be a fabricated story."

She almost sat back as if she was done, but frowned and added, "In addition, gentlemen, the position the Braxtons reported finding him was approximately 40 miles too far north of his expected position if he had just been drifting in a raft. The breeze was light, he had no sail, not even paddles. He had no form of propulsion. Something external transported him that additional 40 miles. His story about a sub caught in fishing net seems—" she paused, searching for the word— "preposterous. But it must be true." Now she sat back, looking around the table for their reaction.

The officers were mostly studying their notes, but Commander Behrens spoke up. "There are really two parts to the story, aren't there? The first is your man being towed up the coast by a submarine. I reluctantly must agree that we can't explain the evidence any better way." He went on, "But this is an Iranian sub. That raises international issues."

An officer raised his hand. "What about radar? Did you see it on radar?"

Captain Martin said, "Not that I know of. Our efforts that night were focused on rescuing the crew of the sinking sailboat. If we'd gotten an image of the submarine's snorkel, it would have been very faint at best."

Another officer asked, "So who is this Philip Shepherd? What's he doing sailing across the Gulfstream with a bunch of college kids?"

Captain Martin looked at Saxby. "Would you like to answer that, Lieutenant?"

"Certainly," she said. "Mr. Shepherd's a high school history teacher from Kokomo, Indiana. He's widowed and takes his sons and their friends sailing during spring vacation from Florida to the Bahamas. He's done this, they told me at the charter company, six times."

Commander Behrens asked, "So what do you think we should do next?"

Alisha looked at Captain Martin and asked sweetly, to the amusement of the men, "Would you like to answer that, Captain?"

He almost grinned. "Happy to. Obviously, the most important thing is to find Mr. Shepherd. Our search was too far south. We've made corrections with the new information and put out a new search pattern. As you can imagine, finding a little life raft at night in an area this large will be extremely difficult."

The lieutenant had taken a quick call on her cell as he spoke. She scribbled a note and slid it to the captain. He read it and looked up. "My lieutenant says she has new information." He looked at Saxby. "Share it, please."

"I just got a text from my station," she said. "That's the Port Everglades Boat Station. They interviewed David Shepherd this morning, and as it turns out, he calculated his father's approximate location. Since the sub is a diesel electric, he's even farther north than we predicted."

She continued, "We're notifying District 7 to rework the coordinates and update the air search, which, by the way, is now being run out of Clearwater."

The officers looked satisfied. Commander Behrens glanced at a wall- clock and came to his feet. "I'm convinced. I don't know anything about this Iranian stuff, but a sub is enough for me. As you know, these days we have few anti-submarine assets in the Coast Guard, and as far as I know, none readily available on the East Coast." He looked around with a sober expression. "Time to contact the navy." He paused and added, "Unless there's anything else, I'll adjourn this meeting and ask our friends from Florida to join me while we call our navy brethren."

A minute later, Commander Behrens slid behind his desk and pointed to side chairs for the captain and lieutenant.

"To be honest, folks, I've never done this before," he said. "I'll start with the OOD at the Norfolk Naval Station and see where that gets us. It's Sunday evening, and I don't think we're gonna get very far. But—we need to start." He paused. "Tomorrow, when they're fully open for business, we'll get a lot of help from our respective hierarchies. So, when we're finished here, I suggest you make it an early evening."

He made a call and followed an automated menu until he got someone.

"Seaman French. May I help you?" A voice answered.

"Seaman French, this is Commander Roger Behrens, United States Coast Guard. I need to speak to the officer of the day, please."

"He's not available. What is this about?" he asked, grumpily.

The commander gave the others a look and proceeded. "It's about an *Iranian* submarine coming up the East Coast of the United States with hostile intentions," he said, slowly and deliberately.

There was a long pause. "Say that again please?"

The commander repeated it. *"Have you got that?"* he asked, growing angry himself.

"Yes, sir, got it! Hang on a minute." They heard him calling, "Get the captain! We got a major situation here!" Sounds of garbled voices followed. *"Then go find him!"* Seaman French cried, and then came back on. In a calm voice, he said, "He'll be with you in just a moment, sir. Please stand by."

Behrens smiled at the officers—and waited—and waited. Several minutes later a new voice came on. "This is Captain Perkins, may I help you?"

Commander Behrens explained the situation and ended with, "Captain, I know this is an unusual story, so I'd like to send you the photographs of Mr. Shepherd and the raft, a little video of it being towed by the submarine, and a transcript of the interview that our lieutenant had today with the people who spoke with him."

"Yeah, I guess you better, because right now I say 'not possible.' Give me your number, and I'll see what I can do. We'll call you back. Hey, one question: how far offshore is this alleged submarine, anyway?"

Behrens said, "We estimate approximately 30 to 40 miles." He looked at the officers, who nodded in agreement.

"Thirty to forty miles! That's practically on the beach! I'm sure you can appreciate, Commander, that it's Sunday night and peacetime. I'll have to call you back. I don't know what we'll be able to do this evening."

Later, as they were preparing to go up to their rooms at a local motel, Captain Martin turned to Lieutenant Saxby. "You know why they believed us? Because of you. You sold it. You had your facts and were firm and convincing."

"Thank you, sir. I appreciate that."

"You deserve it. But I bet we wind up repeating this story for days."

"I hope *not*," she said with feeling. "I think we have one, maybe two days at best."

CHAPTER 44

Phil awoke groggily, having to pry his eyes open. Dawn had arrived, but the sky was again blanketed in clouds. He missed the bright sunshine of the earlier days.

The raft was soft, even worse than last night, so he re-inflated it with the tube. The slow leak was survivable, but a nuisance. And if it got worse? What then?

It was 7 AM. Phil stifled a yawn, considering going back to sleep, but he was too awake. Looking about, a line from an old poem crossed his mind. *Water, water everywhere, and not a drop to drink.* Fortunately, the jug from the Braxtons was still about half full. He took a sip to wash the grumbles out of his mouth.

The sea was relatively calm. Luckily the crosswind from the west had not grown worse. Would have been hard to sleep with waves washing over him. He scanned the southern skies for a sign of Coast Guard. A high dot far off brought him to his knees. *A plane!* And closer than any he'd seen before. He resisted the urge to wave and yell. Wasting energy wouldn't be wise. *Thank you, Lord! They'll find me today!*

Waiting for the plane to get closer, Phil considered getting a last gourmet sushi breakfast. He thought of Dave and what he might be doing. Just in case, he checked his cell phone, and even kept it on for a few minutes, hoping by some miracle for a message. There was none.

He checked his location with the phone app and felt greatly reassured that he could. Though to those on shore he might have been lost, to him it was heartening to know where he was lost. They were north of Wilmington, North Carolina, coming up on Cape Hatteras! As best he could tell, it looked like they'd come closer to land. Maybe he'd soon be able to get a cell connection. He sure hoped so.

Better yet, maybe he wouldn't need one. The Coast Guard should have him safe and sound—someplace. He checked on that plane he'd seen earlier, but it was still circling to the south. *Might as well find that leak.*

He had no good idea of how to do it. A slow leak—though better than a fast one! —was hard to detect. He needed more light. The sky was still evenly covered with clouds scudding above. No dice. He thought about what might cause a leak to start. Damage, obviously, such as a sharp fish spine. Probably not his knife. That would have made a faster leak. He searched the side of the raft alongside the net, looking for a scrape or laceration. The fabric was old but looked intact.

Would friction wear it thin? Such as where the net rubbed the raft near its tie line? He got on his knees and cautiously peeked over the edge of the raft. He had to be careful of the cross waves, which posed the risk of rolling him right into the ocean.

He pulled up on the net to get some slack, and then lifted the tie-lines. From what he could see, the fabric looked fine. He noticed that the net's float line was getting gummy, though, from ocean trash—probably crude oil or boat discharge. He checked the other side of the raft but saw nothing suspicious there either.

Time to check the front. He stuck his nose practically in the water to check the bow ring. The metal was pulling away from the fabric—this had to be the source! And he could let the ocean show him the leak. He pushed the tow ring under the water's surface and held it, watching for telltale bubbles. He'd have to keep it there for some time since the leak was so slow. And he did. After forty-five minutes, his arms felt like they were coming out of their sockets. He gave up and let go. Not a single bubble. It wasn't the tow ring.

Please, Lord, don't let this leak be underwater, on the bottom of the raft. There's no way I could find it much less fix it!

There were numerous folds and creases in the raft from being stored, each one a possible source of the leak. He couldn't even remember storing this raft. Maybe Dave had. Phil realized his mind wasn't as sharp as usual. He was getting run down.

The idea stressed him out and his pulse picked up. This leak might get dire, and the Coast Guard was taking an awfully long time to find him! *Seriously, how hard could it be?* He saw their plane still flying back and forth to the south. Was it even getting closer? He wasn't sure. And even when it got overhead, they couldn't do anything to get him out of the raft. They'd have to call a helicopter or send a boat. That could take all day.

Okay Phil, relax. God has watched over you this far. He's kept you safe, reasonably dry, provided food and water. He will never leave you or abandon you. "Okay, Lord," he prayed. "I trust in you. Help me to find this leak."

He inflated the raft as hard as he dared, realizing he should have done that to begin with. He'd look at the folds and creases with meticulous care, on his hands and knees. Moving a few inches at a time, he examined the fabric. Some spots were discolored from years of storage, but not leaking. When he got to the foot of the raft, he noticed a dark "V"—another storage crease. But it looked suspicious.

He worked up some saliva and smeared it over the V. After five or ten minutes, with eyes sore from staring at the spot, he saw a bubble forming! He put some more spit on and waited, this time squeezing the tubes of the raft to increase the pressure—hoping that wasn't a poor idea. The bubble persisted and got bigger. This was it! He wished he had a pen to mark the spot and remembered that he might just have one. He checked the pocket of his shorts and found he did. *Phil, Baby, you might be getting run down, but you've still got it. Kudos to me for always carrying a pen!*

He thanked the Lord as he drew a ring around the spot, then wiped the area clean of spit. He couldn't see the defect in the material—that leak was awfully small. Or perhaps the fabric was porous from age and rubbing.

As he sat back to think how to fix it, he glanced up to check on the Coast Guard plane. It must have been flying a swath 30 or 40 miles wide. With no exact location on him, they had to cover a lot of territory.

He hoped they found him soon. Because he could think of nothing, absolutely nothing, to fix that leak.

CHAPTER 45

Earlier that day

Connie had dropped Dave at Wal-Mart, put together her article at a nearby coffee shop and submitted it via email. She picked up Dave and they caught a quick lunch before they returned to close up the charter boat. She got a call as they entered the dock. Dave went ahead to change into new clothes while she took it.

When she joined him shortly afterward, she wore a big grin.

"They accepted the article?" he asked.

She nodded. "I got a text about that. It'll run in the late edition. But that call was even better news—" She searched his eyes. "If we can postpone the trip to Clearwater just a bit?"

"Actually, I've been re-thinking that," Dave said. "My dad's moving north at a pretty good clip. And I bet the Coast Guard's shifted their search base to keep up with him. It doesn't make sense to drive to Clearwater if they're flying out of Savannah."

"Savannah?"

"That's the next air station. After that, I think it's Elizabeth City, North Carolina. What do you think?"

Connie smiled. "I think you're smart, Mr. Shepherd. When do you think they'll find him?"

"Today, for sure. With the search adjusted for the sub's day and night speeds, they ought to. I'd love to be there when they bring him in."

Connie's face scrunched in thought. "I'm hoping you might be able to hang around a few hours. Our TV affiliate in Miami wants to interview you! That's what the call was about. They like the human-interest angle on your dad's story." She paused and bit her lip, looking at him with hope-filled eyes. "And they asked *me* to line it up! What do you think?"

Dave looked daunted. "Wow! What would I have to do? And when do they want to do this?"

Connie squeezed Dave's hand. "You mean you'll do it?"

"This is important to you, isn't it?" he asked gently.

"It is," she said.

"If it doesn't take all day, I think I can manage it before heading north."

Her eyes shone as she said, "Thank you! You'll be great. And all you have to do is answer questions. If you don't know an answer, just say so. It'll be edited before going live."

"When do they want me? It's gotta be today."

"This afternoon! They'll put it on the evening news."

He took a breath. "Okay, let's do it. The sooner the better."

Connie was thrilled and gave him an impulsive hug. "Thank you," she said again, into his ear.

With a grin, he added, "Let me bag up my precious Wal-Mart belongings, say thank you and goodbye to Larry for letting me stay here, and we'll get going." He looked around at the catamaran. "This was great. I like living on the water."

On the drive to the studio, Dave turned to Connie with a grin. "Are they gonna put makeup on me?" he asked.

Connie laughed but kept her eyes on the road. "Of course! They'll want your rugged good looks at their absolute best." She shot him a smiling glance.

Dave bristled with pleasure but said, "I guess I can deal with it. Tom Cruise must deal with it, all those actors must."

Two hours later, Dave was seated in an easy chair on the set of the station. He'd survived makeup with only mild discomfort and was both eager and nervous about sharing his story. An attractive lady in her early thirties introduced herself as Katie Lynn, offering her hand with a camera-ready smile. Dave stood to receive her hand.

"Oh my, a gentleman," she said, still smiling.

Katie quickly reviewed his story, explained how the interview would go, and gave instructions about lights and cameras. She opened the segment by introducing him to the audience as a "Special Guest, an Asbury Seminary student from Kokomo, Indiana." Dave was on live TV!

Staring soberly into the camera Katie said, "David's father, Phil Shepherd, is somewhere out in the ocean tonight as we speak—in a one-person raft, hoping the Coast Guard finds him." She turned to Dave, her face filled with concern. "Mr. Shepherd, how did this happen?"

Dave went through the story again from the time the *Amazing Grace* sank, guided by occasional clarifying questions from Katie. She was a pro. She made the Q&A downright relaxing like a conversation with a friend. Soon he was saying, "Dad'll be okay. He was found once on Saturday afternoon by a British couple. They took some pictures and video and offered to take him aboard. They were going to Fort Lauderdale, which is where he wanted to go anyway."

Katie looked surprised. "But he turned them down? Why on earth would he do that?"

Dave smiled. "Katie, this is gonna sound crazy, but it's true. My dad *refused* to get off his raft until the Coast Guard could show up and take over tracking a *submarine* that was towing him."

"Submarine?" Katie stared at the audience. "This is getting better and better!" She turned back to Dave. "You can't be serious."

"I'm serious!" He went on to explain the details, ending with, "This pipe from the sub had got caught in a massive drift net and my dad caught onto it, too. They've been towing him ever since."

The studio director Ted Kershaw in the control booth reached for a phone after hearing that. "Jerry, get down here, pronto. Got a breaking story of a submarine towing some guy from a sailboat that sank Friday night. The story's breaking right on our set."

Katie had Dave go through the story again to be sure she and her listeners—all of Miami—understood. Turning back to the audience she said, "Stay tuned for more on this incredible story." The studio lights dimmed to normal, and Ted's voice came over a speaker. "Katie, this is a lead headliner—if we can verify it. Hang on a minute."

Ted came down to the set and introduced himself. "Dave, this story is national news if it's true. Do you have the photos and video?"

Dave replied, "Sure. Connie has a copy. The newspaper and the Coast Guard have copies."

"Who's Connie?"

"Connie Morello—a reporter for the Miami Herald." He pointed her out, sitting off the set. "Connie, you got your flash drive with you?"

"Sure do." She dug in her purse. "Here it is!"

Dave said, "Call the Coast Guard. They believe it's a sub, but I don't think they're so sure about it being Iranian. Anyway, that's why they haven't found Dad yet. They didn't allow for the sub pulling him."

"*Iranian?*" Ted and Katie exchanged looks. Ted introduced another man, the station manager, Jerry Markinson. Jerry said, "I hope we can keep you for the afternoon. We want to get on top of this."

Dave looked at Connie, "We were hoping to get to Savannah…I want to be up there when they bring in my dad."

"Savannah?" Jerry asked.

"The Coast Guard's search is probably based from there by now. I'll call to confirm before heading up, but I figure Dad's somewhere near Wilmington, North Carolina."

Jerry shook his head. "Wait, wait. We'll get you up there later if you give us time. Can we move to my office? I want to put you on speaker to our network in New York. Ted, get that flash drive and get me the pictures and especially the video.

And call the Coast Guard and see if they'll confirm it's a sub."

He stopped and looked at Katie. "Sorry to take this from you, but this is huge. Don't leave though, we may want you to run the story for network."

Katie eventually did the interview over, carefully scripted this time. Dave had mentioned missiles off air, but that mention was kept out when it aired on the six o'clock national news.

Their switchboard was immediately swamped with people asking questions. The network asked Dave to fly to New York to be interviewed again there, but he refused.

At the end of the news that evening, Harlan Morrison, national news vice president, came into the broadcast booth. "Great story, people. There may be a Pulitzer lurking in here someplace. Frank—just thinking out loud here. This kid seems to think he knows where his father is—right?"

"Yeah, he seemed pretty confident."

"So even though the Guard hasn't found him—you think we could get to him, first?"

The men shared a smile.

CHAPTER 46

Lieutenant Saxby could hardly believe all the attention she was getting. She, Captain Bob Martin, and now Vice Admiral Edward G. Pierce—Commander Atlantic Area Defense Force East—had just left the office of the big kahuna, Coast Guard Commandant Walter S. Marriott. Martin had warned that she'd have to tell the story over and over, and he'd been right.

Vice Admiral Pierce and the commandant were quick to catch on to the ramifications of the submarine. Her next meeting was with somebody from the navy. Commandant Marriott said, "I've got Dirk Hunter, CNO, coming to join us and Martha." To Saxby's questioning expression he said, "CNO is chief of naval operations. Normally I'd get the secretary of the navy here too, but he's in the Philippines."

"And Martha?" she asked.

The commandant chuckled, "Martha Saslow, secretary of DHS—Homeland Security. She's an interesting lady, an Israeli with military experience. I don't know which branch. She's also my boss."

"I see," the lieutenant said, feeling overwhelmed and worn out. Perhaps she'd get to go home after this next meeting. She hadn't had a chance to get into a fresh uniform, not to mention take a shower since it all started.

She was amazed—and relieved—at how fast the navy guy showed up. Admiral Dirk Hunter burst into the conference room, resplendent in his gold-adorned uniform and service ribbons. "Good morning, Coast Guard!" He bowed jocularly to Commandant Marriott. "Okay—talk to me of submarines. I got a little heads-up from Norfolk, but I couldn't make sense of it. They claim a foreign sub is prowling our shores without us having a clue. I doubt that's possible." He plopped in a chair, leaned back, laced his hands behind his head, and smiled. "So, this had better be good." He was a large, muscular man, looking as if he'd be ready to step into a ring for a few rounds.

Commandant Marriott wasn't in a jocular mood. He said, "Dirk, this could be a serious situation. We're convinced there's a foreign sub coming up the East Coast, and with unfriendly intentions. Let me introduce my team, and they'll tell you the whole story."

Lieutenant Saxby thought, *showtime.* She got out the photos and transcript.

Ten minutes later, Admiral Hunter's smile was replaced by a frown. "The submarine, I get. But Iranian? Venezuelan possibly—but Iran, how would they do it?"

"Has anybody alerted DHS yet?" the CNO asked.

"That's next," the commandant replied.

Dirk held up a hand, "I need to call Norfolk and get them looking for this sub. No one's found the guy in the raft, right?"

Captain Martin said, "Not yet, Admiral, but I'm confident we'll find him today."

"And your best guess as to where he's located?"

Martin looked at Lieutenant Saxby, who said, "Coming up on Cape Hatteras, sir."

The CNO grabbed his cell phone but turned to the captain and Saxby. "I'm getting Martha on the line. Not to worry, she's quick."

"Martha? Dirk Hunter. What would you say if we told you we have evidence of a foreign sub coming up our East Coast, reportedly Iranian?" He paused, listening, "Really?" He eyed the rest of the room with his brows raised. "Amazing. Okay, we're coming up ASAP."

To the questioning faces around him, Hunter said, "The FBI just took an Iranian sailor in custody in Nassau—accused of murdering three people. The guy came from a submarine." He stood up, scooped up the materials the lieutenant had given him and snapped them in his briefcase. "Come on, folks. Time to defend the country."

Martha Saslow filled them in on the details of Hesam's capture and that he'd eventually confessed coming off an Iranian sub in the area. Looking at Dirk she said quietly, "We have to tell him—right away."

Martin and Saxby looked at each other. *Tell who*, they wondered.

"Absolutely," Dirk said, nodding. "This may go to a DefCon alert."

She said, "I'll get DOD, state, justice, joint chiefs—all that I can." She looked at her watch. "One hour, max."

Bob Martin could no longer contain his curiosity. "Tell who?"

The CNO and Secretary Saslow responded in unison, "The president."

CHAPTER 47

"Nigel, take a look at this," Olivia Braxton said.

Nigel came on deck from below and looked overhead. He'd heard the Coast Guard Learjet racing low and now saw it make a tight turn, coming back.

"Dear Lord. They want us to come back to the States. We can't, Livvy. We're not going back to Fort Lauderdale." He and Olivia nodded at each other. "I wonder what they'll do next? Send a boat? It would take hours."

"They might enlist the Bahamians to get us."

The *Wanderlust* was 70 miles from Fort Lauderdale, on the western coast of the Bahamas.

The plane flew off, but thirty minutes later they heard the fluck-a-ta-fluck-a-ta of a helicopter and soon spotted the red Coast Guard HC 65 approaching.

"Here it comes," Nigel said. "I suppose they'll want to put somebody aboard. Might as well drop sail." He glanced at the depth gauge. "Move into shore and drop anchor."

A few minutes later, with the helicopter hovering overhead, a loudspeaker announced, *"Wanderlust, Wanderlust.* This is the U.S. Coast Guard. We're putting an officer on board. Please cooperate." After a pause, they heard, "And thank you for anchoring to receive us."

A young lieutenant swung down on the end of a cable and slipped into the boat's cockpit. After introducing himself, they learned he'd been sent on behalf of the Commandant of the Coast Guard to ask them to return to the United States, specifically to Washington DC! And at Coast Guard expense, for their testimony about Phil was extremely important.

Olivia and Nigel shared a smile. "Well, Mr. Hackett," said Olivia, "Thank you for dropping in on us, er, *pun intended.* My husband and I have already discussed this, and it would very much interfere with our plans. We told that nice young lady, I think Saxby was her name, everything we have to say. We have nothing to add. She recorded it all, so nothing was missed."

Nigel added, "There's nothing more we can contribute."

The young lieutenant looked distressed. He said quietly, "I was afraid this might happen. If you'll excuse me." He pulled out a satellite phone.

"Commander? Lieutenant Hackett. The Braxtons refuse to return to the U.S. They say they told Lieutenant Saxby everything and have nothing more to contribute." Hackett listened, then looked around. "We're anchored—that is, they're anchored—off a small island south of the Bimini chain... I don't know the name of it. It's not on our charts; it's uninhabited... What's that?" He listened again. "Yes, definitely in Bahamian waters." After listening again for a long minute, he said, "Yes, sir," and shut the phone.

"Okay," he said solemnly, "Please take a phone number. Do you have a satellite phone?" Nigel and Olivia shook their heads, *no.*

"Hmm, well if you think of anything—anything at all— that you might add to what you told the lieutenant, please contact us."

He signaled to the helicopter. Just as he reattached the hoisting harness to the cable that was lowered for him, Olivia raised her hand.

"Lieutenant. One thing we did not tell that other lieutenant. Mr. Shepherd said it is a Kilo." As Lieutenant Hackett started to rise above them, he shouted down, "A Kilo, ma'am?"

Olivia shouted back, "Yes—the submarine is a Kilo."

CHAPTER 48

The leak was growing. Water sloshed around him. Phil's pulse raced. With a dry mouth, he thought frantically of what to do—and remembered a Scripture verse. "If any man lacks wisdom, let him ask of the Lord." Why hadn't he thought of that sooner?

Lord, I'm asking! You've been with me from the start of this crazy journey. I believe this is Your will, not just mine. And now my raft is losing air. So please, please, Lord, show me a way to fix it! In Jesus' name. Amen.

Nothing immediately came to mind, but his heart rate was slowing down. If this was a test of faith, he wouldn't say he'd aced it. But he did trust God. He believed His Word. The Lord wouldn't leave him. He wouldn't forsake him. *Thank you, Jesus.*

He scanned the horizon and saw off to the west, a long container ship heading south—probably staying out of the Gulfstream to make time. He glanced at the sky and was heartened to see sunlight breaking through the clouds. He could use the warmth. And the Coast Guard's plane—was it finally getting closer?

Please, God, let this be the day! I'm so ready to be out of here!

Now that he'd prayed, he turned his mind to the leak. He forced a couple of puffs into the tube to firm it up. But hunger called. His meals were getting messier and messier—not from his sloppy cleaning, but from all the crud that the net was

229

continually picking up. He was happy to find a nice, fresh pompano in it, though. When he'd had enough, he threw the remains to dolphins, glad to see they'd returned. They were a friendly presence in this lonely outpost. *Thank you, Jesus.*

He was cleaning gooey net sludge from his hands when he took a good look at it. It reminded him of tar—roofing repair tar. And it hit him—if it might patch up a hole on the roof, it should patch up a hole in the raft! Here was his answer! His thanks rang out loud as he looked up at the heavens and called, "Thank you, Jesus!"

"Okay, tar—we're no longer enemies." The sound of his voice—any voice—was reassuring "Now we're friends." He took a nice gooey glob and pulled up yards of the float rope. With the gunky black stuff in hand, he slid to the foot of the raft where, fortunately, his mark—the ring around the leak— was still legible. Slapping the gunk over it, he troweled back and forth with his fingers, then sat back to observe his handiwork. "Lord, let this patch hold. No more leaks!"

He washed the tar from his hands in the ocean as best he could. Mary wouldn't have approved of the results, he thought ruefully, but he'd need soap to do better. On a whim, he pulled up a couple of handfuls of net without gunk on it, bunched it up and used it as a scrub brush. *Ha—better!* Not what you'd call clean—but cleaner than before.

Sunlight washed over him, and he looked up gratefully, leaning back to soak it in. If it warmed up the patch, he could work the tar further into the fabric and really seal that leak. His spirits lifted. It might have been the sunlight, or maybe the successful patch; maybe it was faith; but he felt good. Today would be the day, he was sure!

With the sun out, he remembered he had a mirror—he could flash it again! He tried not to think how bad the odds were of reflecting the sun into the eyes of a pilot 2,000 or 3,000 feet above as he flew by at a couple hundred miles an hour. Probably about as good as winning the Irish Sweepstakes without buying a ticket. But he watched the plane approach and did his best. "Okay, mirror, do your thing!" Holding it as steadily as possible, he sighted the plane's cockpit in the center of the little cross.

Oops. Lost him. He looked around the mirror and his heart soared. The plane was coming his way! He laughed out loud. Was the mirror working? He signaled again, trying to sight in the cockpit window.

The plane dipped toward him. Phil was sure he'd been seen! He dropped the mirror into his bag and waved his hands like mad. "Thank you, Jesus! Thank you, Lord! I knew today was gonna be the day!"

The plane dropped even lower, but it wasn't a seaplane. It couldn't land and pick him up—spectacular as that would be. When it flew over at only about 700 feet, Phil was still waving madly. He watched as it went by and then made a turn in the air and passed over again, even lower. *This is great!*

When it made yet another pass, throttling its engines, a ramp dropped down at the approach and a dark, cylindrical object dropped out. Phil could even see the man who'd released it and waved at him. When he waved back, a sense of relief swept over Phil.

"Yes! Human contact." *Thank you, Lord*! He hadn't realized how much he'd missed it, but he was blinking back tears. A saying from his former pastor came to mind: "A man in isolation is a man in crisis."

That did it—Phil decided that when he got home, he'd ditch the hermit stuff. He'd get out—he'd call Louise!

He couldn't wait to find out what they'd left in the water, a dark object which had surfaced about fifty yards from the raft. As he watched, something like blades opened up. Was it a buoy to mark the spot? How would they rescue him? With a boat? A helicopter? He was pretty far out for a boat—were there Coast Guard boat stations anywhere nearby? No, they'd probably send a helicopter. They liked helicopters.

The plane circled back for a final pass, dropping a bulky package as it went by. Phil watched with excitement as it popped to the surface and unfolded itself. It was a raft, a *big* raft! A six or eight-man raft. He figured they expected him to paddle over to it and ditch this little guy. Right after he'd fixed it, too—but maybe his fix wouldn't hold.

But disappointment quickly followed his elation. If he got into their raft, he'd lose the sub. And if he lost the sub, this whole caper was pointless. Deal-breaker. *Sorry, Coast Guard—appreciate the offer but he'd stay where he was. For better or worse.*

He watched the raft and buoy as they gradually went out of sight behind him. The search plane made another pass above him, wagged its wings, and headed back toward the coast.

Phil realized he'd just said goodbye to a safer craft but hoped it wouldn't delay his rescue. He dreamed of food, real food—pizza, or steak! Clean sheets, warmth—a cup of coffee. *Man, hot, black coffee would be really nice.* No sense denying it—he wasn't born to be a pioneer.

He noted the time. In less than an hour, they should have a helicopter overhead.

Sometime later, way over on the horizon, he saw the helicopter! Small at this distance as a horsefly. It hovered to the south—by the beacon, no doubt. And then turned in Phil's direction! "Follow the net, boys," he murmured, watching. "Just follow the net!"

A few minutes later, a beautiful red Coast Guard helicopter hovered overhead. A man in a wetsuit, fins, and snorkel descended on a cable. He'd swim to Phil. The little raft was too small for him to climb on, and Phil wondered how this was gonna go down. Still above the water, the man pushed up his mouthpiece and spoke to the pilot of the helicopter on his little hand-held radio.

Finally, he dropped in the water a few feet behind Phil's raft and quickly stroked to the net. He grabbed it, reeled up to the back of the raft, and took out his snorkel. "Did you call for a cab? I'm Johnny Watson, your friendly neighborhood Coast Guard rescue swimmer."

Phil grinned. "At this point, I'd take a garbage scow."

He grinned back. "I thought so. Okay, let me tell you how this is gonna work. You have to let go of your raft and get in the water. We'll lower a basket, and I'll help you in it. Then we'll hoist you to the helicopter. Then it's home to the US of A. How's that sound?"

Phil's elation died in his breast. "What happens to this net—and the submarine?"

"What do you mean? They'll keep on going."

"How are you gonna follow them? If you fly me back, how will you know where they are?"

The man looked perplexed. "Do we need to? Our job is to rescue *you*. Nobody said anything about following the sub."

"Can you get somebody to come out and track the submarine first? Before I leave?"

He frowned. "I don't have a clue. Let me call the skipper." He pulled out a waterproof VHF radio. "Do you mind if I hang onto your raft while I do this? It's a lot easier than swimming."

"Not at all but watch my patch there." Phil pointed to it. "I had a leak, but I think I've got it fixed."

The man talked with the pilot. "Got it!" He looked at Phil. "Mr. Shepherd, we don't have the capability to follow your submarine after we pick you up. I hope that is satisfactory."

"No," Phil said slowly, "No, it isn't" He looked at Phil in amazement. He continued, "I'm sorry, young man, but the reason I've been out here since Friday night is that I'm being pulled by an Iranian sub that wants to *launch missiles on the US* in the next day or two. I believe the Lord has brought me this far, and I'm not gonna bail on Him now. Thank you very much, but I have to stay here."

CHAPTER 49

The Yunes

Ensign Navid Sharifi, the *Yunes's* medic, approached Captain Golzar. "Can we speak privately, please, sir?" Slight to begin with, Sharifi seemed even smaller next to the captain. Like most all the crew, his facial hair had grown to a full mustache and beard, but pale skin still peeked out.

The captain forced a smile. *Now what?* He'd thought the crew was generally healthy despite the long, arduous passage. He led the way to his private cabin. He hoped it was important, not being in the mood to settle some petty dispute.

"Well, sir," Sharifi began, "You may not have heard, but the men are grumbling and scared. A few of them have had nose bleeds, a few more, skin rashes. They're saying it's radiation from the missiles. The crew in engineering are complaining most, since they're directly below the missiles."

"I've not heard. Tell me, Ensign, what is your opinion?"

"I'm not sure. Nosebleeds aren't common aboard a submarine, and I've seen three crewmen with one. But they were mild; easily stopped."

"And the skin rash?" The captain asked.

"Not unusual, sir. With decreasing air quality and limited water for bathing, skin ailments are expected. However, this voyage is three times longer than anything previously attempted by us, so I have no basis for comparison. But as you know, I'm not an MD, just a medical ensign."

The captain thought. "Have you talked to our missile officer, Lieutenant Commander Okhovat?"

"I thought I would bring it to your attention first." The lieutenant wasn't in the ensign's chain of command, and he had reasons for not taking it to him. He hesitated.

"Is there more?" the captain asked.

"Perhaps I shouldn't say this," he answered slowly, "but it's possible that he may be the problem. You know how he periodically sweeps the boat with his Geiger counter? The men aren't used to that. It puts ideas in their heads. They're asking questions like, 'Am I going to be able to have children after this?' and more direct questions—about their anatomy. Okhovat reassures them, but…you know, sailors tend to be superstitious." He paused. "I thought you ought to know, sir."

"I'm glad you told me. I can't have the men afraid of the missiles. We launch in two days."

Sharifi gasped. "Two days?"

The captain grinned. "That's right." He clapped Sharifi's shoulder. "Okay, Ensign, we'll get on top of this. Meet me in the wardroom. I'll call for the exec and Lieutenant Commander Okhovat."

Minutes later after the ensign repeated his story to the assembled officers, Executive Officer Pourali exclaimed, "I knew it! I thought the men were acting uneasy—I just didn't know why. This is serious, very serious!"

Lieutenant Commander Okhovat seemed amused. "No, it's not, Pourali. It's nothing. I already told them it was nothing."

The captain half rose from his chair and glowered at his missile expert. "No, Lieutenant Commander, it is not 'nothing' as you claim. In two days, this crew must swarm on deck and launch two missiles as quickly as humanly possible. How will they do that if they're afraid of the missiles? They won't get close to them."

Okhovat stared at the captain. He stammered, "But sir, we have all the shielding we need from radiation in the missile casings."

"So what are your Geiger counter measurements for? To verify *nothing?* You can't have it both ways, Lieutenant Commander."

Okhovat flushed. "I can see how that may have given the men the wrong idea. I never got anything more than normal background readings—as expected."

Golzar's eyes narrowed. "You're not a submariner, not Academy, not even a blue water sailor. I had to accept you on this crew; they said you were the best missile man. But your rank is strictly honorary. You and your two helpers are guests on this boat. So listen carefully Mister Ohkovat; the exec and I handpicked this crew—every one of them. And they are excellent—Iran's best. This is the most important and difficult mission the Islamic Republic's navy has ever undertaken. So you are upsetting excellent sailors and still haven't answered why you took the readings." Okhovat cowered under his glare.

"I'm sorry, sir. As you say, I'm a guest here. As such, I have little to do. Since the radioactive materials are contained in the missile casings I surveyed periodically to ensure they were intact. There's no other way to inspect them." He took a breath. "Besides, it's good practice to take readings occasionally whenever there's nuclear material around. I'm sorry, sir, very sorry if I caused confusion."

Captain Golzar relaxed. "This has been a strain on all of us." He looked around at his men, "Okay, Lieutenant Commander, here's what you're going to do: You will conduct a meeting—perhaps a few meetings—with the crew. You'll explain everything they want to know about the missiles, how they work, and why they are 100 percent safe for us. Can you do that?"

Ohkovat hesitated. "That's confidential information, sir."

The captain leaned forward and stared. "What?"

Ohkovat met his gaze and hurriedly said, "Yes sir, I can do that, sir, certainly." He forced a smile and nodded, but with a troubled expression.

"Good. You can start by explaining to my other officers here why your missiles are so safe."

"Gladly, sir. We're launching what are known as 'dirty bombs.' They're not atomic bombs. There won't be a nuclear detonation. Instead, conventional explosives will scatter significant radioactive material into the atmosphere. It will disperse with the wind and contaminate the area—rendering it uninhabitable."

"For how long?" Ensign Sharifi asked.

Ohkovat gave his first genuine smile of the day. "Ah! That's the beauty of it. You may know that radioactive materials are measured in half-life—the time it takes for them to lose half of their radioactivity. For some materials, this is just a few minutes. For ours? We're using radium, with a half-life of seventy-seven thousand years, and thorium, with an expected half-life of four and a half billion years."

"Praise Allah!" the exec exclaimed. "That's forever." Then he asked cautiously, "And why isn't this radiating us right now?"

"Good question, Executive Officer. Our two materials were specifically chosen because they emit primarily alpha waves. Alpha waves—how shall I say this—have very little penetrating power. A little bit of lead, which we have in the missile launch tubes, keeps them comfortably contained. And the other beauty of alpha waves is that they carry very well in air—to people."

The exec interrupted, "But I'm confused, if they have very little penetrating power, so what if they land on people? What's the harm?"

"The primary hazard is not skin penetration, it's inhalation—breathing."

"And if I breathe it?"

"You die."

CHAPTER 50

"Connie!" Dave knocked at the motel door next to his the following morning in Savanna, Georgia, where they'd arrived somewhere near 4:30 a.m. Right near the Coast Guard station coordinating the search for Phil.

"Connie, you in there?" He banged again, urgency in his voice.

Connie had gone to the Coast Guard, done an early interview, then filed her story, "Missing Man Refuses Rescue." She'd returned and tried to rest but came to the door still groggy.

"Is something wrong?" she asked, blinking sleepily.

Dave held up his cell phone. "No! Look what I got!"

Connie squinted, trying to sweep away cobwebs in the bright sun and focus on his phone. "Come on in. I was falling back asleep. I've been to the Coast Guard and interviewed them; they found your dad, but he wouldn't come!" She smiled wanly up at him, "And I'm not even a morning person."

"He wouldn't come? I had no idea. I can't say I'm surprised, but I sure want to see him. At least they know where he is."

"Well, they did," Connie replied, "Now…" She stood back from the door. "Come on. Let me see what you've got."

Dave hesitated but entered the room. "I guess it's okay—but let's not be in here long. My dad always said, 'Avoid all appearance of wrongdoing.' Look! I've got pictures from him!"

Connie's eyes opened fully. "Are you sure?"

"Look! He took these a couple of nights ago. They must've been stuck in his outbox until I guess he came into a freak signal or something from a cell tower, so now we've got them." He sat beside her on the bed, trying not to look around at her personal things. "Here's the snorkel—the submarine's snorkel! And here's dad next to it." He grinned. "He took a selfie. And here's some writing on top of the snorkel, but it's a foreign language."

Connie grabbed Dave's arm. "These look great. Let me freshen up and we'll decide what to do with them."

When she returned minutes later, she looked more alert—and very pretty in a bright flowery blouse, capris and sandals. She plopped next to him. "Okay, *mi cariño*. Show me again."

Dave flushed with pleasure and handed her the phone, again going over what each portrayed.

Connie said, "This is another story! When did he take these pictures?"

"They're dated Saturday night. I'm psyched," Dave said, springing to his feet. "This is like, more proof for the naysayers."

"It sure is. Send them to me. I'll do another story and get it to my editor. Sound good?"

"Sounds great, beautiful lady," Dave said, looking up long enough to wink at her as he forwarded the photos. "I'll send these to the others, and, what the heck—post them on Facebook." In another second he looked up again. "We should show these to the Coast Guard, too. Maybe they'll get them to the Navy."

Connie nodded.

Dave said, "We can't exactly go to the Navy and knock on the door and say "By the way, you want some pictures of my dad on an Iranian submarine snorkel off the Florida coast?"

Connie's eyes sparkled, "Not unless you're ready to go into custody." Her face sobered. "They'll want your photographs for sure. They'll want to analyze the writing on top of the snorkel. And they really are going to want something else."

Dave looked at her questioningly.

"You."

"You think?"

She nodded again. "Uh-hum. You're their best connection with your father and that sub."

Dave paced the room. "Well, I have no choice. But I have one condition to going forward."

"Which is…?"

He stopped in front of her. "That you'll come too." He gently pulled her to her feet and put his hands lightly about her waist. "It means a lot that you've been with me through this." Gingerly, he moved a stray curl to the side of her face. "I couldn't have asked for a better—or prettier—reporter. Or friend."

His eyes sent warmth running through her, and Connie sank into his arms. "I couldn't have asked for a better story to get my career off the ground," she said into his shirt. And then, looking up at him, she added, "And the fact that it came with you…" She blinked, unable to continue.

Dave bent his head. They shared a sweet, long, kiss.

CHAPTER 51

Washington, D.C.

Lieutenant Saxby followed Captain Martin, Vice Admiral Pierce, and Commandant Marriott into the cabinet room adjacent to the Oval Office, along with Secretary DHS Saslow and CNO Dirk Hunter. Sun streamed through the tall, draped windows from the Rose Garden, giving the room a look of quiet elegance.

The lieutenant was surprised they'd seated her at the conference table, rather than in one of the side chairs that lined the room. Especially when, in minutes, the chairs were nearly full. Franklin Grant, Secretary of the Department of Defense, Devonne Jones, Director of the FBI, Marsha Williams, Secretary of State, and a cast of subordinates were now seated, and a collective hush fell over the room as they waited expectantly for the president.

When he entered from an end door, President Mitchell Brandenburg was preceded by the Attorney General, Zachary Crawford. The president looked the part of a consummate politician; tall, strong-jawed, with sparkling blue eyes and silver-streaked hair.

Cordially he said, "Good morning, ladies and gentlemen. Since this meeting is urgent, I will dispense with personal greetings and handshakes; I hope you vote for me next time in any case." The roomful of dignitaries chuckled. A white-jacketed steward entered the room, rolling a cart of refreshments.

"Milo, I'll have my usual, thank you," he said.

Although Milo Dumlao, a Filipino American, was more than eighty years old, he was spry and attentive. He reached across the president to place a decaf amaretto latte next to his pad.

The president turned to DHS Saslow. "Marsha, you called this meeting," he said, looking around the room. "And I guess it's a popular one." Another murmur of chuckles went round. "Why don't you introduce your people, and then tell us what this is about?"

After introducing the Coast Guard, Saslow looked around and said, "I think you know everyone else, Mr. President."

"Some of you too well," he rejoined, with a grin. "Okay, what have you got?"

Saslow said, "I'll turn this over to the Coast Guard."

Lieutenant Saxby squirmed with nerves, but thankfully Commandant Marriott began. "Mr. President. Friday night a sailboat sank off the Miami coast on its way to the Bahamas..." Saxby and the rest of the room listened as he detailed the rescue, the missing man, Phil Shepherd, and the fishing net linking him to a sub, which turned out to be an Iranian vessel—a diesel-electric, not nuclear—but apparently on a mission of harmful intent to the United States.

The president said, "So it's not one of ours."

CNO Hunter interjected. "That's right sir, and it doesn't belong to any of our allies." He added a quick rundown of how they'd obtained photos from the Braxtons, then turned to the lieutenant and asked her to continue.

Saxby's heart jumped. She was about to convey information to the *president!* She showed the photos on a large screen, followed by the short video of the submarine pulling Phil through the water. "Our Savannah search team found Mr. Shepherd this morning. However, he refused to be rescued without the reassurance that we would follow the submarine."

"Good grief!" the president exclaimed, "Dirk, this has to be a submarine, right?"

The CNO responded, "Yes, Mr. President."

"Whose is it?" the president asked him.

"We have strong reason to believe it's from Iran."

FBI Director Jones jumped in. "Mr. President, our liaison in Nassau reports that the Royal Bahamian Police Force apprehended a man accused of murdering three people off the coast of the Bahamas. Turns out he's a sailor from an Iranian submarine."

"Unbelievable," the president murmured.

The CNO continued, "As you heard from Lieutenant Saxby, Mr. Shepherd claims the sub is carrying missiles which they intend to fire on this country." He paused. "Frankly, sir, I doubt it's possible to take to a deck-mounted missile all the way from Iran, then surface and launch, especially undetected."

The white-jacketed steward suddenly leaned into the president's ear and spoke. The Filipino's years of stewarding high-level meetings had trained him to be virtually invisible. He was never to interrupt the proceedings. But something compelled him. His words, spoken softly but clearly were, "Mr. President, I was on a U.S. submarine that did exactly what this gentleman is talking about."

The president turned and surveyed his steward. "Really, Milo?" He turned to the room. "Say it loud enough so everybody can hear you, please."

Milo looked shyly at the assemblage. "In 1963, I was assigned as a steward on the submarine *Growler,* a diesel-electric—like the kind of sub you are talking about."

"It was equipped with two deck-mounted Regulus cruise missiles. We went on cruises as far as Japan. We did what this gentleman says the Iranian sub can do." He motioned at the CNO. "We'd surface, take the missiles out of their containers, and fire them. I believe the *Grayback* was also similarly equipped." He bowed to the assembly and said meekly, "Please excuse my interruption."

The room responded with quiet appreciation and thanks as heads nodded and eyes followed the steward gratefully. CNO Hunter said, "Mr. President, I stand corrected. I can see there is great value in keeping people in the Navy for extended tours of service."

Franklin Grant, Secretary of Defense, asked, "So, Dirk, are you saying this is real? And if it is real, what can the Navy do about it?"

The CNO said "I've already put Norfolk and Jacksonville on alert to find this sub. According to our best information," he looked at Lieutenant Saxby, "it's coming up on Cape Hatteras." Saxby nodded in agreement.

Secretary of State Marsha Williams said, "Mr. President, if I may. According to what I've just heard, this is a foreign vessel operating in international waters outside our 12-mile limit. To date, they have done nothing hostile or threatening.

We can't exactly blow them out of the water just because we think they have bad intentions."

"Good point, Marsha," the president said. He looked out at the room. "What are your suggestions?"

CNO Hunter said, "Mr. President, our first course of action is to find the sub. I'm fully confident we'll do that shortly, sir, within hours. Then we need to track it. If it continues up the coast and surfaces, we'll observe, and if necessary, interdict."

The president turned to his steward again. "Milo, first let me say, I've never appreciated the full range of your talents." Everyone laughed. "If you can dig again into your memory, how long did it take the *Growler* to surface and launch a missile?"

The room waited with a heavy silence. The steward thought about it, took a deep breath, and said slowly, "I would say about ten minutes, Mr. President."

Some of the listeners gasped.

The Secretary of Defense blurted, "That's a small window, especially at night! You've got to find that bad boy and toast him in ten minutes."

Lieutenant Saxby's nerves were still on edge, but she had something that had to be shared. Raising her hand with a staccato heartbeat, she waited for the president to notice her. When he pointed at her and said, "Go," she cleared her throat. "It hasn't been brought out yet—and I don't mean to complicate all this—but you need to know that Mr. Shepherd and his son Dave, are becoming well known. Dave has been on network news, which is now being re-run everywhere. He's on YouTube and Facebook. Photos of Phil Shepherd on the sub's snorkel are going viral as we speak."

Secretary of State Williams said, "So if we sink the sub, we also sink him—a national hero."

The president stood. "All right! Lieutenant Saxby, thank you very much for that. Now, unless there is anything else, people…?"

No one spoke up.

"Marsha and Zachary, come with me," he said.

"Mr. President?" they both asked simultaneously.

"Let's make this the Iranians' problem. I'm going to call their new president—what's his name—Akbari, on the telephone, open channel, and tell him we know the name of his submarine, where it is, and why it's there. And if there are any acts of hostility against this country, we will take that as an open declaration of war by Iran."

CHAPTER 52

Patrol Commander Adrian Zook pulled back on the yoke of his P-3 Orion aircraft to lift off the runway at the Naval Air Station in Jacksonville, Florida. He wasn't feeling confident about the flight. His crew had been hastily thrown together and he lacked his usual men. And this wasn't a training exercise, but a real mission. He'd been told only to find a foreign submarine off the East Coast, close to shore somewhere around Cape Hatteras. Although the information was sketchy, the note of urgency about it was crystal clear: something big was going down.

Over the intercom, he said, "Pilot to crew. Get settled quickly. This is *not* a drill." Since they were airborne, he went on to brief them about their purpose.

The uniqueness of the P-3 Orion, that it carried a magnetic anomaly detector or MAD, was why he'd got this mission. The P-3 was a modified version of the old Lockheed Electra—the one whose wings fell off from time to time. The MAD sensor head was at the trailing end of a long tube out the tail. It was so sensitive it would confuse its own plane with a target if it wasn't positioned properly. The MAD detected variations in the Earth's magnetic field that ran from the North to the South Pole—variations caused by large concentrations of magnetic material such as iron or steel—or a sub.

At the rear of Orion, Petty Officer Albert Cosby sat at his

consul waiting for his equipment to warm up. In front of him was an array of screens, dials, and controls. He keyed his mic. "Coming online, Commander."

"Thanks, Albert," Zook replied. Albert, at least, was his regular operator. The plane today included a full crew of ten, but only two of them—he and Albert—were experienced.

He headed north at cruising speed until he approached the North Carolina border. Shortly thereafter he eased the yoke forward, dropped down to 500 feet, and throttled back to search speed. It helped that it was fairly sunny with plenty of daylight hours left.

He keyed his mic. "Okay folks, if you're near a window, keep your eyes peeled. If we're lucky, we might actually see this thing." Submerged submarines were sometimes visible under these conditions. Zook wasn't hopeful, though.

"Commander, I'm getting a hit. Not sure what it is," Albert's voice crackled over the intercom.

"Roger that. But I'll keep going north for a bit. We're too far south for this to be our sub. Maybe it's a wreck."

"It could be," Albert replied.

A new voice came on. The tactical coordinator, Captain Edward Duleave, said, "Confirming a wreck. Water's shallow here. We may find more."

Petty Officer LaShawn Lennert, the in-flight tech for ordinance came on. "Commander? Do I need the rules of engagement? I've got a full complement here." The P-3's bomb bays could drop a variety of missiles and torpedoes.

"We're instructed to not engage, just to identify and report the location. If and when we find it, I'll call in for further instructions. They'll probably want to get some helos out of

Norfolk to sit on it."

Lennert relaxed and pulled out a paperback. Long idle hours—interrupted by short periods of high tension when they practiced dropping torpedoes on simulated submarines—weren't unusual.

They were approaching Cape Hatteras. Zook said, "Heads up, Albert, this is where our bad boy is supposed to be."

Albert studied the display screen intently. "Commander, we must be flying over a marine graveyard! I'll stop calling out every hit." He ran a hand through his hair "Lord! I'm recording so we can compare the hits with a chart of wrecks." He paused and muttered, "If there is such a thing."

Duleave interjected, "I've seen one, but we don't have one on board. Probably have to go to the Coast Guard. Good idea, PO Cosby."

Zook frowned. A shooter would call the area target-rich, though only one of the targets was moving—but they had no way to tell which one. He decided to fly 100 miles north and circle back doing a north-south weave, gradually moving further from the coast. "Albert? You still getting lots of hits?"

"They're coming faster than my system can record, sir. I've never seen anything like this."

Duleave came on. "I think we can thank the Germans. This is the World War II graveyard of commercial shipping. Their U-boats had a field day at the beginning of the war. Their sub captains even called this 'happy time' because the shooting was so easy. There are hundreds of wrecks all along the East Coast here."

"Well, that explains it, Ed, thanks," said Zook. "I wasn't aware of that. Albert? You holding it together back there?"

"That's why I get the big bucks," he said, jovially. "Another day, another dollar."

On the third weave pass, they were about 100 miles from the coast. Albert said, "Commander, since our last turn, I'm getting nothing back here."

"Good. I think we'll head for the barn," Zook replied. He called Jacksonville as he put the plane over to head south. "Commander? We have an unusual situation. The bottom here is littered with wrecks, probably from World War II; we can't tell a live sub from the hulks. We recorded the positions of the hits, but we'll need to go over them with a chart to see if one is our guy. Request permission to return to base."

"Permission granted," Air Station Commander Captain Harold Anderson responded. With compressed lips, he called his Norfolk boss, Rear Admiral Nathan St. Clair. He explained the situation, adding, "I don't know whether the bad guys thought about it, but this sub couldn't have picked a better place to hide."

St. Clair put the phone down gently "Lord, have mercy," he said. He made another call. "Joe? How soon will you be ready to go?"

Commander Joe Burgin, captain of the Los Angeles Class Attack Submarine *Tuscaloosa*, responded. "Still assembling our crew, sir. We're bringing the reactor up. I would say…ready in three hours, minimum. By the way, Admiral, what do we do if we find the sub?"

The admiral hesitated. The answer to that question was highly political. "At this point, just track and report," he said. Slowly he added, "But be ready to engage on very short notice."

"Yes, sir. But I'll need all my people here. I'm still two officers, five CPOs, and eleven crew short."

"Okay, Joe, thanks. I'll see what Ollie Jenkins can do."

Moments later, he had Oliver Jenkins, captain of the USS *Steel*, an Arleigh Burke Class Destroyer, on the phone. "Ollie? How close are you to getting underway? Remember, this is only anti-sub. You won't need crew for any more than that."

"We're just about there, sir. I'm assuming two or three days for this at most, so I won't need more than depth charges and torpedoes?"

"Affirmative," St. Clair replied. "I'll get out of your hair. Send me a confirm when you're leaving the dock." He made one more call.

"Hunter," CNO Dirk Hunter answered. "Talk to me here, Nate."

"Yes, sir. He gave him the sitrep about the wrecks, about Jenkins being almost ready to set out, and about Joe Burgin and the *Tuscaloosa* still three hours to leave dock at best."

He paused, troubled, and added, "You said the president was gonna telephone the Iranian president and get their sub to abort mission? I have to say, sir, that even if Iran tries to do that, they could fail. I don't know what the Iranians have in the way of communications, but they're halfway around the world from their guy. And the sub commander sure isn't riding around on the surface with his radio on. Also, it's possible that even if he does get an abort message, he'll think it's a ruse from us. I thought I should share those concerns, sir. "

CNO Hunter frowned, nodding. "I've had the same thoughts, Nate. Okay," he sighed. I'll tell the president. I'll tell the president his idea probably won't work."

CHAPTER 53

Iran

President Akbai was relaxing in front of a flickering fire at home, enjoying a privileged snifter of Courvoisier brandy and a fine Cohiba Cuban cigar. It had been a productive day, but a long one.

There was a gentle knock on the door, cautiously opened to reveal Farouk, his aide. "Mr. President? President Brandenberg of the United States is on the telephone. I have an English interpreter on his way." The wide eyes of the aide spoke volumes.

Akbari dropped his cigar and practically choked on the brandy. "President Brandenberg? Of the United States?"

"Yes, sir. He's on the telephone; and demanding to speak to you. It came through our general switchboard."

Akbari pulled himself together. He sat up and took a deep breath. "I'll take it in my office." He stood. "Get Minister Zamani—immediately. And I don't need an interpreter for English. I thought you knew that."

In his office, Akbari sat behind his desk, thinking about President Brandenberg. He knew a little of the man—but not enough. He was a conservative, an adept politician, with strong support in the U.S.

He hesitantly picked up the phone. "This is President Akbari," he said in a tone as calmly as possible. "Mr. President, how can I help you?" His tone belied the fact that he could barely take a good breath and one hand gripped the phone while his other held to the desk to keep it from shaking.

"Mr. President, this is President Mitchell Brandenberg of the United States. As I recall, you speak English. Can we dispense with interpreters?"

Akbari relaxed a notch. "I was educated at Cambridge. I have no interpreter here. I hope you find my English satisfactory. May I ask, sir, what brings you to call me tonight? This is a surprise, to say the least."

There was a pause. Then in firm, measured tones, Brandenberg said, "I'll come right to the point. We know about your submarine, the *Yunes*, number 903. We know where it is and why it is just a few miles off the coast of the United States. My message is very simple, Mr. President: if your sub does anything that can be interpreted as a hostile action against the United States, we will consider that a declaration of war by the nation of Iran. Do I make myself clear?"

Akbari was stunned. How could they know? How much did they know? How should he respond? He couldn't deny it if they already knew about it. "Mr. President, I assure you, Iran has no hostile intentions toward the United States. I know nothing of a submarine of which you speak. I will contact our navy people, and I guarantee, Mr. President, that if there is any truth in what you say to me, it will immediately be taken care of."

"Thank you, sir," Brandenberg said. "That is exactly what I wanted to hear. But I must tell you that as we speak, our military is on full alert. We'll do whatever is necessary to protect our nation. Any questions?"

Akbari stammered, "No, no. No questions. You have been abundantly clear. I must assure you again that we have no hostile intentions, but thank you for alerting me about this sub. If it is there, it is not with my authority or approval, sir."

"I hope not," President Brandenberg said. "Good night, sir."

"Good night, Mr. President," he said, as strongly as he could manage. He gently replaced the receiver, stood, and punched his intercom. "Farouk!" he yelled, raking a hand through his hair. "I want Admiral Radan and Minister Zamani in here—now! This is an extreme emergency!"

Akbari sank back in his chair. How did the U.S. know? The mission was out of control. He'd had bad feelings about it from the beginning, but now—. The door opened again to Farouk who said, "Minister Zamani is on the way. Commander Radan is happily here in Teheran. We're locating him now."

Akbari wanted another healthy swig of brandy, but he needed a clear head. He'd been increasingly confident about his presidency and the fate of the country, particularly since the West seemed to be responding to his friendly overtures. But now, tonight, the future of Iran hung by a thread. If they didn't stop this sub—if it launched on New York and Washington—Iran would soon be little more than a smoldering spot on the map.

Zamani appeared, casually dressed. "Mr. President, is there a problem? How may I serve you?"

Akbari said, "I don't want to explain this twice." He pressed his intercom, "Farouk? How soon for Radan?"

The aide reappeared. "We found him. He should be here in a few minutes." Already they could hear the sound of sirens approaching the Presidential Palace.

Within minutes, Admiral Radan, Commander of the Iranian Navy, entered the president's office. He, too, was casually dressed. "Mr. President?"

Akbari glared at him. "Sit!" He pointed to the chair in front of his desk. In staccato tones, he said, "I just received a call from the President of the United States! They know about your infernal submarine! He told me it was the *Yunes*, number 903! They know where it is, and what it's doing, and to quote him exactly, 'If your sub does anything that can be interpreted as a hostile action against the United States, we will consider that a declaration of war by the nation of Iran.'"

The two men were dumbstruck, jaws dropped, their eyes wide. Zamani looked at Radan, who said, "How?"

"I don't know how!" Akbari barked. "But they know everything! They probably know what I had for breakfast and the name of my dog! And since they know it is us, if this mission is completed, they will obliterate us from the face of the earth!" He glared at the admiral. "Stop this mission *now*. I never liked it in the first place, and my instincts were correct. This was trouble from the start." He shifted bloodshot eyes to Zamani, "And there will be a thorough investigation of the affair when this is over—if we survive."

He jabbed his finger back at Radan. "You! Get out of here and stop your submarine. Do you understand?"

Radan jumped to his feet. "Yes, Mr. President." He hesitated. "You should know, though, sir, as I explained when we last spoke, that it's extremely difficult to communicate with a submerged sub halfway around the world." Before

Akbari could explode, he hurriedly added, "But we'll do everything possible!"

"And how many days before they launch, Mr. Admiral?" Akbari's voice was silky calm.

"The day after tomorrow, sir," Radan said. He swallowed.

Akbari suppressed his rage. "I don't care how you do it—that sub must be stopped! If you can't reach them, then get over there and blow them up yourself!"

Radan said, "We'll send abort messages immediately, open transmission, uncoded, so they won't have to decode them—the Americans will know we're doing it. The *Yunes* should receive these messages when they surface to snorkel. They'll confirm the order with us, so we'll know they got it." Radan bowed lightly. "If there's nothing else, sir—I'll get on this." He turned on his heel without waiting for an answer and strode out of the office.

Radan was in utter turmoil. He had two problems. The first was how to tell the *Yunes* to abort mission and come home when they might not get the message. And would they confirm receipt or try to avoid detection?

Secondly, Captain Golzar was a wild card. Even if he got the message, would he trust it? Would he obey? Radan could only pray.

CHAPTER 54

As the sub and Phil's raft neared Cape Hatteras, Phil thought, what the heck; he tried his phone. When he heard a ring at the other end, a thrill ran through him. Contact! He'd called his son. *Please, answer your phone, Dave!*

When Dave got on, he said calmly, "Hi son, it's Dad."

"Dad?" Dave turned to Connie and gave her a thumbs up. Once again, he and Connie had taken side-by-side motel rooms. She bit her lip and nodded excitedly at him.

"How are ya, Dad? And where are you?"

"We're nearing Cape Hatteras; I'm doing good. I've got food and water; I'm almost comfortable. How are you doing?"

"I'm fine! Listen, I'm with a special friend of mine— Connie Morello. She's a reporter from the Miami Herald." He shot her a warm glance. "She's covering your story. She even got me an interview on TV in Miami! We're in Savannah. We figured the Coast Guard rescue would happen here. Connie interviewed the Guard this morning. That's when we found out you decided to stay in the raft! I can't say I'm glad, Dad."

"To tell the truth, neither am I. I was ready to get off this thing and get to shore. But they had no way to follow the submarine. And that's what this is about—getting this sub before she does damage."

"I figured you'd say that. I get it. You're gonna be a hero, Dad."

Phil snorted. "I just want to protect my country."

"Get his location," Connie said.

"Can you text me your position?" Dave asked.

"I'll try. The sub is following the Gulfstream, probably for extra speed. So it'll come close to the Cape. By the way, did you get my photos?"

"We sure did! They were great. Connie put them in her latest story about you."

Phil shook his head. He'd no idea that he was a newspaper feature. He was gripping the phone—the tie to his son. "It is so good to talk to you," he said, trying not to get teary. "I miss you."

"I miss you too."

Connie squeezed Dave's hand.

"You know," Phil said. "I've realized a few things while I've been out here floating around by myself." He paused. "I've been living vicariously through your life and your brother's. It's not healthy—not healthy for me, not healthy for you. I'm socializing when I get back. I'm gonna reach out to people." He added his biggest decision. "I may even start dating."

"Dad, that is so right on!" Dave shook his head, wondering at this enormous change in his father. "I think you're absolutely right about that. Mom would have wanted it."

Phil nodded, but had no words, though he was grateful for the support.

"By the way, Dad, I have us on speakerphone so Connie can hear. I hope you don't mind."

Phil smirked. "Not at all. Hi Connie. Hope to meet you soon."

"Hi, Mr. Shepherd!" Connie said with gusto. "I'm looking forward to meeting you. I know you're special to be Dave's dad. Good job on your son." She and Dave grinned at each other.

Phil had to smile. This Connie sounded serious about Dave.

"Dad? Have you seen anybody looking for you? The Navy is supposed to be taking over from the Coast Guard."

"Let's put it this way," Phil said. "If they are, they're being subtle about it. The Coast Guard flew back and forth numerous times, but way too far south. Today a fine-looking Navy plane flew past me a couple of times and then disappeared. I tried to flash them with my signal mirror, but no go. The plane had a long pipe or something hanging out the back. I have no idea what it was, but it was definitely U.S. Navy. Flying low and slow." He paused and added, "You know what? I bet they're looking for the sub, not for me! How about you tell them I'm still tied to it and I'm a lot easier to find?"

Dave said, "Good idea! But we're not sure how to communicate with the Navy, so we've been going through the Coast Guard. But I think we need to step it up."

He and Phil chatted for a few minutes longer, discussing food and water sources, the weather, and the state of the raft.

Before Phil let Dave go, he said, "Hey—keep praying. God has His hand upon this."

Dave said, "Are you kidding? I've been emailing and texting everybody I can think of. They're all praying for you."

Phil said, "They say God chooses the least likely of people. I would say a high school history teacher from Kokomo, Indiana, falls in that category!"

Dave and Connie chuckled. Figuring his father was ready for it, Dave said, "That lady friend of yours—uh, Louise? She's been really following this and asking about you. Says she's praying hard for you."

Phil's heart lifted. It was music to his ears. "That's great!"

"OK, Dad. Connie and I'll try to contact the Navy. I hope we see you soon! Stay safe. And send me your coordinates."

"Sure thing."

More softly, Dave added, "And call me again when you can. I love you, Dad."

"I love you too. Good night. And good night to you, Connie."

Before she could reply, Phil had clicked off.

He sat back in the raft, feeling both happy and sad. But suddenly it occurred to him that there were other calls he could make—one in particular. He scrolled through his contacts. Holding the phone to his ear, Phil felt a frisson of nerves and excitement. Was he really doing this?

As it rang on the other end, he felt more and more like a school kid with a crush. He checked the time. Maybe she wasn't home.

Finally, a soft voice answered, "Hello?"

His heart swelled—this was it. "Louise? Hi, it's Phil, Phil Shepherd."

CHAPTER 55

To call Franklin Grant, Secretary of Defense, Dirk Hunter had to go out of his normal chain of command. His boss, the Secretary of the Navy, was in the Philippines. "Mr. Secretary? CNO Dirk Hunter. Got a minute?" Silence was tacit permission to continue, so he said, "I just got off the phone with my people at Norfolk. They believe—and I'm in agreement—that even if the Iranians try to get their sub to abort and come home, it probably won't work."

"Uh-oh. Because...?"

"First, it's a heck of a long way to transmit anything without relay stations—which we don't believe they have—and second, nothing gets through while a sub's underwater. The earliest they'd get the message is tonight if they come up to snorkel. And third, their skipper might interpret it as a U.S. trick. The good news? We should find him before he gets any messages, and we won't be shy about letting him know. We'll be sonar pinging him ten ways from Sunday."

The Secretary fell silent but finally said, "What do your people suggest?"

"They want permission to engage. At least cripple them, if not send them all to their seventy-two virgins."

"No plan B?"

"Negative, sir."

Franklin hesitated, then said, "Dirk, I can't give the green light for this. This has to go to the top."

"I figured as much. Can you set it up? Our destroyer is already out and we're dropping sonobuoys from copters. Their hearing range isn't great against a Kilo. Plus, our sub is going to be ready in another hour or two. I want to give him the rules of engagement before he leaves port and goes under."

"Got it," Grant said. "I want to recommend going to DEFCON 2 for you and the Air Force. Gotta get the joint chiefs in on this."

"Should I come over?" Dick asked.

"No, go to the White House. There's gonna be a crowd; better get your Coast Guard lady to bring newcomers up to speed. I guess her handlers will have to come, too. Okay—I'm out."

Handlers—Dirk chuckled. He rounded up the Coast Guard and got to the White House where they were escorted to the cabinet room. Lieutenant Saxby was armed with copies of the photos and the Braxton transcripts. Twenty minutes later, the room was packed.

General Vernon Swartley, chairman of the Joint Chiefs of Staff, exuded a commanding presence in full uniform with row after row of service ribbons. As he shook hands with the lieutenant he said, "I've read your interview. Good work. You've stirred things up here, Lieutenant."

Alicia Saxby smiled and colored. "Thank you, General. Unfortunately, I don't think we're done being stirred up."

The general's response was interrupted by President Brandenburg's entrance. "Good evening, people." He looked around the room. "Something tells me this is not a victory celebration."

Secretary Grant replied, "Unfortunately, sir. I assume you contacted President Akbari and told him to get his submarine out of our front yard?"

The president smiled. "I sure did. If it weren't so darned serious, I'd say it was fun. So—it's not resolved? Who wants to tell me the hole in my idea?"

Dirk Hunter raised his hand and went on to explain the concerns they had with long-distance communications with the sub.

"Franklin, do you agree with this?" the president asked Grant.

"I do, sir. It's high risk to depend upon them getting—and believing—the message."

The president turned to General Swartley, "General, what's your take?"

"Mr. President, I have no reason to quibble with the navy's assessment here."

"Okay, gentlemen—and ladies—what should we do?"

Dirk cleared his throat. "Mr. President, we recommend allowing our forces to engage the sub—cripple it, or, if necessary, sink it."

The President held up a hand and the room fell silent. He stared down at a blank pad in front of him, his lips moving silently in prayer. He looked at Dirk. "I'm no submarine expert, but there's something I don't understand. When you say cripple this sub, would they still be able to surface for air?"

"Yes, sir, it would have to."

"And how would we cripple them? With what?"

"We're working on that, sir. We're examining an option using SEALs. They'd get on the deck while submerged and sabotage the missiles."

"The stuff movies are made of," the President murmured. How soon can we do it?"

"Wednesday, soonest." That was in two days.

"And if that fails, they only need ten minutes to fire those missiles. Am I right?"

"Correct, sir. We'd have to sink them before they do it."

"If we can," Secretary of Defense Grant added quietly.

"Can we talk to them?" The president asked. "While they're underwater? I remember underwater music at a ritzy pool I once swam in."

Dirk nodded thoughtfully. "There is a system for that. Hydrophones. It's not used much, but, yes, technically, we could talk to the sub. Their sonar guy would blast it out. In fact, the whole crew would probably hear it through the hull if the transmitting sub was close."

"Good!" The President responded. "Tell your sub to stay at dock until we can figure out who to put on board. Someone who'll talk the *Yunes* into going home."

CHAPTER 56

Phil spent the afternoon looking for a plane, a ship, anything. He was amazed—and discouraged—that they hadn't appeared. Were they deliberately ignoring him? At least his calls with Dave and Louise were wonderfully heartening. Louise was surprised to hear from him but genuinely grateful for the call. She'd been worried about him! It felt great having a woman worrying about him. She'd even assured him that he was in her prayers. He thanked her and hinted—his heart pounding—that he'd be happy if she'd have dinner with him when he got back. And she'd agreed!

He hoped he'd be back soon. The app showed they were right off Cape Hatteras, but he'd lost the cell signal. Happily, there was enough sun for his little Levin Solstar charger to put juice in it.

Suddenly a new hissing sound greeted his ears. Compressed air? When he heard it again, he turned to watch for the sub. Was it surfacing? It was too early for that.

When he heard it a third time, he saw two jets of steamy water squirt out of the ocean in a V pattern. A *whale*? He didn't know much about whales and had seen them only from long distances while sailing. He thought their spray would shoot straight up. He was half scared, half intrigued.

There! Further—another jet of water. Then, looking north, he saw many more of them—straight in their path. They were gaining on them. He'd get a close-up look! A glance at the western sky revealed the start of a beautiful sunset but an ache in his stomach reminded him it was time for dinner. *What do whales eat,* he wondered. Surely not history teachers.

The spouting was getting close. A terrible thought hit him. What if they got tangled in the net? They'd probably shred it instantly. *Lord, let them pass by the net without any problems!*

Trusting for the best, he grabbed his camera. What a photo op! *Come on, Baby, pose for papa.* Sure enough, practically underneath him, a behemoth rose to the surface. He steadied himself. When the whale's blowhole surfaced, he was so close he could see why it blew in a V. It was split down the middle. Probably a separate hole for each lung. And—*woosh!*—out she came! The spray rose at least 15 feet. He snapped photos madly and then jammed the phone below the shroud for protection. But he wasn't protected and found himself drenched. He was surprised by an awful stench. *Was that on purpose, whale?*

With the camera safely out of the way, Phil relaxed to enjoy the show. The creatures were majestic and peaceful. Their giant tails rose with regal height as the beautiful animals turned again for the deep. Fourteen of them, by his count.

As the sun approached the horizon, he heard a helicopter. *Finally! Yes! Spare me another night out here, please!* He watched its approach, turning on the little Maglite to guide them in. It was a commercial helicopter, not navy. There was a logo on the side—a TV station! He waved and smiled. Maybe he was on TV!

A blinding spotlight circled around him and suddenly Phil was self-conscious. What was he—the local sideshow? He could imagine the broadcast: "Tune in at 11:00 and see the wild man chasing a submarine up the coast."

A loudspeaker blared, "Mr. Shepherd, I'm Bret Kohler, Channel 12 Network News. Since we can't land, we'd like to lower a satellite phone to you for an interview. Is that all right?"

What the heck. He nodded and motioned them to drop it. A rear door slid open, a man lowered a plastic bag on a cord, and, swinging wildly, Phil made a grab for it. Good thing they had that blasted light. There—almost got it. *Sorry, guys, but I'm not falling in the drink to get your phone.* The next pass almost clunked him in the head, but he grabbed the bag and pulled out the phone.

Kohler called, "Turn it on! I'll call you!" Phil gave him a thumbs up.

He felt suddenly foolish when it rang, knowing the caller was a mere 50 feet above him. "Mr. Kohler?"

"Call me Bret, and I'll call you Phil if that's okay." He explained that the interview would be taped, edited, and aired nationally, not just locally. Phil was daunted—he hadn't chased the sub to become a celebrity. In fact, as soon as the navy showed up, he wanted out—big time.

Kohler was particularly interested in the enemy sailor who'd told him they had missiles and were prepared to launch them at the U.S. "Did he say when this is supposed to happen, Phil? Or what the targets will be?"

"Sorry, I don't think he knew. He didn't have—what do you call it—a need to know."

After discussing this, he came back to Phil's routine and asked how he would spend the night.

"The way I usually do," Phil said. "When the sub comes up to snorkel, I move the raft up close to get in the warm exhaust."

"Snorkel? Can you explain that? Many of our viewers won't be familiar with submarines." Phil gave a quick explanation about diesel-electrics and their nightly snorkeling.

"So, this Iranian snorkel will come up to the surface where we can see it?"

"Has to. That's how this started for me in the first place."

"How soon?"

Phil glanced at his backlit watch. "Not for an hour or more. They like it to be really dark."

The man paused to speak with somebody. When he came back, he said, "I'd love to get a shot of you and the snorkel, but we'd run out of fuel by then. In fact, we need to head back. It's been a pleasure, Phil. We'll be back tomorrow for an update."

"Good. Not much happening here. It's contemplative. It's convinced me I don't have a future as a cloistered monk."

Bret laughed, "Good that you have a sense of humor in the face of all this."

"I'm not worried. I'm in the Lord's hands. He won't let me down."

"I admire your faith, Phil."

"I recommend it, Bret." He paused, "What about the phone here?"

"Keep it. There's no way to get it back and we'll need it to talk to you anyway. Call a few friends if you like. It's got a full charge, good for three or four hours. Save enough for us, of course."

"I'd like to call the navy. Any chance you got their number?" If the news could find him, he wondered why the navy hadn't.

"Sorry, Phil." The chopper wheeled away to the west.

Phil watched it go with pangs of loneliness. The wind had dropped and was veering south, but a heavy cloud cover was coming with it. The last of the sunset glowed over the horizon, turning the undersides of the clouds pink, red, and yellow. He took a couple photos. They wouldn't come close to capturing the beauty, but he had to try. *So, I'm still out here, Lord. Thank you, for being here with me. Just you and me. But I'm ready to go home, Lord.* He thought of Louise. *I'm more than ready.*

CHAPTER 57

Louise placed the phone back in its cradle as if it were a sleeping baby, tears pooling in her eyes. She hated to lose the connection with Phil. She was lonely, but hadn't realized how much she'd come to care for her optimistic, easy-going choir friend until now. In fact, it seemed she'd cared for him for a long time. His call had crashed through her loneliness and denial like a runaway truck. Yet he was gentle, his voice soft and kind. It swept away any doubts about how she felt for him. She put her head in her hands, and then realized the best thing she could do for him was pray.

"Oh Lord, keep Phil safe, keep him well, keep him protected. Jesus, Jesus, Jesus, put your warring angels around this dear man and bring him back to me!"

She smiled as she entertained wild thoughts about flying out to meet him. The government would probably isolate him for endless questioning. But eventually, he'd be available. How she looked forward to that—she'd walk right into his arms—and stay there as long as he'd have her.

Commander Joe Burgin, Captain of the *Tuscaloosa*, knew his sub had been selected for this mission only because it was the sole boat at the Norfolk dock with a ready and powerful enough reactor. But he didn't know what the mission was. It seemed that Washington was making it up on the fly.

He told his Lieutenant Commander Ben Rothan to call a meeting and then waited at the wardroom table with coffee and an East Coast chart. His typically jocular expression was pinched. As the men arrived, the executive officer scurried them to their posts. Some asked if this was about "the guy in the raft they had seen on TV." The officer pleaded ignorance. Joe, too, had no idea what the men referred to.

Just then, an order came through the secure radio: "Captain's eyes only."

A minute later, Burgin returned to the meeting with new energy. "Ben, can you get Josh and Dutch in here? It's time to tell what we're looking at."

Ben nodded, "Yes, sir!" and called for the navigator and COB Dutch Stoller, Chief of Boat, to join them. They arrived smiling. An actual mission was an exciting rarity in the peacetime navy. Stoller's enthusiasm about the mission was evident. He'd seen the interview of Phil on Network News and was pretty sure what the *Tuscaloosa* would be doing.

Burgin relaxed. His deep blue eyes sparkled beneath sandy eyebrows and a square jaw. "Gentlemen, I suspect you know why I called this meeting. This guy in the raft being towed by a sub was on TV?"

Dutch and Josh raised their hands, nodding.

"Hmm, seems Ben and I need to watch the news more often. Okay, our mission is to find that sub—it's Iranian—and track it. There may be deck-mounted missiles aboard. Targets unknown—but we assume it's our coast. That part wasn't on TV, was it?" Dutch and Josh shook their heads.

"Good." He stopped and surveyed the room, then pointed at the chart in front of him. "We're gonna have our hands full. This water is shallow. I'm told we have a destroyer trying to find them, but we're it for a sub—a Virginia class boat would be better, but we're the only game in town with a hot reactor."

"I'm also told Jacksonville Air flew a hunting mission over the area, but there are too many wrecks; they can't tell a live sub from all the dead ones." He paused.

An officer asked, "That's all we do? Find it?"

Joe motioned for silence. "The CNO said we need to be ready to 'engage at very short notice.' His exact words."

The men nodded, and the captain continued, "There are complications. First, this sub is a Russian-built Kilo. Dutch, you may be familiar with Kilos, but some of us aren't."

Dutch winced, "Oh yeah, Skip. They're quiet, real quiet."

"That's right," Joe replied. "When they're on battery—especially in shallow water—" he swept his hand across the chart, "they're almost impossible to find."

The captain continued, "Intelligence says this one had a complete refit last year, so we can bet they have the latest anechoic tiles available to mute our sonar." He took a breath. "The second problem is this net. Did that TV broadcast give a good look at the net?"

The navigator answered with an Alabama drawl. "Naw, you could see a couple of lines with floats on each side of his raft. The net went below the surface to the sub."

"How far was it from the raft where it dipped down?" Joe asked.

"Maybe fifty yards—give or take," Josh said.

Dutch added, "It looked like a deep drift net. The guy said he'd been eating fish that got caught in it." He grinned.

"But how long is that net?" Burgin asked. "Some of these things go for miles."

Ben answered, "We don't know how long, so we can't afford to get close behind this guy."

"That's one way of putting it," Navigator Josh said. The steward stuck his head in the door. "Captain—CNO on the line."

When he left to take the call, the three remaining men sat silently around the table. Josh noted, "They're probably following the Gulfstream. We normally don't submerge that close in, XO."

The officer said, "We will tonight. We'll do what we need to do."

Burgin returned. "There's more," he said. "This Phil Shepherd that's tied to the sub is becoming a kind of folk hero. He's been communicating with his son—sends him pictures, which the son posts on Facebook and YouTube—he's getting TV interviews now. So we can't find the sub and send it to its happy hunting grounds without a national outcry. We haven't been authorized—yet—to get Mr. Shepherd. But we might be."

Burgin looked at his XO. "Ben, we'll have two civilian guests aboard: an Iranian national, and an FBI translator—a female."

His team's jaws dropped. Women were common in the navy these days, but not on old subs like *Tuscaloosa*.

"When we find this Kilo," the captain continued, "the president wants our guests to talk to it on the Gertrude, the Hydra-speaker—tell it to go home."

CHAPTER 58

When CNO Dirk Hunter's phone rang, the last thing he expected to hear was, "This is the White House operator. President Brandenberg calling for Dirk Hunter."

His pulse jumped. "This is Hunter."

In an irritated tone, the president barked, "Dirk—turn on the National News. There's a helicopter right over this Shepherd guy. If they can find him, why can't the navy?"

Dirk swallowed. "Um. I don't know, Mr. President, but I'll sure find out."

"Don't bother, Dirk, we're on it. Look, we're gonna set up a command post in the Situation Room. You and Franklin are to gather your team and get them here pronto. We're running out of time. Also, thought you should know, Marsha—the Secretary of State—and I are getting the Iranian Ambassador to talk to the sub."

"Got it, Mr. President."

With trepidation, Dirk turned on his TV. Sure enough, there was Phil Shepherd in his little raft talking to a reporter on a phone. It was dark outside but not on the screen, so he knew it wasn't live coverage.

Dirk mentally prepared a team. He'd get that Coast Guard lady and Shepherd's son. The Secret Service would have kittens about them not being cleared, but they'd have to suck it up on this one. Should he get someone from Norfolk? Nah, better leave the sub hunters to the search. But he'd open a video link to them.

President Akbari was awakened from a sound sleep to take a call from the United States' president.

In alarm, Akbari snapped on his bedside lamp, grabbed a robe and scooted to his office, wide awake now. "Mr. President, this is President Akbari. What can I do for you? We are sending urgent messages to our submarine to abort mission and come home."

"That's what I'm calling about," President Brandenburg replied. "My people are highly concerned that they won't get your message. They tell me that radio communications all the way from Teheran to our East Coast are not reliable; and even if your captain gets the message, he may not believe it's from you. We want more than one approach."

"I understand," Akbari said, though he was uncertain what else could be done. "What do you propose?"

"Mr. President, I cannot overstate that we are extremely concerned about this situation. We do not want war. We want your ambassador on one of our subs to talk directly to the *Yunes* on an underwater speaker."

Akbari was impressed. This was unprecedented, though under the circumstances, a good idea. "Mr. President, when would you like to do this?" Akbari knew they had less than forty-eight hours before the *Yunes* was to launch their missiles.

"At once. Our sub is waiting for your ambassador as we speak. Please call him immediately to be ready within thirty minutes. We'll pick him up at home and fly him to the base." Brandenberg paused. Hearing no response, he asked, "Is there a problem, Mr. President?"

"No, I agree, it is urgent. Okay."

Brandenberg blanched. Akbari had as much as tacitly admitted that the missile threat was real. "Thank you, Mr. President. I'm sure your people appreciate it, as do the American people—although they probably will never know."

45 minutes later

A U.S. Navy car whisked the very rattled U.N. Ambassador Ahmad Shakiba to the 34th Street heliport on the East River and into a waiting NYPD helicopter. Shakiba, the "Permanent Representative of the Islamic Republic of Iran to the United Nations," had the additional rank and status of Ambassador Extraordinary and Plenipotentiary. He'd been Iran's man at the U.N. since the fall of the Shah and was enjoying the pleasures of New York and the U.S. immensely ever since.

At sixty years old, the tall, distinguished, white-haired gentleman was still piecing together what his president had told him. After this, he'd be ready to retire—assuming he still had a home nation to retire to.

Fifteen minutes later they escorted him out of the helicopter onto a runway at the Teterboro, New Jersey airport, and rushed him into a Navy C-20 Gulfstream IV jet. As the plane leaped into the sky, he dearly wished he could contact someone in Iran for more details on this mission; but that wasn't possible.

Ahmad accepted an American coffee from a nice young officer during the short flight to Virginia. At least they were treating him with respect—so far. He could not fathom what it was like on a nuclear submarine, but he was about to find out. As he stepped down the stairs of the jet, he was met by a handsome naval officer.

"Ambassador Shakiba, I'm Commander Joseph Burgin—Joe for short. I'm captain of the submarine *Tuscaloosa*."

Burgin escorted him to a waiting car that would take them to the dock, filling him in on procedures and what to expect when they boarded the sub.

"Thank you, Commander, I appreciate that. Two hours ago, I was sleeping peacefully in my New York apartment, so I am still largely in the dark here—no pun intended."

Joe laughed. Good thing this guy had a sense of humor. Before this was over, they were all going to need one.

CHAPTER 59

Dave awoke groggily to pounding on the door of his motel room.

"Mr. Shepherd? Mr. Shepherd, it's the Coast Guard."

When the words registered, he jumped from bed and hurried to fling open the door, eager to hear news of his dad.

A young ensign peered in at him beneath the motel's shadowy night lighting. "Mr. David Shepherd?"

"Yes.,

"Mr. Shepherd, I'm Ensign Ted Lawson, Savannah Coast Guard Air Station. I've been sent to escort you to a plane to Washington, D.C. per the request of Admiral Hunter, Chief of Naval Operations."

Dave shook his head to clear away cobwebs. "Is this about my dad?" he asked.

"I don't really know. My orders are to take you to the plane. It's waiting at the air station."

The door to the next room opened a crack, and Connie peeked out. Dave said, "Um. If I go, I need to bring Connie, Connie Morello." He motioned with his head toward her. To the ensign's questioning look, he added. "We're a team."

The crack of Connie's door widened and Dave caught a grin on her face. "They want us in Washington. Some Admiral. I assume you want to come too—right?"

Connie's smile broadened. "Absolutely. I'll get dressed and pack up," she said. The door closed.

The ensign seemed disturbed. "I don't know about this. I need to call my commander. Excuse me."

Call done, they made driving arrangements. Connie didn't want to leave her car in the lot, so Dave said he'd drive with her. They'd follow the ensign in his Coast Guard Jeep.

As they drove, Connie said, "I appreciate you bringing me along, but you know, you don't have to insist that I come. They really want you, not me."

Dave studied his pretty companion. He loved having her along. "We've come this far together. I see no reason to stop." He paused and added softly, "I like having you with me."

Connie stifled a happy grin. "I like being with you." She took a breath and said shyly, "You know you're toying with my heart, don't you?"

"Not toying. I don't do that," Dave said seriously, leveling earnest eyes upon her. "But if you're saying your heart's on the line here, don't worry, you're not alone. Mine's right there with yours."

She gave his hand a quick squeeze and then returned hers to the steering wheel. Connie drove with both hands planted on it—Dave liked that. Soon they were at the base.

"I wonder what kinda plane they'll put us on. I hope not a helicopter. You can't hear yourself think on those."

"Look!" Connie cried as her headlight swept past a Gulfstream V. "First class."

Minutes later, as the plane left the ground and steeply angled skyward, a crewman said, "Welcome aboard. You must be special people. We don't get requests like this often—like, ever. We'll be flying into Andrews Air Base, and then you'll go on to the White House."

"The White House?" Dave and Connie said simultaneously. They looked at each other and grinned.

"Are you sure?" Dave asked.

"Admiral Hunter wants you there. Must be something top priority at this hour. Want me to try and call him for you?"

Dave looked at Connie, who smiled and said, "Why not? Forewarned is forearmed, somebody once said."

The crewman disappeared into the front of the plane and returned in a few minutes. "His deputy says Admiral Hunter's preparing a meeting in the White House Situation Room— that's where you're going." He paused. "Might I suggest that you prepare for whatever's ahead by catching more sleep? You can tilt your seats back, and I'll get you some blankets and pillows, and dim the lights. We've got about fifty more minutes in the air."

"Works for me," Dave said as he pushed his seat back. Connie did the same.

But they were still awake when the plane touched down at Andrews. Dave stretched and yawned. "Showtime. Sure hope this gets Dad back soon—and safe."

"I'm sure it will," Connie said, placing a reassuring hand on Dave's arm.

They boarded a government car which soon stopped at the White House gate. A uniformed guard came to the passenger window with a clipboard. "May I see some I.D. please?"

After Dave and Connie handed him their driver's licenses, the guard said, "I have Mr. Shepherd on my list, but no one else. I'm afraid Ms. Morello cannot go through."

Dave winked at Connie and said, "Then you can call Admiral Hunter and tell him I won't be coming, either."

CHAPTER 60

Phil awoke up from a nap, glanced at his watch, and waited for the snorkel to come up. Should be any time now. The night was dark, not a glimmer in the sky—not even a glow on the horizon from a passing town. He couldn't remember a darker night out there. But wait—he saw a faint stern light on a small freighter ahead of them. Funny how reassuring that was. But something seemed strange about the net. He shone his Maglite and saw it splayed out on the surface of the water, not curving down to the snorkel like it usually did. And where was that snorkel? The periscope was up—uh oh—he covered the lens and twisted off the light.

Something unusual was happening—but what? He watched, slowly reeling himself closer to the sub. He'd be ready for the snorkel when it came up, and now it was easier to see the periscope. But something else was sticking out of the water—a second periscope? It was different than the first one. He wondered if it was a radio or radar antenna.

The sub changed course, veering toward the path of the freighter. And they were picking up speed—almost as though trying to catch it. Phil wondered if he could reach someone on the freighter and get help somehow—a long shot. If they had a watch on duty, he'd be looking ahead, not behind.

They got close enough that he could almost read the name of the ship. Were they gonna ram him? No, that's why the periscope was up.

The snorkel finally came up, the valve popped open, and the usual roar of the diesels hit the air. Could they hear it on the freighter? Probably not.

Suddenly he understood what was happening. They were shadowing the freighter to mask the sound of the engine while they snorkeled. Phil had seen some helicopters earlier that day flying back and forth to the south. They'd dropped things in the water. He realized now they were probably sonar gizmos looking for the sub. Maybe the sub knew. He was glad the navy was looking for it—though it still seemed easier if they had simply looked for him in the raft.

Okay, Phil, enough sightseeing. Time to get some shut-eye. He pulled up behind the snorkel, set his usual quick-release knot to the net, and slid under the shroud.

The next thing Phil knew, something was vibrating next to his hip—the sat phone! He was getting a call!

"Phil? I can't believe it," a woman's soft voice said.

"Louise? Is that you?" Gladness filled his heart. "What a wonderful surprise," he said, coming fully awake.

"I hope I'm not calling too late. It's just that you were so much on my mind and heart tonight that I had to try. I thought you'd probably turn off your phone when you wanted to sleep."

"I do—except I forgot. I'm glad I forgot." He smiled. "Hey, how'd you get this number?"

"Pastor Hendricks was able to get the number from those television people. You know how persuasive he is. So—how's life on the ocean?" she asked. "I saw you on television."

Phil was amazed. "I was on TV in Kokomo? I had no idea. Well, you saw my entire world—a little raft, a net, and water—lots and lots of water."

"You're very brave," Louise said.

"Thanks, but I think stubborn might be the better word," Phil joked. "Anyway, it's dark here tonight, but I've been spoiled with beautiful sunsets and blankets of stars and moonlight."

"It must be beautiful," murmured Louise.

Phil caught a wistful sound in her voice. Almost holding his breath, he said, "When I get back, I'd love to take you out some time so you can see for yourself."

"I would love that!"

Phil sighed with relief. "Other than that, there's been some excitement; the sub's shadowing a freighter—I think to mask the sound of its engine to avoid detection."

"Oh, dear," Louise said worriedly. "That sounds dangerous. Do you really have to do this? Can't you let go somehow and let them find you?"

Phil was touched. Softly he said, "I'll be okay. I'm sure the navy'll find the sub tomorrow and take over."

"But they're taking so long!" she cried.

In his heart, he agreed. But he said, "God's done so many things since Friday night that I know He's got my back. I feel like David going up against Goliath—except I don't have to kill him—that's the navy's job."

"I guess so," she said. She cleared her throat. "You've been a good friend. You're important to me."

"I appreciate that," Phil replied. He plunged ahead. "You've been a good friend, too. I hope—" he hesitated, choosing his words. "I hope we get to become better friends."

"I do, too," she said, softly.

His heart swelled. For the next few minutes, they talked about her life, church, her grown children, and then circled back to him out on the ocean.

"Remember our church is praying for you," Louise said. "I think the whole country is! Be safe, dear man, please be safe." She paused. "And get a good night's sleep. Sweet dreams."

Phil thanked her, adding that he could feel the prayers going out for him. He shut the phone marveling at how sweet that call had been. Here he was out in the middle of the ocean, making headway in a relationship that hadn't advanced for years. He and Louise had only been comfortable, distant friends, even standing side-by-side in the choir. He pictured the beautiful music teacher in his mind and suddenly longed to get back to his life—real life, off the ocean and away from this darn sub.

627 miles away, in Kokomo, Indiana, that beautiful music teacher fell to her knees in prayer, blinking back tears. "Keep him safe, Lord! Bring him back for me!"

CHAPTER 61

The Yunes

Chief Sonar Technician Emad Jabrani came alert as the sound of a faint sonar pinging reached his ears from the south. Their diesel engines were running while snorkeling, which was like a cat burglar blowing a bugle, but there was no way to hide that sound. All subs had libraries of sonar recordings to electronically match every conceivable engine sound, so someone had probably identified the sound of the Kilo within seconds of hearing it.

He alerted Captain Golzar, who ordered silent running. All non-essential motors and equipment were turned off. The crew was confined to their bunks, and the galley told to prepare only cold food. Life would be more uncomfortable than usual for a sub, but caution was necessary. The sound of a single wrench dropping on the deck or a galley pot hitting the stove, could be the difference between escape and doom—between mission success and failure.

Fortunately, Jabrani had detected a slow-moving ship, probably a small freighter, close to their path. Using Jabrani's ears as a guide, Golzar slowly guided the sub up behind the freighter. He rose to snorkel depth and raised the periscope. After a quick sweep around the horizon, he focused on the freighter's stern. It was the MV Joosten, out of Rotterdam. As long as it wasn't going to turn off to Chesapeake Bay and go to Baltimore, they were fine.

Golzar ordered them to slowly edge the *Yunes* closer and closer to the unsuspecting freighter. The batteries would drain faster than he liked in order to match the freighter's speed, but it couldn't be helped. They'd have to recharge a bit longer.

They would snorkel and shadow the Dutch guide all night. He ordered the communications mast to be raised to check for possible messages.

In minutes Radioman Nikahd approached. "Captain?" he said quietly, "I just got this—from Teheran. It was a bit garbled, but I think I got it properly."

Golzar read it quickly. "Have you told anyone else what this says?"

"No, sir."

"Are you sure of that?"

Nikahd blanched under the captain's sharp scrutiny. "Yes, sir. Completely. It just came in. It's repeating and repeating."

"Was it in our usual code?"

"Only our authentication, sir, then clear transmission. Anyone could understand it."

The captain's lips curled. "And I know why. It's an American trick, nothing more. That's why they didn't encode it. They don't know all of our codes. And you didn't send a response or confirmation?"

"No, sir. Your orders were for strict radio silence."

Golzar patted him on the shoulder. "Well done, Nikahd. Return to your station and speak to no one about this. I'm going to pull the coms mast down, but we may want it back up later." Part of silent running included suspension of the intercom. He saw his executive officer Purali, and motioned him to follow to his cabin, where Golzar handed him the paper. "This just came, open transmission—not encoded."

"Captain!" Purali exclaimed, "We must leave now—head out to sea. I will give the order."

As he turned to open the cabin door, Golzar clamped a vice-like grip on his arm, turning him back to face him. Eye to eye, he said icily, "No, Massoud, it's a fake. The Americans are desperate. They can't find us. They don't know why we are here, and they are trying this trick. They sent it in open transmission because they don't know our code. We will do nothing. We will ignore it."

"Then we should send a coded message asking for clarification, Captain."

"No!" Golzar hissed. "We have not come all this way to be frightened off by our enemy. We will maintain absolute radio silence, Massoud." He studied his subordinate's face. "We've become casual on this long trip, but I am captain, and this is my decision. The radioman is scared out of his wits but will be silent about it. Can you do the same?"

The officer responded meekly, "Yes, sir."

"Good. Now, go look at our new freighter friend and be sure we're still in proper position." He opened the door for the officer to leave.

After closing it again, he stepped to the small safe mounted over the foot of his bunk and entered the combination. He swung it open and removed a PC-9 Zoaf semi-automatic pistol—an Iranian knock-off of a Sig Sauer. He cycled it once to advance a shell into the firing chamber and slipped it under his pillow for quick access.

CHAPTER 62

Dirk Hunter led Dave and Connie into an empty Situation Room. "This is where it all happens, folks. This is where they watched Osama Bin Laden go down and Saddam Hussein's capture." He looked at Connie. "Ms. Morelli, have you made your peace with the White House Office of Information? No photos, no recordings, clear all copy first?"

"Yes," Connie smiled up at him. "I got the drill."

"Hey, would you two like a little rundown of the facilities?"

"That would be great!" Dave said.

"The first thing to know is that this building is operated by the United States Navy," he said with a proud smile. Motioning at a door he said, "Through that are the watch commander and technicians who set up the video conferencing capabilities, among other things. You see these various screens around the room? They can be connected to any of thousands of screens that we and our allies have stationed around the world. Today we'll be connecting to ComSubLant in Norfolk."

He saw their confused looks. "Sorry, that's Submarine Command Atlantic. They're in communication with the *Tuscaloosa* and the Iranian ambassador." He saw more confused looks. "I guess you didn't know about that. The president asked if we could speak to the Iranian sub—talk to them underwater. Last night we put their ambassador aboard the *Tuscaloosa*—that's an atomic sub—and they're out in the Atlantic looking for the *Yunes* right now. Connie, you know this is classified information, right?"

Connie nodded. "I know—but it would make an incredible story!"

"Maybe later," Dirk replied. "Okay, through that door on the other side is the president's breakout room. He takes people in there for private conversations—or whatever else he wants to do. On the way in, did you notice the glass booths along the wall?"

They nodded. "I was wondering what those were," Dave said.

"Telephone booths. Totally secure; they've got an open public line, and a secure line."

"So," Dave said with a grin, "I could call out for pizza?"

"You could, but I recommend you take orders first," Dirk quipped. He rubbed his hands together. "If you go back out the way we came in and turn right, you'll find the restrooms, and just beyond them is the dining room. Food's quite good. As you can imagine, some people spend very long periods of time here."

"Admiral," Connie asked, "Do you know how long we'll be here?"

He shook his head. "I imagine until the issue is resolved."

The door opened to admit a steady stream of people. Dirk knew almost all of them and made introductions to Dave and Connie. Everyone seemed to know where to sit. Connie marveled that DHS, State and Attorney Generals, FBI, Joint Chiefs, NSA, and DoD were all represented.

When everyone was settled, they waited expectantly until, minutes later, President Brandenburg came in. He was followed by the vice president and press secretary. The president looked over the room. "A very early good morning to you all. Let's get down to business. Dirk, what's our status?"

"Mr. President, the bottom line is we are still looking for the *Yunes*. *The Tuscaloosa* left Norfolk with Ambassador Shakiba about four hours ago and should be in the search area. I regret to say that because it has been so long since this country's coast has been under submarine threat, we're not overflowing with sonobuoys. So we're using them judiciously."

Dave whispered in Connie's ear, "I'll be back in a couple of minutes," and quietly ushered himself out of the room. Dirk and some others looked up in surprise but said nothing.

Franklin Grant said "Mr. President, we're on DEF CON two for the East Coast air force and navy. I'm wondering if we should consider evacuation procedures for potential target areas."

"And those would be?" the President asked.

Franklin and Dirk looked at each other. Dirk said, "We believe there are three possibilities, sir. Norfolk Navy Base, Washington, D.C., and New York City." A collective gasp was heard. Dirk hurried to explain, "The *Yunes* is likely to fire both her missiles from the same location, probably simultaneously or as close to that as they can get. We don't think they're capable of carrying long-range missiles, which is why those targets are most likely." He continued, "The missiles have a range of 200 or 300 miles, so those three locations can be reached rather easily from a number of spots off the coast of New Jersey."

DHS Secretary Martha Saslow cried, "Evacuate New York City? You've got to be kidding. What are we giving them—twenty-four-hour notice? Or less? That wouldn't be an evacuation—that would be mass panic. Admiral, there's only one solution. You have to stop that submarine."

They were interrupted by Dave quietly returning. He strode purposefully down the length of the room and slipped a piece of paper to CNO Hunter. "That's the position of the Iranian submarine, sir," Dave said quietly in his ear.

The president said irritably, "Speak up, please!"

Dave rose and faced him. "I'm sorry, sir. I just gave Admiral Hunter the coordinates of the position of the Iranian submarine."

The room filled with surprised murmurs.

"Quiet!" the President said. "How did you get the position?"

Dave smiled at him and said, "I just called my dad on his sat phone. He got the position from the GPS app on his cell phone."

CHAPTER 63

Normally Ambassador Shakiba avoided what he called, 'testosterone-laden military types,' much preferring the gentility of the diplomatic corps. He had misgivings about boarding a sub, but no choice. He hoped it would be a short run. And, no sense denying it, he was curious to see the inside of a U.S. nuclear submarine.

Captain Burgin led him across a gangplank to the *Tuscaloosa*. The deck, he noticed, was covered with squares of a spongelike material. In fact, as they went on, he saw the whole boat was covered with them. The captain motioned at a doorway. "Through here, please." He pointed at a tall, wide, metal protrusion. This is the sail. You may have heard it referred to as a conning tower in old war movies." They moved on to a ladder. The ambassador couldn't remember the last time he'd descended one, but down he went. He had no choice.

As he made his way, above him the crew cast off the mooring lines. XO Ben Rothan on top of the sail guided the boat smartly out of its berth.

The ambassador found himself in a brightly lit corridor in pastel colors. He almost expected elevator music but checked himself with a smile. The air was fresher, happily, than the muggy atmosphere outside. The captain ushered him down a set of stairs, to his relief—he disliked ladders—and then through another doorway.

Burgin explained, "You'll have my cabin during the cruise. You can go to the officer's wardroom and the galley if you want coffee or something. Ensign Gerber here will help you with anything else you need—food, clothing, entertainment. I notice you brought no baggage." He paused. "He'll also keep you safe from wandering into areas that are off-limits."

A baby-faced young man in a fresh uniform smiled and said, "I hope you enjoy your stay with us, Ambassador. Let me know whatever you need."

"Thank you," he said, nodding, "And thank you, Captain. I appreciate the sacrifice of giving me your quarters. I hope it does not inconvenience you too much."

Burgin nodded. "Not at all, Ambassador. Now if you would please get settled, I need to attend to affairs of the boat." He was doing his best to maintain a confident demeanor with the crew as well as the ambassador. But he was uncharacteristically nervous due to the vague nature of the mission, and at having an ambassador—an Iranian—on board.

Rothan found him. "I've got the interpreter bunked down in officer country, Joe, with an ensign to keep her out of trouble and get what she needs. Looks like she brought her own stuff, though," he added.

"Good," Burgin said. "The ambassador only has the clothing on his back—a business suit. I don't think he has any idea what may be in store."

The submarine hummed as they picked up speed and exited Hampton Roads for the open Atlantic. It began to roll when it hit the first swell. Burgin said, "Okay, let's get this beast underwater and get out of here as soon as we can. I don't need our guests getting seasick."

Twenty-five minutes later, the Farsi interpreter Evelyn Zarin and the Ambassador were ushered into the wardroom, both looking green. Fortunately, the *Tuscaloosa* had submerged, and the boat was now running smoothly and quietly.

After they were introduced, the ambassador gave Evelyn a perfunctory handshake, but asked, "Is an interpreter necessary, Captain?"

Burgin nodded. "I'm afraid so, Mr. Ambassador. These are my orders. Might I suggest you two get some sleep? We don't know when we'll find the *Yunes*." The captain went into the control room and told the executive officer, "Send the usual confirmation to ComSubLant and see if there are any last-minute instructions."

"Aye, aye, Joe," Rothan said with a grin.

The captain sat on his stool watching while his crew went to work, performing their tasks seamlessly. He had strong confidence and pride in this group. An officer came in excitedly with a piece of paper. "Skipper, we've got the *Yunes's* exact coordinates as of thirty-two minutes ago." He showed him the decoded message, received before they'd left the dock.

"Great; let's plot where he should be now. How did we get this?"

The officer nodded wryly. "You won't believe it. Shepherd's son called him on the sat phone that the news station left him!"

"Amazing. Okay, plot a course for the *Yunes*. Assume he's snorkeling and allow for the Gulfstream; and assume he's still heading a little east of north."

Ensign Gerber stepped into the room. "Captain, the Ambassador wants to speak with you. Says it's urgent."

"Thank you, Ensign." Burgin followed him to the officers' wardroom, where he saw the Ambassador had removed his jacket and tie. "What can I do for you Ambassador?"

"Captain, I'm afraid that when we find the *Yunes*, even if I'm able to speak to them using your system, they may well think it's an American hoax. I don't know Captain Golzar, and he's probably never heard of me."

Burgin took a seat and pushed himself back before settling a thoughtful look upon the ambassador. "You might have a point there," he said. "We've been focused on getting you on board and I hadn't considered that possibility. But I'm sure we didn't get orders to take you if you couldn't handle it." *Might as well make it Iran's problem, not theirs.* He shrugged. "What's your plan, Ambassador?"

A wave of uncertainty crossed the ambassador's face. "I need more information, sir. About the *Yunes*. I need something to prove I'm truly an Iranian official. I'd like to tell Captain Golzar some personal information that could only come from Iran, not from your espionage—like the name of his wife or children or primary school or—I don't know what."

Joe pursed his lips. "Ambassador, we're underwater. We can't even talk to our own headquarters. What would you have me do? Even if I surface, I have no idea how to send a message to Iran. I don't know the frequencies. I don't know your passwords. Do you know any of these?"

Shakiba bit his lip and slowly shook his head. "Frankly, I was hoping your people might have that information. In my office, my staff handles all that."

They sat in silence, both thinking. Burgin got a cup of coffee. "Okay, Ambassador, I can share with you that we've been given the coordinates of the *Yunes* as of about thirty-five minutes ago. This means we'll be able to close in on him. I will bring the boat up to..." Joe stopped—the ambassador didn't deal with the technical aspects of Iran's communications, so he didn't need details of theirs either. "I'll send your thoughts to headquarters, and we'll see what they say. Fair enough?"

Shakiba smiled, stood, and shook Burgin's hand. "Thank you, Captain. I'm relieved, very relieved."

Burgin sprang to his feet. "Yes sir, I'll let you know when we need you." He strode from the room.

The White House Situation Room was filled with bored people tired of waiting for news when the command post officer entered. Brows rose and the room fell silent. "Admiral Hunter, call for you from the *Tuscaloosa*."

Dirk snatched up the phone. "Burgin, this you, Joe? What's going on? Found him yet?" He listened. "Sounds right. Hang on a sec. Let me bounce this off somebody else." He covered the mouthpiece and surveyed the room. "The Iranian ambassador wants to call Iran and get some personal information about the sub captain; says it's the only way to convince him it's not an American trick. He expects our intelligence has the right codes and passwords to get this going." Dirk looked at CIA Director Cosby and NSA Director Delong. Both men looked skeptical, but Cosby grinned. "As a matter of fact, Dirk, we do. But I'm not revealing that to an Iranian. We have someone deep in, ah, Teheran—very deep."

He glanced at Delong, who gave a subtle nod in agreement. "We can't jeopardize our source."

President Brandenberg was watching intently. Director Cosby scribbled something on a pad, tore the page off and folded it, then passed it to the president. Brandenberg read it and then refolded it, putting it in his pocket. "I agree. I'll call President Akbari instead."

The note said, "Akbari's valet."

CHAPTER 64

Phil opened bleary eyes and wiped the sleep out as he sat up to look around. Dreary morning—even eerie. Pea soup fog so thick he couldn't see more than 20 feet. He heard a plane in the sky and his spirits rose—but no way would they find him in this haze! *No pity party, Phil,* he told himself.

He couldn't see the freighter but knew it was ahead in the gloom, for he heard its foghorn. He jerked the quick release knot free of the net and let himself drift farther back than usual—much farther—before tying off. Why? He didn't know; somehow it felt right today.

He'd had a decent sleep as the freighter and the fog gave him an extra hour of warm snooze time. He ran a hand through his hair and was surprised at how clean it felt. The gummy residue of saltwater had been washed out by the rain. He ran a hand over the shroud and found it was also cleaned up. *Thank you, Jesus.*

After another tasty but boring fish breakfast, he checked the position app on his phone. They'd passed Norfolk during the night and were now off the Delaware coast. What came after that—New Jersey? Staying beneath the shroud for warmth, he realized just how handy the raft had been. It had really done its job! He'd never expected to need it to survive when he'd bought it years ago, but now he'd love to meet the people that designed it—tell them they did a great job.

He noticed the charge on his phone was down 50 percent. He'd have to conserve it—especially since there was no sun to recharge it. He zipped it back in its baggie. Without that phone—if he couldn't check where he was—he'd be an anxious mess. He'd have no idea where the submarine was taking him. *Thank you again, Jesus.*

He thought of the satellite phone and fumbled it out of the shroud. Even though he'd had it on standby, the battery was even lower. Should he turn it off? He wouldn't—it was the only way Dave or Louise or even the TV folks could contact him. Right then as he held it, it lit up.

Bret's voice came on—the TV guy, just as Phil thought he heard the helicopter, off to the east. "I can hear you," he said. "You're still far. I would say…" He listened again. "You're west and a little north of me."

Soon the chopper grew loud. "You're close," Phil said, "but you're gonna have to come in real low….no more than 50 feet if you want to see me."

Bret's muffled voice told him he was speaking to the pilot—probably about the low altitude. Then he was back. "Phil—thanks for guiding us in. This is gonna be different than last time. We want to shoot live and broadcast from the chopper. It's gonna take us a couple of minutes to set up with network to break into the newscast. The whole nation is watching, you know."

Phil shook his head. Louise had said as much but he was still floored by it. "I'm not cut out to be a celebrity," he whined. "Look at me—I haven't shaved in three days, never mind a shower."

"That's perfect for a hero stuck out on a raft!" Bret exclaimed.

Phil shook his head. "Okay, let's do it."

Bret said, "Good. But there's one stipulation. We can't have any mention of missiles. Homeland Security made that abundantly clear. The nation knows about you following the sub, but missiles are hush-hush. If it gets out somehow, we'll have mass panic all along the East Coast. So, no mention of them, okay?"

"Sure, Bret. No problem. Everything else is fair game, right?"

"Right. And we have a little surprise for you. I think you'll like it. Okay, help us get down so we can see you. We've got our spotlight on; you see it?"

He searched the skies, could hear them close—there they were! He wondered if it would be difficult to hear them over the roar of the copter.

"I see you. Come down another 50 feet, which will put you a little beyond me. Swing around and come northeast very slowly. Play your light back and forth, if you can do that."

A few moments later, the helicopter came into view. Phil waved.

"Phil, hold that wave until we're on-air if you can. Thanks!" The helicopter took the same position it had last time—sideways, to give the camera a good view. It occurred to Phil that the submarine might hear the copter and was glad now that he'd let the net out so far. He looked sharply to see if the periscope was up. It wasn't—he didn't think so, anyway. Darn, but that fog made it hard to be sure.

"Okay, Phil, you ready?"

Phil made a thumbs up.

"Good morning, America! This is Bret Kohler from National Network News coming to you live off the East Coast. We're looking at Phil Shepherd on his third day in a rubber raft, being towed along by a foreign submarine. Good morning, Phil; how are you?"

Phil waved, smiling, then said into the sat phone, "Good morning, Bret. I'm doing very well, thank you." He motioned at the half-cleaned fish on his lap. "Would you like to join me for breakfast? It's snapper today—very tasty, and very, very fresh."

Bret laughed. "Thank you, Phil. That would be wonderful—another time. Can you explain to us what you're doing? How you manage to feed yourself?"

Phil explained his method, how the fish got caught in the net and all he had to do was pull it up when he was hungry and find fresh fish. "I've learned to filet without cutting myself or nicking the raft."

Bret kept him chatting another minute and Phil told him about the leak in the raft and how he'd fixed it. "Hey, can I say hello to a few people?"

"Sure, Phil."

"Hello to my son Dave! He called me last night asking for my position. And hello to my son, Jerry, although he won't get this for some time since he's backpacking in Alaska. And to all my friends at school, my students, friends at church— and especially my good friend Louise back in Kokomo— hello, folks. Thank you very much for praying for me. I really feel it. You have no idea what an incredible difference that makes. I'd also like to thank all the people who are working on tracking the sub and are gonna take me off of it."

After Bret closed the segment, he thanked Phil and added, "Now we have a little surprise. We'll move the helicopter right overhead and lower it down." A couple of minutes later, a heavy plastic bag slowly descended on a rope.

Phil grabbed it. The rope went slack and fell into the ocean. He put the phone down to open it up and was thrilled to find a box of donuts and a thermos of coffee. He got back on. "This is an answer to prayer! Thank you so much! I was talking to God about how, as much as I love all the fresh fish, a cup of coffee would be really great." He waved, grinning. The sat phone light flashed red, so he added, "The charge is about out! Are you gonna want to talk to me again?"

"We sure are; how about five o'clock this evening? We'll bring a new phone." Bret nodded and the chopper lifted off and headed back to land.

Carefully—this was like contraband, like gold—he opened the thermos and poured out half a cup of the steaming black liquid. Savoring the taste, he wondered how they'd known he liked it black. Maybe they'd asked Dave.

As he munched on a donut—the best donut he'd ever had in his life—he thought about the day ahead. He'd need to pace himself, save some donuts for later. He allowed himself a second—jelly-filled—and slid the package under the shroud down near his feet where it was always dry. What a wonderful new problem—keeping food dry!

"Thank you, thank you, thank you, Lord! You have really provided, as you say you will. I feel isolated without the satellite phone, but I know I'm not alone. You are with me. I have no idea what else is in store today, but I trust You to protect me."

CHAPTER 65

Captain Golzar summoned his officers, crew chiefs, and missile specialists to a meeting in the wardroom. They squeezed in and sat watching him with anticipation. He looked around, searching each man's face, filled with a sense of importance for what he was about to share. "Tomorrow morning we launch the missiles, gentlemen. The weather forecast could not be better: low overcast clouds with negligible winds."

He took a breath. "We've made incredible progress coming this far. I am pleased and proud of each of you and all the crew. But I want to review exactly what will happen. When we surface, as you know, we'll be at our most vulnerable, and will need to act quickly and efficiently."

The men nodded.

"You may have noticed that we had an extra-long snorkel last night; we were able to shadow a freighter during heavy fog. I do not expect to snorkel tonight. We will not start our engines until after we surface to launch." Again, the men nodded.

"Navigator Behzadi, can you show the men, please, where we will be at dawn tomorrow morning?" He spread out a chart of the New Jersey coastline.

The navigator studied the chart and made a small cross in pencil approximately 25 miles off the coast of Atlantic City. "We should be here at dawn, Captain, at our present rate."

Only the privileged three—the missile control officer Okhovat, his executive officer Purali, and he—knew the target cities. "Gentlemen," Golzar said now, looking around. "Our targets are Washington, D.C., and New York City." There was murmuring throughout the room. He waited patiently for them to quiet. "We are launching dirty nuclear bombs. This is the big one, gentlemen. There will be no atomic explosions. Instead, these bombs release radioactive particles into the atmosphere. Done properly, they'll make midtown Washington, D.C., and lower Manhattan in New York City uninhabitable—for hundreds of years." His men reacted with amazed murmurs and smiles.

Golzar's voice rose. "This blow against the great Satan we do in the name of Allah!" The men cheered. "It will be the most definitive act in the history of mankind for the supremacy of Islam in the world!" More cheers.

"Mr. Ohkovat, what heading do you want us to be on when we surface?"

Ohkovat spoke nervously, "Captain, may I?" He reached for the chart and brought out a pair of dividers and a straight edge. He borrowed the navigator's pencil and drew very faint lines from Behzadi's cross to Washington D.C., and the south end of Manhattan. He bisected it with his dividers and said, "If we come upon a course of 297 degrees, we will be able to launch both missiles from the same heading."

"Excellent!" the captain exclaimed, smiling. "That's what I hoped." Then he turned to his engineering officer. "Mr. Rostami. Cruising at our current speed, how much battery charge will we have left?"

Rostami took out a calculator and punched in a few numbers. "Approximately 27 percent, Captain. It would take us at least six hours of top engine speed to bring back a full charge.

"Thank you." The captain turned with a grave expression to his crew chiefs. "The success or failure of this mission now falls to you and your crews. During practice, we couldn't launch or even expose missiles to the atmosphere. Therefore, your deck crews need to be rested and alert. I don't care who's on what watch—reassign them so they can get a good night's sleep and a proper meal before 5:15 tomorrow morning. I want no flashlights on deck; dim their quarters to increase their night vision. Is that clear?"

The crew chiefs glanced at each other and nodded with serious expressions. "Yes, sir."

"Very good," the captain said. "Even though we're on silent running, I'll have galley prepare a good, hot meal." There were murmurs of appreciation.

"Okay, to review. The moment we surface"—he looked at Purali— "we blow all tanks to be at the maximum above-sea level." Purali nodded. "Then we send two teams out the sail door, one for each missile cover."

The men looked suddenly apprehensive. Golzar said, "Some of your crewmen are worried about radioactivity, especially once the nose cones are exposed. Mr. Okhovat reassures us that exposure will be trivial, less than a luminous watch dial emits."

All heads turned to Ohkovat, who nodded. "That's right."

The captain said, "If they are still concerned, pass out facemasks. The masks prevent the inhalation of particles." He gave a rueful grin. "Just don't tell your men they're placebos."

He studied the sober faces of his men. "These preparations should have us on the surface no more than four minutes." To the raised brows watching him, he said, "Yes, that's fast. Speed is key. After Mr. Ohkovat's crew are done with the nose cones, the deck crews will attach the hoists and raise them into position—as we practiced, to their full extent. We must be sure, of course, that the launch tubes are completely free of obstructions—no tools or other gear can be left."

"I'll be on top of the sail in constant communication with the XO in the control room. We will maintain just enough speed to provide steerage. The moment the launch tubes are in position—we launch. Mr. Ohkovat is there anything you would like to remind us of at this point?"

Ohkovat regarded him thoughtfully. "There is, sir." He cleared his throat and looked at the others. "I believe none of you have been near a missile when it's fired. The after deck must be clear of all personnel and the hatch closed. The base of the missiles from the rocket motors are hot enough to melt steel. That's why there are special ceramic bases to prevent damage to the ship."

"These missiles are loud," he continued. "Anyone on deck forward of the sail or on the sail," he looked directly at the captain, "should have hearing protection. I recommend all personnel, including you, sir, return to the safety of the pressure hull, and close the hatch."

He thought a moment and added, "If any personnel remain on deck, they absolutely must not—must not—look at the missile exhaust. It will permanently damage their eyes. Warn your men that although they may have seen missiles on television, that was through heavy filters." He smiled and relaxed. "It will take less than fifteen seconds to complete the launch." He sighed. His hands had been shaking as he spoke.

"Thank you, Mr. Ohkovat," the captain said. "Please go with each crew chief and repeat what you've told us for their men. And don't forget—as soon as we've launched, our deck crews must race topside and get the missile launch tubes down." He paused and added, "If we can afford the time, we'll unbolt the base of the tubes and roll them overboard. If not, we'll submerge and head for home." He smiled. The men nodded and smiled back.

"One thing more, gentlemen. I have evidence that the Americans know we are out here."

CHAPTER 66

Captain Oliver "Ollie" Jenkins was thoroughly frustrated. Standing on the bridge of the destroyer, *USS Steel*, he stared at a thick fog hiding the ship's main deck, never mind the bow. They finally had a real mission—albeit an unusual one—but so far, his updates to the CNO were merely explanations that sounded like excuses for why they'd made little progress.

They'd set sail on zero notice with only two hundred twelve of the normal three hundred needed on board. Then, shortly after leaving Hampton Roads, one of his firemen went down with acute appendicitis and had to be evacuated for emergency surgery. That stopped them while they went through the launch helicopter drill and took his helicopter out of service for the mission.

They resumed sailing, and then hit something solid in the water. It turned out to be a whale. In fact, they found themselves in a pod of migrating Minka whales. Not only was the whale a goner, but they'd sucked pieces of the carcass into the water intakes and fouled the strainers. So their four GE twenty-seven thousand hp turbine engines were impotent until the strainers were cleaned and returned to service. The ailing fireman was particularly missed, as the engine room was now shorthanded.

When they finally achieved actual patrol, their sonar operators found the same bottom of wrecks that the sub-hunting plane had. Scores of false pings echoed off them, making their search for the Kilo slinking its way up the coast virtually impossible. Their visibility was bad and getting worse—Jenkins hoped they could rely on their radar—but not so! This close to shore, they practically ran down fishermen in wooden boats and even pleasure boaters who probably were looking for the *Yunes* too. Irritated at the obstacles, Jenkins was still relieved that so far, they had only hit a whale, not any of the boaters. *The enviros might complain when they eventually hear about it,* he thought, *but at least we'll have no grieving families to contend with.* Their recourse was to sound the foghorn periodically, post lookouts on the bow, and creep along. But he knew they were probably losing the sub, which was likely moving faster than they were.

When the CNO finally sent the *Yunes's* exact position, it was miles from their location. Normally they could get to the *Yunes* in less than two hours but unless the weather cleared, it would take all day. He had to do better than that. "Get me ComSubLant!" he barked.

In a minute he was speaking with Commander Gresso and laid out his plan quickly. "Hi, Larry. Look, I'm totally socked in here and weaving my way past civilians who don't show up on our radar. Unless the fog breaks soon, I propose we head to sea and run north at flank speed for several hours. By then, by the grace of God, this blankety-blank fog will have burned off, and I can come in ahead of the *Yunes* and intercept. What do you think?"

Gresso, in a deep voice, agreed. "You're not doing any good now, and more of the same would be—shall we say—futile." The commander paused, then asked, "I guess you don't get Network News out there?"

"Of course not. Is that raft guy back on?"

"I just watched a live broadcast of him trucking along behind the *Yunes*, eating fish and drinking coffee that the TV crew brought him, plain as day. Their chopper blew away enough fog to get a good picture."

"How the heck did they find him?" Jenkins asked. "I can barely find my own—well, never mind."

"Best I can figure is that he vectored them in on the sat phone they gave him."

"Well—why don't we call him up and ask him where he is now?"

"We think his battery is flat—phone's off."

"Figures. You know, we're coming out of this looking like idiots, aren't we?"

"Careful, Captain. But yes, something like that. I'm gonna tell the CNO that we need to stop thinking about the submarine and look for the raft guy instead."

"Sounds right to me, sir," Jenkins said as he clicked off. He shook his head. "Lord, have mercy."

CHAPTER 67

Commander Burgin of the *Tuscaloosa* studied the chart on the plotting table, noting the position of the *Yunes* as reported eighty-seven minutes prior, and their estimate of where it would be now. They had gone east out of Norfolk to sea, and then followed a curving course north to catch up with the sub. Burgin glanced at his watch. The sub should still be snorkeling, so why hadn't they heard it? The board showed them approximately 2 miles east of it.

He went to the sonar room, adjacent to the control room. His chief technician, Jimmy Glenn from Cincinnati, had the hearing of a bat—a rare capability in these days of mega loud music. And he could read the cryptic sonar displays almost as easily as reading a newspaper.

He found the four operators in front of their BSY-1 displays, which covered different ranges of the sonar spectrum. Wavy green lines on the screens represented what the many microphones around the boat were hearing. A "contact" or suspected vessel, showed up as a white line. The technician would listen to the suspect and try to identify it.

Burgin stood behind Glenn's console and saw several white lines. Glenn saw him in the screen's reflection and slipped off his headphones.

"Skipper, we've got a steady volume of small surface craft, mostly coming from shore. And I've been watching a slow freighter off the port bow. I've never heard a freighter that sounds like this one. It's like it has a wavering harmonic—two different frequencies that drift in and out with each other. I think our bad guy may be shadowing him. If he's snorkeling, his diesel could harmonize with the freighter's."

Burgin cracked a smile. This made sense. "Alright, Jimmy! Let's run up on him and see if we can confirm this. With two diesels running, he probably wouldn't hear a brass band, right?"

"Right on, Captain."

"Where do you think we should be to hear him best?"

"I'd say right behind them, or off their port side."

Burgin returned to the control room and spoke to his XO. "Let's get to periscope depth and run up the coms mast. Jimmy suspects a freighter a couple miles off our port bow has the *Yunes* hiding on the other side of it. I want to get close enough to see him. If we can't, we can still get him on radar long enough for a course and speed. Then we'll duck under that darned net and come up on the other side."

In minutes, despite zero visibility topside, they got a good radar image of the freighter and a ghost that they strongly suspected was the *Yunes*'s snorkel. The diving control officer took the boat to 100 feet and turned 30 degrees to port. He, his helmsman, and the diving plane crewmen were each strapped into bucket seats at their individual consoles with an airplane-style yoke between their knees. Driving a sixty-nine-hundred-ton boat longer than a football field was not like operating a jet ski in three dimensions. It had to be done smoothly and gradually, with great consideration for the boat's momentum.

Twenty minutes later, Jimmy exclaimed, "That's our perpetrator, Captain! No doubt about it. I'd put him about fifteen hundred yards ahead, 15 degrees to starboard."

"Thank you, Jimmy. I'm going to ease up next to him and wait until he stops snorkeling. I want to be sure he can hear us."

Jimmy gave him a quizzical look but said nothing.

Burgin explained back in the control room to Rothan, his XO. "And when he dives, sir, what course then? Probably the same?" Rothan asked.

"Yeah, probably. Why, what are you thinking?"

"I'm thinking if he makes a sharp left, like to clear his baffles, he could drag that net right in front of us. Remember, he doesn't know he has it."

"Right. Can we go under him?" Joe held up his hand. "Scratch that. Only if we can bulldoze a path through the bottom." He thought a moment. "Okay, we trail him by four hundred yards until he does whatever he's gonna do and then resumes his course. Then we come alongside and talk to him."

Rothan scratched his head. "You open for a suggestion, Skipper?"

"Shoot."

"Now that we know it's him, why not come along on the seaward side? Right now, he's got us boxed against the coast, and he's better built for shallow water than we are. If we put him off our port side, if we need room, we can run out to sea.

"Oh, you are a wise man. Make it so," Burgin replied with a twinkle in his eye. He turned his head sharply, "Did you hear their diesel stop?"

"Maybe." They both looked at the sonar shack, "Jimmy?"

Jimmy confirmed. The *Yunes* was securing from snorkeling and clearing their baffles with a left turn.

They were on them like flypaper. Burgin felt the boat turn to starboard, hoping they were under the drift net. Time to get the ambassador. But first, he needed to check in with ComSubLant and see if they had any more info from Iran, per the ambassador's request.

"Larry?" Joe asked the ComSubLant Commander. He wasn't positive they had a secure channel. "Joe Burgin here. Any word from our friends, ah, from the far side? You know, per my guest's request?"

"Joe, we're secure. No, I haven't heard a thing. Why, have you found the *Yunes*?

"Found him? I could almost scratch his belly. He was shadowing a freighter. But we're coming alongside, and if we're gonna talk to him, now is the time."

"Got it. Okay, hold the line. Let me see if Washington's heard anything."

A couple of minutes later, he was back. "DC hasn't heard anything. But if you think about it, if their president called ours and asked for your grade school and dog's name, how long would it take to get that?"

Joe laughed. "A very long time. I never had a dog. But I get the point. Okay, we'll go with what we've got. Back to you when it's over."

"Break a leg, Joe."

Burgin turned to Rothan. "Come up alongside her, no farther than five hundred yards, and I'll get the ambassador and the translator. Cover up anything they shouldn't see."

A few minutes later, Burgin, the ambassador, the translator, and Willie Ott, the radioman, were all crammed into the communications shack, a small, equipment-laden room off the port corridor adjacent to the control room. Willie had draped all the equipment with tablecloths from the officer's wardroom. A microphone cable snaked its way out between two drapes and lay on the desk, which was also covered. After quick introductions, Willie demonstrated the phone to the ambassador. "It's like a telephone except when you want to talk, you have to squeeze the switch on the hand grip. Your voice will go out on a loudspeaker. At this distance, the *Yunes* will hear us easily."

The ambassador turned to Burgin with a pained look, "Captain, please, let us wait to hear from Iran."

Burgin shook his head. "Mr. Ambassador, we've given it our best shot. If the tables were reversed and your president asked for similar information about me, right here, right now, it could take hours to get it, maybe a day. I'm sorry, I must ask you to proceed as best you can."

"Thank you for trying," Shakiba said dejectedly. He pulled notes from a pocket. "Can I sit here?"

"Oh, sure," Willie said. "I'll be outside the door. I've got it all set up for you. Just press and talk."

"Will I hear anything?"

"Only if they talk back, sir."

Ambassador Shakiba took a deep breath, cleared his throat, pressed the button, and began in Farsi. "Submarine *Yunes*, submarine *Yunes*. This is Ambassador Ahmad Shakiba. I am a permanent representative of the Islamic Republic of Iran to the United Nations, Ambassador Extraordinary and Plenipotentiary. I am on board the USS *Tuscaloosa*, a Los

Angeles class atomic submarine traveling beside you." Burgin raised his brows when Zarin, the translator, whispered that last sentence into his ear.

"I bring greetings from our government in Iran. President Akbari has asked me to pass on his orders, and the orders of Admiral Mustafa Radan, to abort your mission, come to the surface, and return to Iran immediately. The Americans have assured me and President Akbari that you will not be harmed. However, if there are any hostile acts toward the United States from the *Yunes*, they will consider this an act of war and retaliate immediately and in great force."

Burgin thought *We're on the verge of nuclear war!*

The ambassador repeated the message to no response. His tone changed. Unlike his earlier formal if forceful approach, it became wheedling, pleading. "Captain, Golzar, please, please abort this mission! Come up and leave this coast immediately. You will be sunk if you don't, and Iran will be devastated! I implore you, turn away." When there was no response, the ambassador's shoulders slumped. He handed the phone back to Willie as he exited the little room. In the hall, he looked at Burgin. "I've done everything I can, Captain. I hope that it is enough."

"So do I, Ambassador, and thank you very much. Now, if you will excuse me, I need to talk to my sonar man and see what the *Yunes* is doing.

Moments later in the sonar room: "Well, Jimmy?"

"Sir, I think they could hear that all the way to Hoboken. I know I sure could." He put his finger on the sonar display. "That's strange," he muttered. He put on his earphones and slowly adjusted a couple of dials. Then he turned to the captain, slid off his earphones, and said "Captain, I've lost him. It's like he dropped into a hole."

"What?"

"Yes, sir, he's gone."

CHAPTER 68

There were no birds with the fog. No dolphins. Phil especially missed them, for their playful presence seemed to connote good luck. He must have read that once—was it an ancient mariners' superstition? An occasional flying fish was some comfort. Otherwise, since the departure of the news crew, the ocean seemed desolate. The oil sludge and trash that sometimes floated by was at least a sign of human life, but today he saw none of that either. He toyed with the idea of putting the raft outside the net just to see if something would bump his bottom. Bad idea.

Although the fog was burning off, he felt like the ocean had become a sensory deprivation chamber. Back in college, he'd been paid a whopping two dollars and fifty cents an hour to lie in a little bed covered with a plastic bubble. A psyche experiment. But a grad student recorded and listened to everything he said. They finally let him out when he threatened to pee in the bed. As it turned out, the experiment didn't work—they couldn't establish a baseline. Nobody reacted the same way.

Phil thought of the coffee and donuts. A faint inner glow reminded him that his stomach still appreciated them. He glanced at his watch to see if it was time for another helping—and laughed. *It's been twenty minutes since your last one.* He'd eaten more donuts on this trip than he had in a year. He wondered if he'd been dropping weight. He couldn't safely stand to tell if his shorts were getting loose. He'd been on the seafood diet for only three days, but it sure felt longer. That old joke had never been truer: "I see food. I eat it."

As the fog continued to disburse, he saw the morning sun glowing through clouds in the east. He turned to see if the freighter was visible yet. Not a glimmer. But they were at snorkel speed—running submerged was a lot slower. He saw the net was curving off to the left, which meant they were turning. He was pretty sure the sub did that after every snorkel. Then they'd straighten after a few minutes and return to the normal course. But hadn't he turned right yesterday? It was like the captain wanted to look behind him somehow—not possible underwater.

Suddenly Phil caught a flash of something rising from the water, but off to the right—not from the sub. A periscope! It had to be the Navy! Halleluiah! Yes! But had they seen him? The scope wasn't turned in his direction. That's okay. They're here.

The periscope slid below the surface. Phil searched the water, trying to see in its depth for a glance of them—and laughed. Get real, Phil. But he was so excited he could hardly contain himself. Could he do anything to help this along? No, like what? It was all happening down there.

Minutes later, something changed. The net seemed looser somehow, riding more gently. Maybe it was the turn they'd made. With the extra net, it was like being towed on the inside of the curve on a water ski boat. If he wasn't careful, the towrope would go slack. He hoped when the sub straightened out again, it would ride tighter like always.

He busied himself searching for donut crumbs on his lap and in the raft. Good thing the gulls weren't there or he'd have competition! Maybe not—pickings were pretty paltry. He tried to relax, watching the net stream out behind him. It was really quite graceful. Now they were turning right again, resuming the regular course. And then it not only stopped turning but slowed down. Phil swiveled to face forward. The haze had cleared enough to see that the net was floating loosely, barely pulling him at all. His heart raced. There was literally no current passing the floats on the net. He put a hand in the water and confirmed it. The raft was barely moving. What was going on?

He could think of only one explanation—the net must have broken loose from the sub. "Oh no!"

Maybe, with its turning back and forth, it had worked off the snorkel—or wore it out so it broke. If he reeled in the net ahead of him, he'd probably find frayed ends. He decided to wait on doing that until he saw if anything else happened.

Good time to try the sat phone. Still low battery. If he chanced a call now and it didn't work, he'd probably exhaust the little juice left. He snapped it off and slid it under the shroud.

Lord, watch over me. You've gotten me this far, and I trust in you. Show me what to do. He sat back and took a deep breath, let it out slowly, and forced a smile. Mary used to say that your body doesn't know when a smile is forced, but you'll feel better. She was right—he felt better. This wasn't a catastrophe. He was relatively safe, with food, and the U.S. Navy was looking for him— they better be!

As he watched the net, it casually meandered in his direction, bunching up, swept along by the Gulfstream. Wait a minute. If the net broke loose of the sub, why would it start bunching up? Wouldn't it just float on the current? This didn't make sense. *Okay, Lord, show me what's happening.*

Now the net was doubling back in his direction. In fact, soon he would float past the dipping point where it went down to the sub. What about that? If it had broken loose, wouldn't both ends float to the surface?

As he pondered this, the net started to pull the raft around. The sub had reversed course! The net was still wrapped around the snorkel.

Okay, sit tight Phil. Let's see what Mister Sub Skipper is doing. He didn't need to figure it out—they'd show him. Sure enough, in the next few minutes, as he floated along, the net gradually reversed completely. Now it was streaming behind him to the north. The current seemed weaker than before, however, so he checked his position on the app, and noted the time.

Five minutes later, he checked again. They hadn't moved! What could have happened? Did the sub hit the freighter and get damaged?

No. Suddenly Phil knew. There could only be one reason—the Navy must have sunk the sub!

CHAPTER 69

The crew of the *Yunes* heard Ambassador Shakiba's message loud and clear —and froze. The message sounded close—was he right next to them? They looked at each other in wonderment. And found the captain.

Captain Golzar, after hearing the message, was bent over the depth gauge. "All stop. Planesman, ten degrees down angle." His firm but quiet tone was somehow reassuring to his men. The planesman turned his wheel until the dial lined up with a negative ten degrees indicator, veering the angle of the large diving planes that extended off the bow and stern like fins on a fish, guiding it down deeper.

"Executive officer—I want all hands in absolute silence. Rostami, tell the engine room and wait there for further orders. Absolute silence."

They felt the boat angling downward, coasting slower and slower. The captain studied the depth gauge again. "Planesman, five degrees down angle." Then, waiting, his eyes glued to the depth gauge, he ordered "Zero angle." He looked around at the wide-eyed crew. "Brace for collision. We'll sit on the bottom. Planesman, two degrees up angle." He'd try to touch bottom with their stern rather than the bow to keep the boat from plowing into the mud and getting embedded. He hoped a gentle slide would do it.

A slight tug at the rear of the boat told them they'd landed well, although they leaned slightly left. Rarely did a sailor feel much motion on a sub, but now there was none at all—the crew felt the difference. The captain stepped over to Emad Jabrani, his lead sonar technician. "Jebrani," he whispered, "Can you tell where the Americans are?"

Jebrani adjusted a dial and pressed on his earphones. "Sir, I believe they're moving right ahead of us." He paused, then jerked his head. "They are pinging actively, sir; but there is something else echoing, too. Can there be another sub in the area?"

"I think not. Just the fruits of our German friends' hunting."

Jebrani had no idea what the captain referred to but wasn't about to ask.

Back in 1942 Ernst-August Rehwinkle, captain of U-578 of the Deutsche Kriegsmarine, put two torpedoes into the USS *Jacob Jones* and blew it into pieces—right where the *Yunes* had settled. Its remains now masked their presence. Captain Golzar had gambled on sinking near one of the plentiful wrecks along the Delaware coast, and he'd won—big time.

XO Purali had been silent during the *Yunes's* trip to the bottom, but he paced the wardroom nervously and now spoke. "Captain."

The captain whipped his hand up. "Not here! Come to my cabin." He led the way down the passageway. Closing the door firmly behind them, Golzar said, "Keep your voice low, Massoud. You can be sure there are ears straining to hear." He put his hands bracingly on Purali's shoulders. "This is not an emergency. We must remain calm." Purali's eyes were anything but.

"Yes, they know we're here," the captain continued. But that's all they know—nothing more. They do not know what our mission is. It's not possible."

Purali's anxiety wasn't appeased. "But Captain, what the ambassador said …a war…"

"It's a bluff. They said nothing specific, nothing about our missiles. Their intel is good. But we are better. Their sub is a lumbering bus compared to ours, especially in shallow water. I am not deterred, Massoud. It's all a bluff. Everything he said can be found on the Internet."

"But Captain…"

Golzar squeezed Purali's shoulders. "Ask yourself; have you ever in all history heard of a submarine warning an enemy sub to leave an area? Of course not. If they wanted us out of here, they wouldn't try coaxing us out; they would put torpedoes into us, and you and I would be fish food."

The captain studied Purali, wishing Hesam Asgari was still on board. Hesam was a true believer and fearless. But he would have to rely on Purali to help him calm the crew. "The Americans have the courage of rabbits. You and I need to reassure the crew. Our mission is on. Tomorrow morning we strike the blow that we've all worked so hard and long for. Allah and Iran will be proud!" He paused. "Whoever spoke to us made a mistake. He said he was on a Los Angeles class submarine."

"I don't understand, Captain, how is that a mistake?"

"It means that we now know we can do something they can't. The Los Angeles class are open ocean boats. We can go very slowly. They are unstable below 5 knots. The lion does not hunt the cobra."

CHAPTER 70

In the White House Situation Room, despite its excellent ventilation, a gamey atmosphere developed. Bodies, heated conversations, and plenty of coffee had that effect. Admiral Hunter was summoned to the phone, with the *Tuscaloosa* on the line.

"Speaker, please," the president called as Dirk reached for the phone.

"Burgin!" Dirk said. "You're on speaker."

All focus shifted from personal electronics to Dirk.

"Here's the situation," Burgin's voice crackled over the line. "We found the *Yunes* and came alongside him—no more than four hundred yards away—in shallow water. Ambassador Shakiba gave him the full message, 'leave or die,' which of course was recorded and translated. We'll have the transcript for you in a few minutes. Shakiba gave a personal plea for the sake of Iran to abort and leave—but there's a kicker."

"What is it?" Dirk asked.

"He's gone. The *Yunes*—disappeared. We're actively pinging, but all we get are false echoes from all the wrecks. The best I can figure is that he's on full silence and moving slow and low. It's quite shallow here."

The room was silent, all eyes on Dirk. "That must be it, Captain." He paused. "If he's just creeping along, he's gonna be a long way from his destination for a while. That gives us time. We're putting together a SEAL team on the Monford with an ASDS. They should be in theater by mid-morning tomorrow. Keep looking. Thanks for the report."

"Excellent—that's what we need, actual visual on this guy. And if the missile on deck story is true, the SEALS can neutralize them."

"That's the idea. Anything else?"

"Now that we've tried our 'friendly persuasion' approach, what are my rules of engagement?"

"Captain, we're gonna have to talk that one over here. Stay on coms a few more minutes, and I'll get back to you."

"Aye, aye, Admiral. *Tuscaloosa* standing by."

The room burst into conversation. Somebody called out, "What's an ASDS?"

"Advanced Seal Delivery System," said Dirk. "Basically, a midget sub mounted on the deck of a full-size one, the Monford in this case. The parent sub takes the SEALS as close as they can to their target, then they go the rest of the way in the ASDS. It wasn't designed for this kind of operation, but it's ideal. The Monford'll get close to the *Yunes*, and SEALS will sabotage the missiles," he said, nodding.

"We don't know how fast the *Yunes* is moving," he continued, "which could be a problem—faster than the SEALS can swim. We have propulsion units available for them, but it's easy to get separated, especially if visibility is low. Also, at high speeds the units' battery life is low." He surveyed the room.

The president asked, "That's the good news, Dirk. What's the bad news?"

Dirk took a deep breath. "We may be too late. We need to

decide the rules of engagement, not only for the *Tuscaloosa*, but for all our forces."

Secretary of Defense Franklin Grant met eyes with General Vernon Swartly, Chairman of the Joint Chiefs, and moved his hand across his neck. The general nodded and cleared his throat. "Mr. President, if the Iranians surface in the least threatening position, then we must sink them immediately. We have no other option."

Secretary of State Marsha Williams cried, "Excuse me, but I don't understand something. We just heard that the ambassador told the sub to stop pursuing their course, surface, and sail for Iran—correct?" Several heads nodded. "So my question is this: 'If they do decide to follow the ambassador's instructions, and come to the surface to return to Iran, and we sink them, aren't we exposing ourselves to a major international incident?"

All eyes turned to Secretary of Defense Grant. "Good question, Marsha. I'd say it depends on our interpretation of his intentions. Dirk, correct me if I'm wrong, but if he comes up headed out to sea, then we'd assume he was going to leave the scene."

"That's right, General. And we'll help him keep that intention by escorting him until he's hundreds of miles offshore," Dirk said.

"If he comes up facing the U.S., or turns toward it shortly after surfacing?"

"Then we blow him out of the water," Dirk said. Around the room, heads nodded in agreement—except one. Dave Shepherd, listening with great concern to all this, suddenly cried, "What about my DAD?"

CHAPTER 71

Submarine Tuscaloosa

Captain Burgin's sonar tech Jimmy hadn't been able to find the *Yunes* since they'd lost contact. But he had to admire the action. "This guy is good—fast and good," he said about the *Yunes*'s captain.

"He didn't sail into a hole, Jimmy," Burgin said. "I think he's sitting on the bottom. It's so darned shallow here it would be easy." Joe patted Jimmy's shoulder. "Keep listening. But I bet it'll be hours before he moves, maybe longer. And stop pinging. No need to give more information than necessary about where we are."

Burgin turned to Rothan, standing just outside the sonar shack. He nodded toward the wardroom. "Let's go. Get Sabin, too, with his chart." He'd need the navigator to help determine their next moves.

In minutes, the three settled at the wardroom table over the Atlantic Coast chart—covered in tracing paper for their markups—and coffee. "Is this where we lost him?" he asked Sabin, pointing to a dot at the end of a short line.

"Yes, sir. That's when he pulled off snorkeling behind that freighter. The *Tuscaloosa*'s path was a blue line on the chart, showing they'd passed the last known position of the *Yunes*.

Burgin put his pencil on the end of the line and drew an X. "I say that's our boy, sitting pretty on the bottom." He looked at Rothan, who nodded.

"The question is, how long is that net he's attached to? Since we don't know, we'll assume it's long." He surveyed the men. "You guys know much about drift nets? I sure don't."

Rothan and Sabin shook their heads, but Sabin said, "Skipper, I think…I was talking to somebody on board who grew up in Alaska and used to fish as a kid."

"Get Dutch," Burgin said. "He'll know who it is if anyone does."

He was summoned over the intercom. In less than a minute, Dutch Stoller's ruddy face and twinkling eyes appeared around the edge of the wardroom door. "What's up, Captain?"

"Dutch, our bad guy is sitting on the bottom, waiting us out. We need to know how long the net is that he's hooked onto. Sabin here seems to think there's somebody on board who grew up in Alaska and used to fish as a kid."

Dutch grinned. "Marty Harelson. Some little place on the Aleutians, I think. Should I get him?"

Minutes later a very nervous young seaman stepped into the officer's wardroom, eyes wide. "Yes, sir?" he said, stiffening to attention.

Burgin said, "Have a seat. Relax, Harelson, you're not in trouble. Want a cup of coffee or a Danish?"

The youth relaxed enough to ease into a seat opposite the captain, but he took no refreshments. Burgin said, "Dutch says you grew up in a fishing town in Alaska and may have spent time on commercial fishing boats. Is that right?"

Marty smiled self-consciously, "Yes, sir. My dad is the skipper of the Sea Eagle," he said proudly. "We'd drift net for salmon, and then put out crab pots too."

"Great. Do you know how long your drift net was, and how deep?"

"Oh yeah, I had to repair it. Ours wasn't that long, just a couple miles. And it was about 60 feet deep, starting 10 feet below the float line."

"Wow. When you say, 'not that long,' do you have any idea how long they can be?"

"I don't know, sir. I heard my dad talking once about some Chinese guys with nets like 25 or 30 miles long—for open-ocean fishing. We were coastal."

Joe leaned back in his chair and took a deep breath. "Okay, son. That helps. I suppose you're wondering what this is all about."

"Sure, sir, if you'd like to tell me." The young sailor grinned.

"We can't afford to run into a net the sub we're following is dragging. It would foul our diving planes, and probably our propeller too. It would put us out of action. Our idea is to sneak up on him without getting caught in the net—but it's gonna be tricky."

He turned to the other officers. "I'm gonna assume he snagged this net somewhere in the Caribbean, probably off Cuba. That would make it a coastal fishing situation. So let's say his net is no longer than two miles long." He paused. "That sound reasonable, Harelson?"

Marty's head jerked up in surprise. He hadn't expected to be advising the captain on anything, much less the length of drift nets. *Wait until the guys hear this one*, he thought. "Yes sir, that sounds about right. I don't think any boats ran nets much longer than ours. Of course, that's Alaska. I don't know nothing about Cuba."

Burgin nodded with a smile. "Okay, seaman, we'll take it from here. Help yourself to a donut if you want one. It's on the Navy."

"Thank you, sir. Thank you very much," Harelson said as he rose and paused at the pastry tray on his way out.

Burgin said, "Nice kid. Okay, navigator, draw a line one-and-a-half miles from the X. Both north and south."

Rothan asked, "North, sir?"

Burgin nodded. "Think about it. If he's sitting on the bottom, the current will carry his net north. So we've got about a three-mile circle around this guy that we need to stay out of. Sabin, plot us a course and let's get on it." He stood and then added, "Don't forget we've got our towed array about half a mile behind us; we don't want that to get stuck in his net either." To Rothan he said, "Let's go to periscope depth. I want to see if I can make out our marker."

"Sir?"

"The raft guy. We should have been looking for him from the get-go. I'm calling ComSubLant and telling them that. Find the raft guy!"

CHAPTER 72

Had the navy sunk the Iranian sub? That was Phil's question as the hazy morning dispersed into a sunny afternoon, and still his position didn't change. He took the phone out to let it charge beneath the welcome rays, noticing that even the dolphins had returned. He wondered if they were the same ones that had escorted him down in Florida. Probably not. Since he was turned around from the usual position, he faced north with the sun on his back. It felt good

He'd passed time by praying, singing, and napping, not necessarily in that order, with an occasional donut as a treat.

He thought a lot about the people in the sub, especially Ace. If it had sunk, were they still alive? All he knew about submarines was from Hollywood. Were they down there gasping for air, and trying to stop huge gushers of water as they did in the movies? Somehow, he didn't think so. And if they had sunk, why wasn't there any evidence on the surface? He remembered something about oil slicks, huge bubbles of air and debris from a dying submarine. Some of his prayers were for the sub and its crew. *Love your enemies, right?*

He played with the signal mirror—to no avail. Occasionally he saw a ship in the distance and tried to flash the bridge, but the operative word at those times was "tried." It would be hard to do even from a steady dock.

He thought about cutting loose from the sub and drifting

north, but that didn't make sense. The navy wanted the sub first and foremost, not him. So he was theoretically doing them a service by staying on top of it. The breeze from the Atlantic was chilly, and he hoped it wasn't bringing bad weather. The swell was gentle, but the waves looked like they might be in the mood to get bigger.

He studied the net and saw it wasn't as straight as it had been, but there was little tension on it. He looked closer but saw nothing to make him think it had broken loose of the ship. He checked GPS and noted his position. Five minutes later, he checked again. This time they'd moved slightly north.

Phil, you peanut brain, he's not sunk. He's playing possum, hiding on the bottom! Had a U.S. sub come up and forced him into hiding? If he remembered correctly, the water was shallow here—the Atlantic shelf, he thought they called it. He wished he had a cell signal to look it up online.

That sub captain was determined. Phil bet they'd be going right back to their old course up the coast as soon as they deemed it safe. They were now off Delaware. The net began making its way around him, turning the raft as it went, which Phil enjoyed. Now he faced south again. This felt better somehow, the way it should be. But out there on the water, any change, anything different, was welcome entertainment.

Phil must have dozed; he was jolted from a nap when the raft almost flipped over in the wake of a huge freighter that passed about 100 feet away. Nobody had seen him, he was sure.

Almost TV time. He searched the eastern skies for a helicopter but saw nothing. He pulled out the sat phone and waited. It lit up about the same time he heard a chopper. "Bret?"

"Phil, we're on the way—with more surprises!"

"Great! Look, the phone's almost dead, but I can see you. Turn slightly to your right and come in." He listened for confirmation, but the phone died. He hoped they'd find him. *The signal mirror.* He positioned it carefully, tucking his elbows around it for extra stability. To his joy, the copter turned toward him. Soon they were overhead.

When the door opened, two bags were lowered. A new sat phone in the first one—yes! And a jug of water in the other. Good thing—he'd just run out. He switched on the phone. "Just in time, Bret. The old one just died. You want it back?"

Bret was talking to someone but then said, "We're not set up to take things up. Hey, were you flashing us with a mirror? Man, that thing is bright."

"Glad I finally got it to work," Phil said, grinning while waving the mirror.

"Hang on, we're about to go live again. Remember, no mention of missiles."

He introduced Phil and they chatted. Phil told about seeing the U.S. submarine periscope and the Iranian sub stopping. He told him he'd at first thought they'd sunk the Iranians, but now he realized they were hiding on the bottom.

"That's fascinating, Phil. What do you make of it?"

"I think the captain is down there deciding what to do—he really wants to continue his mission. He's determined. I don't suppose I'll ever meet him—but it would be interesting."

"Phil, the whole nation is following your story. How do you feel about that?"

Phil chuckled. "I'm amazed. You know I'm a high school history teacher back in Kokomo—right? It occurs to me that instead of just teaching history, now I'm part of it… It's gonna be hard to settle down and get the students back into a regular lesson plan." After more chatting, Phil took pictures of the copter. Bret said, "I've got a little something you might like."

Another bag came swinging down on a light line. This one had a full meal take-out from a steak house! Bacon-wrapped filet mignon, mashed potatoes, grilled asparagus, a salad, and a brownie. "Bret, this is wonderful! Thank you so much. I really appreciate it." Phil was almost choked up at the thought of not having to eat another sushi dinner.

"Happy to oblige, Phil. You should see all the emails we're getting with suggestions of what we should bring you. People are really into this."

"Amazing," said Phil. He asked if they'd heard from the navy. Bret said they hadn't, but perhaps the network had. He'd find out.

"Please ask them to pick me up." Phil had just given the perfect human-interest moment that all TV stations love, without even knowing it.

"Will do, Phil, for sure. Anything else?"

Phil paused. "My heartfelt appreciation for all the prayers coming my way. I can really feel them. And the usual hello to my sons, my colleagues and classes, my friend Louise, and I guess now, the whole country." Phil smiled and waved. "You've been great! Thanks so much."

Phil tried to admire the sunset in the ensuing loneliness once the copter had wheeled out of sight. He ate the meal with excruciating appreciation, but even the dolphins seemed to have retired early, and not a bird was in sight. As he thought about what was next—New Jersey—his stomach tightened.

Staring at the little chart on his phone, somehow Phil felt this would be his last night out there on the raft. The sub captain must know he'd been spotted and was under pressure to do his thing and get out of town.

Lord, You choose the least likely of people. I don't know what you want me to do from here, but I still rest and trust in you. As Jesus prayed in the Garden of Gethsemane, he prayed now: *Father, if it is your will, take this cup from me.* Reluctantly, he completed it: *Nevertheless, not my will, but yours be done.*

He thought about the Iranians—they could be preparing to surface and nuke the U.S. Watching the last of the evening light, he thought about courage. Somebody once said it was doing the right thing even if you're scared to death. He pleaded, *Lord, grant me courage!*

That was it! Doggone it, he was not going to just sit back and watch them lob missiles at the U.S. He pulled the raft up to where the net dipped below the surface. From there, he'd be able to jump on the snorkel, wedge its valve open again, and force the sub to surface to fix it. That's all he could do. He rummaged around the foot of the raft for the anchor parts and the line he'd used to lash the mechanism the last time.

Touching the sat phone by accident, he thanked God for it and called Dave. They chatted, but Phil didn't tell him his plan. He called Louise, his hand again shaking like a schoolboy's. He hoped his voice wouldn't shake as well.

"Phil! From the Atlantic! I just saw the news," Louise gushed, sounding very excited, and maybe concerned.

"How are things in Kokomo?" he asked, trying to sound cheery.

"Oh Phil, we're fine. But how about you?

"I'm fine. Did you see the steak dinner? First class." They continued with small talk, but Phil felt a compulsion to share his plan with Louise. "I've decided if the navy doesn't show up tonight, when the sub comes up to snorkel, I'm gonna jam it open. They'll be forced to surface to fix it. That should make them easy to find!"

"Oh, dear. That sounds dangerous. Are you sure about this? You know, I never thought of you as the daredevil type."

"I'm not, trust me. But I believe I need to finish what the Lord put me out here for. So I guess I'm as ready as I can be."

After a long pause—with some sniffling—*was Louise actually crying for him?* Phil was touched deeply. She said, "Please, please be careful," almost in a whisper.

"I will, my sweet." He could just imagine getting a warm embrace from her, how he wished—he broke up at the thought. "I just wanted to say that if I don't make it for some reason, it was the Lord's decision, not mine. So we'll have to accept it. Okay?"

"I guess so," she choked out.

"And—I hadn't intended to say this just yet, but I want you to know that I, er..." Phil swallowed and continued. "I think I've fallen in love with you."

A sob escaped her. He could picture Louise's sweet face, rounder than long, her still pretty features, blue eyes filled with concern, her arms open to him, as she replied, "And I love you, Phil. Actually, I have for a long time."

There was a phrase for that—*music to one's ears!* She'd loved him for a long time? He'd been too distracted to notice. He couldn't wait to get back home and let her know that he was sure noticing her now.

CHAPTER 73

Golzar was tired. He'd been on high alert for hours since the so-called ambassador spoke to them. In his heart of hearts, he thought it probably was their UN ambassador, proving their new president wasn't a true believer—he'd chickened out. But it changed nothing. He was ready to die, even if his officers and crew hadn't figured out theirs was a one-way mission.

His problem was evading the Americans. He crouched down next to Jabrani at the sonar station. "Can you tell what he's doing?"

"Yes, sir, he's circling us. I lose him when he goes through the baffles behind us, but then he appears out the other side. He's made almost two full circles so far."

Golzar glanced at his watch. They'd been on the bottom for four hours and fifteen minutes. "Can you tell how far out he is, how big his circle?"

"It's large. I estimate a radius of about five kilometers when he's in front of us, but six when he's behind."

Golzar grew thoughtful. "Thank you, Jabrani." He signaled XO Purali to follow him to the wardroom. "Bring the chart. Get Behzadi too."

They sat at the table with the chart between them. The captain held coffee in one hand while pointing to the chart as he spoke with the other, explaining what sonar revealed about the American sub's path. "I think they know what we're doing—because they're not widening their search. So, we need to get out of here somehow without being detected." His colleagues nodded agreement but looked perplexed.

Purali said, "If we start-up, he'll hear us for sure, Captain."

Golzar smiled, "Then we won't. We'll let the current take us out. Behzadi, what do you estimate the current to be here?"

The navigation officer studied the chart, then replied confidently, "2.5 knots, sir. However, I believe based on our earlier progress, that it's actually a shade less than this, but not much. Perhaps 2.3 knots."

"Excellent!" the captain replied as he lightly sketched an oval around their present position. "The Yankees have made almost two circles around us and are about to cross our bow. Therefore, I propose that we very slowly blow just enough ballast to lift us off the bottom by about ten meters."

"And then?" Purali asked.

Golzar chafed under Purali's lack of imagination. "Then *nothing*. We drift—north. The Americans will be headed south in their circle and moving away from us."

"But how do we steer, Captain?" Purali asked.

"We don't. We let the Gulfstream take us out of their circle—and when we're far enough away, then we power up and continue. I don't even want a GPS float until we're well away from them. The secret to success is that we cannot sound any different than the water moving past the wrecks along the bottom here." He stopped and looked both of his colleagues in the eye. "It will be difficult to maintain depth. Ballast adjustments will have to be done very, very carefully."

"How will we know when we're out of his circle, Captain? And how far should we go before we can return to power?" Purali asked.

"The clock. We know it takes him about two hours and ten minutes to make one circle. Jabrani can tell us when he's directly ahead. So, I say we wait for one and a half more circles before we power up."

"One and a half, Captain?"

"He'll be farthest away from us then. Then we'll need to get back on power immediately for the launch tomorrow morning." He paused to give Purali time to catch up. "Do you understand?"

"Oh yes, sir, perfectly. It is a very clever plan."

"Good," the captain responded, trying to be as patient as he could. "Because you will be in command during the entire procedure." Purali might not have been the sharpest knife in the drawer, but he was an excellent boat handler and had the men's confidence. "I'm going to check our latest sonar readings and then get some sleep," Golzar added. "Wake me when you're ready to power up, or, of course, if there are any problems."

They returned to the control room where Purali gave the order to begin blowing ballast. Moments later, they heard the faint hiss of air moving into the ballast tanks, expelling water that had held them to the bottom. The boat stirred and lifted off. Four sets of eyes were glued to the depth gauge. Purali whispered, "Secure ballast, but be ready to bleed a little in if we rise higher than 15 feet. Adjust depth gradually to maintain that distance and control—and silence."

Golzar watched his crew at work with satisfaction. This plan would work.

At the sonar station, he asked Jabrani, "And where is he now?"

The tech looked up and smiled. "He'll cross our bow in about three minutes, Captain. This would be a perfect position to put a couple of torpedoes into him. He wouldn't have a chance."

CHAPTER 74

The White House

President Brandenberg went from the break-out room back into the situation room, followed by Secretary of State Marsha Williams and Attorney General Zachary Crawford. Everyone looked up in expectation as they got seated. Weary but determined, the president shed his jacket and tie and rolled up his shirtsleeves. He cleared his throat. "Thank you all for your patience. I know this has been an ordeal—and it's not over. Marsha, Zach, and I have reached a decision regarding the rules of engagement. We'll write them out and send them to the relevant forces immediately." He looked down the table at Dave. "This will address Mr. Shepherd's concern about his father."

"Thank you, sir—Mr. President," Dave said, somberly. He'd been swallowing down tears, looking distraught. Connie had a comforting hand on his arm. She whispered, "Your dad will be okay. We have great SEALS—they'll get him out."

Dave nodded at her appreciatively but raised a hand. When the president nodded at him, he said, "I talked to my dad while you all were in your huddle room. He said that if he's still out there tonight when the sub comes up to snorkel, he's gonna jam the valve open and force them to surface to fix it."

"What?" CNO Dirk Hunter exclaimed in disbelief. "How's he going to do that?"

Dave smiled. "I don't know, sir. But he did it once before, the night after our boat sank. My dad's pretty determined when he puts his mind to something."

Dirk was taken aback. "Was that in the report? I must have missed it." He raked a hand through his hair. Softly, he added, "I never heard of anything like that."

"None of us have, Dirk." Secretary of Defense Franklin Grant added. "But doesn't this help? If the sub is forced to the surface to make a repair, won't he be more vulnerable than if he surfaces to launch his missiles?"

Dirk nodded, "Absolutely. The trick will be to know exactly when he comes up—and where. Then we can be on him like white on rice." He looked at Dave. "Can you call your dad and have him call us as soon as the *Yunes* surfaces?"

President Brandenberg cleared his throat. "Actually, Dirk, I think it's time for us to have direct communication with Mr. Shepherd. Marsha, Zach, and I believe we'd be wise to let him stay with the *Yunes*—he's a reliable source for their location and actions—but there's no sense going through Dave when we can speak to him ourselves."

Grant nodded, "I agree, sir." He paused. "But if this sub comes up to launch their missiles, if that's their plan, it's gonna be very tricky to get Mr. Shepherd off safely, as well as take it out of action. Our window is only a few minutes. This will call for air assets."

General Swartley of the joint chiefs said, "We need to get Eddie Hipps in here pronto, with an open link to air squadrons. And Josh Allen, of course."

The president nodded confirmation to a watch commander through the control room window, who immediately reached for a phone.

Dirk Hunter offered, "You know, General, the navy can get those guys out of our base at Oceana."

General Swartley swiveled his chair to look at Dirk. "What's the sub's last reported position?"

"Off the Delaware Coast, coming up on Cape May, New Jersey."

"And we expect he'll continue north throughout the night?"

"Yes, sir."

"That will put him mid-Jersey."

Dirk nodded. "I see what you mean. Okay, let's see what the Air Force can do. This may need to be a joint exercise."

"Yes," the general replied.

"Gentlemen," Marsha Williams interjected. "Why don't we ask Mr. Shepherd to call us when the *Yunes* comes up, and immediately release himself from their net? In fact, can't he put a lot of net between himself and the sub? Couldn't he just follow from a safe distance?"

Dave pumped his fist and exclaimed, "Yes!" making others chuckle.

"Marsha, are you angling for a career in the military?" the president quipped.

"I believe, Mr. President, they have enough to deal with," she said smiling.

The president said. "Okay people, let's take a break. We'll get the Air Force up to speed and figure out how they'll do this." He looked at Dave, "And then, sir, if you don't mind, I think it's time for me to talk to your father. Think he'll take my call?"

Dave laughed, "I sure do, sir. I have his new sat number here from the TV people."

As people stood, stretched, and headed out of the room, several came and expressed appreciation to Dave for his being there. Connie smiled, turning shining eyes to Dave. "I'm so proud of him."

When they returned to the Situation Room sometime later with fresh coffee, they found Air Force Chief of Staff General Eddie Hipps and Secretary of the Air Force Josh Allen there. Grant explained the situation and what they hoped to do.

"Will this be day or nighttime?" Hipps asked.

The CNO answered. "We believe they'll need natural light on deck to see what they're doing. If they use artificial light at night, it'll be like a beacon at sea; makes it very easy to find ships."

General Hipps said, "I'm calling Andrews to ready some F-18 squadrons. In addition, we'll get a Global Hawk out of MacDill in Tampa to survey the area. I'd love to use a Predator, but there are none immediately available in theater."

"Translation please?" Marsha asked.

"The F-18 is a fighter aircraft, which we equip with Hellfire air-to-surface missiles. It also has a 20-millimeter cannon. The Global Hawk is a drone with synthetic-aperture radar and an electro-optical infrared camera. It can stay up over twenty-four hours and read a headline from 60,000 feet. A Predator is a drone with precision weapons capabilities. It's what we've been using to take out the Taliban and Al-Qaeda leadership in Afghanistan. The Global Hawk can find this sub when it comes up and call in the F-18s for the kill."

"Sounds lethal Eddie, thank you," the president said. "And now I'll call Mr. Shepherd and introduce myself." He gave the number to the technician. "Put it on speaker, please."

The room fell silent as they all listened for Phil's phone to ring. There were a couple of clicks, and then a voice.

It said, "This number is currently not available."

CHAPTER 75

Phil's heart was still thumping after talking with Louise. It was difficult to be so far when he wanted to see her, touch her, hold her—kiss her. *Thank you, Lord, for bringing Louise into my life.* His sudden transition from emotional isolation to declaring his love was unsettling, but despite the nerves, he knew in his heart that it was right—Louise was right. Right for him in every way.

Above him was a glorious sky, a blanket of stars, and he thanked God for the view, especially after the last few nights when clouds had hidden it. Suddenly he felt comfortable in the little raft and realized he was smiling. In fact, he wanted to jump up and cheer, run around, do some push-ups—anything to express the excitement of the moment. *Louise loved him!* He considered going for a quick swim. Dumb, Phil, very dumb.

As the euphoria settled, he had the presence of mind to switch off the sat phone. He didn't believe he'd be out there much longer, but it was his only link with the world, and he had to conserve the battery. He was surprised how quickly the first one had run down.

A glance at his watch told him it wasn't quite time for the snorkel to come up. Since they seemed to be back on the usual course and speed, he pulled the raft up close to the sub and gathered the line and anchor parts to jimmy the snorkel open. Okay, Captain Whoever-you-are, I'm ready for you to get my little surprise and show yourself. In the meantime, he thought he might as well get some rest until the snorkel woke him up.

Sometime later he awoke, freezing. *What?* Dawn was peeking over the horizon. It was almost five AM, and the sub hadn't snorkeled! So much for his brilliant sabotage. He gulped a swig of water and a donut. And then sensed something changing. Turning around, he saw the net rising. It was still pulling the raft along, so the sub was coming up too! Was this a last-minute snorkel? As he pondered this, the top of the submarine's sail came visible just below the surface. He tensed, readying himself to get on top when it came up. Just then the periscope popped up—and did a full 360-degree turn! Phil ducked low in the raft, hoping they hadn't seen him. But the periscope was way up—sub captain wanted to see as far as he could.

Phil scanned the horizon and didn't see anything—not that he had much of a view—maybe a few miles at most. And then suddenly, he was hanging on—the submarine was surfacing and lifting the raft right out of the water. Phil got his bearings, took the anchor parts and line, and leaped on top of the sail. It was wet and slick; he almost slid into the water. But then his foot found a "personnel well," and he slipped down into it. It was where the officers stood when the sub was on the surface. Oh no! They might be coming up right now!

He grabbed the Maglite from a lanyard around his neck and saw a large round hatch in the middle of the well. It had a big crank handle that must secure it. Just as he grabbed the anchor line to lash it shut, it started to move. Phil dropped back into the well and braced his feet against the crank. If they got it open, he was a dead man.

He could feel someone below, probably standing on a ladder, trying to open the hatch. He heard him yelling. He seemed to release his grip on the crank, so Phil quickly lashed it to a support in the well. The crank jerked again, but his lashing held. The raft—he had to get rid of it. They'd see it and know he was there. He jumped up and cut it free from the net with his sheath knife. As it slid overboard, Phil felt a touch of sadness. Goodbye, good buddy.

The sub had turned west as it surfaced, so the net was pulled to the left. Phil figured they wanted to face the coast to launch. He cautiously peered over the edge of the well and saw he was about 15 feet above the deserted forward deck.

Glancing at the afterdeck he saw two large cylinders with sailors swarming around their ends. He couldn't see all the men, but the ones right below him were unbolting covers from the cylinders, exposing missile nose cones. He guessed they would raise them up somehow to fire them off.

What should he do? What could he do? Try to get help! He hunkered down, yanked out both phones, and turned them on, praying they'd boot up quickly. The sat phone came up first. He punched in Dave's number, hoping he was still in the White House. Or that he'd at least get to some navy people. As it connected, he thumbed up the GPS app.

"Dad?"

"Dave—get a pencil. I'm on top of the sub and they're getting ready to fire the missiles," he said, in sharp staccato.

He heard the rattle of chain hoists and quickly told Dave the GPS coordinates. "Gotta run, son!"

"Dad, the president wants to talk to you!"

"Hey, sorry—I'm kind of busy here. I'll call later—if I can." He hung up and looked around. He saw the two missile housings rising up beside the sail—practically within arm's distance—with the noses sticking out! There was no time! The navy would never make it. If they were going to be stopped, then Phil would have to stop them. "Lord, help me!" he cried aloud, not caring if they heard.

He could reach out and touch the missiles. Phil got an idea. He recalled reading once that missiles were most vulnerable before they got going; once in the sky they were freight trains on steroids, but these hadn't taken off yet. He grabbed a handful of net, hauled up a few yards, and wrapped several turns of it over the end of the left side missile tube. That took care of one of them—he hoped. The other one, he had to contain in its launch tube. But how could he do it?

The tethers! He had two safety tethers clipped to the bottom of his safety harness. He'd been wearing it since the first night. They were 6 feet long with 6,000-pound carabiner clips at each end. He formed a loop at one end and dropped it over the nose cone. He clipped the other end to a bolt hole on the missile housing. He did the same with the other tether, spacing it out as far as he could reach.

Somebody below yelled at him. He'd been seen! *Too late, guys.* He hoped it was too late. He ducked back down in the well, covered his ears, and crouched low. Just in time! They fired a missile. It was deafening. He peeked up to see it lift out of its tube, dragging the net with it. He looked over the edge just in time to see it flounder and crash into the sea with the net. Yes!

Almost immediately, the other missile fired. It rose up in its tube and—stopped! The tethers were steel rod tight, but they held. *Thank you, Jesus!* He peeked over the edge. The outside bottom of the missile tube was glowing cherry red—the missile was melting the tube! The rubber anti-sonar coating melted, smoldered, and poured out billows of black smoke and stink. The tube softened and sagged. Just as he thought the weight was becoming too much for the hoist, sure enough, it ripped free of the sail. Slowly the whole missile and tube slumped off the side into the sea, boiling the water as it sank.

Phil slid down in the well. *Thank you, Jesus! Thank you! You are the King!*

Suddenly there was yelling on deck, and the submarine slowed, then stopped. He peered out and couldn't believe what he saw. The sub had caused the net to straighten out—it was now wrapped up in their propeller. The big sickle-shaped blades had wound it up around them like a giant ball of yarn, and now the floats and more netting bobbed around the stern of the boat. The sub wasn't going anywhere.

He slid down again and called Dave. But a new voice answered.

"This is President Brandenberg. Is this Mr. Shepherd?"

Phil was momentarily shocked. Finally, he blurted, "Yes, sir, it is!"

"Mr. Shepherd, get off that submarine. We have forces on the way to sink it."

"That won't be necessary, sir. The sub is no longer a threat."

CHAPTER 76

Every person in the Situation Room sat transfixed by the Global Hawk's images displayed on six screens circling the room. Using the coordinates Phil had given Dave, the drone's cameras located the sub with Phil on top of the sail just before the first missile fired. When the second one fell into the sea, Dave jumped from his seat. "Way to go, Dad!" He was accompanied by spontaneous applause and cheering throughout the room.

The president, still holding the phone, stared at the screens. "Mr. Shepherd, I see what you mean." He paused. "The nation can never thank you enough." CNO Hunter and Secretary of the Air Force Hipps both stood and signaled to him. "Hang on just a minute."

Hunter came up to him. "Mr. President, he's still at high risk. The Iranians are gonna figure out he's up there. Our F-18s are strafing them now, holding all munitions. We suggest he lay low until the Steele can get there—about twenty minutes."

The president could hear the roar of a fighter plane passing above the sub. "Mr. Shepherd? Phil?"

"Yes, sir?"

"We're strafing the sub, as you already know, and will do so until our destroyer can take you off—in about twenty minutes. Please stay low until then."

"Not to worry, sir. But tell them to hurry. These guys down there are yelling up a storm. I think they're trying to get a ladder or grappling hooks up here. I've blocked their hatch."

Hipps motioned to take the phone, so the president handed it over. "Mr. Shepherd, this is the Air Force Chief of Staff, General Hipps. Can you tell me how high you are off the sub's deck?"

"About 15 feet."

"And are you in some sort of recess or well?"

"Yes, sir."

"How deep is it?

"About 4 feet."

"So that leaves an eleven-foot window for us to put some cannon shells into. Not very big. Can you lie on top somehow and give us a little more leeway?"

"I guess I can. Are you gonna shoot at them?"

"That's the idea. Better them than you."

"Sounds good. Er, please tell the president I need to hang up here so I can use both hands to hang on. Good to talk to you, sir."

The president nodded with a small smile, as General Hipps took another phone and barked orders into it.

As Phil scrambled out of the well, a grappling hook angled overhead and hooked onto the side. Phil whipped out his sheath knife and cut the rope, letting it drop off. He threw the hook in the sea. He glanced over his shoulder just in time to see a U.S. fighter skimming along the surface with its cannon blazing. He heard thunderous booms underneath him, screams of pain, and then silence as the fighter raced off in the distance. He called the White House again.

"You're on speaker, Phil," the president said.

"I think that stopped them, sir. They tried to get up with a grapple, but I cut it off."

"We saw it from our drone. We can see you plain as day and any activity on the submarine. Please, just stay out of sight a few more minutes until we can get you off."

"Will do, Mr. President. Thank you!"

"We thank you, Mr. Shepherd."

Phil lay down as another fighter screamed overhead, this time without firing its cannon. In the distance, he saw a helicopter hovering, its side door open. Was that his ride?

Several strafings later, the USS *Steele* pulled alongside the *Yunes*, leveled its cannons and announced, "*Yunes*, stand by for boarding." The words were repeated in what Phil assumed was Farsi. As he watched, the destroyer hoisted a small boat from its side with six armed sailors, an officer in tan dress uniform, and two motormen. It came alongside the *Yunes* just forward of the sail, and they threw docking lines to a couple of Iranian sailors on the sub.

A short, stocky Iranian officer with a gold embroidered hat came out of the sail door and stood stiffly on the forward deck wearing a sidearm. The American officer stepped aboard and saluted him. The Iranian officer returned the salute, spoke a few words, and handed his pistol—butt first—to the American. He then turned and looked directly at Phil. "Navy Seal?" he asked bitterly, in accented English.

"No, Captain; high school history teacher."

CHAPTER 77

The White House Rose Garden was particularly lush and beautiful, the sky a clear blue—presidential blue, one might say—with wispy white clouds, as Phil and his sons assembled for an award ceremony. Magnolias and crab apples were in full bloom. Tulips and hyacinths filled the air with sweet fragrances—and it was sure gonna be a sweet day, Phil thought.

President Brandenberg stood at a podium flanked by Phil and his sons Dave and Jerry. Louise and Connie had center front seats. Next to them were uniformed representatives of all the services, plus the secretary of state, the attorney general, the White House press secretary, speaker of the house, the governor of Indiana, the two Indiana senators, and nine more representatives. Phil's pastor and his wife, the Kokomo High School principal, and the student body president sat further back. Last was the press—there in droves, with reporters representing places from the Kokomo Tribune clear through *Pravda*. A literal bank of cameras lined the back row.

Phil had resisted most interviews since his return to shore, but he figured he'd be cornered after the ceremony. Since Network News had broadcast *Yunes*'s surrender, it had gone viral worldwide. The White House called the missiles rockets instead of missiles to reduce public concern and attributed the danger to a rogue captain, which the Iranians confirmed. Thus far they'd suppressed any mention of nuclear materials.

However, with the number of U.S. Navy personnel involved, it would be a real challenge to bottle all leaks, Phil thought. Moreover, since salvage efforts were underway to recover the missiles from the shallow water, the question of their design and capabilities was far from over.

President Brandenberg cleared his throat. "Ladies and Gentlemen, today we are gathered to present the Presidential Medal of Freedom to a most unusual man for his heroic efforts in thwarting a rocket attack on the United States. I need to explain that this is the first time this medal has ever been awarded for valor. As you know, we have the Congressional Medal of Honor, our nation's highest award of valor for men and women in our military. We also have the Medal of Valor for exceptional acts of bravery in public safety and for firefighters. Frankly, I'd like to award all three to Mr. Shepherd, but I'm told I must pick just one. The Presidential Medal of Freedom is our nation's highest award for civilians, so it is the obvious choice."

In the second row, Connie squeezed Louise's arm. "Isn't this exciting?" she whispered. The two ladies had only met briefly but had already established a sweet rapport as each of them loved a Shepherd—one the father, one the son. Connie blinked back tears. "I can hardly believe it," she agreed. "I'm so proud of him—I could just—cry!"

The president continued, "Not only is today's award appropriate for Mr. Shepherd's bravery, but I must say, for his determination. I'd like to point out certain actions that have struck me as particularly significant. First, I believe no other person in history has refused to be rescued by the Coast Guard. Some may have resisted, but they tell me there's no record of outright refusal. Second, I believe no other president has had a citizen tell him to call back later because he was too busy." Phil smiled sheepishly, but the crowd roared.

"Last, I'd like to thank the press for allowing us to follow Mr. Shepherd's efforts, through fine reporting by people such as Connie Morello and Bret Kohler."

Connie rippled with pride. Her name, mentioned by the president!

President Brandenburg beckoned to Phil. "Step forward please, Mr. Shepherd." He held the award medal aloft for all to see—a blue field with thirteen stars, it was similar to the Congressional Medal of Honor. He cleared his throat and turned to Phil. "Mr. Phillip Shepherd, on behalf of the grateful people of the United States, I present you with the Presidential Medal of Freedom in appreciation for your exceptional acts of heroism in singlehandedly thwarting an enemy rocket attack on our shores." He removed the ribbon and medal from the case, stood behind Phil, and clipped the ribbon together. "Ladies and Gentlemen, I give you Phil Shepherd, a national hero." His clapping was joined by an immediate flood of applause. The audience came to their feet and cheered and clapped more. Phil had to wipe his eyes, and Louise was outright crying.

Blinking hard, Phil moved behind the podium. He shook his head and cleared his throat. "Thank you, Mr. President, thank you for this high honor. I never, ever expected anything like this." He surveyed the crowd. "Many of you may be wondering why I did this, and how." He paused. His eyes met Louise's teary ones. She smiled at him through the tears.

"All I can say is—my sons would call it a God thing. I call it the Lord's blessing. I believe the Lord had His hand on me through it all—from the time our sailboat sank to the surrender of the Iranian submarine. He answered every one of my prayers in that little raft—even for a cup of coffee." Chuckles rippled through the audience.

"The president mentioned my fearless bravery, and most of the time I truly felt safe. But I got scared when the Iranians started firing their rockets and when they tried to get at me afterward. A big shark the first night was scary, too; I don't think that made it to the news." He took a deep breath. "But the Lord was right there with solutions whenever I needed one. I especially liked the F-18 solution." That brought a laugh from the benches. "They were awesome. I'm glad they were on my side." Another wave of mirth.

"So—despite all, I will continue to preach this message to my sons and anyone who will listen: Do not do dangerous things carefully—don't do them at all! And I hope I'm about to return to practicing that myself!" Everyone laughed again. "Most of all I will urge them to rely on the Lord, always and forever, through thick and thin. I pray that for our whole country." He nodded his head. "To God be the glory."

Acknowledgments

I would like to thank the following people who helped me with *Mayday USA (*former edition of *The Accidental Spy)*:My wife Peggy who read and/or listened to the book and both steered me away from precipices and cheered me on throughout the writing process.

Jocelyn Godfrey Carbonara, my friend and niece, who commented and provided untold corrections, tips, and enthusiasm for the original edition of the book;

My son Jeff, who read, commented, and provided a number of helpful inputs, the most cogent of which was "Hogwash;"

My friend, Pastor Jody Burgin, who provided encouragement, questions, and interest throughout the project;

Jerry Gilkey, USN Ret. Jerry served on a diesel-electric sub similar to the one in the book, and confirmed the validity of my basic thesis, as well as that the U.S. had experimented with deck-mounted sub missiles;

Inspector Michael Checkely, Royal Bahamas Police, Bimini station, who was very helpful in providing realistic details for the Bahamian scenes;

Lt. Nathan Shakespeare and Lt Cmd. Brent Schmadeke, U.S. Coast Guard, Traverse City Air Station. These helicopter pilots gave generously of their time to help, particularly with the search and rescue scenes;

Dr. Peter Sandwall II, medical physicist, provided valuable expertise on the radiation aspects of the book. And finally, with particular appreciation, Linore Rose Burkard, who edited this edition with major input to strengthen, tighten and shorten it.

About the Author

Tom Rattray is a retired Engineer/Associate Director from Procter and Gamble with a Master's in engineering. A veteran sailor, he's enjoyed sailing to the Bahamas and Bermuda from Florida numerous times, as well as many trips on Lakes Michigan, Erie, and Huron, the Gulf of Mexico, and Chesapeake Bay. Tom has three sons who enjoy sailing, and lives in Ohio with his wife Peggy, who does not. When he isn't writing, Tom enjoys reading, wood working, day sailing, and a good meal! Active in his church, Tom is also a Healing Rooms Volunteer.